Honoré de Balzac

# About Catherine de'Medici

And other Stories

Honoré de Balzac

**About Catherine de'Medici**
*And other Stories*

ISBN/EAN: 9783744751247

Printed in Europe, USA, Canada, Australia, Japan

Cover: Foto ©Andreas Hilbeck / pixelio.de

More available books at **www.hansebooks.com**

H. DE BALZAC

———

ABOUT

# CATHERINE DE' MEDICI

AND OTHER STORIES

TRANSLATED BY

CLARA BELL

WITH A PREFACE BY

GEORGE SAINTSBURY

PHILADELPHIA

THE GEBBIE PUBLISHING CO., Ltd.

1898

# CONTENTS

# LIST OF ILLUSTRATIONS



*Drawn by D. Murray-Smith.*

# PREFACE.

THIS book (as to which it is important to remember the *Sur** if injustice is not to be done to the intentions of the author) has plenty of interest of more kinds than one; but it is perhaps more interesting because of the place it holds in Balzac's work than for itself. He had always considerable hankerings after the historical novel: his early and lifelong devotion to Scott would sufficiently account for that. More than one of the *Œuvres de Jeunesse* (youthful works) attempts the form in a more or less conscious way: the " Chouans," the first successful book, definitely attempts it; but by far the most ambitious attempt is to be found in the book before us. It is most probable that it was of this, if of anything of his own, that Balzac was thinking when, in 1846, he wrote disdainfully to Madame Hanska about Dumas, and expressed himself toward " Les Trois Mousquetaires " (which had whiled him through a day of cold and inability to work) nearly as ungratefully as Carlyle did toward Captain Marryat. And though it is, let it be repeated, a mistake, and a rather unfair mistake, to give such a title to the book as might induce readers to regard it as a single and definite novel, of which Catherine is the heroine, though it is made up of three parts written at very different times, it has a unity which the introduction shows to some extent, and which a rejected preface given by M. de Lovenjoul shows still better.

To understand this, we must remember that Balzac, though not exactly an historical scholar, was a considerable student of history; and that, although rather an amateur politician, he was a constant thinker and writer on political subjects. We must add to these remembrances the fact of his intense interest

* About.

(ix)

in all such matters as Alchemy, the Elixir of Life, and so forth, to which the sixteenth century in general, and Catherine de' Medici in particular, were known to be devoted. All these interests of his met in the present book, the parts of which appeared in inverse order, and the genesis of which is important enough to make it desirable to incorporate some of the usual bibliographical matter in the substance of this preface. The third and shortest, "Les Deux Rêves" (The Two Dreams), a piece partly suggestive of the famous "Prophecy of Cazotte" and other legends of the Revolution (but with more retrospective than prospective view), is dated as early as 1828 (before the turning-point), and was actually published in a periodical in 1830. "La Confidence des Ruggieri," written in 1836 (and, as I have noted in the general introduction, according to its author, in a single night), followed, and "Le Martyr Calviniste," which had several titles, and was advertised as in preparation for a long time, did not come till 1841.

It is unnecessary to say that all are interesting. The personages, both imaginary and historical, appear at times in a manner worthy of Balzac; many separate scenes are excellent; and, to those who care to perceive them, the various occupations of the author appear in the most interesting manner. Politically, his object was, at least by his own account, to defend the maxim that private and public morality are different; that the policy of a state cannot be, and ought not to be, governed by the same considerations of duty to its neighbors as those which ought to govern the conduct of an individual. The very best men—those least liable to the slightest imputation of corrupt morals and motives—have indorsed this principle; though it has been screamed at by a few fanatics, a somewhat larger number of persons who found their account in so doing, and a great multitude of hasty, dense, or foolish folk. But it was something of a mark of that amateurishness which spoilt Balzac's dealing with the subject to choose the sixteenth century for his text. For every cool-headed student of history and ethics will admit that it was precisely the abuse of this principle at this time, and by persons of whom Catherine de' Medici, if not the most blamable, has had the most blame put on her, that brought the principle itself into discredit. Between the assertion that the strictest morality of the Sermon on the Mount must obtain between nation and nation, between governor and governed, and the maxim that in politics the end of public safety justifies *any* means whatever, there is a perfectly immense gulf fixed.

If, however, we turn from this somewhat academic point, and do not dwell very much on the occult and magical sides of the matter, interesting as they are, we shall be brought at once face to face with the question, Is the handling of this book the right and proper one for an historical novel? Can we in virtue of it rank Balzac (this is the test which he would himself, beyond all question, have accepted) a long way above Dumas and near Scott?

I must say that I can see no possibility of answer except, "Certainly not." For the historical novel depends almost more than any other division of the kind upon interest of story. Interest of story is not, as has been several times pointed out, at any time Balzac's main appeal, and he has succeeded in it here less than in most other places. He has discussed too much; he has brought in too many personages without sufficient interest of plot; but, above all, he exhibits throughout an incapacity to handle his materials in the peculiar way required. How long he was before he grasped "the way to do it," even on his own special lines, is the commonplace and refrain of all writing about him. Now, to this special kind he gave comparatively little attention, and the result is that he mastered it less than any other. In the best stories of Dumas (and the best number some fifteen or twenty at least) the interest of narrative, of adventure, of what will happen to the personages, takes you by the throat at once, and never lets you go till the end. There is little or nothing of this sort here. The three stories are excellently well-informed studies, very curious and interesting in divers ways. The "Ruggieri" is perhaps something more; but it is, as its author no doubt honestly entitled it, much more an "Étude Philosophique"(Philosophical Study) than an historical novelette. In short, this was not Balzac's way. We need not be sorry—it is very rarely necessary to be that—that he tried it; we may easily forgive him for not recognizing the ease and certainty with which Dumas trod the path. But we should be most of all thankful that he did not himself enter it frequently or ever pursue it far.

The most important part of the bibliography of the book has been given above. The rest is a little complicated, and for its ins and outs reference must be made to the usual authority. It should be enough to say that the "Martyr," under the title of "Les Lecamus," first appeared in the "Siècle" during the spring of 1841. Sovverain published it as a book two years later with the other two, as "Catherine de Medicis Expliquée." The second part, entitled, not "La Confidence," but "Le Secret des Ruggieri," had appeared much earlier in the "Chronique de Paris" during the winter of 1836–37, and had been published as a book in the latter year; it was joined to "Catharine de Medicis Expliquée" as above. The third part, after appearing in the "Monde" as early as May, 1830, also appeared in the "Deux Mondes" for December of the same year, then became one of the "Romans et Contes Philosophiques" (Philosophical Romances and Stories), then an "Étude Philosophique," and in 1843 joined "Catherine de Medicis Expliquée." The whole was inserted in the Comédie in 1846.

"The Exiles" (Les Proscrits) first appeared in the "Revue de Paris" for May, 1831, and was almost immediately included in the "Romans et Contes Philosophiques." Its fortunes will be more fully given in the preface to "Seraphita."

Sensibility claims us in "Le Message," a story which, by the way, was much twisted about in its author's hands, and underwent transformations too long to be summarized here. There is a point of irony in it which commends itself to its author, and which keeps it sweet and prevents it from sharing the mawkishness of the earlier stories. But it is slight.

G. S.

# ABOUT CATHERINE DE' MEDICI.

*To Monsieur le Marquis de Pastoret,*
*Member of the Académie des Beaux-Arts.*

*When we consider the amazing number of volumes written to ascertain the spot where Hannibal crossed the Alps, without our knowing to this day whether it was, as Whitaker and Rivaz say, by Lyons, Geneva, the Saint-Bernard, and the Valley of Aosta; or, as we are told by Letronne, Follard, Saint-Simon, and Fortia d'Urban, by the Isère, Grenoble, Saint-Bonnet, Mont Genèvre, Fenestrella, and the Pass of Susa; or, according to Larauza, by the Mont Cenis and Susa; or, as Strabo, Polybius, and de Luc tell us, by the Rhône, Vienne, Yenne, and the Mont du Chat; or, as certain clever people opine, by Genoa, la Bochetta, and la Scrivia—the view I hold, and which Napoleon had adopted—to say nothing of the vinegar with which some learned men have dressed the Alpine rocks, can we wonder, Monsieur le Marquis, to find modern history so much neglected that some most important points remain obscure, and that the most odious calumnies still weigh on names which ought to be revered? And it may be noted incidentally that by dint of explanations it has become problematical whether Hannibal ever crossed the Alps at all. Father Ménestrier believes that the Scoras spoken of by Polybius was the Saône; Letronne, Larauza, and Schweighauser believe it to be the Isère; Cochard, a learned man of Lyons, identifies it with the Drôme. But, to any one who has eyes, are there not striking geographical and linguistic affinities between Scoras and Scrivia, to say nothing of the almost certain fact that the Carthaginian fleet lay at la Spezzia or in the Gulf of Genoa?*

*I could understand all this patient research if the battle of Cannae could be doubted; but since its consequences are well known, what is the use of blackening so much paper with theories that are but the Arabesque of hypothesis, so to speak; while the most important history of later times, that of the Reformation, is so full of obscurities that the name remains unknown of the man* who was making a boat move by steam at Barcelona at the time when Luther and Calvin were inventing the revolt of mind?*

*We, I believe, after having made, each in his own way, the same investigations as to the great and noble character of Catherine de' Medici, have come to the same opinion.  So I thought that my historical studies on the subject might be suitably dedicated to a writer who has labored so long on the history of the Reformation; and that I should thus do public homage, precious perhaps for its rarity, to the character and fidelity of a man true to the Monarchy.*

PARIS, *January*, 1842.

---

* The inventor of this experiment was probably Salomon of Caux, not of Caus.  This great man was always unlucky; after his death even his name was misspelt.  Salomon, whose original portrait, at the age of forty-six, was discovered by the author of the " Human Comedy," was born at Caux, in Normandy.

# INTRODUCTION.

WHEN men of learning are struck by a historical blunder, and try to correct it, " Paradox ! " is generally the cry; but to those who thoroughly examine the history of modern times, it is evident that historians are privileged liars, who lend their pen to popular beliefs, exactly as most of the newspapers of the day express nothing but the opinions of their readers.

Historical independence of thought has been far less conspicuous among lay writers than among the priesthood. The purest light thrown on history has come from the Benedictines, one of the glories of France—so long, that is to say, as the interests of the monastic orders are not in question. Since the middle of the eighteenth century, some great and learned controversialists have arisen who, struck by the need for rectifying certain popular errors to which historians have lent credit, have published some remarkable works. Thus Monsieur Launoy, nicknamed the Evicter of Saints, made ruthless war on certain saints who have sneaked into the Church Calendar. Thus the rivals of the Benedictines, the too little known members of the Académie des Inscriptions et Belles-lettres, began their memoirs, their studious notes, full of patience, erudition, and logic, on certain obscure passages of history. Thus Voltaire, with an unfortunate bias and sadly perverted passions, often brought the light of his intellect to bear on historical prejudices. Diderot, with this end in view, began a book—much too long—on a period of the history of Imperial Rome. But for the French Revolution, criticism, as applied to history, might perhaps have laid up the materials for a good and true history of France, for which evidence has long been amassed by the great French Benedictines. Louis XVI., a man of clear mind, himself translated the English work, which so much agitated the last century, in which Walpole tried to explain the career of Richard III.

How is it that persons so famous as kings and queens, so important as generals of great armies, become objects of aversion or derision?   Half the world hesitates between the song on Marlborough and the history of England, as they do between popular tradition and history as concerning King Charles IX.

At all the periods when great battles are fought between the masses and the authorities, the populace creates an *ogresque* figure—to coin a word for the sake of its exactitude.   Thus in our own time, but for the "Memorials of Saint-Helena," and the controversies of Royalists and Bonapartists, there was scarcely a chance but that Napoleon would have been misunderstood.   Another Abbé de Pradt or two, a few more newspaper articles, and Napoleon from an Emperor would have become an ogre.

How is error propagated and accredited?   The mystery is accomplished under our eyes without our discerning the process.   No one suspects how greatly printing has helped to give body both to the envy which attends persons in high places, and to the popular irony which sums up the converse view of every great historical fact.   For instance, every bad horse in France that needs flogging is called after the Prince de Polignac; and so who knows what opinion the future may hold as to the Prince de Polignac's *coup d'Etat?*   In consequence of a caprice of Shakespeare's—a stroke of revenge, perhaps, like that of Beaumarchais on Bergasse (Begearss)— Falstaff, in England, is a type of the grotesque; his name raises a laugh, he is the King of Buffoons.   Now, instead of being enormously fat, ridiculously amorous, vain, old, drunken, and a corrupter of youth, Falstaff was one of the most important figures of his time, a Knight of the Garter, holding high command.   At the date of Henry V.'s accession, Falstaff was at most four-and-thirty.   This general, who distinguished himself at the battle of Agincourt, where he took the Duc d'Alençon prisoner, in 1420 took the town of Montereau, which was stoutly defended. Finally, under Henry VI., he beat ten thousand Frenchmen with fifteen hundred men who were dropping with fatigue and hunger. So much for valor!

If we turn to literature, Rabelais, among the French, a sober man who drank nothing but water, is thought of as a lover of good-cheer and a persistent sot. Hundreds of absurd stories have been coined concerning the author of one of the finest books in French literature: "Pantagruel."

Aretino, Titian's friend, and the Voltaire of his day, is now credited with a reputation, in complete antagonism with his works and character, which he acquired by his over-free wit, characteristic of the writings of an age when gross jests were held in honor, and queens and cardinals indited tales which are now considered licentious. Instances might be infinitely multiplied.

In France, and at the most important period of our history, Catherine de' Medici has suffered more from popular error than any other woman, unless it be Brunehaut or Frédégonde; while Marie de' Medici, whose every action was prejudicial to France, has escaped the disgrace that should cover her name. Marie dissipated the treasure amassed by Henry IV.; she never purged herself of the suspicion that she was cognizant of his murder; Epernon, who had long known Ravaillac, and who did not parry his blow, was *intimate* with the Queen; she compelled her son to banish her from France, where she was fostering the rebellion of her other son, Gaston; and Richelieu's triumph over her on the "Journée des Dupes" was due solely to the cardinal's revealing to Louis XIII. certain documents secreted after the death of Henry IV.

Catherine de' Medici, on the contrary, saved the throne of France, she maintained the Royal authority under circumstances to which more than one great prince would have succumbed. Face to face with such leaders of the factions and ambitions of the houses of Guise and of Bourbon as the two Cardinals de Lorraine and the two "Balafrés," the two Princes de Condé, Queen Jeanne d'Albret, Henri IV., the Connétable* de Montmorency, Calvin, the Colignys, and Théodore de Bèze, she was forced to put forth the rarest fine qualities, the most essential gifts of statesmanship, under the fire of the Calvinist press. These, at any rate, are indisputable facts. And to the student who digs deep into the history of the sixteenth century in France the figure of Catherine de' Medici stands out as that of a great king.

When once calumnies are undermined by facts laboriously brought to light from under the contradictions of pamphlets and false anecdotes, everything is explained to the glory of this wonderful woman, who had none of the weaknesses of her sex, who lived chaste in the midst of the gallantries of the most licentious Court in Europe, and who, notwithstanding her lack of money, erected noble buildings, as if to make good the losses caused by the destructive Calvinists, who injured art as deeply as they did the body politic.

Hemmed in between a race of princes who proclaimed themselves the heirs of Charlemagne, and a factious younger branch that was eager to bury the Connétable de Bourbon's treason under the throne; obliged, too, to fight down a heresy on the verge of devouring the Monarchy, without friends, and aware of treachery in the chiefs of the Catholic party and of republicanism in the Calvinists, Catherine used the most dangerous but the surest of political weapons—Craft. She determined to deceive by turns the party that was anxious to secure the downfall of the House of Valois, the Bourbons who aimed at the Crown, and the Reformers—the Radicals of that day, who dreamed of an impossible republic, like those of our own day, who, however, have nothing to reform. Indeed, so long as she lived, the Valois sat on the throne. The great de Thou

* Constable ; at that time the highest military officer.

understood the worth of this woman when he exclaimed, on hearing of her death—

"It is not a woman, it is Royalty that dies in her!"

Catherine had, in fact, the sense of Royalty in the highest degree, and she defended it with admirable courage and per- sistency. The reproaches flung at her by Calvinist writers are indeed her glory; she earned them solely by her triumphs. And how was she to triumph but by cunning? Here lies the whole question.

As to violence—that method beats on one of the most hotly disputed points of policy, which, in recent days, has been answered here, on the spot where a big stone from Egypt has been placed to wipe out the memory of regicide, and to stand as an emblem of the materialistic policy which now rules us; it was answered at les Carmes and at the Abbaye; it was answered on the steps of Saint Roch; it was answered in front of the Louvre in 1830, and again by the people against the King, as it has since been answered once more by la Fayette's "best of all republics" against the republican rebellion, at Saint-Merri and the Rue Transnonnain.

Every power, whether legitimate or illegitimate, must de- fend itself when it is attacked; but, strange to say, while the people are heroic when they triumph over the nobility, the au- thorities are murderers when they oppose the people! And, finally, if after their appeal to force they succumb, they are regarded as effete idiots. The present Government (1840) will try to save itself, by two laws, from the same evil as at- tacked Charles X., and which he tried to scotch by two de- crees. Is not this a bitter mockery? May those in power meet cunning with cunning? Ought they to kill those who try to kill them?

The massacres of the Revolution are the reply to the mas- sacre of Saint-Bartholomew. The People, being King, did by the nobility and the King as the King and the nobility did by the rebels in the sixteenth century. And popular writers, who know full well that, under similar conditions, the people would do the same again, are inexcusable when they blame Catherine de' Medici and Charles IX.

"All power is a permanent conspiracy," said Casimir Périer when teaching what power ought to be. We admire the anti-social maxims published by audacious writers; why, then, are social truths received in France with such disfavor when they are boldly stated? This question alone sufficiently accounts for historical mistakes. Apply the solution of this problem to the devastating doctrines which flatter popular passion, and to the conservative doctrines which would repress the ferocious or foolish attempts of the populace, and you will see the reason why certain personages are popular or unpopular. Laubardemont and Laffemas, like some people now living, were devoted to the maintenance of the power they believed in. Soldiers and judges, they obeyed a Royal authority. D'Orthez, in our day, would be discharged from office for misinterpreting orders from the Ministry, but Charles X. left him to govern his province. The power of the masses is accountable to no one; the power of one is obliged to account to its subjects, great and small alike.

Catherine, like Philip II. and the Duke of Alva, like the Guises and Cardinal Granvelle, foresaw the future to which the Reformation was dooming Europe. They saw monarchies, religion, and power all overthrown. Catherine, from the Cabinet of the French kings, forthwith issued sentence of death on that inquiring spirit which threatened modern society —a sentence which Louis XIV. finally carried out. The revocation of the Edict of Nantes was a measure that proved unfortunate, simply in consequence of the irritation Louis XIV. had aroused in Europe. At any other time England, Holland, and the German Empire would not have encouraged on their territory French exiles and French rebels.

Why, in these days, refuse to recognize the greatness which the majestic adversary of that most barren heresy derived from the struggle itself? Calvinists have written strongly against Charles IX.'s stratagems; but travel through France: as you see the ruins of so many destroyed fine churches, and consider the vast breaches made by religious fanatics in the social body; when you learn the revenges they took, while deploring the mischief of individualism—the plague of France to-day, of which the germ lay in the questions of liberty of conscience which they stirred up—you will ask yourself on which side were the barbarians. There are always, as Catherine says in the third part of this Study, "unluckily, in all ages, hypocritical writers ready to bewail two hundred scoundrels killed in due season." Cæsar, who tried to incite the Senate to pity for Catiline's party, would very likely have conquered Cicero if he had had newspapers and an Opposition at his service.

Another consideration accounts for Catherine's historical and popular disfavor. In France the Opposition has always been Protestant, because its policy has never been anything but negative; it has inherited the theories of the Lutherans, the Calvinists, and the Protestants on the terrible texts of liberty, tolerance, progress, and philanthropy. The opponents of power spent two centuries in establishing the very doubtful doctrine of freewill. Two more centuries were spent in working out the first corollary of freewill—liberty of conscience. Our age is striving to prove the second—political liberty.

Standing between the fields already traversed and the fields as yet untrodden, Catherine and the church proclaimed the salutary principle of modern communities: One faith, one Lord; but asserting their right of life and death over all innovators. Even if she had been conquered, succeeding times have shown that Catherine was right. The outcome of freewill, religious liberty, and political liberty (note, this does not mean *civil* liberty) is France as we now see it.

And what is France in 1840? A country exclusively absorbed in material interests, devoid of patriotism, devoid of conscience; where authority is powerless; where electoral rights, the fruit of freewill and political liberty, raise none but mediocrities; where brute force is necessary to oppose the violence of the populace; where discussion, brought to bear on the smallest matter, checks every action of the body politic; and where individualism—the odious result of the indefinite subdivision of property, which destroys family cohesion—will devour everything, even the nation, which sheer selfishness will some day lay open to invasion. Men will say, "Why not the Czar?" as they now say, "Why not the Duc d'Orléans?" We do not care for many things even now; fifty years hence we shall care for nothing.

Therefore, according to Catherine—and according to all who wish to see society soundly organized—man as a social unit, as a subject, has no freewill, has no right to accept the dogma of liberty of conscience, or to have political liberty. Still, as no community can subsist without some guarantee given to the subject against the sovereign, the subject derives from that certain liberties under restrictions. Liberty—no; but liberties—yes; well-defined and circumscribed liberties. This is in the nature of things. For instance, it is beyond human power to fetter freedom of thought; and no sovereign may ever tamper with money.

The great politicians who have failed in this long contest— it has gone on for five centuries—have allowed their subjects wide liberties; but they never recognize their liberty to publish anti-social opinions, nor the unlimited freedom of the subject. To them the words *subject* and *free* are, politically speaking, a contradiction in terms; and, in the same way, the statement that all citizens are equal is pure nonsense and contradicted by nature every hour. To acknowledge the need for religion, the need for authority, and at the same time to leave all men at liberty to deny religion, to attack its services, to oppose the exercise of authority by the public and published expression of opinion, is an impossibility such as the Catholics of the sixteenth century would have nothing to say to. Alas! the triumph of Calvinism will cost France more yet than it has ever done; for the sects of to-day—religious, political, humanitarian, and leveling—are the train of Calvinism; and, when we see the blunders of those in power, their contempt for intelligence, their devotion to those material interests in which they seek support, and which are the most delusive of all props, unless by the special aid of providence, the genius of destruction must certainly win the day from the genius of conservatism. The attacking forces, who have nothing to lose and everything to win, are thoroughly in agreement; whereas their wealthy opponents refuse to make any sacrifice of money or of self-conceit to secure defenders.

Printing came to the aid of the resistance inaugurated by the Vaudois and the Albigenses. As soon as human thought —no longer condensed, as it had necessarily been in order to preserve the most communicable form—had assumed a multitude of garbs and become the very people, instead of remaining in some sense divinely axiomatic, there were two vast armies to contend with—that of ideas and that of men. Royal power perished in the struggle, and we, in France, at this day are looking on at its last coalition with elements which make it difficult, not to say impossible.

Power is action; the electoral principle is discussion. No political action is possible when discussion is permanently established. So we ought to regard the woman as truly great who foresaw that future, and fought it so bravely. The House of Bourbon was able to succeed to the House of Valois, and owed it to Catherine de' Medici that it found that crown to wear. If the second Balafré had been alive, it is very doubtful that the Béarnais, strong as he was, could have seized the throne, seeing how dearly it was sold by the Duc de Mayenne and the remnant of the Guise faction. The necessary steps taken by Catherine, who had the deaths of François II. and Charles IX. on her soul—both dying opportunely for her safety—are not, it must be noted, what the Calvinist and modern writers blame her for! Though there was no poisoning, as some serious authors have asserted, there were other not less criminal plots. It is beyond question that she hindered Paré from saving one, and murdered the other morally by inches.

But the swift death of François II. and the skillfully contrived end of Charles IX. did no injury to Calvinist interests. The causes of these two events concerned only the uppermost sphere, and were never suspected by writers or by the lower orders at the time; they were guessed only by de Thou, by l'Hôpital, by men of the highest talents, or the chiefs of the two parties who coveted and clung to the Crown, and who thought such means indispensable.

Popular songs, strange to say, fell foul of Catherine's morality. The anecdote is known of a soldier who was roasting a goose in the guardroom of the Château de Tours while Catherine and Henry IV. were holding a conference there, and who sang a ballad in which the Queen was insultingly cómpared to the largest cannon in the hands of the Calvinists. Henri IV. drew his sword to go out and kill the man; Catherine stopped him, and only shouted out—

"It is Catherine who provides the goose!"

Though the executions at Amboise were attributed to Catherine, and the Calvinists made that able woman responsible for all the inevitable disasters of the struggle, she must be judged by posterity, like Robespierre, at a future date.

And Catherine was cruelly punished for her preference for the Duc d'Anjou, which made her hold her two elder sons so cheap. Henri III. having ceased, like all spoilt children, to care for his mother, rushed voluntarily into such debauchery as made him what the mother had made Charles IX., a childless husband, a king without an heir. Unhappily, Catherine's youngest son, the Duc d'Alençon, died—a natural death. The Queen-mother made every effort to control her son's passions. History preserves the tradition of a supper to nude women given in the banqueting-hall at Chenonceaux on his return from Poland, but it did not cure Henri III. of his bad habits.

This great Queen's last words summed up her policy, which was indeed so governed by good sense that we see the Cabinets of every country putting it into practice in similar circumstances.

"Well cut, my son," said she, when Henri III. came to her, on her death-bed, to announce that the enemy of the throne had been put to death. "Now you must sew up again."

She thus expressed her opinion that the sovereign must make friends with the House of Lorraine, and make it useful, as the only way to hinder the effects of the Guises' hatred, by giving them a hope of circumventing the King. But this indefatigable cunning of the Italian and the woman was incompatible with Henry III.'s life of debauchery. When once the Great Mother was dead, the Mother of Armies (*Mater castrorum*), the policy of the Valois died too.

Before attempting to write this picture of manners in action, the author patiently and minutely studied the principal reigns of French history, the quarrels of the Burgundians and the Armagnacs, and those of the Guises and the Valois, each in the forefront of a century. His purpose was to write a picturesque history of France. Isabella of Bavaria, Catherine and Marie de' Medici, each fills a conspicuous place, dominating from the fourteenth to the seventeenth centuries, and leading up to Louis XIV.

Of these three queens, Catherine was the most interesting and the most beautiful. Hers was a manly rule, not disgraced by the terrible amours of Isabella, nor those, even more terrible though less known, of Marie de' Medici. Isabella brought the English into France to oppose her son, was in love with her brother-in-law, the Duc d'Orléans, and with Boisbourdon. Marie de' Medici's account is still heavier. Neither of them had any political genius.

In the course of these studies and comparisons, the author became convinced of Catherine's greatness; by initiating himself into the peculiar difficulties of her position, he discerned how unjust historians, biased by Protestantism, had been to this Queen; and the outcome was the three sketches here presented, in which some erroneous opinions of her, of those who were about her, and of the aspect of the times, are combated.

The work is placed among my Philosophical Studies, because it illustrates the spirit of a period, and plainly shows the influence of opinions.

But, before depicting the political arena in which Catherine comes into collision with the two great obstacles in her career, it is necessary to give a short account of her previous life from the point of view of an impartial critic, so that the reader may form a general idea of this large and royal life up to the time when the first part of this narrative opens.

Never at any period, in any country or in any ruling family, was there more contempt felt for legitimacy than by the famous race of the Medici (in French commonly written and pronounced Medicis). They held the same opinion of monarchy as is now professed in Russia: the ruler on whom the crown devolves is the real and legitimate monarch. Mirabeau was justified in saying, "There has been but one mésalliance in my family—that with the Medici;" for, notwithstanding the exertions of well-paid genealogists, it is certain that the Medici, till the time of Avérardo de' Medici, gonfaloniere of Florence in 1314, were no more than Florentine merchants of great wealth. The first personage of the family who filled a conspicuous place in the history of the great

Tuscan Republic was Salvestro de' Medici, gonfaloniere in 1378. This Salvestro had two sons—Cosmo and Lorenzo de' Medici.

From Cosmo descended Lorenzo the Magnificent, the Duc de Nemours, the Duke of Urbino (Catherine's father), Pope Leo X., Pope Clement VII., and Alessandro, not indeed Duke of Florence, as he is sometimes called, but Duke of the City of Penna, a title created by Pope Clement VII. as a step toward that of Grand Duke of Tuscany.

Lorenzo's descendants were Lorenzino — the Brutus of Florence—who killed Duke Alessandro; Cosmo, the first Grand Duke, and all the rulers of Florence till 1737, when the family became extinct.

But neither of the two branches—that of Cosmo or that of Lorenzo—succeeded in a direct line, till the time when Marie de' Medici's father subjugated Tuscany, and the Grand Dukes inherited in regular succession. Thus Alessandro de' Medici, who assumed the title of Duke of the City of Penna, and whom Lorenzino assassinated, was the son of the Duke of Urbino, Catherine's father, by a Moorish slave. Hence Lorenzino, the legitimate son of Lorenzo, had a double right to kill Alessandro, both as a usurper in the family and as an oppressor of the city. Some historians have indeed supposed that Alessandro was the son of Clement VII. The event that led to the recognition of this bastard as head of the Republic was his marriage with Margaret of Austria, the natural daughter of Charles V.

Francesco de' Medici, the husband of Bianca Capello, recognized as his son a child of low birth bought by that notorious Venetian lady ; and, strange to say, Fernando, succeeding Francesco, upheld the hypothetical rights of this boy. Indeed, this youth, known as Don Antonio de' Medici, was recognized by the family during four ducal reigns ; he won the affection of all, did them important service, and was universally regretted.

Almost all the early Medici had natural children, whose lot was in every case splendid. The Cardinal Giulio de' Medici, Pope Clement VII., was the illegitimate son of Giuliano I. Cardinal Ippolito de' Medici was also a bastard, and he was within an ace of being Pope and head of the family.

Certain inventors of anecdote have a story that the Duke of Urbino, Catherine's father, told her: *"A figlia d'inganno non manca mai figliuolanza"* (A clever woman can always have children, *à propos* to some natural defect in Henri, the second son of François I., to whom she was betrothed). This Lor-enzo de' Medici, Catherine's father, had married, for the second time, in 1518, Madeleine de la Tour d'Auvergne, and died in 1519, a few days after his wife, who died in giving birth to Catherine. Catherine was thus fatherless and mother-less as soon as she saw the light. Hence the strange events of her childhood, checkered by the violent struggles of the Florentines, in the attempt to recover their liberty, against the Medici who were determined to govern Florence, but who were so circumspect in their policy that Catherine's father took the title of Duke of Urbino.

At his death, the legitimate head of the House of the Medici was Pope Leo X., who appointed Giuliano's illegiti-mate son, Giulio de' Medici, then cardinal, Governor of Florence. Leo X. was Catherine's grand-uncle, and this Cardinal Giulio, afterward Clement VII., was her *left-handed* uncle only. This it was which made Brantôme so wittily speak of that Pope as an "uncle in Our Lady."

During the siege by the Medici to regain possession of Florence, the Republican party, not satisfied with having shut up Catherine, then nine years old, in a convent, after strip-ping her of all her possessions, proposed to expose her to the fire of the artillery, between two battlements—the suggestion of a certain Battista Cei. Bernardo Castiglione went even further in a council held to determine on some conclusion to the business; he advised that, rather than surrender Catherine to the Pope who demanded it, she should be handed over to the tender mercies of the soldiers. All revolutions of the populace are alike. Catherine's policy, always in favor of Royal authority, may have been fostered by such scenes, which an Italian girl of nine could not fail to understand.

Alessandro's promotion, to which Clement VII., himself a bastard, largely contributed, was no doubt owing partly to the fact of his being illegitimate, and to Charles V.'s affection for his famous natural daughter Margaret. Thus the Pope and the Emperor were moved by similar feelings. At this period Venice was mistress of the commerce of the world; Rome governed its morals; Italy was still supreme, by the poets, the generals, and the statesmen who were her sons. At no other time has any one country had so curious or so various a multitude of men of genius. There were so many that the smallest princelings were superior men. Italy was overflowing with talent, daring, science, poetry, wealth, and gallantry, though rent by constant internal wars, and at all times the arena in which conquerors met to fight for her fairest provinces.

When men are so great they are not afraid to confess their weakness; hence, no doubt, this golden age for bastards. And it is but justice to declare that these illegitimate sons of the Medici were ardent for the glory and the advancement of the family, alike in possessions and in power. And as soon as the Duke of the City of Penna, the Moorish slave's son, was established as Tyrant of Florence, he took up the interest shown by Pope Clement VII. for Lorenzo II.'s daughter, now eleven years of age.

As we study the march of events and of men in that strange sixteenth century, we must never forget that the chief element of political conduct was unremitting craft, destroying in every nature the upright conduct, the *square-ness* which imagination looks for in eminent men. In this,

2

especially, lies Catherine's absolution.  This observation, in fact, disposes of all the mean and foolish accusations brought against her by the writers of the reformed faith.  It was indeed the golden age of this type of policy, of which Machiavelli and Spinoza formulated the code, and Hobbes and Montesquieu; for the Dialogue of "Sylla and Eucrates" expresses Montesquieu's real mind, which he could not set forth in any other form in consequence of his connection with the Encylopædists.  These principles are to this day the unconfessed morality of every Cabinet where schemes of vast dominion are worked out.  In France we were severe on Napoleon when he exerted this Italian genius which was in his blood, and its plots did not always succeed; but Charles V., Catherine, Philip II., Giulio II., would have done just as he did in the affairs of Spain.

At the time when Catherine was born, history, if related from the point of view of honesty, would seem an impossible romance.  Charles V., while forced to uphold the Catholic Church against the attacks of Luther, who by threatening the tiara threatened his throne, allowed Rome to be besieged, and kept Pope Clement VII. in prison.  This same Pope, who had no more bitter foe than Charles V., cringed to him that he might place Alessandro de' Medici at Florence, and the Emperor gave his daughter in marriage to the bastard Duke.  No sooner was he firmly settled there than Alessandro, in concert with the Pope, attempted to injure Charles V. by an alliance, through Catherine de' Medici, with Francis I., and both promised to assist the French King to conquer Italy.

Lorenzino de' Medici became Alessandro's boon companion, and pandered to him to get an opportunity of killing him; and Filippo Strozzi, one of the loftiest spirits of that age, regarded this murder with such high esteem that he vowed that each of his sons should marry one of the assassin's daughters. The sons religiously fulfilled the father's pledge at a time when each of them, under Catherine's protection, could have made a splendid alliance; for one was Doria's rival, and the other Marshal of France.

Cosmo de' Medici, Alessandro's successor, avenged the death of the tyrant with great cruelty, and persistently for twelve years, during which his hatred never flagged against the people who had, after all, placed him in power. He was eighteen years of age when he succeeded to the government; his first act was to annul the rights of Alessandro's legitimate sons, at the time when he was avenging Alessandro! Charles V. confirmed the dispossession of his grandson, and recognized Cosmo instead of Alessandro's son.

Cosmo, raised to the throne by Cardinal Cibo, at once sent the prelate into exile. Then Cardinal Cibo accused his creature, Cosmo, the first Grand Duke, of having tried to poison Alessandro's son. The Grand Duke, as jealous of his authority as Charles V. was of his, abdicated, like the Emperor, in favor of his son Francesco, after ordering the death of Don Garcias, his other son, in revenge for that of Cardinal Giovanni de' Medici, whom Garcias had assassinated.

Cosmo I. and his son Francesco, who ought to have been devoted, soul and body, to the Royal House of France, the only power able to lend them support, were the humble servants of Charles V. and Philip II., and consequently the secret, perfidious, and cowardly foes of Catherine de' Medici, one of the glories of their race.

Such are the more important features—contradictory and illogical indeed—the dishonest acts, the dark intrigues of the House of the Medici alone. From this sketch some idea may be formed of the other princes of Italy and Europe. Every envoy from Cosmo I. to the Court of France had secret instructions to poison Strozzi, Queen Catherine's relation, when he should find him there. Charles V. had three ambassadors from Francis I. murdered.

It was early in October, 1533, that the Duke *della cittàdi*

*Penna* (of the City of Penna) left Florence for Leghorn, accompanied by Catherine de' Medici, sole heiress of Lorenzo II. The Duke and the Princess of Florence, for this was the title borne by the girl, now fourteen years of age, left the city with a large following of servants, officials, and secretaries, preceded by men-at-arms, and escorted by a mounted guard. The young princess as yet knew nothing of her fate, excepting that the Pope and Duke Alessandro were to have an interview at Leghorn; but her uncle, Filippo Strozzi, soon told her of the future that lay before her.

Filippo Strozzi had married Clarissa de' Medici, whole sister to Lorenzo de' Medici, Duke of Urbino, Catherine's father; but this union, arranged quite as much with a view to converting one of the stoutest champions of the popular cause to the support of Medici as to secure the recall of that then exiled family, never shook the tenets of the rough soldier who was persecuted by his party for having consented to it. In spite of some superficial change of conduct, somewhat over·ruled by this alliance, he remained faithful to the popular side, and declared against the Medici as soon as he perceived their scheme of subjugating Florence. This great man even refused the offer of a principality from Pope Leo X. At that time Filippo Strozzi was a victim to the policy of the Medici, so shifty in its means, so unvarying in its aim.

After sharing the Pope's misfortunes and captivity, when, surprised by Colonna, he took refuge in the castle of Saint-Angelo, he was given up by Clement VII. as a hostage and carried to Naples. As soon as the Pope was free, he fell upon his foes, and Strozzi was then near being killed; he was forced to pay an enormous bribe to get out of the prison, where he was closely guarded. As soon as he was at liberty, with the natural trustfulness of an honest man, he was simple enough to appear before Clement VII., who, perhaps, had flattered himself that he was rid of him. The Pope had so much to be ashamed of that he received Strozzi very ungraciously.

Thus Strozzi had very early begun his apprenticeship to the life of disaster, which is that of a man who is honest in politics, and whose conscience will not lend itself to the caprices of opportunity, whose actions are pleasing only to virtue, which is persecuted by all—by the populace, because it withstands their blind passions; by authority, because it resists its usurpations.

The life of these great citizens is a martyrdom, through which they have nothing to support them but the strong voice of conscience, and the sense of social duty, which in all cases dictates their conduct.

There were many such men in the Republic of Florence, all as great as Strozzi and as masterly as their adversaries on the Medici side, though beaten by Florentine cunning.  In the conspiracy of the Pazzi, what can be finer than the attitude of the head of that house?  His trade was immense, and he settled all his accounts with Asia, the Levant, and Europe before carrying out that great plot, to the end that his correspondents should not be the losers if he should fail.

And the history of the rise of the Medici family in the fourteenth and fifteenth centuries is one of the finest that remains unwritten, though men of great genius have attempted it.  It is not the history of a republic, or of any particular community or phase of civilization; it is the history of political man, and the eternal history of political developments, that of usurpers and conquerors.

On his return to Florence, Filippo Strozzi restored the ancient form of government, and banished Ippolito de' Medici, another bastard, as well as Alessandro, with whom he was now acting.  But he was then afraid of the inconstancy of the populace; and, as he dreaded Pope Clement's vengeance, he went to take charge of a large commercial house he had at Lyons in correspondence with his bankers at Venice and Rome, in France, and in Spain.  A strange fact!  These men, who bore the burden of public affairs as well as that of a perennial struggle with the Medici, to say nothing of their squabbles with their own party, could also endure the cares of commerce and speculation, of banking with all its complications, which the vast multiplicity of coinages and frequent forgeries made far more difficult then than now. The word banker is derived from the bench on which they sat, and which served also to ring the gold and silver pieces on. Strozzi found in his adored wife's death a pretext to offer to the Republican party, whose police is always all the more terrible because everybody is a voluntary spy in the name of Liberty, which justifies all things.

Filippo's return to Florence happened just at the time when the city was compelled to bow to Alessandro's yoke; but he had previously been to see Pope Clement, with whom matters were so promising that his feelings toward Strozzi had changed. In the moment of triumph the Medici so badly needed such a man as Strozzi, were it only to lend a grace to Alessandro's assumption of dignity, that Clement persuaded him to sit on the bastard's council, which was about to take oppressive measures, and Filippo had accepted a diploma as senator. But for the last two years and a half—like Seneca and Burrhus with Nero — he had noted the beginnings of tyranny. He had found himself the object of distrust to the populace, and so little in favor with the Medici, whom he opposed, that he foresaw a catastrophe. And as soon as he heard from Alessandro of the negotiations for the marriage of Catherine with a French Prince, which were, perhaps, to be concluded at Leghorn, where the contracting powers had agreed to meet, he resolved to go to France and follow the fortunes of his niece, who would need a guardian. Alessandro, delighted to be quit of a man so difficult to manage in what concerned Florence, applauded this decision, which spared him a murder, and advised Strozzi to place himself at the head of Catherine's household.

In point of fact, to dazzle the French Court, the Medici

had constituted a brilliant suite for the young girl whom they quite incorrectly styled the Princess of Florence, and who was also called the Duchess of Urbino. The procession, at the head of it Duke Alessandro, Catherine, and Strozzi, consisted of more than a thousand persons, exclusive of the escort and serving-men ; and when the last of them were still at the gate of Florence, the foremost had already got beyond the first village outside the town—where straw plait for hats is now made.

It was beginning to be generally known that Catherine was to marry a son of Francis the First, but as yet it was no more than a rumor which found confirmation in the country from this triumphant progress from Florence to Leghorn. From the preparations required, Catherine suspected that her marriage was in question, and her uncle revealed to her the abortive scheme of her ambitious family, who had aspired to the hand of the Dauphin. Duke Alessandro still hoped that the Duke of Albany might succeed in changing the determination of the French King, who, though anxious to secure the aid of the Medici in Italy, would only give them the Duc d'Orléans. This narrowness lost Italy to France, and did not hinder Catherine from being Queen.

This Duke of Albany, the son of Alexander Stewart, brother of James III.* of Scotland, had married Anne de la Tour de Boulogne, sister to Madeleine, Catherine's mother; he was thus her maternal uncle. It was through her mother that Catherine was so rich and connected with so many families ; for, strangely enough, Diane de Poitiers, her rival, was also her cousin. Jean de Poitiers, Diane's father, was the son of Jeanne de la Tour de Boulogne, the Duchess of Urbino's aunt. Catherine was also related to Mary Stewart, her daughter-in-law.

Catherine was now informed that her dower in money would amount to a hundred thousand ducats. The ducat was

* Great-uncle to Mary, Queen of Scots.

a gold-piece as large as one of our old louis d'or, but only half as thick.  Thus a hundred thousand ducats in those days represented, in consequence of the high value of gold, six millions of francs at the present time, the ducat being worth about twelve francs.  The importance of the banking-house of Strozzi, at Lyons, may be imagined from this, as it was his factor there who paid over the twelve hundred thousand livres in gold.  The counties of Auvergne and Lauraguais also formed part of Catherine's portion, and the Pope, Clement VII., made her a gift of a hundred thousand ducats more in jewels, precious stones, and other wedding gifts, to which Duke Alessandro contributed.

On reaching Leghorn, Catherine, still so young, must have been flattered by the extraordinary magnificence displayed by Pope Clement VII., her "uncle in Our Lady," then the head of the House of Medici, to crush the Court of France.  He had arrived at the port in one of his galleys hung with crimson satin trimmed with gold fringe, and covered with an awning of cloth of gold.  This barge, of which the decorations had cost nearly twenty thousand ducats, contained several rooms for the use of Henri de France's future bride, furnished with the choicest curiosities the Medici had been able to collect. The oarsmen, magnificently dressed, and the seamen were under the captaincy of a prior of the order of the Knights of Rhodes.  The Pope's household filled three more barges.

The Duke of Albany's galleys, moored by the side of the Pope's, formed, with these, a considerable flotilla.

Duke Alessandro presented the officers of Catherine's household to the Pope, with whom he held a secret conference, introducing to him, as seems probable, Count Sebastian Montecuculi, who had just left the Emperor's service—rather suddenly, it was said—and the two generals, Antonio de Leyva and Fernando Gonzaga.  Was there a premeditated plan between these two bastards to make the Duc d'Orléans the Dauphin?  What was the reward promised to Count Sebastian Montecuculi, who, before entering the service of Charles V., had studied medicine? History is silent on these points. We shall see, indeed, in what obscurity the subject is wrapped. It is so great that some serious and conscientious historians have recently recognized Montecuculi's innocence.

Catherine was now officially informed by the Pope himself of the alliance proposed for her. The Duke of Albany had had great difficulty in keeping the King of France to his promise of giving even his second son to Catherine de' Medici; and Clement's impatience was so great, he was so much afraid of seeing his schemes upset either by some intrigue on the part of the Emperor or by the haughtiness of France, where the great nobles cast an evil eye on this union, that he embarked forthwith and made for Marseilles. He arrived there at the end of October, 1533.

In spite of this splendor, the House of the Medici was eclipsed by the sovereign of France. To show to what a pitch these great bankers carried their magnificence, the dozen pieces given by the Pope in the bride's wedding purse consisted of gold medals of inestimable historical interest, for they were at that time unique. But Francis I., who loved festivity and display, distinguished himself on this occasion. The wedding feasts for Henri de Valois and Catherine went on for thirty-four days. It is useless to repeat here details which may be read in every history of Provence and Marseilles as to this famous meeting between the Pope and the King of France, which was the occasion of a jest of the Duke of Albany's as to the duty of fasting; a retort recorded by Brantôme which vastly amused the Court, and shows the tone of manners at that time.

Though Henri de Valois was but three weeks older than Catherine, the Pope insisted on the immediate consummation of the marriage between these two children, so greatly did he dread the subterfuges of diplomacy and the trickery commonly practiced at that period. Clement, indeed, very anxious for proof, remained thirty-four days at Marseilles, in the hope, it is said, of some visible evidence in his young relation, who at fourteen was marriageable. And it was, no doubt, when questioning Catherine before his departure, that he tried to console her by the famous speech ascribed to Catherine's father: *"A figlia d'inganno non manca mai la figliuolanza."* *

The strangest conjectures have been given to the world as to the causes of Catherine's barrenness during ten years. Few persons nowadays are aware that various medical works contain suppositions as to this matter, so grossly indecent that they could not be repeated.† This gives some clue to the strange calumnies which still blacken this Queen, whose every action was distorted to her injury. The reason lay simply with her husband. It is sufficient evidence that, at a time when no prince was shy of having natural children, Diane de Poitiers, far more highly favored than his wife, had no children ; and nothing is commoner in surgical experience than such a malformation as this Prince's, which gave rise to a jest of the ladies of the Court, who would have made him abbé of Saint-Victor, at a time when the French language was as free as the Latin tongue. After the Prince was operated on, Catherine had ten children.

The delay was a happy thing for France. If Henri II. had had children by Diane de Poitiers, it would have caused serious political complications. At the time of his treatment, the Duchesse de Valentinois was in the second youth of womanhood. These facts alone show that the history of Catherine de' Medici remains to be entirely re-written ; and that, as Napoleon very shrewdly remarked, the history of France should be in one volume only, or in a thousand.

When we compare the conduct of Charles V. with that of the King of France during the Pope's stay at Marseilles, it is greatly to the advantage of Francis—as indeed in every in-

---

* See page 16.　　　　　　† See *Bayle.* Art. *Fernel.*

stance.  Here is a brief report of this meeting as given by a contemporary :

" His Holiness the Pope, having been conducted to the Palace prepared for him, as I have said, outside the port, each one withdrew to his chamber until the morrow, when his said Holiness prepared to make his entry.  Which was done with great sumptuousness and magnificence, he being set on a throne borne on the shoulders of two men in his pontifical habit, saving only the tiara, while before him went a white palfrey bearing the Holy Sacrament, the said palfrey being led by two men on foot in very fine raiment holding a bridle of white silk.  After him came all the cardinals in their habit, riding their pontifical asses, and Madame the Duchess of Urbino in great magnificence, with a goodly company of ladies and gentlemen alike of France and of Italy.  And the Pope, with all this company, being come to the place prepared where they should lodge, each one withdrew ; and all this was ordered and done without any disorder or tumult. Now, while as the Pope was making his entry, the King crossed the water in his frigate and went to lodge there whence the Pope had come, to the end that on the morrow he might come from thence to pay homage to the Holy Father, as beseemed a most Christian King.

" The King, being then ready, set forth to go to the Palace where the Pope was, accompanied by the Princes of his blood, Monsieur the Duc de Vendosmois (father of the Vidame de Chartres), the Comte de Saint-Pol, Monsieur de Montmorency, and Monsieur de la Roche-sur-Yon, the Duc de Nemours (brother to the Duke of Savoy who died at that place), the Duke of Albany, and many others, counts, barons, and nobles, the Duc de Montmorency being at all times about the King's person.  The King, being come to the Palace, was received by the Pope and all the College of Cardinals assembled in consistory, with much civility (*fort humainement*). This done, each one went to the place appointed to him, and the King took with him many cardinals to feast them, and among them Cardinal de' Medici, the Pope's nephew, a very magnificent lord with a fine escort.  On the morrow, those deputed by his Holiness and by the King began to treat of those matters whereon they had met to agree.  First of all, they treated of the question of faith, and a bull was read for the repression of heresy, and to hinder things from coming to a greater combustion (*une plus grande combustion*) than they are in already.  Then was performed the marriage ceremony between the Duc d'Orléans, the King's second son, and Catherine de' Medici, Duchess of Urbino, his Holiness' niece, under conditions the same, or nearly the same, as had been formerly proposed to the Duke of Albany.  The said marriage was concluded with great magnificence, and our Holy Father married them.*  This marriage being thus concluded, the Holy Father held a consistory, wherein he created four cardinals to wait on the King, to wit: Cardinal le Veneur, heretofore Bishop of Lisieux and High Almoner; Cardinal de Boulogne, of the family of la Chambre, half-brother on his mother's side to the Duke of Albany; Cardinal de Châtillon, of the family of Coligny, nephew to the Sire de Montmorency; and Cardinal de Givry.''

When Strozzi paid down the marriage portion in the presence of the Court, he observed some surprise on the part of the French nobles; they said pretty loudly that it was a small price for such a mésalliance—what would they say to-day? Cardinal Ippolito replied—

"Then you are not informed as to your King's secrets. His holiness consents to bestow on France three pearls of inestimable price—Genoa, Milan, and Naples."

The Pope left Count Sebastian Montecuculi to present himself at the French Court, where he made an offer of his

---

* At that time in French, as in Italian, the words *marry* and *espouse* were used in a contrary sense to their present meaning.  *Marier* was the fact of being married, *épouser* was the priestly function.

services, complaining of Antonio de Leyva and Fernando Gonzaga, for which reason he was accepted. Montecuculi was not one of Catherine's household, which was composed entirely of French ladies and gentlemen; for, by a law of the realm which the Pope was rejoiced to see carried out, Catherine was naturalized by letters patent before her marriage. Montecuculi was at first attached to the household of the Queen, Charles V.'s sister. Then, not long after, he entered the Dauphin's service in the capacity of cup-bearer.

The Duchesse d'Orléans found herself entirely swamped at the Court of Francis I. Her young husband was in love with Diane de Poitiers, who was certainly her equal in point of birth, and a far greater lady. The daughter of the Medici took rank below Queen Eleanor, Charles V.'s sister, and the Duchesse d'Etampes, whose marriage to the head of the family of de Brosse had given her one of the most powerful positions and highest titles in France. Her aunt, the Duchess of Albany, the Queen of Navarre, the Duchesse de Guise, the Duchesse de Vendôme, the wife of the Connétable, and many other women, by their birth and privileges as well as by their influence in the most sumptuous Court ever held by a French King—not excepting Louis XIV.—wholly eclipsed the daughter of the Florentine merchants, who was indeed more illustrious and richer through the Tour de Boulogne family than through her descent from the Medici.

Filippo Strozzi, a republican at heart, regarded his niece's position as so critical and difficult that he felt himself incapable of directing her in the midst of conflicting interests, and deserted her at the end of a year, being indeed recalled to Italy by the death of Clement VII. Catherine's conduct, when we remember that she was but just fifteen, was a marvel of prudence. She very adroitly attached herself to the King, her father-in-law, leaving him as rarely as possible; she was with him on horseback, in hunting, and in war.

Her adoration of Francis I. saved the house of Medici from all suspicion when the Dauphin died poisoned. At that time Catherine and the Duc d'Orléans were at the King's head-quarters in Provence, for France had already been invaded by Charles V., the King's brother-in-law. The whole Court had remained on the scene of the wedding festivities, now the theatre of the most barbarous war. Just as Charles V., compelled to retreat, had fled, leaving the bones of his army in Provence, the Dauphin was returning to Lyons by the Rhone. Stopping at Tournon for the night, to amuse himself, he went through some athletic exercises, such as formed almost the sole education he or his brother received, in consequence of their long detention as hostages. The Prince being very hot—it was in the month of August—was so rash as to ask for a glass of water, which was given to him, iced, by Montecuculi. The Dauphin died almost instantaneously.

The King idolized his son. The Dauphin was indeed, as historians are agreed, a very accomplished Prince. His father, in despair, gave the utmost publicity to the proceedings against Montecuculi, and placed the matter in the hands of the most learned judges of the day.

After heroically enduring the first tests of torture without confessing anything, the Count made an avowal by which he fully implicated the Emperor and his two generals, Antonio de Leyva and Fernando Gonzago. This, however, did not satisfy Francis I. Never was a case more solemnly thrashed out than this. An eye-witness gives the following account of what the King did:

" The King called all the Princes of the Blood, and all the Knights of his Order, and many other high personages of the realm, to meet at Lyons; the Pope's Legate and Nuncio, the cardinals who were of his Court, and the ambassadors of England, Scotland, Portugal, Venice, Ferrara, and others; together with all the princes and great nobles of foreign countries, both of Italy and of Germany, who were at that

time residing at his Court, to wit : The Duke of Wittemberg,
in Allemaigne ; the Dukes of Somma, of Arianna, and of
Atria ; the Princes of Melphe [Malfi?] (who had desired to
marry Catherine), and of Stilliano, Neapolitan ; the Marquis
di Vigevo, of the House of Trivulzio, Milanese ; the Signor
Giovanni Paolo di Ceri, Roman ; the Signor Césare Fregose,
Genoese ; the Signor Annibale Gonzaga, Mantuan, and many
more.   Who being assembled, he. caused to be read in their
presence, from the beginning to the end, the trial of that
wretched man who had poisoned his late Highness the
Dauphin, with all the interrogations, confessions, confront-
ings, and other proceedings usual in criminal trials, not choosing that the sentence should be carried out until all those
present had given their opinion on this monstrous and miserable matter.''

Count Montecuculi's fidelity and devotion may seem extraordinary in our day of universal indiscretion, when everybody, and even ministers, talk over the most trivial incidents
in which they have put a finger ; but in those times princes
could command devoted servants, or knew how to choose
them.   There were monarchical Moreys then, because there
was faith.   Never look for great things from self-interest :
interests may change ; but look for anything from feeling,
from religious faith, monarchical faith, patriotic faith.   These
three beliefs alone can produce a Berthereau of Geneva, a
Sydney or a Strafford in England, assassins to murder
Thomas à Becket, or a Montecuculi ; Jacques Cœur and
Jeanne d'Arc, or Richelieu and Danton ; a Bonchamp, a
Talmont, a Clément, or a Chabot.

Charles V. made use of the highest personages to carry
out the murder of three ambassadors from Francis I.   A year
later Lorenzino, Catherine's cousin, assassinated Duke Alessandro after three years of dissimulation and in circumstances
which gained him the surname of the Florentine Brutus.   The
rank of the victim was so little a check on such undertakings

that neither Leo X. nor Clement VII. seems to have died a
natural death.    Mariana, the historian of Philip II., almost
jests in speaking of the death of the Queen of Spain, a
Princess of France, saying that "for the greater glory of the
Spanish throne God suffered the blindness of the doctors who
treated the Queen for dropsy."    When King Henri II.
allowed himself to utter a scandal which deserved a sword-
thrust, he could find la Châtaignerie willing to take it.    At
that time royal personages had their meals served to them in
padlocked boxes of which they had the key.    Hence the
*droit de cadenas*, the *right of the padlock*, an honor which
ceased to exist in the reign of Louis XIV.

The Dauphin died of poison, the same perhaps as caused
the death of MADAME, under Louis XIV.    Pope Clement
had been dead two years; Duke Alessandro, steeped in debauchery, seemed to have no interest in the Duc d'Orléans'
elevation.    Catherine, now seventeen years old, was with her
father-in-law, whom she devotedly admired; Charles V.
alone seemed to have an interest in the Dauphin's death,
because Francis I. intended his son to form an alliance which
would have extended the power of France.    Thus the Count's
confession was very ingeniously based on the passions and
policy of the day.    Charles V. had fled after seeing his troops
overwhelmed in Provence, and with them his good fortune,
his reputation, and his hopes of aggrandizement.    And note
that, even if an innocent man had confessed under torture,
the King afterward gave him freedom of speech before an
august assembly, and in the presence of men with whom innocence had a fair chance of a hearing.    The King wanted
the truth, and sought it in good faith.

In spite of her now brilliant prospects, Catherine's position
at Court was unchanged by the Dauphin's death; her child-
lessness made a divorce seem probable when her husband
should become king.    The Dauphin was now enslaved by
Diane de Poitiers, who dared to be the rival of Madame

d'Etampes. Catherine was therefore doubly attentive and insinuating to her father-in-law, understanding that he was her sole mainstay.

Thus the first ten years of Catherine's married life were spent in the unceasing regrets caused by repeated disappointments when she hoped to have a child, and the vexations of her rivalry with Diane. Imagine what the life must be of a princess constantly spied on by a jealous mistress who was favored by the Catholic party, and by the strong support the Sénéchale had acquired through the marriage of her daughters —one to Robert de la Mark, Duc de Bouillon, Prince de Sédan ; the other to Claude de Lorraine, Duc d'Aumale.

Swamped between the party of the Duchesse d'Etampes and that of the Sénéchale (the title born by Diane de Poitiers during the reign of Francis I.), who divided the Court and political feeling between the two mortal foes, Catherine tried to be the friend of both the Duchess and Diane de Poitiers. She, who was to become so great a queen, played the part of a subaltern. Thus she served her apprenticeship to the double-faced policy which afterward was the secret clue to her life. At a later date the Queen found herself between the Catholics and the Calvinists, as the woman had been, for ten years, between Madame d'Etampes and Madame de Poitiers.

She studied the contradictions of French policy. Francis upheld Calvin and the Lutherans to annoy Charles V. Then, after having covertly and patiently fostered the Reformation in Germany, after tolerating Calvin's presence at the Court of Navarre, he turned against it with undisguised severity. So Catherine could see the Court and the women of the Court playing with the fire of heresy ; Diane at the head of the Catholic party with the Guises, only because the Duchesse d'Etampes was on the side of Calvin and the Protestants.

This was Catherine's political education ; and in the King's private circle she could study the mistakes made by the Medici. The Dauphin was antagonistic to his father on

every point ; he was a bad son.  He forgot the hardest but
the truest axiom of Royalty, namely, that the throne is a
responsible entity, and that a son who may oppose his father
during his lifetime must carry out his policy on succeeding to
the throne.  Spinoza, who was as deep a politician as he was
a great philosopher, says, in treating of the case of a king
who has succeeded to another by a revolution or by treason :
"If the new King hopes to secure his throne and protect his
life, he must display so much zeal in avenging his predecessor's
death that no one shall feel tempted to repeat such a crime.
But to avenge him worthily it is not enough that he should
shed the blood of his subjects ; he must confirm the maxims
of him whose place he fills, and walk in the same ways of
government."

It was the application of this principle which gave the
Medici to Florence.  Cosmo I., Alessandro's successor, eleven
years later, instigated the murder, at Venice, of the Florentine
Brutus, and, as has been said, persecuted the Strozzi without
mercy.  It was the neglect of this principle that overthrew
Louis XVI.  That King was false to every principle of government when he reinstated the Parlements suppressed by his
grandfather.  Louis XV. had been clear-sighted ; the Parlements, and especially that of Paris, were quite half to blame
for the disorders that necessitated the assembling of the States-
General.  Louis XV.'s mistake was that when he threw down
that barrier between the throne and the people, he did not
erect a stronger one, that he did not substitute for the Parlements a strong constitutional rule in the provinces.  There
lay the remedy for the evils of the Monarchy, the voting
power for taxation and the incidence of the taxes, with consent gradually won to the reforms needed in the monarchical
rule.

Henri II.'s first act was to give all his confidence to the
Connétable de Montmorency, whom his father had desired

him to leave in banishment. The Connétable de Montmorency, with Diane de Poitiers, to whom he was closely attached, was master of the kingdom. Hence Catherine was even less powerful and happy as Queen of France than she had been as the Dauphiness.

At first, from the year 1543, she had a child every year for ten years, and was fully taken up by her maternal functions during that time, which included the last years of Francis I.'s reign, and almost the whole of her husband's. It is impossible not to detect in this constant child-bearing the malicious influence of a rival who thus kept the legitimate wife out of the way. This feminine and barbarous policy was no doubt one of Catherine's grievances against Diane. Being thus kept out of the tide of affairs, this clever woman spent her time in observing all the interests of the persons at Court, and all the parties formed there. The Italians who had followed her excited violent suspicions. After the execution of Montecuculi, the Connétable de Montmorency, Diane, and most of the crafty politicians at Court were racked with doubts of the Medici; but Francis I. always scouted them. Still the Gondi, the Biraguas, the Strozzi, the Ruggieri, the Sardini, in short, all who were classed as the Italians who had arrived in Catherine's wake, were compelled to exercise every faculty of wit, policy, and courage to enable them to remain at Court under the burden of disfavor that weighed on them. During the supremacy of Diane de Poitiers, Catherine's obligingness went so far that some clever folk have seen in it an evidence of the profound dissimulation to which she was compelled by men and circumstances and by the conduct of Henri II. But it is going too far to say that she never asserted her rights as a wife and a queen. Her ten children (beside one miscarriage) were a sufficient explanation of the King's conduct, who was thus set free to spend his time with Diane de Poitiers. But the King certainly never fell short of what he owed to himself; he gave the Queen an entry worthy of any that had previously taken place, on the occasion of her coronation.  The records of the Parlement and of the Exchequer prove that these two important bodies went to meet Catherine outside Paris, as far as Saint-Lazare.  Here, indeed, is a passage from du Tillet's narrative :

"A scaffolding had been erected at Saint-Lazare, whereon was a throne (which du Tillet calls a chair of state, *chaire de parement*).  Catherine seated herself on this, dressed in a sur-coat, or sort of cape of ermine, covered with jewels ; beneath it a bodice, with a court train, and on her head a crown of pearls and diamonds ; she was supported by the Maréchale de la Mark, her lady of honor.  Around her, standing, were the princes of the Blood and other princes and noblemen richly dressed, with the Chancellor of France in a robe of cloth of gold in a pattern on a ground of red cramoisy.*  In front of the Queen and on the same scaffolding were seated, in two rows, twelve duchesses and countesses, dressed in surcoats of ermine, stomachers, trains, and fillets, that is to say, coronets, whether duchesses or countesses.  There were the Duchesses d'Estouteville, de Montpensier—the elder and the younger—the Princesse de la Roche-sur-Yon ; the Duchesses de Guise, de Nivernois, d'Aumale, de Valentinois (Diane de Poitiers) ; Mademoiselle the legitimized bastard 'of France' (a title given to the King's daughter Diane, who became Duchesse de Castro-Farnese, and afterward Duchesse de Montmorency-Damville), Madame la Connétable, and Mademoiselle de Nemours, not to mention the other ladies who could find no room.  The four *capped* Presidents (*à mortier*), with some other members of the Court and the chief clerk, du Tillet, went up on to the platform and did their service, and the First President Lizet, kneeling on one knee, addressed the Queen.  The Chancellor, likewise on one knee, made re-sponse.  She made her entrance into Paris at about three in

---

* The old French word *cramoisi* did not mean merely a crimson red, but denoted a special excellence of the dye.  (See Rabelais.)

the afternoon, riding in an open litter, Madame Marguerite de France sitting opposite to her, and by the side of the litter came the Cardinals d'Amboise, de Châtillon, de Boulogne, and de Lenoncourt, in their rochets. She got out at the Church of Notre-Dame, and was received by the clergy. After she had made her prayer, she was carried along the Rue de la Calandre to the Palace, where the royal supper was spread in the great hall. She sat there in the middle at a marble table, under a canopy of velvet powdered with gold fleurs de lys.''

It will here be fitting to controvert a popular error which some persons have perpetuated, following Sauval in the mistake. It has been said that Henri II. carried his oblivion of decency so far as to place his mistress' initials even on the buildings which Catherine had advised him to undertake or to carry on at such lavish expense. But the cypher, which is to be seen at the Louvre, amply refutes those who have so little comprehension as to lend credit to such nonsense, a gratuitous slur on the honor of our kings and queens. The H for Henri and the two Cs, face to face, for Catherine seem indeed to make two Ds for Diane ; and this coincidence was no doubt pleasing to the King. But it is not the less certain that the royal cypher was officially constructed of the initials of the King and the Queen. And this is so true that the same cypher is still to be seen on the corn-market in Paris which Catherine herself had built. It may also be found in the crypt of Saint-Denis on Catherine's tomb, which she caused to be constructed during her lifetime by the side of that of Henri II., and on which she is represented from life by the sculptor to whom she sat.

On a solemn occasion, when he was setting out on an expedition to Germany, Henri II. proclaimed Catherine Regent during his absence, as also in the event of his death—on March 25, 1552. Catherine's bitterest enemy, the author of the *Discours merveilleux sur les déportements de Catherine II.*

("Strange Discourses on the Conduct of Catherine II."), admits that she acquitted herself of these functions to the general approbation, and that the King was satisfied with her administration.   Henri II. had men and money at the right moment. And after the disastrous day of Saint-Quentin, Catherine obtained from the Parisians considerable sums, which she forwarded to Compiègne, whither the King had come.

In politics Catherine made immense efforts to acquire some little influence.   She was clever enough to gain over to her interests the Connétable de Montmorency, who was all-powerful under Henri II.   The King's terrible reply to Montmorency's insistency is well known.   This answer was the result of the good advice given by Catherine in the rare moments when she was alone with the King, and could explain to him the policy of the Florentines, which was to set the magnates of a kingdom by the ears and build up the sovereign authority on the ruins—Louis XI.'s system, subsequently carried out by Richelieu.   Henri II., who saw only through the eyes of Diane and the Connétable, was quite a feudal King, and on friendly terms with the great Houses of the realm.

After an ineffectual effort in her favor made by the Connétable, probably in the year 1556, Catherine paid great court to the Guises, and schemed to detach them from Diane's party so as to set them in opposition to Montmorency.   But, unfortunately, Diane and the Connétable were as virulent against the Protestants as the Guises were.   Hence their antagonism lacked the virus which religious feeling would have given it.   Beside, Diane boldly defied the Queen's plans by coquetting with the Guises and giving her daughter to the Duc d'Aumale.   She went so far that she has been accused by some writers of granting more than smiles to the gallant Cardinal de Lorraine.*

* Some satirist of the time has left the following lines on Henry II. [in which the pun on the words Sire and Cire (wax) would be lost in translation]:

The signs of grief and the ostentatious regret displayed by Catherine on the King's death cannot be regarded as genuine. The fact that Henri II. had been so passionately and faithfully attached to Diane de Poitiers made it incumbent on Catherine that she should play the part of a neglected wife who idolized her husband; but, like every clever woman, she carried on her dissimulation, and never ceased to speak with tender regret of Henri II. Diane herself, it is well known, wore mourning all her life for her husband, Monsieur de Brézé. Her colors were black and white, and the King was wearing them at the tournament where he was fatally wounded. Catherine, in imitation no doubt of her rival, wore mourning for the King to the end of her life.

On the King's death, the Duchesse de Valentintois was shamelessly deserted and dishonored by the Connétable de Montmorency, a man in every respect beneath his reputation. Diane sent to offer her estate and château of Chenonceaux to the Queen. Catherine then replied in the presence of witnesses, "I can never forget that she was all the joy of my dear Henri; I should be ashamed to accept, I will give her an estate in exchange. I would propose that of Chaumont-on-the-Loire." The deed of exchange was, in fact, signed at Blois in 1559. Diane, whose sons-in-law were the Duc d'Aumale and the Duc de Bouillon, kept her whole fortune and died peacefully in 1566 at the age of sixty-six. She was thus nineteen years older than Henri II. These dates, copied from the epitaph on her tomb by a historian who studied the question at the end of the last century, clear up many historical difficulties; for many writers have said she was forty when

> "Sire, si vous laissez, comme Charles désire,
>  Comme Diane veut, par trop vous gouverner,
>  Fondre, pétrir, mollir, refondre, retourner,
>  Sire, vous n'êtes plus, vous n'êtes plus que cire."

Charles was the Cardinal de Lorraine.

her father was sentenced in 1523, while others have said she
was but sixteen.   She was, in fact, four-and-twenty.

After reading everything both for and against her conduct
with Francis I., at the time when the House of Poitiers was
in the greatest danger, we can neither confirm nor deny anything.   It is a passage of history that still remains obscure.
We can see by what happens in our own day how history is
falsified, as it were, in the making.

Catherine, who founded great hopes on her rival's age,
several times made an attempt to overthrow her.   On one occasion she was very near the accomplishment of her hopes.
In 1554, Madame Diane, being ill, begged the King to go to
Saint-Germain pending her recovery.   This sovereign co-
quette would not be seen in the midst of the paraphernalia of
doctors, nor bereft of the adjuncts of dress.   To receive the
King on his return, Catherine arranged a splendid *ballet*, in
which five or six young ladies were to address him in verse.
She selected for the purpose Miss Fleming, related to her
uncle, the Duke of Albany, and one of the loveliest girls im-
aginable, fair and golden-haired ; then a young connection of
her own, Clarissa Strozzi, with magnificent black hair and
rarely fine hands ; Miss Lewiston, maid of honor to Mary
Stewart ; Mary Stewart herself ; Madame Elisabeth de France,
the unhappy Queen of Spain ; and Madame Claude.   Elisabeth was nine years old, Claude eight, and Mary Stewart
twelve.   Obviously, the Queen aimed at showing off Clarissa
Strozzi and Miss Fleming without other rivals in the King's
eyes.   The King succumbed : he fell in love with Miss
Fleming, and she bore him a son, Henri de Valois, Comte
d'Angoulême, Grand Prior of France.

But Diane's influence and position remained unshaken.
Like Madame de Pompadour later with Louis XV., the
Duchesse de Valentinois was forgiving.   But to what sort of
love are we to ascribe this scheme on Catherine's part ?   Love
of power or love of her husband ?   Women must decide.

A great deal is said in these days as to the license of the press; but it is difficult to imagine to what a pitch it was carried when printing was a new thing. Aretino, the Voltaire of his time, as is well known, made monarchs tremble, and foremost of them all Charles V. But few people know, perhaps, how far the audacity of pamphleteers could go. This château of Chenonceaux had been given to Diane, nay, she was entreated to accept it, to induce her to overlook one of the most horrible publications ever hurled at a woman, one which shows how violent was the animosity between her and Madame d'Etampes. In 1537, when she was eight-and-thirty, a poet of Champagne, named Jean Voûté, published a collection of Latin verses, and among them three epigrams aimed at her. We must conclude that the poet was under high patronage from the fact that his volume is introduced by an *eulogium* written by Simon Macrin, the King's First Gentleman· of the Bedchamber. Here is the only passage quotable to-day from these epigrams, which bear the title: *In Pictaviam, anum aulicam.* (Against *la Poitiers*, an old woman of the Court.)

"Non trahit esca ficta prædam."

"A painted bait catches no game," says the poet, after telling her that she paints her face and buys her teeth and hair; and he goes on: "Even if you could buy the finest essence that makes a woman, you would not get what you want of your lover, for you would need to be living, and you are dead."

This volume, printed by Simon de Colines, was dedicated "To a Bishop!"—To François Bohier, the brother of the man who, to save his credit at Court and atone for his crime, made an offering on the accession of Henri II. of the château of Chenonceaux, built by his father, Thomas Bohier, Councilor of State under four Kings: Louis XI., Charles VIII., Louis XII., and Francis I. What were the pamphlets published against Madame de Pompadour and Marie Antoinette in comparison with verses that might have been written by Martial! Voûté must have come to a bad end. Thus the estate and château of Chenonceaux cost Diane nothing but the forgiveness of an offense—a duty enjoined by the Gospel. Not being assessed by a jury, the penalties inflicted on the press were rather severer then than they are now.

The widowed Queens of France were required to remain for forty days in the King's bedchamber, seeing no light but that of the tapers; they might not come out till after the funeral. This inviolable custom annoyed Catherine greatly; she was afraid of cabals. She found a way to evade it. The Cardinal de Lorraine coming out one morning—at such a time! at such a juncture!—from the house of "the Fair Roman," a famous courtesan of that day, who lived in the Rue Culture-Sainte-Catherine, was roughly handled by a party of roisterers. "Whereat his holiness was much amazed," says Henri Estienne, "and gave it out that heretics were lying in wait for him." And on this account the Court moved from Paris to Saint-Germain. The Queen would not leave the King her son behind, but took him with her.

The accession of Francis II., the moment when Catherine proposed to seize the reins of power, was a disappointment that formed a cruel climax to the twenty-six years of endurance she had already spent at the French Court. The Guises, with incredible audacity, at once usurped the sovereign power. The Duc de Guise was placed in command of the army and the Connétable de Montmorency was shelved. The cardinal took the control of the finances and the clergy.

Catherine's political career opened with one of those dramas which, though it was less notorious than some others, was not the less horrible, and initiated her no doubt into the agitating shocks of her life. Whether it was that Catherine, after vainly trying the most violent remedies, had thought she might bring the King back to her through jealousy;

whether on coming to her second youth she had felt it hard never to have known love, she had shown a warm interest in a gentleman of royal blood, François de Vendôme, son of Louis de Vendôme—the parent House of the Bourbons—the Vidame de Chartres, the name by which he is known to history. Catherine's covert hatred of Diane betrayed itself in many ways, which historians, studying only political developments, have failed to note with due attention. Catherine's attachment to the Vidame arose from an insult offered by the young man to the favorite. Diane looked for the most splendid matches for her daughters, who were indeed of the best blood in the kingdom. Above all, she was ambitious of an alliance with the Royal family. And her second daughter, who became the Duchesse d'Aumale, was proposed in marriage to the Vidame, whom Francis I., with sage policy, kept in poverty. For, in fact, when the Vidame de Chartres and the Prince de Condé first came to Court, Francis I. gave them appointments! What? the office of chamberlains in ordinary, with twelve hundred crowns a year, as much as he bestowed on the humblest of his gentlemen. And yet, though Diane offered him immense wealth, some high office under the Crown, and the King's personal favor, the Vidame refused. And then this Bourbon, factious as he was, married Jeanne, daughter of the Baron d'Estissac, by whom he had no children.

This proud demeanor naturally commended the Vidame to Catherine, who received him with marked favor, and made him her devoted friend. Historians have compared the last Duc de Montmorency, who was beheaded at Toulouse, with the Vidame de Chartres for his power of charming, his merits, and his talents.

Henri II. was not jealous; he did not apparently think it possible that a Queen of France could fail in her duty, or that a Medici could forget the honor done her by a Valois. When the Queen was said to be flirting with the Vidame de

Chartres, she had been almost deserted by the King since the birth of her last child.   So this attempt came to nothing—as the King died wearing the colors of Diane de Poitiers.

So, at the King's death, Catherine was on terms of gallant familiarity with the Vidame, a state of things in no way out of harmony with the manners of the time, when love was at once so chivalrous and so licentious that the finest actions seemed as natural as the most blamable.   But, as usual, historians have blundered by regarding exceptional cases as the rule.

Henri II.'s four sons nullified every pretension of the Bourbons, who were all miserably poor, and crushed under the scorn brought upon them by the Connétable de Montmorency's treason, in spite of the reasons which had led him to quit the country.   The Vidame de Chartres, who was to the Prince de Condé what Richelieu was to Mazarin, a father in politics, a model, and yet more a master in gallantry, hid the vast ambition of his family under a semblance of levity. Being unable to contend with the Guises, the Montmorencys, the Princes of Scotland, the cardinals, and the Bouillons, he aimed at distinction by his gracious manners, his elegance, and his wit, which won him the favors of the most charming women, and the hearts of many he never thought about.   He was a man privileged by nature, whose fascinations were irresistible, and who owed to his love affairs the means of keeping up his rank.   The Bourbons would not have taken offense, like Jarnac, at la Châtaignerie's scandal ; they were very ready to accept lands and houses from their mistresses—witness the Prince de Condé, who had the estate of Saint-Valery from Madame la Maréchale de Saint-André.

During the first twenty days of mourning for Henri II., a sudden change came over the Vidame's prospects.   Courted by the Queen-mother, and courting her as a man may court a queen, in the utmost secrecy, he seemed fated to play an important part ; and Catherine, in fact, resolved to make him useful. The Prince received letters from her to the Prince de Condé, in which she pointed out the necessity for a coalition against the Guises. The Guises, informed of this intrigue, made their way into the Queen's chamber to compel her to sign an order consigning the Vidame to the Bastille, and Catherine found herself under the cruel necessity of submitting. The Vidame died after a few months' captivity, on the day when he came out of prison, a short time before the Amboise conspiracy.

This was the end of Catherine de' Medici's first and only love affair. Protestant writers declare that the Queen had had him poisoned to bury the secret of her gallantries in the tomb.

Such was this woman's apprenticeship to the exercise of royal power.

# PART I.

### THE CALVINIST MARTYR.

Few persons in these days know how artless were the dwellings of the citizens of Paris in the sixteenth century, and how simple their lives. This very simplicity of habits and thought, perhaps, was the cause of the greatness of this primitive citizen class—for they were certainly great, free, and noble; more so, perhaps, than the citizens of our time. Their history remains to be written; it requires and awaits a man of genius. Inspired by an incident which, though little known, forms the basis of this narrative, and is one of the most remarkable in the history of the citizen class, this reflection will no doubt occur to every one who shall read it to the end. Is it the first time in history that the conclusion has come before the facts?

In 1560, the houses of the Rue de la Vicille-Pelleterie (old furrieries) lay close to the left bank of the Seine, between the Notre-Dame Bridge and the bridge to the Exchange. The public way and the houses occupied the ground now given up to the single path of the present quay. Each house, rising from the river, had a way down to it by stone or wooden steps, defended by strong iron gates or doors of nail-studded timber. These houses, like those of Venice, had a door to the land and one to the water. At the moment of writing this sketch, only one house remains of this kind as a reminiscence of old Paris, and that is doomed soon to disappear; it stands at the corner of the Petit-Pont, the *little bridge* facing the guard-house of the Hôtel-Dieu.

Of old each dwelling presented, on the river-side, the peculiar physiognomy stamped on it either by the trade and the habits of its owners, or by the eccentricity of the constructions devised by them for utilizing or defiling the Seine. The

(46)

bridges being built, and almost all choked up by more mills than were convenient for the requirements of navigation, the Seine in Paris was divided into as many pools as there were bridges. Some of these old Paris basins would have afforded delightful studies of color for the painter. What a forest of timbers was built into the cross-beams that supported the mills, with their immense sails and wheels! What curious effects were to be found in the joists that shored up the houses from the river. Genre painting as yet, unfortunately, was not, and engraving in its infancy; so we have no record of the curious scenes which may still be found, on a small scale, in some provincial towns where the rivers are fringed with wooden houses, and where, as at Vendôme, for instance, the pools, overgrown with tall grasses, are divided by railings to separate the various properties on each bank.

The name of this street, which has now vanished from the map, sufficiently indicates the kind of business carried on there. At that time the merchants engaged in any particular trade, far from dispersing themselves about the city, gathered together for mutual protection. Being socially bound by the guild which limited their increase, they were also united into a brotherhood by the church. This kept up prices. And then the masters were not at the mercy of their workmen and did not yield, as they do now, to all their vagaries; on the contrary, they took charge of them, treated them as their children, and taught them the finer mysteries of their craft. A workman, to become a master, was required to produce a masterpiece—always an offering to the patron saint of the guild. And will you venture to assert that the absence of competition diminished their sense of perfection or hindered beauty of workmanship, when your admiration of the work of the older craftsmen has created the new trade of dealers in *bric-a-brac?*

In the fifteenth and sixteenth centuries, the fur trade was one of the most flourishing industries. The difficulty of obtaining furs, which, coming from the North, necessitated

long and dangerous voyages, gave a high value to skins and
furriers' work.   Then, as now, high prices led to demand,
for vanity knows no obstacles.

In France, and in other kingdoms, not only was the use of
furs restricted by law to the great nobility, as is proved by
the part played by ermine in ancient coats-of-arms; but
certain rare furs, such as *vair*, which was beyond doubt imperial sable, might be worn only by kings, dukes, and men
of high rank holding certain offices.   *Vair* (a name still used
in heraldry, *vair* and *counter vair*) was subdivided into *grand
vair* and *menu vair*.   The word has within the last hundred
years fallen so completely into disuse, that in hundreds of
editions of Perrault's fairy tales, Cinderella's famous slipper,
probably of fur, *menu vair*, has become a glass slipper,
*pantoufle de verre*.   Not long since a distinguished French
poet was obliged to restore and explain the original spelling
of this word, for the edification of his brethren of the press,
when giving an account of the "Cenerentola," in which a
ring is substituted for the symbolical slipper—an unmeaning
change.

The laws against the use of fur were, of course, perpetually
transgressed, to the great advantage of the furriers.   The
high price of textiles and of furs made a garment in those days
a durable thing, in keeping with the furniture, armor, and
general details of the sturdy life of the time.   A nobleman
or lady, every rich man as well as every citizen, possessed at
most two dresses for each season, and they lasted a lifetime
or more.   These articles were bequeathed to their children.
Indeed, the clauses relating to weapons and raiment in
marriage-contracts, in these days unimportant by reason of
the small value of clothes that are constantly renewed, were
at that period of great interest.   High prices had led to
durability.

A lady's outfit represented a vast sum of money; it was
included in her fortune, and safely bestowed in those enor-

mous chests which endanger the ceilings of modern houses. The full dress of a lady in 1840 would have been the dishabille of a fine lady of 1540. The discovery of America, the facility of transport, the destruction of social distinctions, which has led to the effacement of visible distinctions, have all contributed to reduce the furrier's craft to the low ebb at which it stands, almost to nothing. The article sold by a furrier at the same price as of old—say twenty livres—has fallen in value with the money: the livre or franc was then worth twenty of our present money. The citizen's wife or the courtesan who, in our day, trims her cloak with sable, does not know that in 1440 a malignant constable of the watch would have taken her forthwith into custody, and hailed her before the judge at le Châtelet. The English ladies who are so fond of ermine are unconscious of the fact that formerly none but queens, duchesses, and the Chancellor of France were permitted to wear this royal fur. There are at this day various ennobled families bearing the name of Pelletier or Lepelletier, whose forebears were obviously wealthy furriers; for most of our citizen names were originally surnames of that kind.

This digression not only explains the long squabbles as to precedence which the Drapers' Guild carried on for two centuries with the Mercers and the Furriers, each insisting on marching first, as being the most important, but also accounts for the consequence of one Master Lecamus, a furrier honored with the patronage of the two Queens, Catherine de' Medici and Mary Stewart, as well as that of the legal profession, who for twenty years had been the Syndic of his corporation, and who lived in this street. The house occupied by Lecamus was one of the three forming the three corners of the crossroads at the end of the bridge to the Exchange, where only the tower now remains that formed the fourth corner. At the angle this house, forming the corner of the bridge and of the quay, now called the Quai aux Fleurs, the architect had placed a niche for a Madonna, before whom tapers constantly burned, with posies of real flowers in their season and artificial flowers in the winter.

On the side toward the Rue du Pont, as well as on that to the Rue de la Vieille-Pelleterie, the house was supported on wooden pillars. All the houses of the trading quarters were thus constructed, with an arcade beneath, where foot passengers walked under cover on a floor hardened by the mud they brought in, which made it a rather rough pavement. In all the towns of France these arcades have been called *piliers*—in England *rows*—a general term to which the name of a trade is commonly added, as "Piliers des Halles," "Piliers de la Boucherie." These covered ways, required by the changeable and rainy climate of Paris, gave the town a highly characteristic feature, but they have entirely disappeared. Just as there now remains one house only on the river bank, so no more than about a hundred feet are left of the old *piliers* in the market, the last that have survived until now ; and in a few days this remnant of the gloomy labyrinth of old Paris will also be destroyed. The existence of these relics of the Middle Ages is, no doubt, incompatible with the splendor of modern Paris. And these remarks are not intended as a lament over those fragments of the old city, but as a verification of this picture by the last surviving examples now falling into dust, and to win forgiveness for such descriptions, which will be precious in the future which is following hard on the heels of this age.

The walls were of timber covered with slates. The spaces between the timbers had been filled up with bricks, in a way that may still be seen in some provincial towns, laid in a zigzag pattern known as *Point de Hongrie.* The window-sills and lintels, also of wood, were handsomely carved, as were the corner tabernacle above the Madonna, and the pillars in front of the store. Every window, every beam dividing the stories, was graced with arabesques of fantastic figures and animals wreathed in scrolls of foliage.  On the street-side, as on the river-side, the house was crowned with a high-pitched roof having a gable to the river and one to the street.  This roof, like that of a Swiss chalet, projected far enough to cover a balcony on the third floor with an ornamental balustrade; here the mistress might walk under shelter and command a view of the street, or of the pool shut in between two bridges and two rows of houses.

Houses by the river were at that time highly valued.  The system of drainage and water-supply was not yet invented; the only main drain was one around Paris, constructed by Aubriot, the first man of genius and determination who—in the time of Charles V.—thought of sanitation for Paris. Houses situated like this of the Sieur Lecamus found in the river a necessary water-supply, and a natural outlet for rain-water and waste.  The vast works of this kind under the direction of the Trade Provosts are only now disappearing. None but octogenarians can still remember having seen the pits which swallowed up the surface-waters, in the Rue Montmartre, Rue du Temple, etc.  These hideous yawning culverts were in their day of inestimable utility.  Their place will probably be for ever marked by the sudden rising of the roadway over what was their open channel—another archæological detail which, in a couple of centuries, the historian will find inexplicable.

One day, in 1816, a little girl, who had been sent to an actress at the Ambigu with some diamonds for the part of a queen, was caught in a storm, and so irresistibly swept away by the waters to the opening of the drain in the Rue du Temple, that she would have been drowned in it but for the help of a passer-by, who was touched by her cries.  But she had dropped the jewels, which were found in a man-hole. This accident made a great commotion and gave weight to the demands for the closing of these gulfs for swallowing water and little girls.  These curious structures, five feet high, had more or less movable gratings, which led to the flooding of cellars when the stream produced by heavy rain was checked by the grating being choked with rubbish, which the residents often forgot to remove.

The front of Master Lecamus' store was a large window, but filled in with small panes of leaded glass, which made the place very dark.  The furs for wealthy purchasers were carried to them for inspection.  To those who came to buy in the store, the goods were displayed outside between the pillars, which, during the day, were always more or less blocked by tables and salesmen sitting on stools, as they could still be seen doing under the arcade of the Halles some fifteen years since.  From these outposts the clerks, apprentices, and sewing girls could chat, question, and answer each other, and hail the passer-by in a way which Walter Scott has depicted in the "Fortunes of Nigel."  The signboard, representing an ermine, was hung out as we still see those of village inns, swinging from a handsome arm of pierced and gilt ironwork.  Over the ermine were these words:

## LECAMUS

### FURRIER

### TO HER MAJESTY THE QUEEN AND THE KING OUR SOVEREIGN LORD

On one side, and on the other:

### TO HER MAJESTY THE QUEEN-MOTHER AND TO THE GENTLEMEN OF THE PARLEMENT.

The words "To Her Majesty the Queen" had been lately added ; the gilt letters were new.  This addition was a consequence of the recent changes produced by Henri II.'s sudden and violent death, which overthrew many fortunes at Court and began that of the Guises.

The back store looked over the river. In this room sat the worthy citizen and his wife, Mademoiselle Lecamus. The wife of a man who was not noble had not at that time any right to the title of Dame, or lady ; but the wives of the citizens of Paris were allowed to call themselves Demoiselle (as we might say Mistress), as part of the privileges granted and confirmed to their husbands by many kings to whom they had rendered great services. Between this back room and the front store was a spiral ladder or staircase of wood, a sort of corkscrew leading up to the next story, where the furs were stored, to the old couple's bedroom, and again to the attics, lighted by dormer windows, where their children slept, the maidservant, the clerks, and the apprentices.

This herding of families, servants, and apprentices, and the small space allotted to each in the dwelling, where the apprentices all slept in one large room under the tiles, accounts for the enormous population at that time crowded together in Paris on a tenth of the ground now occupied by the city, and also for the many curious details of mediæval life, and the cunning love affairs, though these, *pace* the grave historian, are nowhere recorded but by the story-writers, and without them would have been lost.

At this time a grand gentleman—such as the Admiral de Coligny, for instance—had three rooms for himself in Paris, and his people lived in a neighboring hostelry. There were not fifty mansions in all Paris, not fifty palaces, that is to say, belonging to the sovereign princes or great vassals, whose existence was far superior to that of the greatest German rulers, such as the Duke of Bavaria or the Elector of Saxony.

The kitchen in the Lecamus' house was on the river-side below the back store. It had a glass door opening on to an ironwork balcony, where the cook could stand to draw up water in a pail and to wash the household linen. Thus the back store was at once the sitting-room, the dining-room, and the counting-house. It was in this important room—always fitted with richly carved wood and adorned by some chest or artistic article of furniture—that the merchant spent most of his life ; there he had jolly suppers after his day's work ; there were held secret debates on the political interests of the citizens and the Royal family. The formidable guilds of Paris could at that time arm a hundred thousand men. Their resolutions were stoutly upheld by their serving-men, their clerks, their apprentices, and their workmen. Their provost was their commander-in-chief, and they had, in the Hôtel de Ville, a palace where they had a right to assemble.

In that famous "citizens' parlor" (*parlouer aux bourgeois*) very solemn decisions were taken. But for the continual sacrifices which had made war unendurable to the guilds, wearied out with losses and famine, Henri IV., a rebel-made king, might never have entered Paris.

Every reader may now imagine for himself the characteristic appearance of this corner of Paris where the bridge and the quay now open out, where the trees rise from the Quai aux Fleurs, and where nothing is left of the past but the lofty and famous clock-tower whence the signal was tolled for the massacre of Saint-Bartholomew. Strange coincidence ! One of the houses built round the foot of that tower—at that time surrounded by wooden stores—the house of the Lecamus, was to be the scene of one of the incidents that led to that night of horrors, which proved, unfortunately, propitious rather than fatal to Calvinism.

At the moment when this story begins, the audacity of the new religious teaching was setting Paris by the ears. A Scotchman, named Stewart, had just assassinated President Minard, that member of the Parlement to whom public opinion attributed a principal share in the execution of Anne du Bourg, a councilor burnt on the Place de Grève after the tailor of the late King, who had been tortured in the presence of Henry II. and Diane de Poitiers. Paris was so closely watched that the archers on guard compelled every passer-by to pray to the Virgin, in order to detect heretics, who yielded unwillingly, or even refused to perform an act opposed to their convictions.

The two archers on guard at the corner of the Lecamus' house had just gone off duty; thus Christophe, the furrier's son, strongly suspected of deserting the Catholic faith, had been able to go out without fear of being compelled to adore the Virgin's image. At seven in the evening of an April day, 1560, night was falling, and the apprentices, seeing only a few persons walking along the arcades on each side of the street, were carrying in the goods laid out for inspection preparatory to closing the house and the store. Christophe Lecamus, an ardent youth of two-and-twenty, was standing in the door, apparently engaged in looking after the apprentices.

"Monsieur," said one of these lads to Christophe, pointing out a man who was pacing two and fro under the arcade with a doubtful expression, "that is probably a spy or a thief, but whatever he is, such a lean wretch cannot be an honest man. If he wanted to speak to us on business, he would come up boldly instead of creeping up and down as he is doing. And what a face!" he went on, mimicking the stranger, "with his nose hidden in his cloak! What a jaundiced eye, and what a starved complexion!"

As soon as the stranger thus described saw Christophe standing alone in the doorway, he hastily crossed from the opposite arcade where he was walking, came under the pillars of the Lecamus' house, and, passing along by the store before the apprentices had come out again to close the shutters, he went up to the young man.

"I am Chaudieu!" he said in a low voice.

On hearing the name of one of the most famous ministers, and one of the most heroic actors in the terrible drama called the Reformation, Christophe felt such a thrill as a faithful peasant would have felt on recognizing his King under a disguise.

"Would you like to see some furs?" said Christophe, to deceive the apprentices whom he heard behind him. "Though it is almost dark, I can show you some myself."

He invited the minister to enter, but the man replied that he would rather speak to him out of doors. Christophe fetched his cap and followed the Calvinist.

Chaudieu, though banished by an edict, as secret plenipotentiary of Théodore de Bèze and Calvin—who directed the Reformation in France from Geneva—went and came, defying the risk of the horrible death inflicted by the Parlement, in concert with the church and the monarch, on a leading reformer, the famous Anne du Bourg. This man, whose brother was a captain in the army and one of Admiral Coligny's best warriors, was the arm used by Calvin to stir up France at the beginning of the twenty-two years of religious wars which were on the eve of an outbreak. This preacher of the reformed faith was one of those secret wheels which may best explain the immense spread of the Reformation.

Chaudieu led Christophe down to the edge of the water by an underground passage like that of the Arche Marion, filled in some ten years since. This tunnel between the house of Lecamus and that next it ran under the Rue de la Vieille-Pelleterie, and was known as le Pont aux Fourreurs. It was used by the dyers of the city as a way down to the river to wash their thread, silk, and materials. A little boat lay there, held and rowed by one man. In the bows sat a stranger, a small man, and very simply dressed. In an instant the boat was in the middle of the river, and the boatman steered it under one of the wooden arches of the Pont au Change, where he quickly secured it to an iron ring. No one had said a word.

"Here we may talk in safety, there are neither spies nor traitors," said Chaudieu to the two others. "Are you filled with the spirit of self-sacrifice that should animate a martyr?   Are you ready to suffer all things for our holy cause?   Do you fear the torments endured by the late King's tailor and the Councilor du Bourg, which of a truth await us all?''   He spoke to Christophe, looking at him with a radiant face.

"I will testify to the Gospel,'' replied Christophe simply, looking up at the windows of the back store.

The familiar lamp standing on a table, where his father was no doubt balancing his books, reminded him by its mild beam of the peaceful life and family joys he was renouncing.   It was a brief but complete vision.   The young man's fancy took in the homely harmony of the whole scene—the places where he had spent his happy childhood, where Babette Lallier lived, his future wife, where everything promised him a calm and busy life; he saw the past, he saw the future, and he sacrificed it all.   At any rate, he staked it.

Such were men in those days.

"We need say no more,'' cried the impetuous boatman. "We know him for one of the saints.   If the Scotchman had not dealt the blow, he would have killed the infamous Minard.''

"Yes,'' said Lecamus, "my life is in the hands of the brethren, and I devote it with joy for the success of the Reformation.   I have thought of it all seriously.   I know what we are doing for the joy of the nations.   In two words, the Papacy makes for celibacy, the Reformation makes for the family.   It is time to purge France of its monks, to restore their possessions to the Crown, which will sell them sooner or later to the middle-classes.   Let us show that we can die for our children and to make our families free and happy!''

The young enthusiast's face, with Chaudieu's, the boatman's, and that of the stranger seated in the bows, formed a picture that deserves to be described, all the more so because such a description entails the whole history of that epoch, if it be true that it is given to some men to sum up in themselves the spirit of their age.

Religious reform, attempted in Germany by Luther, in Scotland by John Knox, and in France by Calvin, found partisans chiefly among those of the lower classes who had begun to think. The great nobles encouraged the movement only to serve other interests quite foreign to the religious question. These parties were joined by adventurers, by gentlemen who had lost all, by youngsters to whom every form of excitement was acceptable. But, among the artisans and men employed in trade, faith was genuine and founded on intelligent interests. The poorer nations at once gave their adherence to a religion which brought the property of the church back to the State, which suppressed the convents, and deprived the dignitaries of the church of their enormous revenues. Everybody in trade calculated the profits from this religious transaction, and devoted themselves to it body, soul, and purse ; and among the youth of the French citizen class the new preaching met that noble disposition for self-sacrifice of every kind which animates the young to whom egoism is unknown.

Eminent men, penetrating minds, such as are always to be found among the masses, foresaw the Republic in the Reformation, and hoped to establish throughout Europe a form of government like that of the United Netherlands, which at last triumphed over the greatest power of the time—Spain, ruled by Philip II., and represented in the Low Countries by the Duke of Alva. Jean Hotoman was at that time planning the famous book in which this scheme is set forth, which diffused through France the leaven of these ideas, stirred up once more by the League,* subdued by Richelieu, and afterward by Louis XIV., to reappear with the Economists and the Encyclopædists under Louis XV., and burst into life under Louis XVI.; ideas which were always approved by the

* Headed by Henry, Duke of Guise, 1576.

younger branches, by the House of Orleans in 1789, as by the House of Bourbon in 1589.

The questioning spirit is the rebellious spirit.  A rebellion is always either a cloak to hide a prince or the swaddling wrapper of a new rule.  The House of Bourbon, a younger branch than the Valois, was busy at the bottom of the Reformation.  At the moment when the little boat lay moored under the arch of the Pont au Change, the question was further complicated by the ambition of the Guises, the rivals of the Bourbons.  Indeed, the Crown, as represented by Catherine de' Medici, could, for thirty years, hold its own in the strife by setting these two factions against each other; whereas later, instead of being clutched at by many hands, the Crown stood face to face with the people without a barrier between; for Richelieu and Louis XIV. had broken down the nobility, and Louis XV. had overthrown the Parlements.  Now a king alone face to face with a nation, as Louis XVI. was, must inevitably succumb.

Christophe Lecamus was very typical of the ardent and devoted sons of the people.  His pale complexion had that warm burnt hue which is seen in some fair people; his hair was of a coppery yellow; his eyes were bluish-gray and sparkled brightly.  In them alone was his noble soul visible, for his clumsy features did not disguise the somewhat triangular shape of a plain face by lending it the look of dignity which a man of rank can assume, and his forehead was low and characteristic only of great energy.  His vitality seemed to be seated no lower down than his chest, which was somewhat hollow.  Sinewy, rather than muscular, Christophe was of tough texture, lean but wiry.  His sharp nose showed homely cunning and his countenance revealed intelligence of the kind that acts wisely on one point of a circle, but that has not the power of commanding the whole circumference.  His eyes, set under brows that projected like a pent-house and faintly outlined with light down, were surrounded with broad light-blue circles, with a sheeny white patch at the root of the nose, almost always a sign of great excitability. Christophe was of the people—the race that fights and allows itself to be deceived; intelligent enough to understand and to serve an idea, too noble to take advantage of it, too magnanimous to sell himself.

By the side of old Lecamus' only son, Chaudieu, the ardent minister, lean from watchfulness, with brown hair, a yellow skin, a contumacious brow, an eloquent mouth, fiery hazel eyes, and a short rounded chin, symbolized that Christian zeal which gave the Reformation so many fanatical and earnest preachers, whose spirit and boldness fired whole communities. This aide-de-camp of Calvin and Théodore de Bèze contrasted well with the furrier's son. He represented the living cause of which Christophe was the effect. You could not have conceived of the active firebrand of the popular machine under any other aspect.

The boatman, an impetuous creature, tanned by the open air, the dews of night, and the heats of the day, with firmly set lips, quick motions, a hungry, tawny eye like a vulture's, and crisp black hair, was the characteristic adventurer who risks his all in an undertaking as a gambler stakes his whole fortune on a card. Everything in the man spoke of terrible passions and a daring that would flinch at nothing. His quivering muscles were as able to keep silence as to speak. His look was assertive rather than noble. His nose, upturned but narrow, scented battle. He seemed active and adroit. In any age you would have known him for a party leader. He might have been Pizarro, Hernando Cortez, or Morgan the Destroyer if there had been no Reformation—a doer of violent deeds.

The stranger who sat on a seat, wrapped in his cloak, evidently belonged to the highest social rank. The fineness of his linen, the cut, material, and perfume of his raiment, the make and texture of his gloves, showed a man of the

Court, as his attitude, his haughtiness, his cool demeanor, and his flashing eye revealed a man of war. His appearance was at first somewhat alarming and inspired respect. We respect a man who respects himself. Though short and hunchbacked, his manner made good all the defects of his figure. The ice once broken, he had the cheerfulness of decisiveness and an indescribable spirit of energy which made him attractive. He had the blue eyes and the hooked nose of the House of Navarre, and the Spanish look of the marked physiognomy that was characteristic of the Bourbon kings.

With three words the scene became of the greatest interest.

"Well, then," said Chaudieu, as Christophe Lecamus made his profession of faith, "this boatman is la Renaudie; and this is Monsiegneur the Prince de Condé," he added turning to the hunchback.

Thus the four men were representative of the faith of the people, the intellect of eloquence, the arm of the soldier, and Royalty cast into the shade.

"You will hear what we require of you," the minister went on, after allowing a pause for the young man's astonishment. "To the end that you may make no mistakes, we are compelled to initiate you into the most important secrets of the Reformation."

The Prince and la Renaudie assented by a gesture, when the minister ceased speaking, to allow the Prince to say something if he should wish it. Like all men of rank engaged in conspiracies, who make it a principle not to appear before some critical moment, the Prince kept silence. Not from cowardice: at such junctures he was the soul of the scheme, shrank from no danger, and risked his head ; but, with a sort of royal dignity, he left the explanation of the enterprise to the preacher, and was content to study the new instrument he was compelled to make use of.

"My son," said Chaudieu in Huguenot phraseology, "we are about to fight the first battle against the Roman whore.

In a few days our soldiers must perish at the stake, or the Guises must be dead. So, ere long, the King and the two Queens will be in our power. This is the first appeal to arms by our religion in France, and France will not lay them down until she has conquered—it is of the nation that I speak, and not of the kingdom. Most of the nobles of the kingdom see what the Cardinal de Lorraine and the Duke his brother are driving at. Under pretense of defending the Catholic faith, the House of Lorraine claims the Crown of France as its inheritance. It leans on the church, and has made it a formidable ally; the monks are its supporters, its acolytes and spies. It asserts itself as a protector of the throne it hopes to usurp, of the Valois whom it hopes to destroy.

"We have decided to rise up in arms, and it is because the liberties of the people are threatened as well as the interests of the nobility. We must stifle in its infancy a faction as atrocious as that of the Bourguignons, who of old put Paris and France to fire and sword. A Louis XI. was needed to end the quarrel between the Burgundians and the Crown, but now a Prince of Condé will prevent the Lorrains from going too far. This is not a civil war; it is a duel between the Guises and the Reformation—a duel to the death! We will see their heads laid low, or they shall crush ours!"

"Well spoken!" said the Prince.

"In these circumstances, Christophe," la Renaudie put in, "we must neglect no means of strengthening our party—for there is a party on the side of the Reformation, the party of offended rights, of the nobles who are sacrificed to the Guises, of the old army leaders so shamefully tricked at Fontainebleau, whence the cardinal banished them by erecting gibbets to hang those who should ask the King for the price of their outfit and arrears of pay."

"Yes, my son," said Chaudieu, seeing some signs of terror in Christophe, "that is what requires us to triumph by fighting instead of triumphing by conviction and martyrdom.

The Queen-mother is ready to enter into our views ; not that she is prepared to abjure the Catholic faith—she has not got so far as that, but she may perhaps be driven to it by our success. Be that as it may, humiliated and desperate as she is at seeing the power she had hoped to wield at the King's death in the grasp of the Guises and alarmed by the influence exerted by the young Queen Marie, who is their niece and partisan, Queen Catherine will be inclined to lend her support to the princes and nobles who are about to strike a blow for her deliverance. At this moment, though apparently devoted to the Guises, she hates them, longs for their ruin, and will make use of us to oppose them ; but Monseigneur can make use of her to oppose all the others. The Queen-mother will consent to all we propose. We have the Connétable on our side—Monseigneur has just seen him at Chantilly, but he will not stir without orders from his superiors. Being Monseigneur's uncle, he will not leave us in the lurch, and our generous Prince will not hesitate to rush into danger to enlist Anne de Montmorency.

"Everything is ready ; and we have cast our eyes on you to communicate to Queen Catherine our treaty of alliance, our schemes for edicts, and the basis of the new rule. The Court is at Blois. Many of our friends are there ; but those are our future chiefs—— and, like Monseigneur," and he bowed to the Prince, "they must never be suspected ; we must sacrifice ourselves for them. The Queen-mother and our friends are under such close espionage that it is impossible to communicate with them through any one who is known or of any consequence. Such a person would be at once suspected, and would never be admitted to speak with Madame Catherine. God should indeed give us at this moment the shepherd David with his sling to attack Goliath de Guise. Your father—a good Catholic, more's the pity—is furrier to the two Queens ; he always has some garment or trimming in hand for them ; persuade him to send you to the Court.

You will arouse no suspicions and will not compromise Queen Catherine.  Any one of our leaders might lose his head for an imprudence which should give rise to a suspicion of the Queen-mother's connivance with us.  But where a man of importance, once caught out, gives a clue to suspicions, a nobody like you escapes scot-free.  You see!  The Guises have so many spies that nowhere but in the middle of the river can we talk without fear.  So you, my son, are like a man on guard, doomed to die at his post.  Understand that, if you are taken, you are abandoned by us all.  If need be, we shall cast opprobrium and disgrace on you.  If we should be forced to it, we should declare that you were a creature of the Guises whom they sent to play a part to implicate us.  So what we ask of you is entire self-sacrifice."

"If you perish," said the Prince de Condé, "I pledge my word as a gentleman that your family shall be a sacred trust to the House of Navarre;  I will bear it in my heart and serve it in every way."

"That word, my lord, is enough," replied Christophe, forgetting that this leader of faction was a Gascon.  "We live in times when every man, prince or citizen, must do his duty."

"That is a true Huguenot!  If all our men were like him," said la Renaudie, laying his hand on Christophe's shoulder, "we should have won by to-morrow."

"Young man," said the Prince, "I meant to show you that while Chaudieu preaches and the gentleman bears arms, the prince fights.  Thus, in so fierce a game, every stake has its value."

"Listen," said la Renaudie;  "I will not give you the papers till we reach Beaugency, for we must run no risks on the road.  You will find me on the quay there; my face, voice, and clothes will be so different that you may not recognize me.  But I will say to you, 'Are you a *Guêpin?*' and you must reply, 'At your service.'  As to the manner of proceeding, I will tell you.   You will find a horse at *la Pinte fleurie*, near Saint-Germain l'Auxerrois.   Ask there for Jean le Breton, who will take you to the stable and mount you on a nag of mine known to cover thirty leagues in eight hours.   Leave Paris by the Bussy Gate.   Breton has a pass for me; take it for yourself and be off, riding round outside the towns.   You should reach Orleans by daybreak."

"And the horse?" asked Lecamus.

"He will hold out till you get to Orleans," replied la Renaudie.   "Leave him outside the suburb of Bannier, for the gates are well guarded; we must not arouse suspicion. You, my friend, must play your part well.   You must make up any story that may seem to you best to enable you to go to the third house on your left on entering Orleans; it is that of one Tourillon, a glover.   Knock three raps on the door and call out, 'In the service of Messieurs de Guise!'   The man affects to be a fanatical *Guisard;* we four only know that he is on our side.   He will find you a boatman, such another as himself of course, but devoted to our cause.   Go down to the river at once, get into a boat painted green with a white border.   You ought to be at Beaugency by noonday to-morrow.   There I will put you in the way of getting a boat to carry you down to Blois without running any danger.   Our enemies the Guises do not command the Loire, only the river-ports.

"You may thus see the Queen in the course of to-morrow or of the next day."

"Your words are graven here," said Christophe, touching his forehead.

Chaudieu embraced his son with religious fervency; he was proud of him.

"The Lord protect you!" he said, pointing to the sunset which crimsoned the old roofs covered with shingles, and shot fiery gleams among the forest of beams round which the waters foamed.

5

"You are of the stock of old Jacques Bonhomme," said la Renaudie to Christophe, wringing his hand.

"We shall meet again, *monsieur*," said the Prince, with a gesture of infinite graciousness, almost of friendliness.

With a stroke of the oar, la Renaudie carried the young conspirator back to the steps leading up to the house, and the boat vanished at once under the arches of the Pont au Change.

Christophe shook the iron gate that closed the entrance from the river-side and called out ; Mademoiselle Lecamus heard him, opened one of the windows of the back store, and asked how he came there. Christophe replied that he was half-frozen and that she must first let him in.

"Young master," said la Bourguignonne, "you went out by the street-door and come in by the river-gate? Your father will be in a pretty rage."

Christophe, bewildered by the secret conference which had brought him into contact with the Prince de Condé, la Renaudie, and Chaudieu, and even more agitated by the expected turmoil of an imminent civil war, made no reply; he hurried up from the kitchen to the back store. There, on seeing him, his mother, who was a bigoted old Catholic, could not contain herself.

"I will wager," she broke out, "that the three men you were talking to were ref——"

"Silence, wife," said the prudent old man, whose white head was bent over a book. "Now, you lazy oafs," he went on to three boys who had long since finished supper, "what are you waiting for to take you to bed? It is eight o'clock. You must be up by five in the morning. And first you have the Président de Thou's robes and cap to carry home. Go all three together, and carry sticks and rapiers. If you meet any more ne'er-do-weels of your own kidney, at any rate there will be three of you."

"And are we to carry the ermine surcoat ordered by the young Queen, which is to be delivered at the Hôtel de

Soissons, from whence there is an express to Blois and to the Queen-mother?" asked one of the lads.

"No," said the Syndic; "Queen Catherine's account amounts to three thousand crowns and I must get the money. I think I will go to Blois myself."

"I should not think of allowing you at your age, father, and in such times as these, to expose yourself on the high-roads. I am two-and-twenty; you may send me on this errand," said Christophe, with an eye on a box which he had no doubt contained the surcoat.

"Are you glued to the bench?" cried the old man to the apprentices, who hastily took up their rapiers and capes and Monsieur de Thou's fur gown.

This illustrious man was to be received on the morrow by the Parlement as their president; he had just signed the death-warrant of the Councilor du Bourg, and was fated, before the year was out, to sit in judgment on the Prince de Condé.

"La Bourguignonne," said the old man, "go and ask my neighbor Lallier if he will sup with us this evening, furnishing the wine; we will give the meal. And, above all, tell him to bring his daughter."

The Syndic of the Guild of Furriers was a handsome old man of sixty, with white hair and a broad high forehead. As furrier to the Court for forty years past, he had witnessed all the revolutions in the reign of Francis I., and had retained his royal patent in spite of feminine rivalries. He had seen the arrival at Court of Catherine de' Medici, then but just fifteen; he had seen her succumb to the Duchesse d'Etampes, her father-in-law's mistress, and to the Duchesse de Valentinois, mistress to the late King, her husband. But through all these changes the furrier had got into no difficulties, though the Court purveyors often fell into disgrace with the ladies they served. His prudence was as great as his wealth. He main-

tained an attitude of excessive humility.    Pride had never
caught him in its snares.    The man was so modest, so meek,
so obliging, so poor—at Court and in the presence of queens,
princesses, and favorites—that his servility had saved his store
sign.

Such a line of policy betrayed, of course, a cunning and
clear-sighted man.    Humble as he was to the outer world, at
home he was a despot.    He was the unquestioned master in
his own house.    He was highly respected by his fellow-mer-
chants, and derived immense consideration from his long
tenure of the first place in business.    Indeed, he was gladly
helpful to others; and, among the services he had done, the
most important perhaps was the support he had long afforded
to the most famous surgeon of the sixteenth century—Ambroise Paré, who owed it to Lecamus that he could pursue his
studies.    In all the disputes that arose between the merchants
of the guild, Lecamus was for conciliatory measures.    Thus
general esteem had confirmed his supremacy among his equals,
while his assumed character had preserved him the favor of
the Court.

Having, for political reasons, manœuvred in his parish for
the glory of his trade, he did what was needful to keep himself in a sufficient odor of sanctity with the priest of the church
of Saint-Pierre aux Bœufs, who regarded him as one of the
men most devoted in all Paris to the Catholic faith.    Consequently, when the States-General were convoked, Lecamus
was unanimously elected to represent the third estate by the
influence of the priests, which was at that time enormous in
Paris.

This old man was one of those deep and silent ambitious
men who for fifty years are submissive to everybody in turn,
creeping up from place to place, no one knowing how, till
they are seen peacefully seated in a position which no one, not
even the boldest, would have dared to admit was the goal of
his ambition at the beginning of his life—so long was the

climb, so many gulfs were there to leap, into which he might fall! Lecamus, who had hidden away a large fortune, would run no risks, and was planning a splendid future for his son. Instead of that personal ambition which often sacrifices the future to the present, he had family ambition, a feeling that seems lost in these days, smothered by the stupid regulation of inheritance by law. Lecamus foresaw himself president of the Paris Parlement in the person of his grandson.

Christophe, the godson of the great historian, de Thou, had received an excellent education, but it had led him to skepticism and inquiry, which indeed were increasing apace among the students and Faculty of the University. Christophe was at present studying for the bar, the first step to a judgeship. The old furrier pretended to be undecided as to his son's career; sometimes he would make Christophe his successor, and sometimes he would have him a pleader; but in his heart he longed to see this son in the seat of a Councilor of the Parlement. The furrier longed to place the house of Lecamus on a par with the old and honored families of Paris citizens which had produced a Pasquier, a Molé, a Miron, a Séguier, Lamoignon, du Tillet, Lecoigneux, Lescalopier, the Goix, the Arnaulds—all the famous sheriffs and high provosts of corporations who had rallied to defend the throne.

To the end that Christophe might in that day do credit to his rank, he wanted him to marry the daughter of the richest goldsmith in the city, his neighbor Lallier, whose nephew, at a later day, presented the keys of Paris to Henri IV. The most deeply rooted purpose in the good man's heart was to spend half his own fortune and half of Lallier's in the purchase of a lordly estate, a long and difficult matter in those days.

But he was too deep a schemer, and knew the times too well, to overlook the great movements that were being hatched; he saw plainly, and saw truly, when he looked forward to the division of the kingdom into two camps. The useless executions on the Place de l'Estrapade, that of Henry II.'s tailor, and that, still more recent, of the Councilor Anne du Bourg, beside the connivance of the reigning favorite in the time of Francis I., and of many nobles now, at the progress of reform, all were alarming indications. The furrier was determined, come what might, to remain faithful to the church, the Monarchy, and the Parlement, but he was secretly well content that his son should join the Reformation. He knew that he had wealth enough to ransom Christophe if the lad should ever compromise himself seriously; and then, if France should turn Calvinist, his son could save the family in any furious outbreaks in the capital such as the citizens could vividly remember, and as would recur again and again through four reigns.

Like Louis XI., the old furrier never confessed these thoughts even to himself; his cunning completely deceived his wife and his son. For many a day this solemn personage had been the recognized head of the most populous quarter of Paris—the heart of the city—bearing the title of *Quartenier*, which became notorious fifteen years later. Clothed in cloth, like every prudent citizen who obeyed the sumptuary laws, Master Lecamus—the Sieur Lecamus, a title he held in virtue of an edict of Charles V. permitting the citizens of Paris to purchase *Seigneuries*, and their wives to assume the fine title of *Demoiselle* or mistress—wore no gold chain, no silk; only a stout doublet with large buttons of blackened silver, wrinkled hose drawn up above his knees, and leather shoes with buckles. His shirt, of fine linen, was pulled out, in the fashion of the time, into full puffs through his half-buttoned vest and slashed trunks.

Though the full light of the lamp fell on the old man's broad and handsome head, Christophe had no inkling of the thoughts hidden behind that rich Dutch-looking complexion; still he understood that his old father meant to take some advantage of his affection for pretty Babette Lallier.

And Christophe, as a man who has laid his own schemes, smiled sadly when he heard the invitation sent to his fair mistress.

As soon as la Bourguignonne and the apprentices were gone, old Lecamus looked at his wife with an expression that fully showed his firm and resolute temper.

"You will never rest till you have got the boy hanged with your damned tongue!" said he in stern tones.

"I would rather see him hanged, but saved, than alive and a Huguenot," was the gloomy reply. "To think that the child I bore within me for nine months should not be a good Catholic, but hanker after the heresies of Colas—that he must spend all eternity in hell——!" and she began to cry.

"You old fool!" said the furrier, "then give him a chance of life, if only to convert him! Why, you said a thing, before the apprentices, which might set our house on fire and roast us all in it like fleas in straw."

The mother crossed herself, but said nothing.

"As for you," said the good man, with a scrutinizing look at his son, "tell me what you were doing out there on the water with—— Come close to me while I speak to you," he added, seizing his son by the arm and drawing him close to him while he whispered in the lad's ear—"with the Prince de Condé." Christophe started. "Do you suppose that the Court furrier does not know all their faces? And do you fancy that I am not aware of what is going on? Monseigneur the Grand Master has ordered out troops to Amboise. And when troops are removed from Paris to Amboise while the Court is at Blois, when they are marched by way of Chartres and Vendôme instead of by Orleans, the meaning is pretty clear, heh? Trouble is brewing.

"If the Queens want their surcoats, they will send for them. The Prince de Condé may be intending to kill the Messieurs de Guise, who on their part mean to get rid of him

perhaps.   Of what use can a furrier's son be in such a broil?
When you are married, when you are a pleader in the Parlement, you will be as cautious as your father.   A furrier's son
has no business to be of the new religion till all the rest of
the world is.   I say nothing against the Reformers; it is no
business of mine; but the Court is Catholic, the two Queens
are Catholic, the Parlement is Catholic: we serve them with
furs, and we must be Catholic.

"You do not stir from here, Christophe, or I will place
you with your godfather the Président de Thou, who will keep
you at it, blackening paper night and day, instead of leaving
you to blacken your soul in the hell-broth of these damned
Genevese."

"Father," said Christophe, leaning on the back of the old
man's chair, "send me off to Blois with Queen Marie's surcoat and to ask for the money, or I am a lost man.   And you
love me——"

"Lost!" echoed his father, without any sign of surprise.
"If you stay here, you will not be lost.   I shall know where
to find you."

"I shall be killed."

"Why?"

"The most zealous Huguenots have cast their eyes on me
to serve them in a certain matter, and if I fail to do what I
have just promised they will kill me in the street, in the face
of day, here, as Minard was killed.   But if you send me to
the Court on business of your own, I shall probably be able to
justify my action to both parties.   Either I shall succeed for
them without running any risk, and so gain a good position in
the party; or, if the danger is too great, I can do your business only."

The old man started to his feet as if his seat were of red-hot
iron.

"Wife," said he, "leave us, and see that no one intrudes
on Christophe and me."

When Mistress Lecamus had left the room, the furrier took his son by a button and led him to the corner of the room which formed the angle toward the bridge.

"Christophe," said he, quite into his son's ear, as he had just now spoken of the Prince de Condé, "be a Huguenot* if that is your pet vice, but with prudence, in your secret heart, and not in such a way as to be pointed at by every one in the neighborhood. What you have just told me shows me what confidence the leaders have in you. What are you to do at the Court?"

"I cannot tell you," said Christophe; "I do not quite know that myself yet."

"H'm, h'm," said the old man, looking at the lad, "the young rascal wants to hoodwink his father. He will go far! Well, well," he went on, in an undertone, "you are not going to Blois to make overtures to the Guises, nor to the little King our Sovereign, nor to little Queen Mary. All these are Catholics; but I could swear that the Italian Queen owes the Scotchwoman and the Lorrains some grudge: I know her. She has been dying to put a finger in the pie. The late King was so much afraid of her that, like the jewelers, he used diamond to cut diamond, one woman against another. Hence Queen Catherine's hatred of the poor Duchesse de Valentinois, from whom she took the fine Château of Chenonceaux. But for Monsieur le Connétable, the Duchess would have had her neck wrung at least——

"Hands off, my boy! Do not trust yourself within reach of the Italian woman, whose only passions are in her head; a bad sort that. Ay, the business you are sent to the Court to do will give you a bad headache, I fear," cried the father, seeing that Christophe was about to speak. "My boy, I have two schemes for your future life; you will not spoil them by being of service to Queen Catherine. But, for God's sake, keep your head on your shoulders! And the Guises would

* A term of unknown origin, applied to the Protestants.

cut it off as la Bourguignonne cuts off a turnip, for the people who are employing you would throw you over at once."

"I know that, father," said Christophe.

"And you are so bold as that! You know it, and you will risk it?"

"Yes, father."

"Why, the devil's in it!" cried the old man, hugging his son, "we may understand each other; you are your father's son. My boy, you will be a credit to the family, and your old father may be plain with you, I see. But do not be more of a Huguenot than the Messieurs de Coligny; and do not draw your sword. You are to be a man of the pen; stick to your part as a sucking lawyer. Well, tell me no more till you have succeeded. If I hear nothing of you for four days after you reach Blois, that silence will tell me that you are in danger. Then the old man will follow to save the young one. I have not sold furs for thirty years without knowing the seamy side of a Court robe. I can readily find means of opening doors."

Christophe stared with amazement at hearing his father speak thus; but he feared some parental snare, and held his tongue.

Then he said—

"Very well, make up the account; write a letter to the Queen. I must be off this moment, or dreadful things will happen."

"Be off? But how?"

"I will buy a horse. Write, for God's sake!"

"Here! Mother! Give your boy some money," the furrier called out to his wife.

She came in, flew to her chest, and gave a purse to Christophe, who excitedly kissed her.

"The account was ready," said his father; "here it is. I will write the letter."

Christophe took the bill and put it in his pocket.

"But at any rate you will sup with us," said the goodman. "In this extremity you and the Lallier girl must exchange rings."

"Well, I will go to fetch her," cried Christophe.

The young man feared some indecision in his father, whose character he did not thoroughly appreciate; he went up to his room, dressed, took out a small trunk, stole downstairs, and placed it with his cloak and rapier under a counter in the shop.

"What the devil are you about?" asked his father, hearing him there.

"I do not want any one to see my preparations for leaving; I have put everything under the counter," he whispered in reply.

"And here is the letter," said his father.

Christophe took the paper and went out as if to fetch their neighbor.

A few moments after Christophe had gone out, old Lallier and his daughter came in, preceded by a woman-servant carrying three bottles of old wine.

"Well, and where is Christophe?" asked the furrier and his wife.

"Christophe?" said Babette; "we have not seen him."

"A pretty rogue is my son!" cried Lecamus. "He tricks me as if I had no beard. Why, old gossip, what will come to us? We live in times when the children are all too clever for their fathers!"

"But he has long been regarded by all the neighbors as a mad follower of Colas," said Lallier.

"Defend him stoutly on that score," said the furrier to the goldsmith. "Youth is foolish, and runs after anything new; but Babette will keep him quiet, she is even newer than Calvin."

Babette smiled. She truly loved Christophe, was affronted by everything that was ever said against him. She was a girl of the good, old middle-class type, brought up under her mother's eye, for she had never left her; her demeanor was as gentle and precise as her features; she was dressed in stuff of harmonious tones of gray; her ruff, plainly pleated, was a contrast by its whiteness to her sober gown; on her head was a black velvet cap, like a child's hood in shape, but trimmed, on each side of her face, with frills and ends of tan-colored gauze. Though she was fair-haired, with a white skin, she seemed cunning and crafty, though trying to hide her willingness under the expression of a simple and honest girl.

As long as the two women remained in the room, coming to and fro to lay the cloth, and place the jugs, the large pewter dishes, and the knives and forks, the goldsmith and his daughter, the furrier and his wife, sat in front of the high chimney-place, hung with red serge and black fringes, talking of nothing. It was in vain that Babette asked where Christophe could be; the young Huguenot's father and mother made ambiguous replies; but as soon as the party had sat down to their meal, and the two maids were in the kitchen, Lecamus said to his future daughter-in-law—

"Christophe is gone to the Court."

"To Blois! What a journey to take without saying good-by to me!" said Babette.

"He was in a great hurry," said his old mother.

"Old friend," said the furrier to Lallier, taking up the thread of the conversation, "we are going to see hot work in France; the Reformers are astir."

"If they win the day it will only be after long fighting, which will be very bad for trade," said Lallier, incapable of looking higher than the commercial point of view.

"My father, who had seen the end of the wars between the Bourguignons and the Armagnacs, told me that our family would never have lived through them if one of his grandfathers—his mother's father—had not been one of the Goix, the famous butchers at the Halle, who were attached to the

Bourguignons, while the other, a Lecamus, was on the side of the Armagnacs; they pretended to be ready to flay each other before the outer world, but at home they were very good friends. So we will try to save Christophe. Perhaps a time may come when he will save us.''

"You are a cunning dog, neighbor,'' said the goldsmith.

"No,'' replied Lecamus. "The citizen class must take care of itself, the populace and the nobility alike owe it a grudge. Everybody is afraid of the middle-class in Paris excepting the King, who knows us to be his friends.''

"You who know so much, and who have seen so much,'' said Babette timidly, "pray tell me what it is that the Reformers want.''

"Ay, tell us that, neighbor!'' cried the goldsmith. "I knew the late King's tailor, and I always took him to be a simple soul, with no great genius; he was much such another as you are, they would have given him the host without requiring him to confess, and all the time he was up to his eyes in this new religion. He! a man whose ears were worth many hundred thousand crowns. He must have known some secrets worth hearing for the King and Madame de Valentinois to be present when he was tortured.''

"Ay! and terrible secrets too,'' said the furrier. "The Reformation, my friends,'' he went on, in a low voice, "will give the church lands back to the citizen class. When ecclesiastical privileges are annulled, the Reformers mean to claim equality of taxation for the nobles and the middle-class, and to have only the King above all alike—if indeed they have a king at all.''

"What, do away with the throne?'' cried Lallier.

"Well, neighbor,'' said Lecamus, "in the Low Countries the citizens govern themselves by provosts over them, who elect a temporary chief.''

"God bless me! Neighbor, we might do all these fine things and still be Catholics,'' said the goldsmith.

"We are too old to see the triumph of the middle-class in Paris, but it will triumph, neighbor, all in good time, all in good time! Why, the King is bound to rely on us to hold his own, and we have always been well paid for our support. And the last time all the citizens were ennobled, and they had leave to buy manors, and take the names of their estates without any special letters patent from the King. You and I, for instance, grandsons of the Goix in the female line, are we not as good as many a nobleman?"

This speech was so alarming to the goldsmith and the two women that it was followed by a long silence. The leaven of 1789 was already germinating in the blood of Lecamus, who was not yet so old but that he lived to see the daring of his class under the League.

"Is business pretty firm in spite of all this turmoil?" Lallier asked the furrier's wife.

"It always upsets trade a little," said she.

"Yes, and so I have a great mind to make a lawyer of my son," added Lecamus. "People are always going to law."

The conversation then dwelt on the commonplace, to the goldsmith's great satisfaction, for he did not like political disturbances or over-boldness of thought.

The banks of the Loire, from Blois as far as Angers, were always greatly favored by the two last branches of the royal family who occupied the throne before the advent of the Bourbons. This beautiful valley so well deserves the preference of kings that one of our most elegant writers describes it as follows: "There is a province in France which is never sufficiently admired. As fragrant as Italy, as flowery as the banks of the Guadalquivir, beautiful beside with its own peculiar beauty. Wholly French, it has always been French, unlike our Northern provinces, debased by Teutonic influence, or our Southern provinces, which have been the concubines of the Moors, of the Spaniards, of every nation that has coveted them—this pure, chaste, brave, and loyal tract is Touraine! There is the seat of historic France.  Auvergne is Auvergne, Languedoc is Languedoc and nothing more; but Touraine is France, and the truly national river to us is the Loire which waters Touraine.  We need not, therefore, be surprised to find such a quantity of monuments in the departments which have taken their names from that of the Loire and its derivations.  At every step in that land of enchantment we come upon a picture of which the foreground is the river, or some calm reach, in whose liquid depths are mirrored a château, with its turrets, its woods, and its dancing springs.  It was only natural that large fortunes should centre around spots where Royalty preferred to live, and where it so long held its Court, and that distinguished birth and merit should crowd thither and build palaces on a par with Royalty itself.''

Is it not strange, indeed, that our sovereigns should never have taken the advice indirectly given them by Louis XI., and have made Tours the capital of the kingdom?  Without any great expenditure, the Loire might have been made navigable so far for trading vessels and light ships of war.  There the seat of Government would have been safe from surprise and high-handed invasion.  There the strongholds of the north would not have needed such sums for their fortifications, which alone have cost as much money as all the splendors of Versailles.  If Louis XIV. had listened to Vauban's advice, and had his palace built at Mont-Louis, between the Loire and the Cher, perhaps the Revolution of 1789 would never have taken place.

So these fair banks bear, at various spots, clear marks of royal favor.  The castles of Chambord, Blois, Amboise, Chenonceaux, Chaumont, Plessis-les-Tours, all the residences built by kings' mistresses, by financiers, and noblemen, at Véretz, Azay-le-Rideau, Ussé, Villandri, Valençay, Chanteloup, and Duretal, some of which have disappeared, though most are still standing, are splendid buildings, full of the wonders of the period that has been so little appreciated by the literary sect of Mediævalists.

Of all these castles, that of Blois, where the Court was then residing, is the one on which the magnificence of the Houses of Orleans and of Valois has most splendidly set its stamp; and it is the most curious to historians, archæologists, and Catholics. At that time it stood quite alone. The town, inclosed in strong walls with towers, lay below the stronghold, for at that time the castle served both as a citadel and as a country residence. Overlooking the town, of which the houses, then as now, climbed the hill on the right bank of the river, their blue slate roofs in close array, there is a triangular plateau, divided by a stream, now unimportant since it runs underground, but in the fifteenth century, as historians tell us, flowing at the bottom of a rather deep ravine, part of which remains as a deep hollow-way, almost a precipice, between the suburb and the castle.

It was on this plateau, with a slope to the north and south, that the Comtes de Blois built themselves a " castel " in the architecture of the twelfth century, where the notorious Thibault le Tricheur, Thibault le Vieux, and many more held a court that became famous. In those days of pure feudal rule, when the King was no more than *inter pares primus* (the first among equals), as a King of Poland finely expressed it, the Counts of Champagne, of Blois, and of Anjou, the mere Barons of Normandy, and the Dukes of Brittany lived in the style of sovereigns and gave kings to the proudest kingdoms. The Plantagenets of Anjou, the Lusignans of Poitou, the Roberts and Williams of Normandy, by their audacious courage mingled their blood with royal races, and sometimes a simple knight, like du Glaicquin (or du Guesclin), refused royal purple and preferred the Constable's sword.

When the Crown had secured Blois as a royal demesne, Louis XII., who took a fancy to the place, perhaps to get away from Plessis and its sinister associations, built on to the castle, at an angle, so as to face east and west, a wing connecting the residence of the Counts of Blois with the older structure, of which nothing now remains but the immense hall where the States-General sat under Henri III. Francis I., before he fell in love with Chambord, intended to finish the castle by building on the other two sides of a square; but he abandoned Blois for Chambord, and erected only one wing, which in his time and in that of his grandsons practically constituted the castle.

This third building of Francis I.'s is much more extensive and more highly decorated than the Louvre *de Henri II.*, as it is called. It is one of the most fantastic efforts of the architecture of the Renaissance. Indeed, at a time when a more reserved style of building prevailed, and no one cared for the Middle Ages, a time when literature was not so intimately allied with art as it now is, La Fontaine wrote of the Castle of Blois in his characteristically artless language: "Looking at it from outside, the part done by order of Francis I. pleased me more than all the rest; there are a number of little windows, little balconies, little colonnades, little ornaments, not regularly ordered, which make up something great which I found very pleasing."

Thus the Castle of Blois had the attraction of representing three different kinds of architecture—three periods, three systems, three dynasties. And there is not, perhaps, any other royal residence which in this respect can compare with it. The vast building shows, in one inclosure, in one courtyard, a complete picture of that great product of national life and manners which architecture always is.

At the time when Christophe was bound for the Court, that portion of the precincts on which a fourth palace now stands —the wing added seventy years later, during his exile, by Gaston, Louis XIII.'s rebellious brother—was laid out in pastures and terraced gardens, picturesquely scattered among the foundation stones and unfinished towers begun by Francis I.

6

These gardens were joined by a bold flying bridge—which
some old inhabitants still alive saw destroyed—to a garden on
the other side of the castle, which by the slope of the ground
lay on the same level.    The gentlemen attached to Queen
Anne of Brittany, or those who approached her with petitions
from her native province, to discuss or to inform her of the
state of affairs there, were wont to await her pleasure here, her
*lever,* or the hour of her walking out.    Hence history has
handed down to us as the name of this pleasaunce *La Perchoir
aux Bretons* (the Bretons' Perch) ; it is now an orchard belonging to some private citizen, projecting beyond the Place
des Jésuites.    That square also was  then included in the domain of this noble residence which had its upper and its lower
gardens.    At some distance from the Place des Jésuites, a
summer-house may still be seen, built by Catherine de' Medici,
as local historians tell us, to accommodate her hot-baths.
This statement enables us to trace the very irregular arrangement of the gardens which went up and down hill, following
the undulations of the soil ; the land about the castle is indeed
very uneven, a fact which added to its strength, and, as we
shall see, caused the difficulties of the Duc de Guise.

The gardens were reached by corridors and terraces ; the
chief corridor was known as the Galerie des Cerfs (or stags),
on account of its decorations.    This passage led to a magnificent staircase, which undoubtedly suggested the famous double
staircase at Chambord, and which led to the apartments on
each floor.

Though La Fontaine preferred the château of Francis I. to
that of Louis XII., the simplicity of the *Père du Peuple*
(Father of the People) may perhaps charm the genuine artist,
much as he may admire the splendor of the more chivalrous
king.    The elegance of the two staircases which lie at the two
extremities of Louis XII.'s building, the quantity of fine and
original carving, of which, though time has damaged them,
the remains are still the delight of antiquaries ; everything, to

the almost cloister-like arrangement of the rooms, points to very simple habits. As yet the Court was evidently non-existent, or had not attained such development as Francis I. and Catherine de' Medici subsequently gave it, to the great detriment of feudal manners. As we admire the brackets, the capitals of some of the columns, and some little figures of exquisite delicacy, it is impossible not to fancy that Michel Colomb, the great sculptor, the Michael Angelo of Brittany, must have passed that way to do his Queen Anne a pleasure before immortalizing her on her father's tomb—the last Duke of Brittany.

Whatever La Fontaine may say, nothing can be more stately than the residence of Francis, the magnificent King. Thanks to I know not what coarse indifference, perhaps to utter forgetfulness, the rooms occupied by Catherine de' Medici and her son Francis II. still remain almost in their original state. The historian may reanimate them with the tragical scenes of the Reformation, of which the struggle of the Guises and the Bourbons against the House of Valois formed a complicated drama played out on this spot.

The buildings of Francis I. quite crush the simpler residence of Louis XII. by sheer mass. From the side of the lower gardens—that is to say, from the modern Place des Jésuites—the castle is twice as lofty as from the side toward the inner court. The first floor, in which are the famous corridors, is the third floor in the garden-front. Thus the second floor, where Queen Catherine resided, is in fact the fourth, and the royal apartments are on the fifth above the lower garden, which at that time was divided from the foundations by a very deep moat. Thus the castle, imposing as it is from the court, seems quite gigantic when seen from the square as La Fontaine saw it, for he owns that he never had been into the court or the rooms. From the Place des Jésuites every detail looks small. The balconies you can walk along, the colonnades of exquisite workmanship, the sculptured windows—their recesses within, as large as small rooms, and used, in fact, at that time as boudoirs—have a general effect resembling the painted fancies of operatic scenery when the artist represents a fairy palace. But, once inside the court, the infinite delicacy of this architectural ornamentation is displayed, to the joy of the amazed spectator, though the stories above the first floor are, even there, as high as the Pavillon de l'Horloge at the Tuileries.

This part of the building, where Catherine and Mary Stewart held magnificent court, had in the middle of the facade a hexagonal hollow tower, up which winds a staircase in stone, an arabesque device invented by giants and executed by dwarfs to give this front the effect of a dream. The balustrade of the stairs rises in a spiral of rectangular panels composing the five walls of the tower, and forming at regular intervals a transverse cornice, enriched outside and in with florid carvings in stone. This bewildering creation, full of delicate and ingenious details and marvels of workmanship, by which these stones speak to us, can only be compared to the overcharged and deeply cut ivory carvings that come from China, or are made at Dieppe. In short, the stone is like lace. Flowers and figures of men and animals creep down the ribs, multiply at every step, and crown the vault with a pendant, in which the chisels of sixteenth-century sculptors have outdone the artless stone-carvers, who, fifty years before, had made the pendants for two staircases in Louis XII.'s building. Though we may be dazzled as we note these varied forms repeated with infinite prolixity, we nevertheless perceive' that Francis I. lacked money for Blois, just as Louis XIV. did for Versailles. In more than one instance a graceful head looks out from a block of stone almost in the rough. More than one fanciful boss is but sketched with a few strokes of the chisel, and then abandoned to the damp, which has overgrown it with green mold. On the facade, by the side of one window carved like lace, another shows us the massive frame eaten into by time, which has carved it after a manner of its own.

The least artistic, the least experienced eye finds here a delightful contrast between this front, rippling with marvels of design, and the inner front of Louis XII.'s castle, consisting on the first floor of arches of the airiest lightness, upheld by slender columns, resting on elegant balustrades, and two stories above with windows wrought with charming severity. Under the arches runs a gallery, of which the walls were painted in fresco; the vaulting, too, must have been painted, for some traces are still visible of that magnificence, imitated from Italian architecture—a reminiscence of our King's journeys thither when the Milanese belonged to them.

Opposite the residence of Francis I. there was at that time the chapel of the Counts of Blois, its facade almost harmonizing with the architecture of Louis XII.'s building. No figure of speech can give an adequate idea of the solid dignity of these three masses of building. In spite of the varieties of style, a certain imposing royalty, showing the extent of its fear by the magnitude of its defenses, held the three buildings together, different as they were; two of them flanking the immense hall of the States-General, as vast and lofty as a church.

And certainly neither the simplicity nor the solidity of those citizen lives which were described at the beginning of this narrative—lives in which art was always represented—was lacking to this royal residence. Blois was the fertile and brilliant example which found a living response from citizens and nobles, from money and rank, alike in the towns and in the country. You could not have wished that the home of the King who ruled Paris as it was in the sixteenth century should be other than this. The splendid raiment of the upper classes, the luxury of feminine attire, must have seemed singularly suited to the elaborate dress of these curiously wrought stones.

From floor to floor, as he mounted the wonderful stairs of his Castle of Blois, the King of France could see farther and farther over the beautiful Loire, which brought him news of all his realm, which it parts into two confronted and almost rival halves.   If, instead of placing Chambord in a dead and gloomy plain two leagues away, Francis I. had built a Chambord to complete Blois on the site of the gardens, where Gaston subsequently erected his palace, Versailles would never have existed and Blois would inevitably have become the capital of France.

Four Valois' and Catherine de' Medici lavished their wealth on the Castle of Blois, but any one can guess how prodigal the sovereigns were only from seeing the thick dividing wall, the spinal column of the building, with deep alcoves cut into its substance, secret stairs and closets contrived within it, surrounding such vast rooms as the council hall, the guard-room, and the royal apartments, in which a company of infantry now finds ample quarters.   Even if the visitor should fail to understand at a first glance that the marvels of the interior are worthy of those of the exterior, the remains of Catherine de' Medici's room—into which Christophe was presently admitted—are sufficient evidence of the elegant art which peopled these rooms with lively fancies, with salamanders sparkling among flowers, with all the most brilliant hues of the palette of the sixteenth century decorating the darkest staircase.   In that room the observer may still see the traces of that love of gilding which Catherine had brought from Italy, for the princesses of her country loved (as the author above quoted delightfully expresses it) to overlay the castles of France with the gold gained in trade by their ancestors, and to stamp the walls of royal rooms with the sign of their wealth.

The Queen-mother occupied the rooms on the first floor that had formerly been those of Queen Claude de France, Francis I.'s wife ; and the delicate sculpture is still to be seen of double C's, with a device in pure white of swans and lilies, signifying *Candidior candidis* (the whitest of the white), the badge of that Queen whose name, like Catherine's, began with C, and equally appropriate to Louis XII.'s daughter and to the mother of the Valois; for notwithstanding the violence of Calvinist slander, no doubt was ever thrown on Catherine de' Medici's enduring fidelity to Henri II.

The Queen-mother, with two young children still on her hands—a boy, afterward the Duc d'Alençon, and Marguerite, who became the wife of Henri IV., and whom Charles IX. called Margot—needed the whole of this second floor.

King Francis II. and his Queen, Mary Stewart, had the royal apartments on the third floor that Francis I. had occupied, and which were also those of Henri III. The royal apartments and those of the Queen-mother are divided from end to end of the castle into two parts by the famous party wall, four feet thick, which supports the thrust of the immensely thick walls of the rooms. Thus on the lower as well as on the upper floors the rooms are in two distinct suites. That half which, facing to the south, is lighted from the court, held the rooms for state receptions and public business; while, to escape the heat, the private rooms had a north aspect, where there is a splendid frontage with arcades and balconies, and a view over the country of the Vendômois, the *Perchoir aux Bretons*, and the moats of the town—the only town mentioned by the great fable writer, the admirable La Fontaine.

Francis I.'s castle at that time ended at an enormous tower, only begun, but intended to mark the vast angle the palace would have formed in turning a flank; Gaston subsequently demolished part of its walls to attach his palace to the tower; but he never finished the work, and the tower remains a ruin. This royal keep was used as a prison, or, according to popular tradition, as *oubliettes* (dungeon cells). What poet could not feel deep regret or weep for France as he wanders now through the hall of this magnificent castle, and sees the exquisite arabesques of Catherine de' Medici's room, whitewashed and almost smothered by order of the governor of the barracks at the time of the cholera—for this royal residence is now a barrack.

The paneling of Catherine de' Medici's closet, of which more particular mention will presently be made, is the last relic of the rich furnishing collected by five artistic kings.

As we make our way through this labyrinth of rooms, halls, staircases, and turrets, we can say with horrible certainty, "Here Mary Stewart cajoled her husband in favor of the Guises. There those Guises insulted Catherine. Later, on this very spot, the younger *Balafré* * fell under the swords of the avengers of the Crown. A century earlier Louis XII. signaled from that window to invite the advance of his friend the Cardinal d'Amboise. From this balcony, d'Épernon, Ravaillac's accomplice, welcomed Queen Marie de' Medici, who, it is said, knew of the intended regicide and left things to take their course!"

In the chapel where Henry IV. and Marguerite de Valois were betrothed—the last remnant of the old castle of the Counts of Blois—the regimental boots are made. This wonderful structure, where so many styles are combined, where such great events have been accomplished, is in a state of ruin which is a disgrace to France. How grievous it is to those who love the memorial buildings of old France to feel that ere long these eloquent stones will have gone the way of the house at the corner of the Rue de la Vieille-Pelleterie: they will survive, perhaps, only in these pages.

It is necessary to observe that, in order to keep a keener eye on the Court, the Guises, though they had a mansion in the town, which is still to be seen, had obtained permission to reside above the rooms of Louis XII. in the apartments

* The gashed or scarred.

since used by the Duchesse de Nemours, in the upper story on the second floor.

Francis II. and his young Queen, Mary Stewart, in love like two children of sixteen, as they were, had been suddenly transferred, one cold winter's day, from Saint-Germain, which the Duc de Guise thought too open to surprise, to the stronghold, as it then was, of Blois, isolated on three sides by precipitous slopes, while its gates were strictly guarded. The Guises, the Queen's uncles, had the strongest reasons for not living in Paris, and for detaining the Court in a place which could be easily guarded and defended.

A struggle for the throne was being carried on, which was not ended until twenty-eight years later, in 1588, when, in this same Castle of Blois, Henri III., bitterly humiliated by the House of Lorraine, under his mother's very eyes, planned the death of the boldest of the Guises, the second Balafré (or scarred), son of the first Balafré, by whom Catherine de' Medici was tricked, imprisoned, spied on, and threatened.

Indeed, the fine Castle of Blois was to Catherine the strictest prison. On the death of her husband, who had always kept her in leading-strings, she had hoped to rule; but, on the contrary, she found herself a slave to strangers, whose politeness was infinitely more cruel than the brutality of gaolers. She could do nothing that was not known. Those of her ladies who were attached to her either had lovers devoted to the Guises, or Argus eyes watching over them. Indeed, at that time the conflict of passions had the capricious vagaries which they always derive from the powerful antagonism of two hostile interests in the State. Love-making, which served Catherine well, was also an instrument in the hands of the Guises. Thus the Prince de Condé, the leader of the Reformed party, was attached to the Maréchale de Saint-André, whose husband was the Grand Master's tool. The cardinal, who had learned from the affair of the Vidame de Chartres that Catherine was unconquered rather than unconquerable, was paying court to

her.   Thus the play of passions brought strange complications
into that of politics, making a double game of chess, as it
were, in which it was necessary to read both the heart and
brain of a man, and to judge, on occasion, whether one would
not belie the other.

Though she lived constantly under the eye of the Cardinal
de Lorraine or of his brother, the Duc François de Guise,
who both distrusted her, Catherine's most immediate and
shrewdest enemy was her daughter-in-law, Queen Mary, a
little, fair girl as mischievous as a waiting-maid, as proud as a
Stewart might be who wore three crowns, as learned as an
ancient scholar, as tricky as a schoolgirl, as much in love
with her husband as a courtesan of her lover, devoted to her
uncles, whom she admired, and delighted to find that King
Francis, by her persuasion, shared her high opinion of them.
A mother-in-law is always a person disliked by her daughter-
in-law, especially when she has won the crown and would like
to keep it—as Catherine had imprudently too plainly shown.
Her former position, when Diane de Poitiers ruled King
Henri II., had been more endurable ; at least she had enjoyed
the homage due to a Queen and the respect of the Court ;
whereas, now, the Duke and the cardinal, having none about
them but their own creatures, seemed to take pleasure in
humiliating her.   Catherine, a prisoner among courtiers, was
the object, not every day, but every hour, of blows offensive
to her dignity ; for the Guises persisted in carrying on the
same system as the late King had employed to thwart her.

The six-and-thirty years of disaster which devastated France
may be said to have begun with the scene in which the most
perilous part had been allotted to the son of the Queen's
furrier—a part which makes him the leading figure in this
narrative.   The danger into which this zealous reformer was
falling became evident in the course of the morning when he
set out from the river-port of Beaugency, carrying precious
documents which compromised the loftiest heads of the

nobility, and embarked for Blois in company with a crafty partisan, the indefatigable la Renaudie, who had arrived on the quay before him.

While the barque conveying Christophe was being wafted down the Loire before a light easterly breeze, the famous Cardinal de Lorraine and the second Duc de Guise, one of the greatest war captains of the time, were considering their position, like two eagles on a rocky peak, and looking cautiously round before striking the first great blow by which they tried to kill the Reformation in France. This was to be struck at Amboise, and it was repeated in Paris twelve years later, on the 24th August, 1572.

In the course of the previous night, three gentlemen, who played an important part in the twelve years' drama that arose from this double plot laid by the Guises on one hand and the Reformers on the other, had arrived at the castle at a furious gallop, leaving their horses half-dead at the postern gate, held by captains and men who were wholly devoted to the Duc de Guise, the idol of the soldiery.

A word must be said as to this great man, and first of all a word to explain his present position.

His mother was Antoinette de Bourbon, great-aunt of Henri IV. But, of what account are alliances? At this moment he aimed at nothing less than his cousin de Condé's head. Mary Stewart was his niece. His wife was Anne, daughter of the Duke of Ferrara. The Grand Connétable Anne de Montmorency addressed the Duc de Guise as "Monseigneur," as he wrote to the King, and signed himself "Your very humble servant." Guise, the Grand Master of the King's household, wrote in reply, "Monsieur le Connétable," and signed, as in writing to the Parlement, "Your faithful friend."

As for the cardinal, nicknamed the Trans-Alpine Pope, and spoken of by Estienne as "His Holiness," the whole monastic church of France was on his side, and he treated with the Pope as his equal. He was vain of his eloquence, and one of the ablest theologians of his time, while he kept watch over France and Italy by the instrumentality of three religious Orders entirely devoted to him, who were on foot for him day and night, serving him as spies and reporters.

These few words are enough to show to what a height of power the cardinal and the Duke had risen. In spite of their wealth and the revenues of their offices, they were so entirely disinterested, or so much carried away by the tide of politics, and so generous too, that both were in debt—no doubt after the manner of Cæsar. Hence, when Henri III. had seen his threatening foe murdered, the second Balafré, the House of Guise was inevitably ruined. Their vast outlay for above a century, in hope of seizing the Crown, accounts for the decay of this great House under Louis XIII. and Louis XIV., when the sudden end of MADAME revealed to all Europe how low a Chevalier de Lorraine had fallen.

So the cardinal and the Duke, proclaiming themselves the heirs of the deposed Carlovingian kings, behaved very insolently to Catherine de' Medici, their niece's mother-in-law. The Duchesse de Guise spared Catherine no mortification ; she was an Este, and Catherine de' Medici was the daughter of self-made Florentine merchants, whom the sovereigns of Europe had not yet admitted to their royal fraternity. Francis I. had regarded his son's marriage with a Medici as a mésalliance, and had only allowed it in the belief that this son would never be the Dauphin. Hence his fury when the Dauphin died, poisoned by the Florentine Montecuculi.

The Estes refused to recognize the Medici as Italian princes. These time-honored merchants were, in fact, struggling with the impossible problem of maintaining a throne in the midst of republican institutions. The title of Grand Duke was not bestowed on the Medici till much later by Philip II., King of Spain ; and they earned it by treason to France, their benefactress, and by a servile attachment to the Court of Spain, which was covertly thwarting them in Italy.

" Flatter none but your enemies! " This great axiom, uttered by Catherine, would seem to have ruled all the policy of this merchant race, which never lacked great men till its destinies had grown great, and which broke down a little too soon under the degeneracy which is always the end of royal dynasties and great families.

For three generations there was a prelate and a warrior of the House of Lorraine; but, which is perhaps not less remarkable, the churchman had always shown—as did the present cardinal—a singular likeness to Cardinal Ximenes, whom the Cardinal de Richelieu also resembled. These five prelates all had faces that were at once mean and terrifying; while the warrior's face was of that Basque and mountain type which reappears in the features of Henri IV. In both the father and the son it was seamed by a scar, which did not destroy the grace and affability that bewitched their soldiers as much as their bravery.

The way and the occasion of the Grand Master's being wounded is not without interest here, for it was healed by the daring of one of the personages of this drama, Ambroise Paré, who was under obligation to the Syndic of the furriers. At the siege of Calais the Duke's head was pierced by a lance which, entering below the right eye, went through to the neck below the left ear; the end broke off and remained in the wound. The Duke was lying in his tent in the midst of the general woe, and would have died but for the bold promptitude and devotion of Ambroise Paré.

" The Duke is not dead, gentlemen," said Paré, turning to the bystanders, who were dissolved in tears. " But he soon will be," he added, " unless I treat him as if he were, and I will try it at the risk of the worst that can befall me—— You see ! "

He set his left foot on the Duke's breast, took the stump of the lance with his nails, loosened it by degrees, and at last drew the spear-head out of the wound, as if it had been from some senseless object instead of a man's head. Though he cured the Prince he had handled so boldly, he could not hinder him from bearing to his grave the terrible scar from which he had his name. His son also had the same nickname for a similar reason.

Having gained entire mastery over the King, who was ruled by his wife, as a result of the passionate and mutual affection which the Guises knew how to turn to account, the two great Princes of Lorraine reigned over France, and had not an enemy at Court but Catherine de' Medici. And no great politician ever played a closer game. The respective attitudes of Henry II.'s ambitious widow, and of the no less ambitious House of Lorraine, was symbolized, as it were, by the positions they held on the terrace of the castle on the very morning when Christophe was about to arrive there. The Queen-mother, feigning extreme affection for the Guises, had asked to be informed as to the news brought by the three gentlemen who had arrived from different parts of the kingdom ; but she had been mortified by a polite dismissal from the cardinal. She was walking at the farther end of the pleasaunce above the Loire, where she was having an observatory erected for her astrologer, Ruggieri ; the building may still be seen, and from it a wide view is to be had over the beautiful valley. The two Guises were on the opposite side overlooking the Vendômois, the upper part of the town, the Perchoir aux Bretons, and the postern gate of the castle.

Catherine had deceived the brothers, tricking them by an assumption of dissatisfaction ; for she was really very glad to be able to speak with one of the gentlemen who had come in hot haste, and who was in her secret confidence ; who boldly played a double game, but who was, to be sure, well paid for it. This gentleman was Chiverni, who affected to be the mere tool of the Cardinal de Lorraine, but who was in reality in Catherine's service. Catherine had two other devoted allies in the two Gondis, creatures of her own ; but they, as Florentines, were too open to the suspicion of the Guises to be sent into the country; she kept them at the Court, where their every word and action was closely watched, but where they, on their side, watched the Guises and reported to Catherine. These two Italians kept a third adherent to the Queen-mother's faction, Birague, a clever Piedmontese, who, like Chiverni, pretended to have abandoned Catherine to attach himself to the Guises, and who encouraged them in their undertakings while spying for Catherine.

Chiverni had arrived from Écouen and Paris. The last to ride in was Saint-André, Marshal of France, who rose to be such an important personage that the Guises adopted him as the third of the triumvirate they formed against Catherine in the following year. But earlier than either of these, Vieilleville, the builder of the Castle of Duretal, who had also by his devotion to the Guises earned the rank of marshal, had secretly come and more secretly gone, without any one knowing what the mission might be that the Grand Master had given him. Saint-André, it was known, had been instructed to take military measures to entice all the reformers who were under arms to Amboise, as the result of a council held by the Cardinal de Lorraine, the Duc de Guise, Birague, Chiverni, Vieilleville, and Saint-André. As the heads of the House of Lorraine thus employed Birague, it is to be supposed that they trusted to their strength, for they knew that he was attached to the Queen-mother; but it is possible that they kept him about them with a view to discovering their rival's secret designs, as she allowed him to attend them. In those strange times the double part played by some political intriguers was known to both the parties who employed them; they were like cards in the hands of players, and the craftiest won the game.

All through this sitting the brothers had been impenetrably guarded. Catherine's conversation with her friends will, however, fully explain the purpose of this meeting, convened by the Guises in the open air, at break of day, in the terraced garden, as though every one feared to speak within the walls full of ears of the Castle of Blois.

The Queen-mother, who had been walking about all the morning with the two Gondi, under pretense of examining the observatory that was being built, but, in fact, anxiously watching the hostile party, was presently joined by Chiverni. She was standing at the angle of the terrace opposite the church of Saint-Nicholas, and there feared no listeners. The wall is as high as the church-towers, and the Guises always held council at the other corner of the terrace, below the dungeon then begun, walking to and from the Perchoir des Bretons and the arcade by the bridge which joined the gardens to the Perchoir. There was nobody at the bottom of the ravine.

Chiverni took the Queen's hand to kiss it, and slipped into her fingers a tiny letter without being seen by the Italians. Catherine quickly turned away, walked to the corner of the parapet, and read as follows:

"You are powerful enough to keep the balance true between the great ones, and to make them contend as to which shall serve you best; you have your house full of kings, and need not fear either Lorrains or Bourbons so long as you set them against each other; for both sides aim at snatching the crown from your children. Be your advisers' mistress, and not their slave; keep up each side by the other; otherwise the kingdom will go from bad to worse and great wars may ensue.

"L'Hôpital."

The Queen placed this letter in the bosom of her stomacher, reminding herself to burn it as soon as she should be alone.

"When did you see him?" she asked Chiverni.

"On returning from seeing the Connétable at Melun; he was going through with the Duchesse de Berri, whom he was most anxious to convey in safety to Savoy, so as to return

here and enlighten the Chancellor Olivier, who is, in fact,
the dupe of the Lorrains. Monsieur de l'Hôpital is resolved
to adhere to your cause, seeing the aims that the Messieurs de
Guise have in view. And he will hasten back as fast as
possible to give you his vote in the council."

"Is he sincere?" said Catherine. "For you know that
when the Lorrains admitted him to the council, it was to
enable them to rule."

"L'Hôpital is a Frenchman of too good a stock not to be
honest," said Chiverni; "beside, that letter is a sufficient
pledge."

"And what answer does the Connétable send to these
gentlemen?"

"He says the King is his master, and he awaits his orders.
On this reply, the cardinal, to prevent any resistance, will propose to appoint his brother lieutenant-general of the realm."

"So soon!" exclaimed Catherine in dismay. "Well, and
did Monsieur de l'Hôpital give you any further message for
me?"

"He told me, madame, that you alone can stand between
the throne and Messieurs de Guise."

"But does he suppose that I will use the Huguenots as a
means of defense?"

"Oh, madame," cried Chiverni, surprised by her perspicacity, "we never thought of placing you in such a difficult
position."

"Did he know what a position I am in?" asked the
Queen calmly.

"Pretty nearly. He thinks you made a dupe's bargain
when, on the death of the late King, you accepted for your
share the fragments saved from the ruin of Madame Diane.
The Messieurs de Guise thought they had paid their debt to
the Queen by gratifying the woman."

"Yes," said Catherine, looking at the two Gondis, "I
made a great mistake there."

7

"A mistake the gods might make!" replied Charles de Gondi.

"Gentlemen," said the Queen, "if I openly take up the cause of the Reformers, I shall be the slave of a party."

"Madame," said Chiverni eagerly, "I entirely agree with you. You must make use of them, but not let them make use of you."

"Although, for the moment, your strength lies there," said Charles de Gondi, "we must not deceive ourselves; success and failure are equally dangerous!"

"I know it," said the Queen. "One false move will be a pretext eagerly seized by the Guises to sweep me off the board!"

"A Pope's niece, the mother of four Valois, the Queen of France, the widow of the most ardent persecutor of the Huguenots, an Italian and a Catholic, the aunt of Leo X.—can you form an alliance with the Reformation?" asked Charles de Gondi.

"On the other hand," Albert replied, "is not seconding the Guises consenting to usurpation? You have to deal with a race that looks to the struggle between the church and the Reformation to give them a crown for the taking. You may avail yourself of Huguenot help without abjuring the faith."

"Remember, madame, that your family, which ought to be wholly devoted to the King of France, is at this moment in the service of the King of Spain," said Chiverni. "And it would go over to the Reformation to-morrow if the Reformation could make the Duke of Florence King!"

"I am very well inclined to give the Huguenots a helping hand for a time," said Catherine, "were it only to be revenged on that soldier, that priest, and that woman!"

And with an Italian glance, her eye turned on the Duke and the cardinal, and then to the upper rooms of the castle where her son lived and Mary Stewart. "Those three snatched the reins of government from my hands," she went on, "when I had waited for them long enough while that old woman held them in my place."

She jerked her head in the direction of Chenonceaux, the castle she had just exchanged for Chaumont with Diane de Poitiers. "*Ma*," she said in Italian, "it would seem that these gentry of the Geneva bands have not wit enough to apply to me! On my honor, I cannot go to meet them! And not one of you would dare to carry them a message." She stamped her foot. "I hoped you might have met the hunchback at Écouen," she said to Chiverni. "He has brains."

"He was there, madame," replied Chiverni, "but he could not induce the Connétable to join him. Monsieur de Montmorency would be glad enough to overthrow the Guises, who obtained his dismissal; but he will have nothing to do with heresy."

"And who, gentlemen, is to crush these private whims that are an offense to royalty? By heaven! these nobles must be made to destroy each other—as Louis XI. made them, the greatest of your kings. In this kingdom there are four or five parties and my son's is the weakest of them all."

"The Reformation is an idea," remarked Charles de Gondi, "and the parties crushed by Louis XI. were based only on interest."

"There is always an idea to back up interest," replied Chiverni. "In Louis XI.'s time the idea was called the Great Fief!"

"Use heresy as an axe," said Albert de Gondi. "You will not incur the odium of executions."

"Ha!" said the Queen, "but I know nothing of the strength or the schemes of these folk, and I cannot communicate with them through any safe channel. If I were found out in any such conspiracy, either by the Queen, who watches me as if I were an infant in arms, or by my two gaolers, who let no one come into the castle, I should then be banished the country, and taken back to Florence under a formidable escort captained by some ruffianly Guisard! Thank you, friends! Oh, daughter-in-law! I hope you may some day be a prisoner in your own house; then you will know what you have inflicted on me!"

"Their schemes!" exclaimed Chiverni. "The Grand Master and the cardinal know them; but those two foxes will not tell. If you, madame, can make them tell, I will devote myself to you, and come to an understanding with the Prince de Condé."

"Which of their plans have they failed to conceal from you?" asked the Queen, glancing toward the brothers de Guise.

"Monsieur de Vieilleville and Monsieur de Saint-André have just had their orders, of which we know nothing; but the Grand Master is concentrating his best troops on the left bank, it would seem. Within a few days you will find yourself at Amboise. The Grand Master came to this terrace to study the position, and he does not think Blois favorable to his private schemes. Well, then, what does he want?" said Chiverni, indicating the steep cliffs that surround the castle. "The Court could nowhere be safer from sudden attack than it is here."

"Abdicate or govern," said Albert de Gondi in the Queen's ear as she stood thinking.

A fearful expression of suppressed rage flashed across the Queen's handsome ivory-pale face. She was not yet forty, and she had lived for twenty-six years in the French Court, absolutely powerless, she who, ever since she had come there, had longed to play the leading part.

"Never so long as this son lives! His wife has bewitched him!"

After a short pause these terrible words broke from her in the language of Dante.

Catherine's exclamation had its inspiration in a strange prediction, spoken a few days before at the Castle of Chaumont, on the opposite bank of the Loire, whither she had gone with her astrologer Ruggieri to consult a famous soothsayer. This woman was brought to meet her by Nostradamus, the chief of those physicians who in that great sixteenth century believed in the occult sciences, with Ruggieri, Cardan, Paracelsus, and many more. This fortune-teller, of whose life history has no record, had fixed the reign of Francis II. at one year's duration.

"And what is your opinion of all this?" Catherine asked Chiverni.

"There will be fighting," said the cautious gentleman. "The King of Navarre——"

"Oh! say the Queen!" Catherine put in.

"Very true, the Queen," said Chiverni, smiling, "has made the Prince de Condé the chief of the Reformed party; he, as a younger son, may dare much; and Monsieur le Cardinal talks of sending for him to come here."

"If only he comes!" cried the Queen, "I am saved!"

So it will be seen that the leaders of the great Reforming movement had been right in thinking of Catherine as an ally.

"This is the jest of it," said the Queen; "the Bourbons are tricking the Huguenots, and Master Calvin, de Bèze, and the rest are cheating the Bourbons; but shall we be strong enough to take in the Huguenots, the Bourbons, and the Guises? In front of three such foes we are justified in feeling our pulse," said she.

"They have not the King," replied Albert. "You must always win, having the King on your side."

"Malediction, Mary!" said Catherine, between her teeth.

"The Guises are already thinking of diverting the affections of the middle-class," said Birague.

The hope of snatching the Crown had not been premedi-

tated by the two heads of the refractory House of Guise;
there was nothing to justify the project or the hope; circumstances suggested such audacity.  The two cardinals and the
two Balafrés were, as it happened, four ambitious men, superior
in political gifts to any of the men about them.  Indeed, the
family was only subdued at last by Henri IV., himself a leader
of faction, brought up in the great school of which Catherine
and the Guises were the teachers—and he had profited by
their lessons.

At this time these two brothers were the arbiters of the
greatest revolution attempted in Europe since that carried
through in England under Henry VIII., which had resulted
from the invention of printing.  They were the enemies of
the Reformation, the power was in their hands, and they
meant to stamp out heresy; but Calvin, their opponent, though
less famous than Luther, was a stronger man.  Calvin saw
government where Luther had only seen dogma.  Where the
burly, beer-drinking, uxorious German fought with the devil,
flinging his inkstand at the fiend, the man of Picardy, frail
and unmarried, dreamed of plans of campaign, of directing
battles, of arming princes, and of raising whole nations by
disseminating republican doctrines in the hearts of the middle-
classes, so as to make up, by increased progress in the spirit
of nations, for his constant defeats on the battlefield.

The Cardinal de Lorraine and the Duc de Guise knew
quite as well as Philip II. and the Duke of Alva where the
Monarchy was aimed at, and how close the connection was
between Catholicism and sovereignty.  Charles V., intoxi-
cated with having drunk too deeply of Charlemagne's cup,
and trusting too much in the strength of his rule, for he believed that he and Soliman might divide the world between
them, was not at first conscious that his front was attacked;
as soon as Cardinal Granvelle showed him the extent of the
festering sore, he abdicated.

The Guises had a startling conception: they would extinguish heresy with a single blow. They tried to strike that blow for the first time at Amboise, and they made a second attempt on Saint-Bartholomew's Day; this time they were in accord with Catherine de' Medici, enlightened as she was by the flames of twelve years' wars, and yet more by the ominous word "Republic" spoken and even published at a later date by the writers of the Reformation, whose ideas Lecamus, the typical citizen of Paris, had already understood. The two Princes, on the eve of striking a fatal blow to the heart of the nobility, in order to cut it off from the first from a religious party whose triumph would be its ruin, were now discussing the means of announcing their stroke of policy to the King, while Catherine was conversing with her four counselors.

"Jeanne d'Albret knew what she was doing when she proclaimed herself the protectress of the Huguenots! She has in the Reformation a battering-ram which she makes good play with!" said the Grand Master, who had measured the depth of the Queen of Navarre's scheming.

Jeanne d'Albret was, in point of fact, one of the cleverest personages of her time.

"Théodore de Bèze is at Nérac, having taken Calvin's orders."

"What men those common folk can lay their hands on!" cried the Duke.

"Ay, we have not a man on our side to match that fellow la Renaudie," said the cardinal. "He is a perfect Catiline."

"Men like him always act on their own account," replied the Duke. "Did not I see la Renaudie's value? I loaded him with favors, I helped him to get away when he was condemned by the Bourgogne Parlement, I got him back into France by obtaining a revision of his trial, and I intended to do all I could for him, while he was plotting a diabolical conspiracy against us. The rascal has effected an alliance between the German Protestants and the heretics in France by smoothing over the discrepancies of dogma between Luther and

Calvin.   He has won over the disaffected nobles to the cause
of the Reformation without asking them to abjure Catholicism.
So long ago as last year he had thirty commanders on his side!
He was everywhere at once: at Lyons, in Languedoc, at
Nantes.   Finally, he drew up the articles settled in Council
and, distributed throughout Germany, in which theologians
declare that it is justifiable to use force to get the King out of
our hands, and this is being disseminated in every town.
Look for him where you will, you will nowhere find him !

"Hitherto I have shown him nothing but kindness !  We
shall have to kill him like a dog, or to make a bridge of gold
for him to cross and come into our house."

"Brittany and Languedoc, the whole kingdom, indeed, is
being worked upon to give us a deadly shock," said the cardinal.   "After yesterday's festival, I spent the rest of the
night in reading all the information sent me by my priest-
hood; but no one is involved but some impoverished gentlemen and artisans, people who may be either hanged or left
alive, it matters not which.   The Colignys and the Condés
are not yet visible, though they hold the threads of the conspiracy."

"Ay," said the Duke ; "and as soon as that lawyer Avenelles had let the cat out of the bag, I told Braguelonne to
give the conspirators their head: they have no suspicions,
they think they can surprise us, and then perhaps the leaders
will show themselves.   My advice would be that we should
allow ourselves to be beaten for forty-eight hours——"

"That would be half-an-hour too long," said the cardinal
in alarm.

"How brave you are ! " retorted le Balafré.

The cardinal went on with calm indifference—

"Whether the Prince de Condé be implicated or not, if
we are assured that he is the leader, cut off his head.   What
we want for that business is judges rather than soldiers, and
there will never be any lack of judges !   Victory in the

Supreme Court is always more certain than on the field of battle, and costs less.''

"I am quite willing," replied the Duke. "But do you believe that the Prince de Condé is powerful enough to inspire such audacity in those who are sent on first to attack us? Is there not——?"

"The King of Navarre,"* said the cardinal.

"A gaby who bows low in my presence," replied the Duke. "That Florentine woman's graces must have blinded you, I think——"

"Oh, I have thought of that already," said the prelate. "If I aim at a gallant intimacy with her, is it not that I may read to the bottom of her heart?"

"She has no heart," said his brother sharply. "She is even more ambitious than we are."

"You are a brave commander," said the cardinal; "but, take my word for it, our skirts are very near touching, and I made Mary Stewart watch her narrowly before you even suspected her. Catherine has no more religion in her than my shoe. If she is not the soul of the conspiracy, it is not for lack of good-will; but we will draw her out and see how far she will support us. Till now I know for certain that she has not held any communication with the heretics."

"It is time that we should lay everything before the King, and the Queen-mother, who knows nothing," said the Duke, "and that is the only proof of her innocence. La Renaudie will understand from my arrangements that we are warned. Last night Nemours must have been following up the detachments of the Reformed party, who were coming in by the cross-roads, and the conspirators will be compelled to attack us at Amboise; I will let them all in. Here," and he pointed to the three steep slopes of rock on which the Château de Blois is built, just as Chiverni had done a moment since, "we should have a fight with no result; the Huguenots could

* Husband of Queen Margaret.

come and go at will.   Blois is a hall with four doors, while Amboise is a sack.''

'' I will not leave the Florentine Queen,'' said the cardinal.

'' We have made one mistake,'' remarked the Duke, playing with his dagger, tossing it in the air, and catching it again by the handle; '' we ought to have behaved to her as to the Reformers, giving her liberty to move, so as to take her in the act.''

The cardinal looked at his brother for a minute, shaking his head.

'' What does Pardaillan want?'' the Duke exclaimed, seeing this young gentleman coming along the terrace.   Pardaillan was to become famous for his fight with la Renaudie, in which both were killed.

'' Monseigneur, a youth sent here by the Queen's furrier is at the gate and says that he has a set of ermine to deliver to her majesty.   Is he to be admitted?''

'' To be sure; an ermine surcoat she spoke of but yesterday,'' said the cardinal.   '' Let the store-clerk in.   She will need the mantle for her journey by the Loire.''

'' Which way did he come, that he was not stopped before reaching the gate?'' asked the Grand Master.

'' I do not know,'' said Pardaillan.

'' I will go to see him in the Queen's room,'' said le Balafré.   '' Tell him to await her *lever* in the guardroom. But, Pardaillan, is he young?''

'' Yes, monseigneur; he says he is Lecamus' son.''

'' Lecamus is a good Catholic,'' said the cardinal, who, like the Duke, was gifted with a memory like Cæsar's.   '' The priest of Saint-Pierre aux Bœufs trusts him, for he is officer of the peace for the Palace.''

'' Make this youth chat with the captain of the Scotch Guard, all the same,'' said the Grand Master, with an emphasis which gave the words a very pointed meaning. '' But Ambroise is at the castle; through him we shall know

"WE HAVE MADE ONE MISTAKE," REMARKED THE DUKE,
PLAYING WITH HIS DAGGER.

at once if he really is the son of Lecamus, who was formerly his very good friend.  Ask for Ambroise Paré."

At this moment the Queen came toward the brothers, who hurried to meet her with marks of respect, in which Catherine never failed to discern deep irony.

"Gentlemen," said she, "will you condescend to inform me of what is going on?  Is the widow of your late sovereign of less account in your esteem than Messieurs de Vieille-ville, Birague, and Chiverni?"

"Madame," said the cardinal, with an air of gallantry, "our first duty as men, before all matters of politics, is not to alarm ladies by false rumors.  This morning, indeed, we have had occasion to confer on State affairs.  You will pardon my brother for having in the first instance given orders on purely military matters which must be indifferent to you—the really important points remain to be discussed.  If you approve, we will all attend the *lever* of the King and Queen; it is close on the hour."

"Why, what is happening, Monsieur le Grand Maître?" asked Catherine, affecting terror.

"The Reformation, madame, is no longer a mere heresy; it is a party which is about to take up arms and seize the King."

Catherine, with the cardinal, the Duke, and the gentlemen, made their way toward the staircase by the corridor, which was crowded with courtiers who had not the right of admission, and who ranged themselves against the wall.

Gondi, who had been studying the Princes of Lorraine while Catherine was conversing with them, said in good Tuscan and in Catherine's ear these two words, which became by-words, and which express one aspect of that royally powerful nature—

"*Odiate e aspettate!*" (Hate and wait.)

Pardaillan, who had delivered to the officer on guard at the gatehouse the order to admit the messenger from the Queen's furrier, found Christophe standing outside the portico and staring at the facade built by good King Louis XII., whereon there was at that time an even more numerous array of sculptured figures of the coarsest buffoonery—if we may judge by what has survived. The curious will detect, for instance, a figure of a woman carved on the capital of one of the columns of the gateway holding up her skirts, and saucily exhibiting "what Brunel displayed to Marphise" to a burly monk crouching in the capital of the corresponding column at the other jamb of this gate, above which once stood a statue of Louis XII. Several of the windows of this front, ornamented in this grotesque taste, and now unfortunately destroyed, amused, or seemed to amuse, Christophe, whom the gunners of the Guard were already pelting with their pleasantries.

"He would like to be lodged there, he would," said the sergeant-at-arms, patting his store of charges for his musket, which hung from his belt in the sugar-loaf-shaped cartridges.

"Halloo, you from Paris, you never saw so much before!" said a soldier.

"He recognizes good King Louis!" said another.

Christophe affected not to hear them, and tried to look even more helplessly amazed, so that his look of blank stupidity was an excellent recommendation to Pardaillan.

"The Queen is not yet risen," said the young officer. "Come and wait in the guardroom."

Christophe slowly followed Pardaillan. He purposely lingered to admire the pretty covered balcony with an arched front, where, in the reign of Louis XII., the courtiers could wait under cover till the hour of reception if the weather was bad, and where at this moment some of the gentlemen attached to the Guises were grouped; for the staircase, still so well preserved, which led to their apartments is at the end of that gallery, in a tower of which the architecture is greatly admired by the curious.

"Now, then! have you come here to study graven images?"

cried Pardaillan, seeing Lecamus riveted in front of the elegant stonework of the outer parapet which unites—or, if you will, separates—the columns of each archway.

Christophe followed the young captain to the grand staircase, not without glancing at this almost Moorish-looking structure from top to bottom with an expression of ecstasy. On this fine morning the court was full of captains-at-arms and of courtiers chatting in groups; and their brilliant costumes gave life to the scene, in itself so bright, for the marvels of the noble architecture that decorated the facade were still quite new.

"Come in here," said Pardaillan to Lecamus, signing to him to follow him through the carved door on the second floor, which was thrown open by a sentry on his recognizing Pardaillan.

Christophe's amazement may easily be imagined on entering this guardroom, so vast that the military genius of our day has cut it across by a partition to form two rooms. It extends, in fact, both on the third floor, where the King lived, and on the second, occupied by the Queen-mother, for a third of the length of the front toward the court, and is lighted by two windows to the left and two to the right of the famous staircase. The young captain made his way toward the door leading to the King's room, which opened out of this hall, and desired one of the pages-in-waiting to tell Madame Dayelle, one of the Queen's ladies, that the furrier was in the guardroom with her surcoats.

At a sign from Pardaillan, Christophe went to stand by the side of an officer seated on a low stool in the corner of a chimney-place as large as his father's shop, at one end of this vast hall opposite another exactly like it at the other end. In talking with this gentleman, Christophe succeeded in interesting him by telling him the trivial details of his trade; and he seemed so completely the craftsman that the officer volunteered this opinion to the captain of the Scotch Guard, who came in to cross-question the lad while scrutinizing him closely out of the corner of his eye.

Though Christophe Lecamus had had ample warning, he still did not understand the cold ferocity of the interested parties between whom Chaudieu had bid him stand. To an observer who should have mastered the secrets of the drama, as the historian knows them now, it would have seemed terrible to see this young fellow, the hope of two families, risking his life between two such powerful and pitiless machines as Catherine and the Guises. But how few brave hearts ever know the extent of their danger! From the way in which the quays of the city and the château were guarded, Christophe had expected to find snares and spies at every step, so he determined to conceal the importance of his errand and the agitation of his mind under the stupid tradesman's stare, which he had put on before Pardaillan, the officer of the Guard, and the captain.

The stir which in a royal residence attends the rising of the King began to be perceptible. The nobles, leaving their horses with their pages or grooms in the outer court, for no one but the King and the Queen was allowed to enter the inner court on horseback, were mounting the splendid stairs in twos and threes and filling the guardroom, a large room with two fireplaces—where the huge mantels are now bereft of adornment, where squalid red tiles have taken the place of the fine mosaic flooring, where royal hangings covered the rough walls now daubed with whitewash, and where every art of an age unique in its splendor was displayed at its best.

Catholics and Protestants poured in as much to hear the news and study each other's faces as to pay their court to the King. His passionate affection for Mary Stewart, which neither the Queen-mother nor the Guises attempted to check, and Mary's politic submissiveness in yielding to it, deprived the King of all power; indeed, though he was now seventeen, he knew nothing of royalty but its indulgences, and of mar-

riage nothing but the raptures of first love.  In point of fact,
everybody tried to ingratiate himself with Queen Mary and
her uncles, the Cardinal de Lorraine and the Grand Master
of the household.

All this bustle went on under the eyes of Christophe, who
watched each fresh arrival with very natural excitement.  A
magnificent curtain, on each side of it a page and a yeoman
of the Scotch Guard, then on duty, showed him the entrance
to that royal chamber, destined to be fatal to the son of the
Grand Master, for the younger Balafré fell dead at the foot
of the bed now occupied by Mary Stewart and Francis II.
The Queen's ladies occupied the chimney-place opposite to
that where Christophe was still chatting with the captain of
the Guard.  This fireplace, by its position, was the seat of
honor, for it is built into the thick wall of the council-room,
between the door into the royal chamber and that into the
council-room, so that the ladies and gentlemen who had a
right to sit there were close to where the King and the Queen
must pass.  The courtiers were certain to see Catherine ; for
her maids of honor, in mourning, like the rest of the Court,
came up from her rooms conducted by the Countess Fieschi,
and took their place on the side next the council-room, facing
those of the young Queen, who, led by the Duchesse de
Guise, took the opposite angle next the royal bedchamber.

Between the courtiers and these young ladies, all belonging
to the first families in the kingdom, a space was kept of some
few paces, which none but the greatest nobles were permitted to cross.  The Countess Fieschi and the Duchesse
de Guise were allowed by right of office to be seated in
the midst of their noble charges, who all remained standing.

One of the first to mingle with these dangerous bevies
was the Duc d'Orléans, the King's brother, who came down
from his rooms above, attended by his tutor, Monsieur de
Cypierre.  This young Prince, who was destined to reign

before the end of the year, under the name of Charles IX., at the age of ten was excessively shy. The Duc d'Anjou and the Duc d'Alençon, his two brothers, and the infant Princess Marguerite, who became the wife of Henri IV., were still too young to appear at Court, and remained in their mother's apartments. The Duc d'Orléans, richly dressed in the fashion of the time, in silk trunk hose, a doublet of cloth of gold, brocaded with flowers in black, and a short cloak of embroidered velvet, all black, for he was still in mourning for the late King his father, bowed to the two elder ladies, and joined the group of his mother's maids of honor. Strongly disliking the Guisards (the adherents of the Guises), he replied coldly to the Duchess' greeting, and went to lean his elbow on the back of the Countess Fieschi's tall chair.

His tutor, Monsieur de Cypierre, one of the finest characters of that age, stood behind him as a shield. Amyot, in a simple abbé's gown, also attended the Prince; he was his instructor as well as being the teacher of the three other royal children, whose favor was afterward so advantageous to him.

Between this chimney-place "of honor" and that at the farther end of the hall—where the Guards stood in groups with their captain, a few courtiers, and Christophe carrying his box—the Chancellor Olivier, l'Hôpital's patron and predecessor, in the costume worn ever since by the chancellors of France, was walking to and fro with Cardinal de Tournon, who had just arrived from Rome, and with whom he exchanged a few phrases in murmurs. On them was centred the general attention of the gentlemen packed against the wall dividing the hall from the King's bedroom, standing like a living tapestry against the rich figured hangings. In spite of the serious state of affairs, the Court presented the same appearance as every Court must, in every country, at every time, and in the midst of the greatest perils. Courtiers always talk of the most trivial subjects while thinking of the gravest, jesting while watching every physiognomy, and considering questions of

love and marriage with heiresses in the midst of the most
sanguinary catastrophes.

"What did you think of yesterday's fête?" asked Bour-
deilles, the Lord of Brantôme, going up to Mademoiselle de
Piennes, one of the elder Queen's maids of honor.

"Monsieur du Baïf and Monsieur du Bellay had had the
most charming ideas," said she, pointing to the two gentlemen who had arranged everything, and who were standing
close at hand.   "I thought it in atrocious taste," she added
in a whisper.

"You had no part in it?" said Miss Lewiston from the
other side.

"What are you reading, madame?" said Amyot to Madame
Fieschi.

"'Amadis de Gaule,' by the Seigneur des Essarts, purveyor-
in-ordinary to the King's Artillery."

"A delightful work," said the handsome girl, who became
famous as la Fosseuse, when she was lady-in-waiting to Queen
Margaret of Navarre.

"The style is quite new," remarked Amyot.   "Shall you
adopt such barbarisms?" he asked, turning to Brantôme.

"The ladies like it!   What is to be said?" cried Brantôme, going forward to bow to Madame de Guise, who had in
her hand Boccaccio's "Famous Ladies."   "There must be
some ladies of your House there, madame," said he.   "But
Master Boccaccio's mistake was that he did not live in these
days; he would have found ample matter to enlarge his
volumes."

"How clever Monsieur de Brantôme is!" said the beautiful Mademoiselle de Limeuil to the Countess Fieschi.   "He
came first to us, but he will stay with the Guises."

"Hush!" said Madame Fieschi, looking at the fair Limeuil.
"Attend to what concerns you——"

The young lady turned to the door.   She was expecting
Sardini, an Italian nobleman, who was subsequently made to

8

marry her after a little accident that overtook her in the Queen's dressing-room, and which procured her the honor of having a queen for her midwife.

"By Saint Alipantin, Mademoiselle Davila seems to grow prettier every morning," said Monsieur de Robertet, Secretary of State, as he bowed to the Queen-mother's ladies.

The advent of the secretary of State, though he was exactly as important as a Cabinet Minister in these days, made no sensation whatever.

"If you think that, monsieur, do lend me the epigram against the Messieurs de Guise; I know you have it," said Mademoiselle Davila to Robertet.

"I have it no longer," replied the secretary, going across to speak to Madame de Guise.

"I have it," said the Comte de Grammont to Mademoiselle Davila; "but I will lend it you only on one condition."

"On condition——?  For shame!" said Madame Fieschi.

"You do not know what I want," replied Grammont.

"Oh, that is easy to guess," said la Limeuil.

The Italian custom of calling ladies, as French peasants call their wives, *la* Such-an-one, was at that time the fashion at the Court of France.

"You are mistaken," the Count replied eagerly; "what I ask is that a letter should be delivered to Mademoiselle de Matha, one of the maids on the other side—a letter from my cousin de Jarnac."

"Do not compromise my maids; I will give it to her myself," said the Countess Fieschi.  "Have you heard any news of what is going on in Flanders?" she asked Cardinal de Tournon.  "Monsieur d'Egmont is at some new pranks, it would seem."

"He and the Prince of Orange," said Cypierre, with a highly expressive shrug.

"The Duke of Alva and Cardinal de Granvelle are going there, are they not, monsieur?" asked Amyot of Cardinal de

Tournon, who stood, uneasy and gloomy, between the two groups after his conversation with the chancellor.

"We, happily, are quiet, and have to defy heresy only on the stage," said the young Duke, alluding to the part he had played the day before, that of a knight subduing a hydra with the word "Reformation" on its brow.

Catherine de' Medici, agreeing on this point with her daughter-in-law, had allowed a theatre to be constructed in the great hall, which was subsequently used for the meetings of the States at Blois, the hall between the buildings of Louis XII. and those of Francis I.

The cardinal made no reply, and resumed his walk in the middle of the hall, talking in a low voice to Monsieur de Robertet and the chancellor. Many persons know nothing of the difficulties that secretaryships of State, now transformed into Cabinet Ministries, met with in the course of their establishment, and how hard the Kings of France found it to create them. At that period a secretary like Robertet was merely a clerk, of hardly any account among the princes and magnates who settled the affairs of State. There were at that time no ministerial functionaries but the superintendent of finance, the chancellor, and the keeper of the king's seals. The King granted a seat in the Council, by letters patent, to such of his subjects as might, in his opinion, give useful advice in the conduct of public affairs. A seat in the Council might be given to a president of a law court in the Parlement, to a bishop, to an untitled favorite. Once admitted to the Council, the subject strengthened his position by getting himself appointed to one of the Crown offices to which a salary was attached—the government of a province, a constable's sword, a marshal's baton, the command of the Artillery, the post of High Admiral, the colonelcy of some military corps, the captaincy of the galleys—or often some function at Court, such as that of Grand Master of the household, then held by the Duc de Guise.

"Do you believe that the Duc de Nemours will marry Françoise?" asked Madame de Guise of the Duc d'Orléans' instructor.

"Indeed, madame, I know nothing but Latin," was the reply.

This made those smile who were near enough to hear it. Just then the seduction of Françoise de Rohan by the Duc de Nemours was the theme of every conversation; but as the Duc de Nemours was cousin to the King, and also allied to the House of Valois through his mother, the Guises regarded him as seduced rather than as a seducer. The influence of the House of Rohan was, however, so great, that after Francis II.'s death the Duc de Nemours was obliged to quit France in consequence of the lawsuit brought against him by the Rohans, which was compromised by the offices of the Guises. His marriage to the Duchesse de Guise, after Poltrot's assassination, may account for the Duchess' question to Amyot, by explaining some rivalry, no doubt, between her and Mademoiselle de Rohan.

"Look, pray, at that party of malcontents," said the Comte de Grammont, pointing to Messieurs de Coligny, Cardinal de Châtillon, Danville, Thoré, Moret, and several other gentlemen suspected of meddling in the Reformation, who were standing all together between two windows at the lower end of the hall.

"The Huguenots are on the move," said Cypierre. "We know that Théodore de Bèze is at Nérac to persuade the Queen of Navarre to declare herself on their side by publicly renouncing the Catholic faith," he added, with a glance at the Bailli d'Orléans, who was chancellor to the Queen of Navarre, and a keen observer of the Court.

"She will do it," said the Bailli d'Orléans drily.

This personage, the Jacques Cœur of his day, and one of the richest middle-class men of his time, was named Groslot, and was envoy from Jeanne d'Albret to the French Court.

"Do you think so?" said the Chancellor of France to the Chancellor of Navarre, quite understanding the full import of Groslot's remark.

"Don't you know," said the rich provincial, "that the Queen of Navarre has nothing of the woman in her but her sex? She is devoted to none but manly things; her mind is strong in important matters and her heart undaunted by the greatest adversities."

"Monsieur le Cardinal," said the Chancellor Olivier to Monsieur de Tournon, who had heard Groslot, "what do you think of such boldness?"

"The Queen of Navarre does well to choose for her chancellor a man from whom the House of Lorraine will need to borrow, and who offers the King his house when there is a talk of moving to Orleans," replied the cardinal.

The chancellor and the cardinal looked at each other, not daring to speak their thoughts; but Robertet expressed them, for he thought it necessary to make a greater display of devotion to the Guises than these great men, since he was so far beneath them.

"It is most unfortunate that the House of Navarre, instead of abjuring the faith of their fathers, do not abjure the spirit of revenge and rebellion inspired by the Connétable de Bourbon. We shall see a repetition of the wars of the Armagnacs and the Bourguignons."

"No," said Groslot, "for there is something of Louis XI. in the Cardinal de Lorraine."

"And in Queen Catherine too," observed Robertet.

At this moment Madame Dayelle, Mary Stewart's favorite waiting-woman, crossed the room and went to the Queen's chamber. The appearance of the waiting-woman made a little stir.

"We shall be admitted directly," said Madame Fieschi.

"I do not think so," said the Duchesse de Guise. "Their majesties will come out, for a State Council is to be held."

La Dayelle slipped into the royal chamber after scratching at the door, a deferential custom introduced by Catherine de' Medici and adopted by the French Court.

"What is the weather like, my dear Dayelle?" asked Queen Mary, putting her fair, fresh face out between the curtains.

"Oh! madame——"

"What is the matter, Dayelle? You might have the bow-men at your heels——"

"Oh! madame—is the King still sleeping?"

"Yes."

"We are to leave the castle, and Monsieur le Cardinal desired me to tell you so, that you might suggest it to the King."

"Do you know why, my good Dayelle?"

"The Reformers mean to carry you off."

"Oh, this new religion leaves me no peace! I dreamed last night that I was in prison—I who shall wear the united crowns of the three finest kingdoms in the world."

"Indeed! but, madame, it was only a dream."

"Carried off! That would be rather amusing. But for the sake of religion, and by heretics—horrible!"

The Queen sprang out of bed and seated herself in front of the fireplace in a large chair covered with red velvet, after wrapping herself in a loose black velvet gown handed to her by Dayelle, which she tied about the waist with a silken cord. Dayelle lighted the fire, for the early May mornings are cool on the banks of the Loire.

"Then did my uncles get this news in the course of the night?" the Queen inquired of Dayelle, with whom she was on familiar terms.

"Early this morning Messieurs de Guise were walking on the terrace to avoid being overheard, and received there some messengers arriving in hot haste from various parts of the kingdom where the Reformers are busy. Her highness the

Queen-mother went out with her Italians hoping to be consulted, but she was not invited to join the little council."

"She must be furious."

"All the more so because she had a little wrath left over from yesterday," replied Dayelle. "They say she was far from rejoiced by the sight of your majesty in your dress of woven gold and your pretty veil of tan-colored crepe——"

"Leave us now, my good Dayelle ; the King is waking. Do not let any one in, not even those who have the *entrée*. There are matters of State in hand and my uncles will not disturb us."

"Why, my dear Mary, are you out of bed already ?  Is it daylight ?" said the young King, rousing himself.

"My dear love, while we were quietly sleeping, malignants have been wide awake, and compel us to leave this pleasant home."

"What do you mean by malignants, my sweetheart ?  Did we not have the most delightful festival last evening, but for the Latin which those gentlemen insisted on dropping into our good French ?"

"Oh !" said Mary, "that is in the best taste, and Rabelais brought Latin into fashion."

"Ah ! you are so learned, and I am only sorry not to be able to do you honor in verse.  If I were not King, I would take back Master Amyot from my brother, who is being made so wise——"

"You have nothing to envy your brother for ; he writes verses and shows them to me, begging me to show him mine. Be content, you are by far the best of the four, and will be as good a king as you are a charming lover.  Indeed, that perhaps is the reason your mother loves you so little.  But be easy ; I, dear heart, will love you for all the world."

"It is no great merit in me to love such a perfect Queen," said the young King.  "I do not know what hindered me from embracing you before the whole Court last night, when you danced the *branle** with tapers.  I could see how all the women looked serving-wenches by you, my sweet Marie ! ''

" For plain prose your language is charming, my dear heart: it is love that speaks, to be sure.  And you know, my dear, that if you were but a poor little page, I should still love you just as much as I now do, and yet it is a good thing to be able to say, ' My sweetheart is a king ! ' ''

" Such a pretty arm !  Why must we get dressed ?  I like to push my fingers through your soft hair and tangle your golden curls.  Listen, pretty one ; I will not allow you to let your women kiss your fair neck and your pretty shoulders any more !  I am jealous of the Scotch mists for having touched them.''

" Will you not come to see my beloved country ?  The Scotch would love you, and there would be no rebellions, as there are here.''

" Who rebels in our kingdom ? '' said François de Valois, wrapping himself in his gown, and drawing his wife on to his knee.

" Yes, this is very pretty play,'' said she, withdrawing her cheek from his kiss.  " But you have to reign, if you please, my liege.''

" Who talks of reigning ?  This morning I want to——''

" Need you say ' I want to,' when you can do what you will ?  That is the language of neither king nor lover.  However, that is not the matter on hand—we have important business to attend to.''

" Oh ! '' said the King, " it is a long time since we have had any business to do.  Is it amusing ? ''

" Not at all,'' said Mary ; " we must make a move.''

" I will wager, my pretty one, that you have seen one of your uncles, who manage matters so well that, at seventeen, I am a king only in name.  I really know not why, since the first Council, I have ever sat at one ; they could do everything

* A swaying, jerky dance.

quite as well by setting a crown on my chair; I see everything through their eyes, and settle matters blindfold."

"Indeed, monsieur," said the Queen, standing up and assuming an air of annoyance, "you had agreed never again to give me the smallest trouble on that score, but to leave my uncles to exercise your royal power for the happiness of your people. A nice people they are! Why, if you tried to govern them unaided, they would swallow you whole like a strawberry. They need warriors to rule them—a stern master gloved with iron; while you—you are a charmer whom I love just as you are, and should not love if you were different—do you hear, my lord?" she added, bending down to kiss the boy, who seemed inclined to rebel against this speech, but who was mollified by the caress.

"Oh, if only they were not your uncles!" cried Francis. "I cannot endure that cardinal; and when he puts on his insinuating air and his submissive ways, and says to me with a bow, 'Sire, the honor of the Crown and the faith of your fathers are at stake, your majesty will never allow——' and this and that—I am certain he toils for nothing but his cursed House of Lorraine."

"How well you mimic him!" cried the Queen. "But why do you not make these Guises inform you of what is going forward, so as to govern by-and-by on your own account when you are of full age? I am your wife, and your honor is mine. We will reign, sweetheart—never fear! But all will not be roses for us till we are free to please ourselves. There is nothing so hard for a king as to govern!

"Am I the Queen now, I ask you? Do you think that your mother ever fails to repay me in evil for what good my uncles may do for the glory of your throne? And mark the difference! My uncles are great princes, descendants of Charlemagne, full of good-will, and ready to die for you; while this daughter of a leech, or a merchant, Queen of France by a mere chance, is as shrewish as a citizen's wife who is not mistress in her house. The Italian woman is provoked that she cannot set every one by the ears, and she is always coming to me with her pale, solemn face, and then with her pinched lips she begins: 'Daughter, you are the Queen; I am only the second lady in the kingdom '—she is furious, you see, dear heart—' but if I were in your place I would not wear crimson velvet while the Court is in mourning, and I would appear in pnblic with my hair plainly dressed and with no jewels, for what is unseemly in any lady is even more so in a queen. Nor would I dance myself; I would only see others dance ! ' That is the kind of thing she says to me."

"Oh, dear heaven ! " cried the King, "I can hear her! Mercy, if she only knew——"

"Why, you still quake before her. She wearies you—say so? We will send her away. By my faith, that she should deceive you might be endured, but to be so tedious——"

"In heaven's name, be silent, Marie," said the King, at once alarmed and delighted. "I would not have you lose her favor."

"Never fear that she will quarrel with me, with the three finest crowns in the world on my head, my little King," said Mary Stewart. "Even though she hates me for a thousand reasons, she flatters me, to win me from my uncles."

"Hates you ? "

"Yes, my angel ! And if I had not a thousand such proofs as women can give each other, and such as women only can understand, her persistent opposition to our happy lovemaking would be enough. Now, is it my fault if your father could never endure Mademoiselle de' Medici? In short, she likes me so little that you had to be quite in a rage to prevent our having separate sets of rooms here and at Saint-Germain. She declared that it was customary for the Kings and Queens of France. Customary ! It was your father's custom; that is quite intelligible. As to your grandfather, Francis, that good man established the practice for the convenience of his love affairs. So be on your guard; if we are obliged to leave this place, do not let the Grand Master divide us."

"If we leave? But I do not intend to leave this pretty castle, whence we see the Loire and all the country round—a town at our feet, the brightest sky in the world above us, and these lovely gardens. Or if I go, it will be to travel with you in Italy and see Raphael's pictures and Saint-Peter's at Rome."

"And the orange trees. Ah, sweet little King, if you could know how your Mary longs to walk under orange trees in flower and fruit! Alas! I may never see one! Oh! to hear an Italian song under those fragrant groves, on the shore of a blue sea, under a cloudless sky, and to clasp each other thus!——"

"Let us be off," said the King.

"Be off!" cried the Grand Master, coming in. "Yes, Sire, you must be off from Blois. Pardon my boldness, but circumstances overrule etiquette, and I have come to beg you to call a Council."

Mary and Francis had started apart on being thus taken by surprise, and they both wore the same expression of offended sovereign majesty.

"You are too much the Grand Master, Monsieur de Guise," said the young King, suppressing his wrath.

"Devil take lovers!" muttered the cardinal in Catherine's ear.

"My son," replied the Queen-mother, appearing behind the cardinal, "the safety of your person is at stake as well as of your kingdom."

"Heresy was awake while you slept, Sire," said the cardinal.

"Withdraw into the hall," said the little King; "we will hold a Council."

"Madame," said the Duke to the Queen, "your furrier's son has come with some furs which are seasonable for your journey, as we shall probably ride by the Loire. But he also

wishes to speak with madame," he added, turning to the
Queen-mother.   "While the King is dressing, would you
and her majesty dismiss him forthwith, so that this trifle may
no further trouble us?"

"With pleasure," replied Catherine; adding to herself,
"If he thinks to be rid of me by such tricks, he little knows
me."

The cardinal and the Duke retired, leaving the two Queens
with the King.   As he went through the guardroom to go to
the council chamber, the Grand Master desired the usher to
bring up the Queen's furrier.

When Christophe saw this official coming toward him from
one end of the room to the other, he took him, from his
dress, to be some one of importance, and his heart sank
within him; but this sensation, natural enough at the approach
of a critical moment, became sheer terror when the usher,
whose advance had the effect of directing the eyes of the
whole splendid assembly to Christophe with his bundles and
his abject looks, said to him—

"Their highnesses the Cardinal de Lorraine and the Grand
Master desire to speak to you in the council-room."

"Has any one betrayed me?" was the thought of this
hapless envoy of the Reformers.

Christophe followed the usher, his eyes bent on the ground,
and never looked up till he found himself in the spacious
council-room—as large almost as the guardroom.   The two
Guises were alone, standing in front of the splendid chimney-
place that backed against that in the guardroom, where the
maids of honor were grouped.

"You have come from Paris?   Which road did you take?"
the cardinal said to Christophe.

"I came by water, monseigneur," replied the lad.

"And how did you get into Blois?" said the Grand
Master.

"By the river-port, monseigneur."

"And no one interfered with you?" said the Duke, who was examining the young man closely.

"No, monseigneur. I told the first soldier, who made as though he would stop me, that I had come on duty to wait on the two Queens, and that my father is furrier to their majesties."

"What is doing in Paris?" asked the cardinal.

"They are still trying to discover the murderer who killed President Minard."

"Are you not the son of my surgeon's greatest friend?" asked the Duc de Guise, deceived by Christophe's expression of candor, now that his fears were allayed.

"Yes, monseigneur."

The Grand Master went out, hastily lifted the curtain which screened the double doors of the council chamber, and showed his face to the crowd, among whom he looked for the King's surgeon-in-chief. Ambroise Paré, standing in a corner, was aware of a glance shot at him by the Duke and went to him. Ambroise, already inclined to the Reformed religion, ended by adopting it; but the friendship of the Guises and of the French kings preserved him from the various disasters that befell the heretics. The Duke, who felt that he owed his life to Ambroise Paré, had appointed him surgeon-in-chief to the King within a few days past.

"What is it, monseigneur," said the leech. "Is the King ill? I should not be surprised."

"Why?"

"The Queen is too fascinating," said the surgeon.

"Ah!" replied the Duke, surprised. "However, that is not the case," he went on after a pause. "Ambroise, I want you to see a friend of yours," and he led him on to the threshold of the council-chamber door and pointed to Christophe.

"Ah, to be sure," cried the surgeon, holding out his hand to the youth. "How is your father, my boy?"

"Very well, Master Ambroise," Christophe replied.

"And what are you doing at Court ?" Paré went on. "It is not your business to carry parcels ; your father wants to make a lawyer of you. Do you want the protection of these two great Princes to become a pleader ?"

"Why, yes, indeed," replied Christophe, "but for my father's sake ; and if you can intercede for us, add your entreaties," he went on, with a piteous air, "to obtain an order from Monseigneur the Grand Master for the payment of the moneys due to my father, for he does not know which way to turn——"

The cardinal and his brother looked at each other, and seemed to be satisfied.

"Leave us now," said the Grand Master to Ambroise with a nod. "And you, my friend," he added to Christophe, "settle your business quickly, and get back to Paris. My secretary will give you a pass, for, by heaven, the roads will not be pleasant to travel on !"

Neither of the brothers had the slightest suspicion of the important interests that lay in Christophe's hands, being now quite assured that he was certainly the son of Lecamus, a good Catholic, purveyor to the Court, and that he had come solely to get his money.

"Take him around to be near the door of the Queen's chamber ; she will ask for him no doubt," said the cardinal to the surgeon.

While the furrier's son was being thus cross-questioned in the council-room, the King had left his mother and the Queen together, having gone into his dressing-room, which was beyond a room adjoining the bedroom.

Catherine, standing in the recess of the deep window, was looking out on the garden, lost in melancholy thought. She foresaw that one of the greatest commanders of the age, in the course of that morning, in the very next hour, would take the place of her son the King, under the terrible title of lieutenant-general of the kingdom.   In the face of such peril she was alone, without a plan, without defense.   Indeed, as she stood there in her mourning, which she had not ceased to wear since the death of Henri II., she might have been compared to a phantom, so still were her pale features as she stood absorbed in thought.   Her black eye seemed to wander in the indecision for which great politicians are so often blamed, which in them is the result of the breadth of sight which enables them to see every difficulty, and to balance one against the other, adding up the sum-total of risk before taking a part.   There was a ringing in her ears, a turmoil in her blood; but she stood there, nevertheless, calm and dignified, while gauging the depths of the political abyss beyond the real gulf that lay at her feet.

Since the day when the Vidame de Chartres had been arrested, this was the second of those terrible days of which there were henceforth to be so many in the course of her royal career; but she never again made a mistake in the school of power.   Though the sceptre seemed always to fly from her grasp, she meant to seize it, and, in fact, did seize it, by that sheer force of will which had never given way to the scorn of her father-in-law, Francis I., and his Court—by whom, though Dauphiness, she had been so little thought of—nor to the constant denials of Henri II., nor to the unresting antagonism of her rival, Diane de Poitiers.   A man would not have understood this Queen in check; but Mary Stewart, so fair, so crafty, so clever, so girlish, and yet so omniscient, watched her out of the corner of her eye while affecting to warble an Italian air with an indifferent countenance.   Without understanding the tempest of ambition which brought a cold moisture to the Florentine Queen's brow, the pretty Scotch girl, with her saucy face, knew that the high position of her uncle the Duc de Guise was filling Catherine with suppressed fury.   Now, nothing amused her so much as watching her mother-in-law, whom she regarded as an intriguing adventuress, who, having been humbled, was always prepared for revenge. The face of the elder was grave and gloomy, a little cadaverous, by reason of the livid complexion of the Italians, which by daylight looks like yellow ivory, though by candlelight it is dazzling; while the younger face was bright and fresh. At sixteen Mary Stewart had that creamy fairness for which she was so famous. Her bright rosy face, with clearly cut features, sparkled with childish mischief, very frankly expressed in the regular arch of her brows, the brightness of her eyes, and the pert smile of her pretty mouth. She had then in perfection that kittenish grace which nothing—neither captivity nor the sight of the horrible block—ever completely quelled.

Thus these two Queens, one in the morning, the other in the summer of life, were at this time a perfect contrast. Catherine was an imposing sovereign, an impenetrable widow, with no passion but the love of power. Mary was a feather-brained and light-hearted wife, who thought of her crowns as playthings. One looked forward to impending misfortunes; she even had a glimpse of the murder of the Guises, guessing that this would be the only way to strike down men who were capable of raising themselves above the throne and the Parlement; she saw rivers of blood in a long struggle—the other little dreamed that she would herself be murdered by form of law.

A curious reflection brought a little calm to the Italian Queen.

"According to the soothsayer and to Ruggieri's forecast, this reign is soon to end. My difficulties will not last," thought she.

And thus, strange to say, an occult science, now forgotten —judicial astrology—was a support to Catherine at this juncture, as it was throughout her life; for the belief grew constantly from seeing the predictions of those who practiced it realized with the greatest exactitude.

"You are very serious, madame," said Mary Stewart, taking from Dayelle's hands her little cap, pinched down over the parting of her hair with two frilled wings of handsome lace beyond the puffs of wavy yellow hair that shadowed her temples.

The painters of the time have so amply perpetuated this cap, that it now belongs essentially to the Queen of Scots, though it was Catherine who invented it when she went into mourning for Henri II.; but she could not wear it with such good effect as her daughter-in-law, to whom it was infinitely more becoming. And this was not the smallest of the grievances harbored by the Queen-mother against the young Queen.

"Does your majesty mean that for a reproof?" said Catherine, turning to her daughter-in-law.

"I owe respect, and should not dare——" said the Scotch-woman meaningly, with a glance at Dayelle.

Between the two Queens the favorite waiting-woman stood like the figure-head on a fire-dog; an approving smile might cost her her life.

"How can I be as gay as you after losing the late King, and when I see my son's kingdom on the eve of a conflagration?"

"Politics do not much concern women," replied Mary Stewart. "Beside, my uncles are there."

These two sentences, in the circumstances, were two poisoned arrows.

"Let us see our furs then," the Italian replied, "and so turn our minds to our own business, while your uncles settle that of the kingdom."

"Oh, but we shall attend the Council, madame; we are of more use there than you suppose."

"We?" said Catherine, with feigned astonishment. "I, for my part, do not know Latin!"

"You fancy me so learned?" said Mary Stewart, with a

9

laugh. "Nay, madame, I swear to you that at this moment I am studying in the hope of rivaling the Medici and of knowing some day how to heal the wounds of the country."

This sharp shaft pierced Catherine to the heart, for it was an allusion to the origin of the Medici, who were descended, as some said, from a leech, or, as others had it, from a rich drug merchant. She had no reply ready. Dayelle colored when her mistress looked to her for the applause which everybody, and even queens, expect from their inferiors when they have no better audience.

"Your witticisms, madame, cannot, unfortunately, heal either the maladies of the State or those of the church," said Catherine, with calm and dignified coldness. "My forefathers' knowledge of such matters won them thrones; while you, if you persist in jesting in the midst of danger, are like enough to lose yours."

At this juncture Dayelle opened the door to Christophe, shown in by the chief physician himself after scratching at the door.

The young Reformer wanted to study Catherine's countenance, and affected a shyness, which was natural enough on finding himself in this place; but he was surprised by Mary's eagerness. She rushed at the boxes to look at her surcoat.

"Madame," said Christophe, addressing Catherine.

He turned his back on the other Queen and Dayelle, promptly taking advantage of the attention the two were devoting to the furs to strike a bold blow.

"What do you want of me?" asked Catherine, looking keenly at him.

Christophe had placed the agreement proposed by the Prince de Condé, with the Reformers' plan of action and an account of their forces, over his heart, between his cloth jerkin and his shirt, wrapped inside the furrier's bill of what Queen Catherine owed him.

"Madame," said he, "my father is in dreadful want of

money, and if you would condescend to look through the accounts," he added, unfolding the paper and slipping the agreement under it, " you will see that your majesty owes him six thousand crowns. May your goodness have pity on us ! See, madame."

And he held out the document.

" Read it. This dates so far back as the accession of the late King."

Catherine was bewildered by the preamble to the address, but she did not lose her presence of mind ; she hastily rolled up the paper, admiring the young man's readiness and daring. She saw from these masterly tactics that he would understand her, so she tapped him on the head with the roll of paper, and said : " You are very ill advised, my young friend, in handing the bill in before the furs. Learn some knowledge of women ! You must never ask for your money until we are perfectly satisfied."

" Is that the tradition ? " said the young Queen to her mother-in-law, who made no reply.

" Ah, mesdames, excuse my father," said Christophe. " If he had not wanted the money, you would not have your furs. The country is up in arms, and there is so much danger on the roads that only our great need induced me to come. No one else would risk his life."

" This lad is quite fresh," said Mary Stewart, smiling.

It is not superfluous to the better understanding of this important little scene to remark that a surcoat was, as the name implies, a sort of close-fitting jacket or spencer which ladies wore over their dress, and which wrapped them closely, shaped down to the hips. This garment protected the back, chest, and throat from the cold. Surcoats were lined with fur which turned up over the stuff, forming a more or less wide border. Mary Stewart while trying on her surcoat was looking at herself in a large Venetian mirror, to see the effect of it at the back ; thus she had left her mother-in-law liberty to glance at the packet of papers, of which the volume might otherwise have excited her suspicions.

"Does a man ever speak to a lady of the dangers he has incurred when he is safe and sound in her presence?" said she, turning around on Christophe.

"Oh, madame, I have your account too," said he, looking at her with well-acted simplicity.

The young Queen looked at him from head to foot without taking the paper; but she observed, without drawing any conclusions at the moment, that he had taken Queen Catherine's bill out of his breast, and drew hers out of his pocket. Nor did she see in the lad's eyes the admiration that her beauty won her from all the world; but she was thinking so much of her surcoat that she did not at once wonder what could be the cause of his indifference.

"Take it, Dayelle," said she to the waiting-woman. "You can give the account to Monsieur de Versailles (Loménie), and desire him, for me, to pay it."

"Indeed, madame, but if you do not give me an order signed by the King, or by his highness the Grand Master, who is at hand, your gracious promise will have no effect."

"You are rather hastier than beseems a subject, my friend," said Mary Stewart. "So you do not believe in royal promises?"

The King came in dressed in his long silk hose and trunks, the breeches of the time, but wore neither doublet nor cloak; he had only a rich wrapper of velvet lined throughout with fur; for wrapper, a word of modern use, can alone describe the *négligé* of his apparel.

"Who is the rascal that doubts your word?" said the young King, who, though at a distance, had heard his wife's speech.

The door of the King's closet was hidden by the bed. This closet was subsequently called the old closet (*le Cabinet vieux*) to distinguish it from the splendid painted closet constructed for Henri III. on the other side of the room adjoining the hall of the States-General.   Henri III. hid the assassins in the old closet, and sent to desire the Duc de Guise to attend him there ; while he, during the murder, remained concealed in the new closet, whence he emerged only to see his overweening subject die—a subject for whom there could be no prison, no tribunal, no judges, no laws in the kingdom. But for these dreadful events, the historian could now hardly identify the former uses of these rooms and halls filled with soldiers.   A sergeant writes to his sweetheart on the spot where Catherine gravely considered her struggle with parties.

"Come, my boy," said the Queen-mother ; "I will see that you are paid.   Trade must flourish, and money is its main sinew."

"Ay, go, my good youth," said the young Queen, laughing ; "my august mother understands matters of trade better than I do."

Catherine was about to leave the room without replying to this innuendo ; but it struck her that her indifference might arouse suspicions, and she retorted on her daughter-in-law—

"And you, my dear, trade in love."

Then she went downstairs.

"Put all those things away, Dayelle.   And come to the council-room, Sire," said the young Queen to the King, enchanted at having to decide the important question of the lieutenancy of the kingdom in her mother-in-law's absence.

Mary Stewart took the King's arm.   Dayelle went out first, speaking a word to the pages, and one of them—young Téligny, fated to perish miserably on the night of Saint-Bartholomew—shouted out—

"The King !"

On hearing the cry, the two musketeers carried arms, and the two pages led the way toward the council chamber between the line of courtiers on one side and the line formed by the maids of honor to the two Queens on the other.   All the members of the Council then gathered round the door of the hall, which was at no great distance from the staircase. The Grand Master, the cardinal, and the chancellor advanced to meet the two young sovereigns, who smiled to some of the maids or answered the inquiries of some of the Court favorites more intimate than the rest.

The Queen, however, evidently impatient, dragged Francis II. on toward the vast council-room.  As soon as the heavy thud of the arquebusses dropping on the floor again announced that the royal pair had gone in, the pages put on their caps, and the conversations in the various groups took their course again on the immense gravity of the business about to be discussed.

"Chiverni was sent to fetch the connétable, and he has not come," said one.

"There is no prince of the blood present," remarked another.

The chancellor and Monsieur de Tournon looked anxious.

"The Grand Master has sent word to the keeper of the seals to be sure not to fail to attend this Council; a good many letters patent will be issued, no doubt."

"How is it that the Queen-mother remains below, in her own rooms, at such a juncture?"

"They are going to make things hot for us," said Groslot to Cardinal de Châtillon.

In short, every one had something to say.  Some were pacing the room from end to end, others were flitting round the maids of honor, as though it could be possible to catch a few words through a wall three feet thick or two doors and the heavy curtains that screened them.

The King, seated at one end of the long table covered with blue velvet, which stood in the middle of the room, his young Queen in an armchair at his side, was waiting for his mother. Robertet was mending his pens.  The two cardinals, the Grand Master, the chancellor, the keeper of the seals—in short, the whole assembly—looked at the little King, wondering why he did not give the word for them all to be seated.

"Are we to sit in council in the absence of the Queen-mother?" the chancellor asked, addressing the young King.

The two Guises ascribed Catherine's absence to some cunning trick of their niece's. Then spurred by a significant look, the much-daring cardinal said to the King—

"Is it your majesty's good-will that we should proceed without madame your mother?"

Francis, not daring to have an opinion of his own, replied—

"Gentlemen, be seated."

The cardinal briefly pointed out the dangers of the situation. This great politician, who showed astounding skill in this business, broached the question of the lieutenancy amid utter silence. The young King was, no doubt, conscious of an awkwardness, and guessed that his mother had a real sense of the rights of the Crown and a knowledge of the danger that threatened his power, for he replied to a direct question on the cardinal's part—

"We will wait for my mother."

Enlightened by this inexplicable delay on Queen Catherine's part, Mary Stewart suddenly recalled in a single flash of thought three incidents which were clear in her memory. In the first place, the bulk of the packet presented to her mother-in-law, which she had seen, though so inattentive at the moment (for a woman who seems to see nothing is still a lynx), then the place where Christophe had carried them to separate them from hers.

"Why?" she said to herself. And then she remembered the boy's cold look, which she at once ascribed to the Reformers' hatred of the Guises' niece. A voice within her cried, "Is he not an envoy from the Huguenots?"

Acting, as all hasty persons do, on the first impulse, she exclaimed—

"I myself will go and fetch my mother."

She rushed away and down the stairs, to the great amazement of the gentlemen and ladies of the Court.  She went down to her mother-in-law's rooms, crossed the guardroom, opened the door of the bedroom as stealthily as a thief, crept noiselessly over the carpet as silently as a shadow, and could see her nowhere.  Then she thought she could surprise her in the splendid private room between the bedroom and the oratory.  The arrangement of this oratory is perfectly recognizable to this day; the fashion of the time then allowed it to serve all the purposes in private life which are now served by a boudoir.

By a piece of good fortune, quite unaccountable when we see in how squalid a state the Crown has left this castle, the beautiful paneling of Catherine's closet exists to this day; in the fine carving the curious may still discern traces of Italian magnificence, and also discover the hiding-places the Queen-mother had contrived there.

A somewhat exact description of these curiosities is indeed indispensable to a comprehension of the scene that took place there.  The woodwork at that time consisted of about a hundred and eighty small oblong panels, of which a hundred or so still remain, each carved with a different design, obviously suggested by the most elegant Italian arabesques.  The wood is holm-oak ; the red ground which is found under the coat of limewash, applied at the time of the cholera—a quite useless precaution—shows plainly that these panels were gilt ; and in spots where the whitewash has rubbed off we see that some portions of the design were in color—blue, red, or green—against a gold background.  The number of these panels shows an evident intention to cheat investigation ; but if there could be a doubt, the keeper of the castle, while holding up Catherine's memory to the execration of all living men, shows to visitors, at the bottom of the paneling, and on a level with the floor, a somewhat heavy skirting which can be raised, and under which there are a number of ingenious springs.  By pressing a knob thus concealed, the Queen could open certain of these panels, known to her alone, behind which lay a hiding-place of the same oblong shape as the panels, but of varying depth. To this day a practiced hand would find it difficult to detect which of these panels would open on its invisible hinges; and when the eye was diverted by the skillfully combined colors and gilding that covered the cracks, it is easy to imagine that it was impossible to discover one or two panels among nearly two hundred.

At the moment when Mary Stewart laid her hand on the somewhat elaborate latch of the door to the closet, the Italian Queen, having convinced herself already of the importance of the Prince de Condé's schemes, had just pressed the spring hidden by the skirting, one of the panels had fallen open, and Catherine had turned to the table to take up the papers and hide them, to turn her attention to the safeguard of the devoted messenger who had brought them to her. When she heard the door open, she at once guessed that no one but Queen Mary would venture to come in unannounced.

"You are lost," she said to Christophe, seeing that she could neither hide the papers nor close the panel promptly enough to preserve the secret of her hiding-place.

Christophe's only reply was a sublime look.

"Poor fellow!" said Catherine, before turning to her daughter-in-law. "Treason, madame!" she exclaimed. "I have them fast. Send for the cardinal and the Duke. And be sure," she added, pointing to Christophe, "that this fellow does not escape!"

Thus, in an instant, this masterful woman saw that it would be necessary to give up the hapless young man; she could not hide him, it was impossible to help him to escape; and, beside, though a week ago he might have been saved, now the Guises had, since that morning, been aware of the conspiracy, and they, too, must have the lists which she held in her hand, and were drawing all the Reformers into a trap. And so, pleased at finding her adversaries in the mind she had hoped for, now that the plot had become known, policy required her to assume the merit of discovering it.

These dreadful considerations flashed through her mind in the brief moment while the young Queen was opening the door.  Mary Stewart stood silent for an instant.  Her expression lost its brightness and assumed that keenness which suspicion always gives the eye, and which in her was terrible by the sudden contrast.  She looked from Christophe to the Queen-mother, and from the Queen-mother to Christophe, with a glance of malignant doubt.  Then she snatched up a bell, which brought in one of Catherine's maids of honor.

"Mademoiselle de Rouet, send in the captain of the Guard," said Mary Stewart, in breach of every law of etiquette, necessarily set aside in such circumstances.

While the young Queen gave her order, Catherine stood looking at Christophe as much as to say, " Courage ! "  The young Reformer understood, and replied by an expression which conveyed, " Sacrifice me, as they have sacrificed me ! "

" Put your trust in me," Catherine answered by a gesture.

Then when her daughter-in-law turned upon her, she was deeply engaged in examining the papers.

" You are of the Reformed religion ? " said Mary Stewart to Christophe.

" Yes, madame."

" Then I was not mistaken," she muttered to herself, as she read in the young man's eyes the same expression in which coldness and aversion lurked behind a look of humility.

Pardaillan appeared at once, sent down by the two Princes of Lorraine and the King.  The captain sent for by Mary Stewart followed this young man—a most devoted adherent of the Guises.

" Go from me to the King, beg him, with the cardinal and the Grand Master, to come here at once, and tell them I would not take such a liberty but that something of serious importance has occurred. Go, Pardaillan. And you, Lewiston, keep guard over this Reformed traitor," she added to the Scotchman in their native tongue, pointing to the wretched Christophe.

The two Queens did not speak till the King came. It was a terrible pause. Mary Stewart had shown her mother-in-law the whole extent of the part her uncles made her play; her unsleeping and habitual distrust stood revealed; and her youthful conscience felt how disgraceful such a part must be to a great Queen. Catherine, on her side, had betrayed herself in her alarm, and feared that she had been understood; she was trembling for the future. The two women, one ashamed and furious, the other vicious but calm, withdrew into the window-bay, one leaning on the right side, the other on the left; but their looks were so expressive that each turned away, and with a common instinct looked out of the window at the sky. These two women, clever as they were, at that moment had no more wit than the commonest. Perhaps it is always so when circumstances overpower men. There is always a moment when even genius is conscious of its smallness in the presence of a great catastrophe.

As for Christophe, he felt like a man falling into an abyss. Lewiston, the Scotch captain, listened in the silence, looking at the furrier's son and the two Queens with a soldier's curiosity. The King's entrance put an end to this painful situation.

The cardinal went straight up to Queen Catherine.

"I have in my hand all the threads of the plot hatched by the heretics; they sent this boy to me carrying this treaty and these documents," said Catherine in an undertone.

While Catherine was explaining matters to the cardinal, Queen Mary was speaking a few words in the Grand Master's ear.

"What is this all about?" asked the young King, standing alone amid this conflict of violent interests.

"The proofs of what I was telling your majesty are already to hand," said the cardinal, seizing the papers.

The Duc de Guise, unmindful of the fact that he was interrupting him, drew his brother aside and said in a whisper—

"This then makes me lieutenant-general without any opposition."

A keen glance was the cardinal's only reply, by which he conveyed to his brother that he had already appreciated the advantages to be derived from Catherine's false position.

"Who sent you?" asked the Duke of Christophe.

"Chaudieu the preacher," he replied.

"Young man, you lie," said the Duke roughly. "It was the Prince de Condé."

"The Prince de Condé, monseigneur," replied Christophe, with a look of surprise. "I never saw him. I belong to the Palais. I am working under Monsieur de Thou. I am his clerk, and he does not know that I have joined the religion. I only submitted to the preacher's entreaties."

"That will do," said the cardinal. "Call Monsieur de Robertet," he added to Lewiston, "for this young villain is craftier than old politicians. He has taken us in, my brother and me, when we should have given him the host without confession."

"You are no child, by heaven!" cried the Duke, "and you shall be treated as a man."

"They hoped to win over your august mother," said the cardinal, turning to the King, and trying to lead him aside to bring him to his way of thinking.

"Alas!" replied Catherine, speaking to her son with a reproachful air, and stopping him just as the cardinal was taking him into the oratory to subjugate him with dangerous eloquence, "you here see the effect of the position I am placed in. I am supposed to rebel against my lack of influence in public affairs—I, the mother of four princes of the House of Valois."

The young King prepared to listen.   Mary Stewart, seeing his brow knit, led him off into the window recess, where she cajoled him with gentle speeches in a low voice; much the same, no doubt, as those she had lavished on him when he arose.

The two brothers meanwhile read the papers handed over to them by the Queen-mother.   Finding in them much information of which their spies and Monsieur de Braguelonne, the governor of the châtelet, knew nothing, they were inclined to believe in Catherine's good faith.   Robertet came in and had private instructions with regard to Christophe. The hapless tool of the leaders of the Reformation was led away by four men of the Scotch Guard, who took him downstairs and handed him over to Monsieur de Montrésor, the provost of the castle.   This terrible personage himself escorted Christophe with five or six sergeants to the prison situated in the vaulted cellars of the now ruined tower, which the verger of the Castle of Blois shows the visitor, and says that these were the *oubliettes* (dungeons).

After such an event the Council could only be an empty form: the King, the young Queen, the Grand Master, and the Cardinal de Lorraine went back to the council-room, taking with them Catherine, quite conquered, who only spoke to approve of the measures demanded by the Guises.   In spite of some slight opposition on the part of the Chancellor Olivier, the only person to utter a word suggesting the independence needful to the exercise of his functions, the Duc de Guise was appointed lieutenant-general of the kingdom. Robertet carried the motions with a promptitude arguing such devotion as might be well called complicity.

The King, with his mother on his arm, once more crossed the guardroom, and announced to the Court that he proposed to move to Amboise on the following day.   This royal residence had been unused since Charles VIII. had very involuntarily killed himself there by striking his head against the pediment of a door that was being carved for him, believing that he could pass under the scaffolding without bending his head.   Catherine, to mask the schemes of the Guises, had announced her intention of finishing the Castle of Amboise on behalf of the Crown at the same time as her own Castle of Chenonceaux.   But no one was deceived by this pretense, and the Court anticipated strange events.

After spending about two hours in accustoming himself to the darkness of his dungeon, Christophe found that it was lined with boards, clumsy indeed, but thick enough to make the square box healthy and habitable.   The door, like that into a pig-sty, had compelled him to bend double to get into it.   On one side of this trap a strong iron grating admitted a little air and light from the passage.   This arrangement, exactly like that of the crypts at Venice, showed very plainly that the architect of the Castle of Blois belonged to the Venetian school, which gave so many builders to Europe in the Middle Ages.   By sounding the wall above the woodwork, Christophe discovered that the two walls which divided this cell from two others, to the right and left, were built of brick; and as he knocked, to estimate the thickness of the wall, he was not a little surprised to hear some one knocking on the other side.

"Who are you?" asked his neighbor, speaking into the corridor.

"I am Christophe Lecamus."

"And I," said the other voice, "am Captain Chaudieu. I was caught this evening at Beaugency; but, happily, there is nothing against me."

"Everything is discovered," said Christophe; "so you are saved from the worst of it."

"We have three thousand men at this present time in the forests of Vendômois, all men determined enough to seize the Queen-mother and the King on their journey.   Happily, la

Renaudie was cleverer than I; he escaped. You had just set out when the Guisards caught us."

"But I know nothing of la Renaudie."

"Pooh! my brother told me everything," replied the captain.

On hearing this, Christophe went back to his bench and made no further reply to anything the so-called captain could say to him, for he had had enough experience of the law to know how necessary it was to be cautious in prison.

In the middle of the night he saw the pale gleam of a lantern in the passage, after hearing the unlocking of the ponderous bolts that closed the iron door of the cellar. The provost himself had come to fetch Christophe. This attention to a man who had been left in the dungeon without food struck Christophe as strange; but the upset at Court had, no doubt, led to his being forgotten. One of the provost's sergeants bound his hands with a cord, which he held till they had reached one of the low rooms in Louis XII.'s part of the castle, which evidently was the anteroom to the apartments of some person of importance. The sergeant and the provost bid him be seated on a bench, where the sergeant tied his feet as he had already tied his hands. At a sign from Monsieur de Montrésor, the sergeant then left them.

"Now listen to me, my young friend," said the provost to Christophe, and the lad observed that he was in full dress at that hour of the night, for his fingers fidgeted with the collar of his Order. This circumstance made the furrier's son thoughtful; he saw that there was more to come. At this moment, certainly, they could not be going either to try him or to hang him.

"My young friend, you may spare yourself much suffering by telling me here and now all you know of the communications between Queen Catherine and Monsieur de Condé. Not only will you not be hurt, but you will be taken into the service of monseigneur, the lieutenant-general of the kingdom, who likes intelligent people, and who was favorably impressed by your looks.   The Queen-mother is to be packed off to Florence, and Monsieur de Condé will no doubt stand his trial.   So, take my word for it, small men will do well to attach themselves to the great men in power.   Tell me everything, and it will be to your advantage."

"Alas, monsieur," replied Christophe, "I have nothing to say.   I have confessed all I know to Messieurs de Guise in the Queen's room.   Chaudieu persuaded me to place those papers in the hands of the Queen-mother, by making me believe that the peace of the country was involved."

"You never saw the Prince de Condé?"

"Never," said Christophe.

Thereupon Monsieur de Montrésor left Christophe and went into an adjoining room.

Christophe was not long left to himself.   The door by which he had entered soon opened for several men to pass in, who did not shut it, letting various far from pleasant sounds come in from the courtyard.   Blocks of wood and instruments were brought in, evidently intended to torture the Reformers' messenger.   Christophe's curiosity soon found matter for reflection in the preparations the new-comers were making under his very eyes.   Two coarse and poorly-clad varlets obeyed the orders of a powerful and thick-set man, who, on coming in, had a look at Christophe like that of a cannibal at his victim; he had scrutinized him from head to foot, taking stock of his sinews, of their strength and power of resistance, with the calculating eye of a connoisseur.   This man was the Blois executioner.   Backward and forward several times, his men brought in a mattress, wooden wedges, planks, and other objects, of which the use seemed neither obvious nor hopeful to the unhappy boy for whom the preparations were being made, and whose blood ran cold in his veins with apprehension, which though vague was appalling.   Two other men came in when Monsieur de Montrésor reappeared.

"What, is nothing ready yet?" said the chief provost, to whom the two new-comers bowed respectfully. "Do you know," he went on to the big man and his two satellites, "that Monsieur le Cardinal supposes you to be getting on with your work? Doctor," he added, turning to one of the new-comers, "there is your man," and he pointed to Christophe.

The doctor went up to the prisoner, untied his hands, and sounded his back and chest. Science quite seriously repeated the torturer's investigation. Meanwhile, a servant in the livery of the House of Guise brought in several chairs, a table, and all the materials for writing.

"Begin your report," said Monsieur de Montrésor to the second person who had come in, dressed in black, who was a clerk.

Then he came back to stand by Christophe, to whom he said very mildly—

"My boy, the chancellor, having learnt that you refuse to give satisfactory replies to my questions, has decided that you must be put to the torture—ordinary and extraordinary."

"Is he in good health, and can he bear it?" the clerk asked of the doctor.

"Yes," said the man of medicine, a physician attached to the House of Lorraine.

"Well, then, retire to the adjoining room; we will send for you if it is necessary to consult you."

The physician left the room.

His first panic past, Christophe collected all his courage. The hour of his martyrdom was come. He now looked on with cold curiosity at the arrangements made by the executioner and his varlets. After hastily making up a bed, they proceeded to prepare a machine called the boot, consisting of boards, between which each leg of the victim was placed, surrounded with pads. The machinery used by bookbinders to press the volumes between two boards, which they tighten with cords, will give a very exact idea of the way in which each

10

leg was encased. It is easy, then, to imagine the effect of a wedge driven home by a mallet between the two cases in which the legs were confined, and which, being tightly bound with rope, could not yield. The wedges were driven in at the knees and ankles, as if to split a log of wood. The choice of these two spots where there is least flesh, and where, in consequence, the wedge found room at the expense of the bones, made this form of torture horribly painful. In ordinary torture four wedges were driven in—two at the knees and two at the ankles; in extraordinary torture as many as eight were employed, if the physician pronounced that the victim's powers of endurance were not exhausted.

At this period the boots were also applied to the hands; but as time pressed, the cardinal, the lieutenant-general of the kingdom, and the chancellor spared Christophe this.

The preamble to the examination was written; the provost himself had dictated a few sentences, walking about the room with a meditative air, and requiring Christophe to tell him his name—Christian name—age, and profession; then he asked him from whom he had received the papers he had delivered to the Queen.

"From Chaudieu the minister," said he.

"Where did he give them to you?"

"At my own home in Paris."

"When he handed them to you, he must have told you whether the Queen-mother would receive you well."

"He told me nothing of the kind," replied Christophe. "He only desired me to give them secretly to Queen Catherine."

"Then have you often seen Chaudieu, that he knew that you were coming here?"

"It was not from me that he heard that I was to carry the furs to the two Queens, and at the same time to ask in my father's behalf for the money owed him by the Queen-mother; nor had I time to ask him who had told him."

"But those papers, given to you without any wrapper or seal, contain a treaty between the rebels and Queen Catherine. You must have known that they exposed you to the risk of suffering the punishment dealt out to those who are implicated in a rebellion."

"Yes."

"The persons who induced you to commit an act of high treason must have promised you some reward and the Queen-mother's patronage."

"I did it out of attachment to Chaudieu, the only person whom I saw."

"Then you persist in declaring that you did not see the Prince de Condé?"

"Yes."

"Did not the Prince de Condé tell you that the Queen-mother was inclined to enter into his views in antagonism to the Guises?"

"I did not see him."

"'Take care. One of your accomplices, la Renaudie, is arrested. Strong as he is, he could not resist the torture that awaits you, and at last confessed that he, as well as the Prince, had had speech with you. If you wish to escape the anguish of torture, I beg you to tell the simple truth. Then, perhaps, you may win your pardon."

Christophe replied that he could not tell anything of which he had no knowledge, nor betray accomplices when he had none. On hearing this, the provost nodded to the executioner, and went back into the adjoining room.

On seeing this, Christophe knit his brows, wrinkling his forehead with a nervous spasm, and preparing to endure. He clenched his fists with such a rigid clutch that the nails ran into the flesh without his feeling it. The three men took him up, carried him to the camp bed, and laid him there, his legs hanging down. While the executioner tied him fast with stout ropes, his two men each fitted a leg into a boot; the cords were tightened by means of a wrench without giving the victim any great pain.   When each leg was thus held in a vise, the executioner took up his mallet and his wedges, and looked alternately at the sufferer and the clerk.

" Do you persist in your denial?" said the clerk.

" I have told the truth," replied Christophe.

" Then go on," said the clerk, shutting his eyes.

The cords were tightened to the utmost, and this moment, perhaps, was the most agonizing of all the torture ; the flesh was so suddenly compressed that the blood was violently thrown back into the trunk.   The poor boy could not help screaming terribly; he seemed about to faint.   The doctor was called back.   He felt Christophe's pulse, and desired the executioner to wait for a quarter of an hour before driving in the wedges, to give time for the blood to recover its circulation and sensation to return.

The clerk charitably told Christophe that if he could not better endure even the beginnings of the suffering he could not escape, he would do better to reveal all he knew; but Christophe's only reply was—

" The King's tailor ! the King's tailor ! "

" What do you mean by saying that ?" asked the clerk.

" Foreseeing the torments I shall go through," said Christophe, slowly, to gain time and to rest, " I am summoning all my strength, and trying to reinforce it by remembering the martyrdom endured for the sacred cause of the Reformation by the late King's tailor, who was tortured in the presence of the King and of Madame de Valentinois ; I will try to be worthy of him ! "

While the physician was advising the hapless man not to drive his torturers to extremities, the cardinal and the Duke, impatient to know the results of this examination, came in and desired Christophe to reveal the truth at once.   The furrier's son repeated the only confession he would allow himself to make, implicating nobody but Chaudieu.

The Princes nodded. On this, the executioner and his foreman seized their mallets, each took a wedge and drove it home between the boots, one standing on the right, and the other on the left. The executioner stood at the knees, the assistant at the ankles, opposite. The eyes of the witnesses of this hideous act were fixed on Christophe's, who, excited no doubt by the presence of these grand personages, flashed such a look at them that his eyes sparkled like flame.

At the two next wedges a horrible groan escaped him. Then when he saw the men take up the wedges for the severer torture, he remained silent ; but his gaze assumed such dreadful fixity, and flashed at the two Princes such a piercing magnetic fluid, that the Duke and the cardinal were both obliged to look down. Philippe le Bel had experienced the same defeat when he presided at the torture by hammer, inflicted in his presence on the Templars. This consisted in hitting the victim on the chest with one arm of the balanced hammer used to coin money, which was covered with a leather pad. There was one knight whose eyes were so fixed on the King that he was fascinated, and could not take his gaze off the sufferer. At the third blow the King rose and went away, after hearing himself called upon to appear before the judgment of God within a year—as he did.

At the fifth wedge, the first of the greater torture, Christophe said to the cardinal—

"Cut my misery short, monseigneur ; it is useless."

The cardinal and the Duke withdrew, and Christophe could hear from the next room these words, spoken by Queen Catherine—

"Go on, go on ; after all, he is only a heretic !"

She thought it prudent to appear more severe to her accomplice than his executioners were.

The sixth and seventh wedge were driven in, and Christophe complained no more, his face shone with a strange radiance, due, no doubt, to the immense strength he derived from fanatical excitement.  In what else but in feeling can we hope to find the fulcrum enabling a man to endure such anguish?  At last, when the executioner was about to insert the eighth wedge, Christophe smiled.  This dreadful torment had lasted one hour.

The clerk went to fetch the leech, to know whether the eighth wedge could be driven in without endangering the sufferer's life.  The Duke meanwhile came in again to see Christophe.

"By our Lady! you are a fine fellow," said he, leaning down to speak in his ear.  "I like a brave man.  Enter my service, you shall be happy and rich, my favors will heal your bruised limbs; I will ask you to do nothing cowardly, like rejoining your own party to betray their plans; there are always plenty of traitors, and the proof is to be found in the prisons of Blois.  Only tell me on what terms are the Queen-mother and the Prince de Condé."

"I know nothing about it, monseigneur," cried Lecamus.

The doctor came in, examined the victim, and pronounced that he could bear the eighth wedge.

"Drive it in," said the cardinal.  "After all, as the Queen says, he is only a heretic," he added, with a hideous smile at Christophe.

Catherine herself slowly came in from the adjoining room, · stood in front of Christophe, and gazed at him coldly.  She was the object of attentive scrutiny to the two brothers, who looked alternately at the Queen-mother and her accomplice.  The whole future life of this ambitious woman depended on this solemn scrutiny; she felt the greatest admiration for Christophe's courage, and she looked at him sternly; she hated the Guises, and she smiled upon them.

"Come," said she, " young man, confess that you saw the Prince de Condé; you will be well rewarded."

"Oh, madame, what a part you are playing!" cried Christophe, in pity for her.

The Queen started.

"He is insulting me!   Is he not to be hanged?" said she to the two brothers, who stood lost in thought.

"What a woman!" cried the Grand Master, who was consulting his brother in the window recess.

"I will stay in France and be revenged," thought the Queen.   "Proceed, he must confess or let him die!" she exclaimed, addressing Monsieur de Montrésor.

The provost turned away, the executioners were busy, Catherine had an opportunity of giving the martyr a look, which no one else saw, and which fell like dew on Christophe. The great Queen's eyes seemed to glisten with moisture; they were, in fact, full of tears, two tears at once repressed and dry.   The wedge was driven home, one of the boards between which it was inserted split.   Christophe uttered a piercing cry; then his face became radiant; he thought he was dying.

"Let him die," said the cardinal, echoing Queen Catherine's words with a sort of irony.   "No, no," he added to the provost, "do not let us lose this clue."

The Duke and the cardinal held a consultation in a low voice.

"What is to be done with him?" asked the executioner.

"Send him to prison at Orleans," said the Duke.   "And, above all," he said to Monsieur de Montrésor, "do not hang him without orders from me."

The excessive sensitiveness of every internal organ, strung to the highest pitch by the endurance which worked upon every nerve in his frame, no less affected every sense in Christophe.   He alone heard these words spoken by the Duc de Guise in the cardinal's ear—

"I have not given up all hope of hearing the truth from this little man."

As soon as the two Princes had left the room, the executioners unpacked the victim's legs, with no attempt at gentle handling.

"Did you ever see a criminal with such fortitude?" said the head man to his assistants. "The rogue has lived through the infliction of the eighth wedge; he ought to have died. I am the loser of the price of his body."

"Untie me without hurting me, my good friends," said poor Christophe. "Some day I will reward you."

"Come, show some humanity," said the doctor. "Monseigneur the Duke esteems the young man, and commended him to my care," cried the leech.

"I am off to Amboise with my men," said the executioner roughly. "Take care of him yourself. And here is the gaoler."

The executioner went off, leaving Christophe in the hands of the smooth-spoken doctor, who, with the help of Christophe's warder, lifted him on to a bed, gave him some broth, which he made him swallow, sat down by his side, felt his pulse, and tried to comfort him.

"You are not dying," he said, "and you must feel a comfort to your mind when you reflect that you have done your duty. The Queen charged me to take good care of you," he added, in a low voice.

"The Queen is very good," said Christophe, in whom acute anguish had developed wonderful lucidity of mind, and who, after enduring so much, was determined not to spoil the results of his devotion. "But she might have saved me so much suffering by not delivering me to my tormentors, and by telling them herself the secrets, of which I most truly know nothing."

On hearing this reply, the doctor put on his cap and cloak and left Christophe to his fate, thinking it vain to hope to gain anything from a man of that temper. The gaoler had the poor boy carried on a litter by four men to the town prison, where Christophe fell asleep, in that deep slumber which, it is said, comes upon almost every mother after the dreadful pains of childbirth.

The two Princes of Lorraine, when they transferred the Court to Amboise, had no hope of finding there the leader of the Reformed party, the Prince de Condé, whom they had ordered to appear in the King's name to take him in a snare. As a vassal of the Crown and as a Prince of the Blood, Condé was bound to obey the behest of the King. Not to come to Amboise would be a felony; but, by coming, he would place himself in the power of the Crown. Now, at this moment, the Crown, the Council, the Court, and every kind of power were in the hands of the Duc de Guise and the Cardinal de Lorraine.

In this difficult dilemma, the Prince de Condé showed the spirit of decisiveness and astuteness, which made him a worthy representative of Jeanne d'Albret and the brave general of the Reformers' forces. He traveled at the heels of the last conspirators to Vendôme to support them in case of success. But when this first rush to arms ended in the brief skirmish in which the flower of the nobility whom Calvin had misled all perished, the Prince, and a following of fifty gentlemen, arrived at the château d'Amboise the very day after this affair, which the Guises, with crafty policy, spoke of as the riots at Amboise. On hearing of the Prince's advance, the Duke sent out the Maréchal de Saint-André to receive him with an escort of a hundred men-at-arms. When the Béarnais came to the gate of the castle, the marshal in command refused to admit the Prince's suite.

"You must come in alone, sir," said the Chancellor Olivier, Cardinal de Tournon, and Birague, who awaited him outside the portcullis.

"And why?"

"You are suspected of felony," replied the chancellor.

The Prince, who saw that his party was being cut off by the Duc de Nemours, quietly replied—

"If that is the case, I will go into my cousin alone and prove my innocence."

He dismounted and conversed with perfect freedom with Birague, Tournon, the Chancellor Olivier, and the Duc de Nemours, from whom he asked details of the riot.

"Monseigneur," said the Duc de Nemours, "the rebels had sympathizers inside Amboise. Captain Lanoue had gotten in some men-at-arms, who opened the gate to them through which they got into the town, and of which they had the command——"

"That is to say, you got them into a sack," replied the Prince, looking at Birague.

"If they had been supported by the attack that was to have been made on the Gate of Bons-Hommes by Captain Chaudieu, the preacher's brother, they would have succeeded," said the Duc de Nemours, "but, from the position I had taken up, in obedience to the Duc de Guise, Captain Chaudieu was obliged to make a detour to avoid fighting me. Instead of arriving at night like the rest, that rebel did not come up till daybreak, just as the King's troops had crushed those who had got into the town."

"And you had a reserve to recapture the gate that had been given up to them?"

"Monsieur le Maréchal de Saint-André was on the spot with five hundred men."

The Prince warmly praised these military manœuvres.

"To have acted thus," said he in conclusion, "the lieutenant-general must certainly have known the Reformers' secrets. They have evidently been betrayed."

The Prince was treated with greater strictness at each step. After being parted from his followers on entering the castle, the cardinal and the chancellor stood in his way when he turned to the stairs leading to the King's apartments.

"We are instructed by the King, sir, to conduct you to your own rooms."

"Am I then a prisoner?"

"If that were the King's purpose, you would not be attended by a prince of the church and by me," replied the chancellor.

The two functionaries led the Prince to an apartment where a guard—of honor so called—was allotted to him, and where he remained for several hours without seeing any one. From his window he looked out on the Loire, the rich country which makes such a beautiful valley between Amboise and Tours, and he was meditating on his situation, wonderiug what the Guises might dare to do to his person, when he heard the door of his room open, and saw the King's fool come in, Chicot, who had once been in his service.

" I heard you were in disgrace," said the Prince.

" You cannot think how sober the Court has become since the death of Henri II."

" And yet the King loves to laugh, surely."

" Which King ?  Francis II. or Francis of Lorraine ? "

" Are you so fearless of the Duke that you speak so ? "

" He will not punish me for that, sir," replied Chicot, smiling.

" And to what do I owe the honor of this visit ? "

" Was it not due to you after your coming here ?  I have brought you my cap and bauble."

" I cannot get out then ? "

" Try ! "

" And if I do get out ? "

" I will confess that you have won the game by playing against the rules."

" Chicot, you frighten me.  Have you been sent by some one who is interested in my fate ? "

Chicot nodded "Yes."  He went nearer to the Prince, and conveyed to him that they were watched and overheard.

" What have you to say to me ? " asked Monsieur de Condé.

" That nothing but daring can get you out of the scrape," said the fool, whispering the words into his ear.  " And this is from the Queen-mother."

"Tell those who have sent you," replied the Prince, "that I should never have come to this castle if I had anything to blame myself for or to fear."

"I fly to carry your bold reply," said the fool.

Two hours later, at one in the afternoon, before the King's dinner, the chancellor and Cardinal de Tournon came to fetch the Prince to conduct him to Francis II. in the great hall where the Council had sat. There, before all the Court, the Prince de Condé affected surprise at the cool reception the King had given him, and he asked the reason.

"You are accused, cousin," said the Queen-mother sternly, "of having meddled with the plots of the Reformers, and you must prove yourself a faithful subject and a good Catholic if you wish to avert the King's anger from your House."

On hearing this speech, spoken by Catherine in the midst of hushed silence, as she stood with her hand in the King's arm and with the Duc d'Orléans on her left hand, the Prince de Condé drew back three steps, and with an impulse of dignified pride laid his hand on his sword, looking at the persons present.

"Those who say so, madame, lie in their throat!" he exclaimed in angry tones.

He flung his glove at the King's feet, saying—

"Let the man who will maintain this calumny stand forth!"

A shiver ran through the whole Court when the Duc de Guise was seen to quit his place; but instead of picking up the glove as they expected, he went up to the intrepid hunchback.

"If you need a second, Prince, I beg of you to accept my services," said he. "I will answer for you, and will show the Reformers how greatly they deceive themselves if they hope to have you for their leader."

The Prince de Condé could not help offering his hand to the lieutenant-general of the kingdom. Chicot picked up the glove and restored it to Monsieur de Condé.

"Cousin," said the boy-King, "you should never draw your sword but in defense of your country. Come to dinner."

The Cardinal de Lorraine, puzzled by his brother's action, led him off to their rooms. The Prince de Condé having weathered the worst danger, gave his hand to Queen Mary Stewart to lead her to the dining-room; but, while making flattering speeches to the young Queen, he was trying to discern what snare was at this moment being laid for him by the Balafré's policy. In vain he racked his brain, he could not divine the Guises' scheme; but Queen Mary betrayed it.

"It would have been a pity," said she, laughing, "to see so clever a head fall; you must allow that my uncle is magnanimous."

"Yes, madame, for my head fits no shoulders but my own, although one is larger than the other. But is it magnanimity in your uncle? Has he not rather gained credit at a cheap rate? Do you think it such an easy matter to have the law of a Prince of the Blood?"

"We have not done yet," replied she. "We shall see how you behave at the execution of the gentlemen, your friends, over which the Council has determined to make the greatest display."

"I shall do as the King does," said Condé.

"The King, the Queen-mother, and I shall all be present, with all the Court and the ambassadors——"

"Quite a high day?" said the Prince ironically.

"Better than that," said the young Queen, "an *auto-da-fé*,* a function of high political purport. The gentlemen of France must be subjugated by the Crown; they must be cured of their taste for faction and manœuvring——"

"You will not cure them of their warlike temper by showing them their danger, madame, and at this game you risk the Crown itself," replied the Prince.

At the end of this dinner, which was gloomy enough, Queen

---

* Lit.: Act of Faith—the ceremony of burning heretics.

Mary was so unfortunately daring as to turn the conversation publicly on the trial which the nobles, taken under arms, were at that moment undergoing, and to speak of the necessity for giving the utmost solemnity to their execution.

" But, madame," said Francis II., " is it not enough for the King of France to know that the blood of so many brave gentlemen must be shed ?   Must it be a cause of triumph ? "

" No, sir, but an example," replied Catherine.

" Your grandfather and your father were in the habit of seeing heretics burned," said Mary Stewart.

" The kings who reigned before me went their way," said Francis, " and I mean to go mine."

" Philip II.," Catherine went on, " who is a great king, lately, when he was in the Netherlands, had an *auto-da-fè* postponed till he should have returned to Valladolid."

" What do you think about it, cousin ? " said the King to the Prince de Condé.

" Sire, you cannot avoid going ; the papal nuncio and the ambassadors must be present.   For my part, I am delighted to go if the ladies are to be of the party."

The Prince, at a glance from Catherine de' Medici, had boldly taken his line.

While the Prince de Condé was being admitted to the Castle of Amboise, the furrier to the two Queens was also arriving from Paris, brought thither by the uneasiness produced by the reports of the rebellion, not only in himself and his family, but also in the Lalliers.

At the gate of the castle, when the old man craved admission, the captain of the Guard, at the words " Queen's furrier," answered at once—

" My good man, if you want to be hanged, you have only to set foot in the courtyard."

On hearing this the unhappy father sat down on a rail a little way off, to wait till some attendant on either of the Queens, or some woman of the Court, should pass him, to ask for some news of his son ; but he remained there the whole day without seeing anybody he knew, and was at last obliged to go down into the town, where he found a lodging, not without difficulty, in an inn on the square where the executions were to take place.    He was obliged to pay a livre a day (then a very large sum) to secure a room looking out on the square.

On the following day he was brave enough to look on from his window at the rebels who had been condemned to the wheel, or to be hanged, as men of minor importance ; and the Syndic of the Furriers' Guild was glad enough not to find his son among the sufferers.

When it was all over, he went to place himself in the clerk's way.    Having mentioned his name and pressed a purse full of crown-pieces into the man's hands, he begged him to see whether, in the three former days of execution, the name of Christophe Lecamus had occurred.    The registrar, touched by the despairing old father's manners and tone of voice, conducted him to his own house.    After carefully comparing notes, he could assure the old man that the said Christophe was not among those who had hitherto been executed, nor was he named among those who were to die within the next few days.

" My dear master," said the clerk to the furrier, " the Parlement is now engaged in trying the lords and gentlemen concerned in the business, and the principal leaders.  So, possibly, your son is imprisoned in the castle, and will be one in the magnificent execution for which my lords the Duc de Guise and the Cardinal de Lorraine are making great preparations.  Twenty-seven barons are to be beheaded, with eleven counts and seven marquises, fifty gentlemen in all, and leaders of the Reformers.  As the administration of justice in Touraine has no connection with that of the Paris Parlement, if you positively must have some news of your son, go to my lord the Chancellor Olivier, who, by the orders of the lieutenant-general of the kingdom, has the management of the proceedings.''

Three times did the poor old man go to the chancellor's house and stand in a file of people in the courtyard in common with an immense number of people who had come to pray for their relations' lives ; but as titled folk were admitted before the middle-class, he was obliged to give up all hope of speaking with the chancellor, though he saw him several times coming out of his house to go either to the château or to the Commission appointed by the Parlement, along a way cleared for him by soldiers, between two hedges of petitioners who were thrust aside.

It was a dreadful scene of misery, for among this crowd were wives, daughters, and mothers, whole families in tears. Old Lecamus gave a great deal of gold to the servants at the castle, enjoining on them that they should deliver certain letters he wrote to la Dayelle, Queen Mary's waiting-woman, or to the Queen-mother's woman ; but the lackeys took the goodman's money, and then, by the cardinal's orders, handed all letters to the provost of the Law Court.  As a consequence of their unprecedented cruelty, the Princes of Lorraine had cause to fear revenge : and they never took greater precautions than during the stay of the Court at Amboise, so that neither the most effectual bribery, that of gold, nor the most diligent inquiries brought the furrier any light as to his son's fate.  He wandered about the little town in a melancholy way, watching the tremendous preparations that the cardinal was making for the shocking spectacle at which the Prince de Condé was to be present.

Public curiosity was being stimulated, by every means in use at the time, from Paris to Nantes.  The execution had been announced from the pulpit by every preacher, in a breath with the King's victory over the heretics.

Three elegant stands, the centre one apparently to be the finest of the three, were being erected against the curtain-wall of the castle, at the foot of which the execution was to take place. All around the open space raised wooden seats were being put up, after the fashion of an amphitheatre, to accommodate the enormous crowd attracted by the notoriety of this *auto-da-fè.* About ten thousand persons were camping out in the fields on the day before this hideous spectacle. The roofs were crowded with spectators, and windows were let for as much as ten livres, an enormous sum at that time.

The unhappy father had, as may be supposed, secured one of the best places for commanding a view of the square where so many men of family were to perish, on a huge scaffold erected in the middle, and covered with black cloth. On the morning of the fatal day, the headsman's block, on which the victim laid his head, kneeling in front of it, was placed on the scaffold, and an armchair, hung with black, for the recorder of the Court, whose duty it was to call the condemned by name and read their sentence. The inclosure was guarded from early morning by the Scotch soldiers and the men-at-arms of the King's household, to keep the crowd out till the hour of the executions.

After a solemn mass in the chapel of the castle and in every church in the town, the gentlemen were led forth, the last survivors of all the conspirators. These men, some of whom had been through the torture chamber, were collected round the foot of the scaffold, and exhorted by monks, who strove to persuade them to renounce the doctrines of Calvin. But not one would listen to these preachers, turned on to them by the Cardinal de Lorraine, among whom, no doubt, these gentlemen feared that there might be some spies on behalf of the Guises.

To escape being persecuted with these exhortations, they began to sing a psalm turned into French verse by Clément Marot. Calvin, as is well known, had decreed that God should be worshiped in the mother-tongue of every country, from motives of commonsense as well as from antagonism to

11

the Roman Church.   It was a pathetic moment for all those among the throng, who felt for these gentlemen, when they heard this verse sung at the moment when the Court appeared on the scene—

> "Lord, help us in our need!
> Lord, bless us with Thy grace!
>     And on the saints in sore distress
> Let shine Thy glorious face!"

The eyes of the Reformers all centred on the Prince de Condé, who was intentionally placed between Queen Mary and the Duc d'Orléans.   Queen Catherine de' Medici sat next her son, with the cardinal on her left.   The papal nuncio stood behind the two Queens.   The lieutenant-general of the kingdom was on horseback, below the royal stand, with two marshals of France and his captains.   As soon as the Prince de Condé appeared, all the gentlemen sentenced to death, to whom he was known, bowed to him, and the brave hunchback returned the salutation.

"It is hard," said he to the Duc d'Orléans, "not to be civil to men who are about to die."

The two other grand stands were filled by invited guests, by courtiers, and the attendants on their majesties; in short, the rank and fashion of the castle from Blois, who thus rushed from festivities to executions, just as they afterward rushed from the pleasures of Court life to the perils of war, with a readiness which to foreigners will always be one of the mainsprings of their policy in France.   The poor Syndic of the Furriers' Guild felt the keenest joy at failing to discern his son among the fifty or so gentlemen condemned to death.

At a signal from the Duc de Guise, the clerk, from the top of the scaffold, called out at once, in a loud voice—

"Jean-Louis-Albéric, Baron de Raunay, guilty of heresy, of the crime of high treason, and of bearing arms against the King's majesty."

A tall, handsome man mounted the scaffold with a firm step, bowed to the people and to the Court, and said—

"The indictment is false; I bore arms to deliver the King from his enemies of Lorraine!"

He laid his head on the block, and it fell.

The Reformers sang—

> "Thou, Lord, hast proved our faith
> And searched our soul's desire,
> And purified our froward hearts,
> As silver proved by fire."

"Robert-Jean-René Briquemaut, Comte de Villemongis, guilty of high treason and rebellion against the King," cried the recorder.

The Count dipped his hands in the Baron de Raunay's blood, and said—

"May this blood be on the heads of those who are truly guilty!"

The Reformers sang on—

> "Thou, Lord, hast led our feet
> Where foes had laid their snare;
> To Thee, O Lord, the glory be,
> Though we should perish there."

"Confess, my lord nuncio," said the Prince de Condé, "that if French gentlemen know how to plot, they also know how to die."

"What hatred you are entailing on the heads of your children, brother," said the Duchesse de Guise to the Cardinal de Lorraine.

"The sight makes me feel sick," said the young King, who had turned pale at the sight of all this bloodshed.

"Pooh! Rebels!" said Catherine de' Medici.

Still the hymn went on, still the axe was plied.   At last the sublime spectacle of men who could die singing, and, above all, the impression produced on the crowd by the gradual dwindling of the voices, became stronger than the terror inspired by the Guises.

"Mercy!" cried the mob, when they heard at last only the feeble chant of a single victim, reserved till the last, as being the most important.

He was standing alone at the foot of the steps leading up to the scaffold, and sang—

> "Lord, help us in our need!
> Lord, bless us with Thy grace!
>     And on the saints in sore distress
> Let shine Thy glorious face!"

"Come, Duc de Nemours," said the Prince de Condé, who was tired of his position; "you to whom the securing of the victory is due, and who helped to entrap all these people —do you not feel that you ought to ask the life of this one? It is Castelnau, who, as I was told, had your promise for courteous treatment when he surrendered——"

"Did I wait to see him here before trying to save him?" said the Duc de Nemours, stung by this bitter reproof.

The clerk spoke slowly, intentionally, no doubt—

"Michel-Jean-Louis, Baron de Castelnau-Chalosse, accused and convicted of the crime of high treason and of fighting against his majesty the King."

"No," retorted Castelnau haughtily; "it can be no crime to oppose the tyranny and intended usurpation of the Guises!"

The headsman, who was tired, seeing some stir in the royal seats, rested on his axe.

"Monsieur le Baron," said he, "I should be glad not to hurt you. One minute may perhaps save you."

And all the people shouted again for mercy.

"Come," said the King, "a pardon for poor Castelnau, who saved the Duc d'Orléans."

The base cardinal intentionally misinterpreted the word
"Come." He nodded to the executioner, and Castelnau's
head fell at the very moment when the King pronounced his
pardon.

"That one goes to your account, cardinal," said Catherine.

On the day after this horrible massacre, the Prince de
Condé set out for Navarre.

This affair made a great sensation throughout France and
in every foreign Court. The torrents of noble blood then
shed caused the Chancellor Olivier such deep grief that this
admirable judge, seeing the end at which the Guises were
aiming, felt that he was not strong enough to hold his own
against them. Although they had made him what he was,
he would not sacrifice his duty and the Monarchy to them;
he retired from public life, suggesting that l'Hôpital should
be his successor. Catherine, on hearing of Olivier's choice,
proposed Birague for the post of chancellor, and urged her
request with great pertinacity. The wily cardinal, who knew
nothing of the note written to Catherine by l'Hôpital, and
who believed him still faithful to the House of Lorraine,
upheld him as Birague's rival, and the Queen-mother affected
to be overridden.

L'Hôpital was no sooner appointed than he took steps to
prevent the introduction into France of the holy office
(Inquisition), which the Cardinal de Lorraine wished to establish; and he so effectually opposed the anti-Gallican measures and policy of the Guises, and showed himself so sturdy a
Frenchman, that within three months of his appointment he
was exiled, to reduce his spirit, to his estate of le Vignay,
near Etampes.

Old Lecamus impatiently waited till the Court should leave
Amboise, for he could find no opportunity of speaking to
either Queen Mary or Queen Catherine; but he hoped to be
able to place himself in their way at the time when the Court
should be moving along the river-bank on the way back to

Blois.   The furrier dressed himself as a poor man, at the risk of being seized as a spy, and, favored by this disguise, he mingled with the beggars who stood by the wayside.

After the departure of the Prince de Condé, the Duke and the cardinal thought that they had silenced the Reformed party, and they left the Queen-mother a little more liberty. Lecamus knew that Catherine, instead of traveling in a litter, liked to ride on horseback on a *planchette*, as it was called, a side-saddle with a foot-rest.   This sort of stirrup was invented by or for Catherine, who, having hurt her leg, rested both feet on a velvet sling, sitting sideways, and supporting one knee in a hollow cut in the saddle.   As the Queen had very fine legs, she was accused of having hit on this device for displaying them.

Thus the old man was able to place himself in sight of the Queen-mother ; but when she saw him she affected anger.

" Go away from hence, good man, and let no one see you speaking to me," she said with some anxiety.   " Get yourself appointed delegate to the States-General from the corporation of Paris Guilds, and be on my side in the Assembly at Orleans, you will then hear something definite about your son——"

" Is he alive ? " said the old man.

" Alas ! " said the Queen, " I hope it."

And Lecamus was obliged to return home with this sad reply and the secret as to the convocation of the States-General, which the Queen had told him.

Some days before this, the Cardinal de Lorraine had received information as to the guilt of the Court of Navarre. At Lyons, and at Mouvans in Dauphiné, the Reformers, commanded by the most enterprising of the Bourbon princes, had tried to inflame the population. This daring attempt, after the dreadful executions at Amboise, astonished the Guises, who, to put an end to heresy, no doubt, by some means of which they kept the secret, proposed to assemble the States-General at Orleans. Catherine de' Medici, who saw a support for her own policy in the representation of the nation, consented with joy. The cardinal, who aimed at recapturing his prey and overthrowing the House of Bourbon, convoked the States solely to secure the presence of the Prince de Condé and of the King of Navarre, Antoine de Bourbon, father of Henri IV. He then meant to make use of Christophe to convict the Prince of high treason if he were able once more to get him into the King's power.

After spending two months in the prison of Blois, Christophe one morning was carried out on a litter lying on a mattress, was embarked on a barge, and taken up the river to Orleans before a westerly breeze. He reached that town the same evening, and was taken to the famous tower of Saint-Aignan. Christophe, who knew not what to make of his transfer, had time enough for meditation on his behavior and on his future prospects. There he remained two months more, on his bed, unable to use his legs. His bones were crushed. When he begged to be allowed the help of a surgeon, the gaoler told him that his orders with regard to his prisoner were so strict that he dared not allow any one else even to bring him his food. This severity, of which the effect was absolutely solitary confinement, surprised Christophe. His idea was that he must either be hanged or released; he knew nothing whatever of the events happening at Amboise.

In spite of the secret warnings to remain at home sent to them by Catherine de' Medici, the two chiefs of the House of Bourbon determined to appear at the meeting of the States-General, since autograph letters from the King were reassuring; and when the Court was settling at Orleans, Groslot, the Chancellor of Navarre, announced their advent, to the surprise of all.

Francis II. took up his quarters in the house of the Chancellor of Navarre, who was also the Bailli or Recorder of Orleans. This man Groslot, whose double appointment is one of the odd features of a time when Reformers were in possession of abbeys—Groslot, the Jacques Cœur of Orleans, one of the richest citizens of his day, did not leave his name to his house. It came to be known as the *Bailliage*, having been purchased, no doubt, from his heirs, by the Crown, or by the provincial authorities, to be the seat of that tribunal. This elegant structure, built by the citizens of the sixteenth century, adds a detail to the history of a time when the King, the nobility, and the middle-class vied with each other in wealth, elegance, and splendor; especially in their dwellings —as may be seen at Varangeville, Ango's magnificent manor-house, and the Hôtel d'Hercules, as it is called, in Paris, which still exists, but in a condition that is the despair of archæologists and of lovers of mediæval art.

Those who have been to Orleans can hardly have failed to observe the Town Hall in the Place de l'Estape. This town-hall is the Old Bailli's Court, the Hôtel Groslot, the most illustrious and most neglected house in Orleans.

The remains of this building plainly show to the archæolo-gist's eye how magnificent it must once have been, at a time when citizens built their houses more of wood than of stone, and the upper ranks alone had the right to build manor-houses, a word of special meaning. Since it served as the King's residence at a time when the Court made so much display of pomp and luxury, the Hôtel Groslot must then have been the largest and finest house in Orleans.

It was on the Place de l'Estape that the Guises and the King held a review of the municipal guard, to which Monsieur de Cypierre was nominated captain during the King's visit. At that time, the cathedral of Sainte-Croix—afterward finished by Henry IV., who desired to set the seal to his conversion— was being built, and the surrounding ground, strewn with blocks of stone and encumbered with piles of timber, was held by the Guises, who lodged in the bishop's palace, now destroyed.

The town was in military occupation, and the measures adopted by the Guises plainly showed how little liberty they intended to give to the States-General, while the delegates flocked into the town and raised the rents of the most wretched lodgings. The Court, the municipal militia, the nobles, and the citizens all alike expected some *Coup d'État;* and their expectations were fulfilled when the Princes of the Blood arrived.

As soon as the two Princes entered the King's room, the Court saw with dismay how insolent was the behavior of the Cardinal de Lorraine, who, to assert his audacious pretensions, kept his head covered, while the King of Navarre before him was beheaded. Catherine de' Medici stood with downcast eyes, not to betray her indignation. A solemn explanation then took place between the young King and the two heads of the younger branch. It was brief, for at the first words spoken by the Prince de Condé, Francis II. closed the discussion by saying—

"My lords and cousins, I fancied the incident of Amboise was at an end; it is not so, and we shall see cause to regret our indulgence!"

"It is not the King who speaks thus," said the Prince de Condé, "but Messieurs de Guise."

"Good-day, monsieur," said the little King, crimson with rage.

As he went through the great hall, the Prince was stopped by the two captains of the Guards. When the officer of the French Guard stepped forward, the Prince took a letter out of the breast of his doublet and said, in the presence of all the Court—

"Can you read me this, Monsieur de Maillé-Brézé?"

"With pleasure," said the French captain to the Prince de Condé.

" ' Cousin, come in all security; I give you my royal word that you may.   If you need a safe-conduct, these presents will serve you.' "

"And signed———? " said the bold and mischievous hunchback.

" Signed ' François,' " said Maillé.

"Nay, nay," replied the Prince, " it is signed ' Your good cousin and friend, François ! '   Gentlemen," he went on, turning to the Scotch Guard, " I will follow you to the prison whither you are to escort me by the King's orders.   There is enough noble spirit, no doubt, in this room to fully understand that."

The utter silence that reigned in the room might have enlightened the Guises, but silence is the last thing that princes listen to.

" Monseigneur," said the Cardinal de Tournon, who was following the Prince, " since the day at Amboise you have taken steps in opposition to royal authority at Lyons and at Mouvans in Dauphiné—things of which the King knew nothing when he addressed you in those terms."

" Rascals ! " cried the Prince, laughing.

" You made a public declaration against the mass and in favor of heresy——"

" We are masters in Navarre," said the Prince.

" In Béarn, you mean !   But you owe homage to the Crown," replied the Président de Thou.

"Ah, you are here, president ! " exclaimed the Prince ironically.   "And is all the Parlement with you ? "

With these words, the Prince flashed a look of contempt at the cardinal and left the room ; he understood that his head was in peril.

On the following day, when Messieurs de Thou, de Viole, d'Espesse, Bourdin, the public prosecutor, and du Tillet, the chief clerk, came into the prison, he kept them standing, and expressed his regrets at seeing them engaged on a business which did not concern them; then he said to the clerk—

"Write."

And he dictated as follows:

"I, Louis de Bourbon, Prince de Condé, peer of the realm, Marquis de Conti, Comte de Soissons, Prince of the Blood of France, formally refuse to recognize any Commission appointed to try me, inasmuch as that by virtue of my rank and the privileges attaching to every member of the royal family, I can only be attainted, heard, and judged by a Parlement of all the peers in their places, the Chambers in full assembly, and the King seated on the bed of justice. You ought to know this better than any one, gentlemen, and this is all you will get of me. For the rest, I trust in God and my Right."

The magistrates proceeded nevertheless, in spite of the determined silence of the Prince.

The King of Navarre was at liberty, but closely watched; his prison was a wider one than the Prince's, and that was the whole difference between his position and his brother's; for the heads of the King and the Prince were to be felled at the same time.

So Christophe was so closely confined by order of the cardinal and the lieutenant-general of the kingdom only to afford proof to the judges of the Prince's guilt. The letters found on the person of La Sagne, the Prince's secretary, intelligible to a statesman, were not clear enough for the judges. The cardinal had thought of bringing the Prince accidentally face to face with Christophe, who had been placed, not without a purpose, in a lower room of the tower of Saint-Aignan, and the window looked out on the yard. Each time he was examined by the magistrates, Christophe intrenched himself in systematic denial, which naturally prolonged the affair till the meeting of the States-General.

Lecamus, who had made a point of getting himself elected by the citizens of Paris as a deputy for the "Third Estate," came to Orleans a few days after the Prince's arrest. This event, of which he had news at Etampes, increased his alarms, for he understood—he who alone in the world knew of his son's interview with the Prince under the Pont au Change—that Christophe's fate was bound up with that of the rashly daring head of the Reformation party. So he determined to study the mysterious interests which had become so entangled at Court since the States had met, so as to hit upon some plan for rescuing his son. It was vain to think of having recourse to Queen Catherine, who refused to receive the furrier. No one of the Court to whom he had access could give him any satisfactory information with regard to Christophe, and he had sunk to such depths of despair that he was about to address himself to the cardinal, when he heard that Monsieur de Thou had accepted the office of one of the judges of the Prince de Condé—a blot on the good fame of that great jurist. The Syndic went to call on his son's patron, and learned that Christophe was alive but a prisoner.

Tourillon, the glover, to whose house la Renaudie had sent Christophe, had offered a room to the Sieur Lecamus for the whole time during which the States-General should be sitting. He believed the furrier to be, like himself, secretly attached to the Reformed religion ; but he soon perceived that a father who fears for his son's life thinks no more of shades of religious dogma ; he throws himself soul and body on the mercy of God, never thinking of the badge he wears before men.

The old man, repulsed at every attempt, wandered half-witless about the streets. Against all his expectations, his gold was of no avail ; Monsieur de Thou had warned him that even if he should bribe some servant of the Guise household, he would only be so much out of pocket, for the Duke and the cardinal allowed nothing to be known concerning Christophe. This judge, whose fair fame is somewhat tarnished by the part he played at this juncture, had tried to give the unhappy father some hope ; but he himself trembled for his godson's life, and his consolations only added to the furrier's alarm.  The old man was always prowling round the house; in three months he grew quite thin.

His only hope now lay in the warm friendship which had so long bound him to the Hippocrates of the sixteenth century.  Ambroise Paré tried to say a word to Queen Mary as he came out of the King's room; but the instant he mentioned Christophe, the daughter of the Stewarts, annoyed by the prospect before her in the event of any ill befalling the King, whom she believed to have been poisoned by the Reformers, as he had been taken suddenly ill, replied—

"If my uncles would take my opinion, such a fanatic would have been hanged before now."

On the evening when this ominous reply had been repeated to Lecamus by his friend Paré, on the Place de l'Estape, he went home half-dead, and retired to his room, refusing to eat any supper.

Tourillon, very uneasy, went upstairs, and found the old man in tears; and as the poor furrier's feeble eyes showed the reddened and wrinkled linings of the lids, the glover believed that they were tears of blood.

"Be comforted, father," said the Huguenot, "the citizens of Orleans are enraged at seeing their town treated as if it had been taken by assault, and guarded by Monsieur de Cypierre's soldiery.  If the Prince de Condé's life should be in danger, we should very soon demolish the tower of Saint-Aignan, for the whole town is on the Reformers' side, and would rise in rebellion, you may be quite certain."

"But even if the Guises were seized, would their death give me back my son?" said the unhappy father.

At this instant there was a timid rap at the outer door; Tourillon went down to open it.  It was quite dark.  In these troubled times the master of every household took elaborate precautions.  Tourillon looked out through the bars of a wicket in the door and saw a stranger, whose accent betrayed him as an Italian.  This man, dressed in black, asked to see Lecamus on matters of business, and Tourillon showed him in.  At the sight of the stranger the old furrier quaked visibly, but the visitor had time to lay a finger on his lips. Lecamus, understanding the gesture, immediately said—

"You have come to offer furs for sale, I suppose?"

"Yes," replied the stranger in Italian, with an air of privity.

This man was, in fact, the famous Ruggieri, the Queen-mother's astrologer.  Tourillon went downstairs, perceiving that he was not wanted.

"Where can we talk without fear of being overheard?" said the astute Florentine.

"Only in the open fields," replied Lecamus.  "But we shall not be allowed out of the town ; you know how strictly the gates are guarded.  No one can pass out without an order from Monsieur de Cypierre, not even a member of the Assembly like myself.  Indeed, at to-morrow's sitting we all intend to complain of this restriction on our liberty."

"Work like a mole, never let your paws be seen in any kind of business," replied the wily Florentine.  "To-morrow will no doubt be a decisive day.  From my calculations, to-morrow, or soon after, you will, perhaps, see your son."

"God grant it !  Though you are said to deal only with the devil ! "

"Come and see me at home," said the astrologer, smiling. "I watch the stars from the tower belonging to the Sieur Touchet du Beauvais, the lieutenant of the bailiwick, whose daughter has found favor in the eyes of the little Duc d'Orléans.  I have cast the girl's horoscope, and it does in fact portend that she will become a great lady and be loved by a king.  The lieutenant is a clever fellow, he is interested in science, and the Queen found me lodgings with the good man, who is cunning enough to be a rabid Guisard till Charles IX. comes to the throne."

The furrier and the astrologer made their way to the Sieur de Beauvais' house without being seen or interfered with ; and, in the event of Lecamus being discovered, Ruggieri meant to afford him a pretext in his desire to consult the astrologer as to his son's fate.

When they had climbed to the top of the turret where the astrologer had established himself, Lecamus said—

" Then my son is really alive ? "

" At present," said the Italian.   " But we must make haste to save him.   Remember, O seller of skins, that I would not give two farthings for yours if in the whole course of your life you breathe one word of what I am about to tell you."

" The warning is not needed, master.   I have been furrier to the Court since the time of the late King Louis XII., and this is the fourth reign I have lived under."

" And you may soon say the fifth," replied Ruggieri.

" What do you know of my son ? "

" Well, he has been through the torture chamber."

" Poor boy ! " sighed the old man, looking up to heaven.

" His knees and ankles are a little damaged, but he has gained royal protection, which will be over him as long as he lives," the Florentine added, on seeing the father's horror. " Your little Christophe has done good service to our great Queen Catherine.   If we can get your son out of the clutches of the cardinal, you will see him councilor in the Parlement yet.   And a man would let his bones be broken three times over to find himself in the good graces of that beloved sovereign—a real genius she, who will triumph over every obstacle.

" I have cast the horoscope of the Duc de Guise ; he will be killed within a year.   Come now, Christophe did meet the Prince de Condé——"

" You know the future, do you not know the past ? " the furrier put in.

" I am not questioning you, I am informing you, goodman. Well, your son will be placed to-morrow where the Prince will pass by. If he recognizes him, or if the Prince recognizes your son, Monsieur de Condé forfeits his head. As to what would become of his accomplice—God only knows! But be easy. Neither your son nor the Prince is doomed to die; I have read their destiny; they will live. But by what means they may escape I know not. Now we will do what we can, apart from the certainty of my calculations. Monsieur de Condé shall get a prayer-book to-morrow, delivered to him by a safe hand, in which he shall find a warning! God grant that your son may be secretive, for he can have no warning! And a mere flash of recognition would cost the Prince his life. Thus, although the Queen-mother has every reason to depend on Christophe's fidelity——"

"He has been put to cruel tests," cried the furrier.

"Do not speak in that way. Do you suppose that the Queen is dancing for joy? She is indeed going to take her measures exactly as though the Guises had decided on the Prince's death; and she is wise, that shrewd and prudent Queen! Now she counts on you to help her in every way. You have some influence in the 'Third Estate,' where you are the representative of the Guilds of Paris; and, even if the Guisards should promise to set your son at liberty, try to deceive them and stir up your class against the Princes of Lorraine. Vote for the Queen-mother as Regent; the King of Navarre will give his assent to that publicly, to-morrow, in the Assembly."

"But the King?"

"The King will die," said Ruggieri; "I have read it in the stars. What the Queen requires of you in the Assembly is very simple; but she needs a greater service from you than that. You maintained the great Ambroise Paré while he was a student; you are his friend——"

"Ambroise loves the Duc de Guise in these days better than he loves me," said the furrier. "And he is right; he owes his place to him. Still, he is faithful to the King. And, although he has a leaning toward the Reformation, he will do nothing but his duty."

"A plague on all honest men!" cried the Florentine. "Ambroise boasted this evening that he could pull the little King through. If the King recovers his health, the Guises must triumph, the Princes are dead men, the House of Bourbon is extinct, we go back to Florence, your son is hanged, and the Guises will make short work of the rest of the royal family——"

"Great God!" cried Lecamus.

"Do not exclaim in that way; it is like a citizen who knows nothing of Court manners; but go forthwith to Ambroise, and find out what he means to do to save the King. If it seems at all certain, come and tell me what the operation is in which he has such faith."

"But——" Lecamus began.

"Obey me blindly, my good friend, otherwise you will be dazed."

"He is right," thought the furrier.

And he went off to the King's surgeon, who lived in an inn in the Place du Martroi.

At this juncture Catherine de' Medici found herself, politically speaking, in the same extremities as she had been in when Christophe had seen her at Blois. Though she had inured herself to the struggle and had exerted her fine intellect in that first defeat, her situation, though precisely the same now as then, was even more critical and dangerous than at the time of the riots at Amboise. Events had grown in magnitude, and the Queen had grown with them. Though she seemed to proceed in agreement with the Princes of Lorraine, Catherine held the threads of a conspiracy skillfully plotted against her terrible associates, and was only waiting for a favorable moment to drop her mask.

The cardinal had just found himself deceived by Catherine.

The crafty Italian had seen in the younger branch of the royal family an obstacle she could use to check the pretensions of the Guises; and, in spite of the counsel of the two Gondis, who advised her to leave the Guises to act with what violence they could against the Bourbons, she had, by warning the Queen of Navarre, brought to naught the plot to seize Béarn concerted by the Guises with the King of Spain. As this State secret was known only to themselves and to Catherine, the Princes of Lorraine were assured of her betrayal, and they wished to send her back to Florence; but to secure proofs of Catherine's treachery to the State—the House of Lorraine was the State—the Duke and cardinal had just made her privy to their scheme for making away with the King of Navarre.

The precautions which were immediately taken by Antoine de Bourbon proved to the brothers that this secret, known but to three people, had been divulged by the Queen-mother. The Cardinal de Lorraine accused Catherine of her breach of faith in the presence of the King, threatening her with banishment if any fresh indiscretions on her part should imperil the State.   Catherine, seeing herself in imminent danger, was compelled to act as a high-handed sovereign.   She gave ample proof indeed of her fine abilities, but it must also be confessed that she was well served by the friends she trusted.

L'Hôpital sent her a letter in these terms:

"Do not allow a Prince of the Blood to be killed by a committee, or you will soon be carried off yourself."

Catherine sent Birague to le Vignay, desiring the chancellor to come to the Assembly of the States-General, although he was in banishment.   Birague returned the same evening with l'Hôpital, halting within three leagues of Orleans, and the chancellor thus declared himself on the side of the Queen-mother.

Chiverni, whose fidelity was with good reason regarded as doubtful by the Guises, had fled from Orleans, and by a forced march, which was nearly his death, he reached Écouen in ten hours. He there told the Connétable de Montmorency of the danger his nephew the Prince de Condé was in, and of the encroachments of the Guises. Anne de Montmorency, furious at learning that the Prince owed his life merely to the sudden illness of which Francis II. was dying, marched up with fifteen hundred horse and a hundred gentlemen under arms. The more effectually to surprise the Guises, he had avoided Paris, coming from Écouen to Corbeil, and from Corbeil to Pithiviers by the valley of the Essonne.

"Man to man, and both to pull, leaves to each but little wool!" he said, on the occasion of this dashing advance.

Anne de Montmorency, who had been the preserver of France when Charles V. invaded Provence, and the Duc de Guise, who had checked the Emperor's second attempt at Metz, were, in fact, the two greatest French warriors of their time.

Catherine had waited for the right moment to stir up the hatred of the man whom the Guises had overthrown. The Marquis de Simeuse, in command of the town of Gien, on hearing of the advance of so considerable a force as the connétable brought with him, sprang to horse, hoping to warn the Duke in time. The Queen-mother, meanwhile, certain that the connétable would come to his nephew's rescue and confident of the chancellor's devotion to the royal cause, had fanned the hopes and encouraged the spirit of the Reformed party. The Colignys and the adherents of the imperiled House of Bourbon had made common cause with the Queen-mother's partisans; a coalition between various antagonistic interests, attacked by a common foe, was silently formed in the Assembly of the States, where the question was boldly broached of making Catherine Regent of France in the event of the young King's death. Catherine herself, whose faith in astrology was far greater than her belief in church dogmas, had ventured to extremes against her foes when she saw her son dying at the end of the time fixed as his term of life by the famous soothsayer brought to the château de Chaumont by Nostradamus.

A few days before the terrible close of his reign, Francis II. had chosen to go out on the Loire, so as not to be in the town at the hour of the Prince de Condé's intended execution.  Having surrendered the Prince's head to the Cardinal de Lorraine, he feared a riot quite as much as he dreaded the supplications of the Princesse de Condé.  As he was embarking, a fresh breeze, such as often sweeps the Loire at the approach of winter, gave him so violent an earache that he was forced to return home; he went to bed, never to leave it alive.

In spite of the disagreement of the physicians, who, all but Chapelain, were his enemies and opponents, Ambroise Paré maintained that an abscess had formed in the head, and that if no outlet were pierced the chances of the King's death were greater every day.

In spite of the late hour and the rigorous enforcement of the curfew at that time in Orleans, which was ruled as in a state of siege, Paré's lamp was shining in his window where he was studying.  Lecamus called to him from below; and when he had announced his name, the surgeon gave orders that his old friend should be admitted.

"You give yourself no rest, Ambroise, and while saving the lives of others you will wear out your own," said the furrier as he went in.

Indeed, there sat the surgeon, his books open, his instruments lying about, and before him a skull not long since buried, dug up from the grave, and perforated.

"I must save the King."

"Then you are very sure you can, Ambroise?" said the old man, shuddering.

"As sure as I am alive. The King, my good old friend, has some evil humor festering on his brain, which will fill it up, and the danger is pressing; but by piercing the skull I let the matter out and free his head. I have already performed this operation three times; it was invented by a Piedmontese, and I have been so lucky as to improve upon it. The first time it was at the siege of Metz, on Monsieur de Pienne, whom I got out of the scrape, and who has only been all the wiser for it; the second time it saved the life of a poor man on whom I wished to test the certainty of this daring operation to which Monsieur de Pienne had submitted; the third time was on a gentleman in Paris, who is now perfectly well. Trepanning—for that is the name given to it—is as yet little known. The sufferers object to it on the score of the imperfection of the instrument, but that I have been able to improve. So now I am experimenting on this head, to be sure of not failing to-morrow on the King's."

"You must be very sure of yourself, for your head will be in danger if you——"

"I will wager my life that he is cured," replied Paré, with the confidence of genius. "Oh, my good friend, what is it to make a hole in a skull with due care? It is what soldiers do every day with no care at all."

"But do you know, my boy," said the citizen, greatly daring, "that if you save the King, you ruin France? Do you know that your instrument will place the crown of the Valois on the head of a Prince of Lorraine, calling himself the direct heir of Charlemagne? Do you know that surgery and politics are, at this moment, at daggers drawn? Yes, the triumph of your genius will be the overthrow of your religion. If the Guises retain the Regency, the blood of the Reformers will flow in streams! Be a great citizen rather than a great surgeon, and sleep through to-morrow morning, leaving the King's room free to those leeches who, if they do not save the King, will save France."

"I!" cried Paré.  "I—leave a man to die when I can cure him?  Never!  If I am to be hanged for a Calvinist, I will go to the castle, all the same, right early to-morrow.  Do you not know that the only favor I mean to ask, when I have savedt he King, is your Christophe's life?  That will surely be a moment when Queen Mary can refuse me nothing."

"Alas, my friend, has not the little King already refused the Princesse de Condé any pardon for her husband?  Do not kill your religion by enabling the man to live who ought to die."

"Are you going to puzzle yourself by trying to find out how God means to dispose of things in the future?" asked Paré.  "Honest folk have but one motto—'Do your duty, come what may.'  I did this at Calais when I set my foot on the Grand Master; I risked being cut down by all his friends and attendants, and here I am, surgeon to the King; I am a Reformer, and yet I can call the Guises my friends.  I will save the King!" cried the surgeon, with the sacred enthusiasm of conviction that genius knows, "and God will take care of France!"

There was a knock at the door, and a few minutes later one of Ambroise Paré's servants gave a note to Lecamus, who read aloud these ominous words:

"A scaffold is being erected at the Convent of the Récollets for the beheading of the Prince de Condé to-morrow."

Ambroise and Lecamus looked at each other, both overpowered with horror.

"I will go and make sure," said the furrier, bidding Ambroise Paré adieu.

Out on the square, Ruggieri took Lecamus by the arm, asking what was Paré's secret for saving the King; but the old man, fearing some treachery, insisted on going to see the scaffold.  So the astrologer and the furrier went together to the Récollets, where, in fact, they found carpenters at work by torchlight.

"Heyday, my friend," said old Lecamus to one of them; "what business is this?"

"We are preparing to hang some heretics, since the bleeding at Amboise did not cure them," said a young friar, who was superintending the workmen.

"Monseigneur the cardinal does well," replied the prudent Ruggieri. "But in my country we do even better."

"What do you do?"

"We burn them, brother."

Lecamus was obliged to lean on the astrologer; his legs refused to carry him, for he thought that his son might next day be swinging on one of those gibbets. The poor old man stood between two sciences—astrology and medicine; each promised to save his son, for whom the scaffold was visibly rising. In this confusion of mind he was as wax in the hands of the Florentine.

"Well, my most respectable vendor of furs, what have you to say to these pleasantries of Lorraine?" asked Ruggieri.

"Woe the day! You know I would give my own skin to see my boy's safe and sound."

"That is what I call talking like a skinner," replied the Italian. "But if you will explain to me the operation that Ambroise proposes to perform on the King, I will guarantee your son's life."

"Truly?" cried the old furrier.

"What shall I swear by?" said Ruggieri.

On this the unhappy old man repeated his conversation with Paré to the Italian, who was off, leaving the disconsolate father in the road the instant he had heard the great surgeon's secret.

"Whom the devil does he mean mischief to?" cried Lecamus, as he saw Ruggieri running at his utmost speed toward the Place de l'Estape.

Lecamus knew nothing of the terrible scene which was going on by the King's bedside, and which had led to the order being given for the erection of the scaffold for the Prince, who had been sentenced in default, as it were, though his execution was postponed for the moment by the King's illness.

There was no one in the hall, on the stairs, or in the court-yard of the bailiff's house but those on actual duty. The crowd of courtiers had resorted to the lodgings of the King of Navarre, who, by the law of the land, was Regent. The French nobles, terrified indeed by the insolence of the Guises, felt an impulse to close their ranks around the chief of the younger branch, seeing that the Queen-mother was subservient to the Guises, and not understanding her Italian policy. Antoine de Bourbon, faithful to his secret compact with Catherine, was not to renounce his claim to the Regency in her favor until the States-General should have voted on the question.

This absolute desertion had struck the Grand Master when, on his return from a walk through the town—as a precautionary measure—he found no one about the King but the friends dependent on his fortunes. The room where Francis II.'s bed had been placed adjoins the great hall of the bailiff's residence, and was at that time lined with oak paneling. The ceiling, formed of narrow boards, skillfully adjusted and painted, showed an arabesque pattern in blue on a gold ground, and a piece of it, pulled down about fifty years ago, has been preserved by a collector of antiquities. This room, hung with tapestry and the floor covered with carpet, was so dark that the burning tapers scarcely gave it light. The enormous bedstead, with four columnar posts and silk curtains, looked like a tomb. On one side of the bed, by the King's pillow, were Queen Mary and the Cardinal de Lorraine; on the other sat Catherine in an armchair. The physician-in-ordinary, the famous Jean Chapelain, afterward in attendance on Charles IX., was standing by the fireplace. Perfect silence reigned.

The young King, pale and slight, lost in the sheets, was hardly to be seen, with his small, puckered face on the pillow. The Duchesse de Guise, seated on a stool, was supporting Mary Stewart; and near Catherine, in a window recess, Madame de Fieschi was watching the Queen-mother's looks and gestures, for she fully understood the great peril of her position.

In the great hall, notwithstanding the late hour, Monsieur de Cypierre, the Duc d'Orléans' tutor, appointed to be governor of the town, occupied a chimney-corner with the two Gondis. Cardinal de Tournon, who at this crisis had taken part with Queen Catherine, on finding himself treated as an inferior by the Cardinal de Lorraine, whose equal he undoubtedly was in the church, was conversing in a low voice with the brothers Gondi. The Maréchal de Vieilleville and Monsieur de Saint-André, keeper of the seals, were discussing in whispers the imminent danger of the Guises.

The Duc de Guise crossed the hall, glancing hastily about him, and bowed to the Duc d'Orléans, whom he recognized.

"Monseigneur," said he, "this may give you a lesson in the knowledge of men. The Catholic nobility of the kingdom have crowded round a heretic prince, believing that the States assembled will place the Regency in the hands of the heir to the traitor who so long kept your illustrious grandfather a prisoner."

And after this speech, which was calculated to make a deep impression on a prince's mind, he went into the bedroom where the young King was lying, not so much asleep as heavily drowsy. As a rule, the Duc de Guise had the art of overcoming, by his affable expression, the sinister appearance of his scarred features; but at this moment he could not force a smile, seeing the instrument of power quite broken. The cardinal, whose civic courage was equal to his brother's military valor, came forward a step or two to meet the lieutenant-general.

"Robertet believes that little Pinard has been bought over by the Queen-mother," he said in his ear, as he led him back into the hall. "He has been made use of to work on the members of the Assembly."

"Bah! what matters our being betrayed by a secretary, when there is treason everywhere?" cried the Duke. "The town is for the Reformers, and we are on the eve of a revolt. Yes! the *Guépins* are malcontents," he added, giving the people of Orleans their common nickname, "and if Paré cannot save the King, we shall see a desperate outbreak. Before long we shall have to lay siege to Orleans, which is a vermin's nest of Huguenots."

"In the last minute," said the cardinal, "I have been watching that Italian woman, who sits there without a spark of feeling. She is waiting for her son's death, God forgive her! I wonder whether it would not be well to arrest her and the King of Navarre too."

"It is more than enough to have the Prince de Condé in prison," replied the Duke.

The sound of a horse ridden at top-speed came up from the gate. The two Princes went to the window, and, by the light of the gatekeeper's torch and of the cresset that was always burning under the gateway, the Duke recognized in the rider's hat the famous cross of Lorraine, which the cardinal had made the badge of their partisans. He sent one of the men-at-arms, who stood in the anteroom, to say that the new-comer was to be admitted; and he went to the head of the stairs to meet him, followed by his brother.

"What is the news, my dear Simeuse?" asked the Duke, with the charming manner he always had for a soldier, as he recognized the Commandant of Gien.

"The connétable is entering Pithiviers; he left Écouen with fifteen hundred horse and a hundred gentlemen——"

"Have they any following?" said the Duke.

"Yes, monseigneur," replied Simeuse. "There are two thousand six hundred of them in all. Some say that Thoré is behind with a troop of infantry. If Montmorency amuses himself with waiting for his son, you have time before you to undo him."

"And that is all you know? Are his motives for this rush to arms commonly reported?"

"Anne speaks as little as he writes; do you go and meet him, brother, while I will greet him here with his nephew's head," said the cardinal, ordering an attendant to fetch Robertet.

"Vieilleville," cried the Duke to the marshal, who came in, "the Connétable de Montmorency has dared to take up arms. If I go out to meet him, will you be responsible for keeping order in the town?"

"The instant you are out of it, the townsfolk will rise; and who can foresee the issue of a fray between horsemen and citizens in such narrow streets?" replied the marshal.

"My lord!" said Robertet, flying up the stairs, "the chancellor is at the gates and insists on coming in; are we to admit him?"

"Yes, admit him," said the Cardinal de Lorraine. "The constable and the chancellor together would be too dangerous; we must keep them apart. We were finely tricked by the Queen-mother when we elected l'Hôpital to that office."

Robertet nodded to a captain who awaited the reply at the foot of the stairs, and returned quickly to take the cardinal's orders.

"My lord," said he, making a last effort, "I take the liberty of representing to you that the sentence requires the approval of the King in Council. If you violate the law for a Prince of the Blood, it will not be respected in favor of a cardinal or of a Duc de Guise."

"Pinard has disturbed your mind, Robertet," said the

cardinal sternly. "Do you not know that the King signed the warrant on the day when he went out, leaving it to us to carry it out?"

"Though you are almost requiring my head of me when you give me this duty—which, however, will be that of the town-provost—I obey, my lord."

The Grand Master heard the debate without wincing; but he took his brother by the arm and led him to a corner of the hall.

"Of course," said he, "the direct heirs of Charlemagne have the right to take back the crown which was snatched from their family by Hugues Capet; but—can they? The pear is not ripe. Our nephew is dying, and all the Court is gone over to the King of Navarre."

"The King's heart failed him; but for that, the Béarnais would have been stabbed," replied the cardinal, "and we could easily have disposed of the children."

"We are in a bad position here," said the Duke. "The revolt in the town will be supported by the States-General. L'Hôpital, whom we have befriended so well and whose elevation Queen Catherine opposed, is now our foe, and we need the law on our side. The Queen-mother has too many adherents now to allow of our sending her away. And, beside, there are three more boys!"

"She is no longer a mother; she is nothing but a queen," said the cardinal. "In my opinion, this is the very moment to be rid of her. Energy, and again energy! that is what I prescribe."

Having said this, the cardinal went back into the King's room, and the Duke followed him. The prelate then went straight up to Catherine.

"The papers found on La Sagne, the Prince de Condé's secretary, have been communicated to you," said he. "You know that the Bourbons mean to dethrone your children?"

"I know it all," said the Queen.

"Well, then, will you not have the King of Navarre arrested?"

"There is a lieutenant-general of the kingdom," replied she.

At this moment Francis complained of the most violent pain in his ear, and began to moan lamentably. The physician left the fireplace, where he was warming himself, and came to examine the patient's head.

"Well, monsieur?" said the Grand Master, addressing him.

"I dare not apply a compress to draw the evil humors. Master Ambroise has undertaken to save his majesty by an operation, and I should annoy him by doing so."

"Put it off till to-morrow," said Catherine calmly, "and be present, all of you medical men; for you know what calumnies the death of a prince gives ground for."

She kissed her son's hands and withdrew.

"How coolly that audacious trader's daughter can speak of the Dauphin's death, poisoned as he was by Montecuculi, a Florentine of her suite!" cried Mary Stewart.

"Marie," said the little King, "my grandfather never cast a suspicion on her innocence."

"Can we not hinder that woman from coming here to-morrow?" said the Queen in an undertone to her two uncles.

"What would become of us if the King should die?" replied the cardinal. "Catherine would hurl us all into his grave."

And so that night the question stood plainly stated between Catherine de' Medici and the House of Lorraine. The arrival of the chancellor and the Connétable de Montmorency pointed to rebellion, and the dawn of the morrow would prove decisive.

On the following day the Queen-mother was the first to appear. She found no one in her son's room but Mary Stewart, pale and fatigued from having passed the night in prayer by the bedside. The Duchesse de Guise had kept the Queen company, and the maids of honor had relieved each other. The young King was asleep.

Neither the Duke nor the cardinal had yet appeared. The prelate, more daring than the soldier, had spent this last night, it is said, in vehement argument, without being able to induce the Duke to proclaim himself King. With the States-General sitting in the town, and the prospect of a battle to be fought with the constable, the Balafré did not think the opportunity favorable; he refused to arrest the Queen-mother, the chancellor, Cardinal de Tournon, the Gondis, Ruggieri, and Birague, in face of the revolt that would inevitably result from such violent measures. He made his brother's schemes dependent on the life of Francis II.

Perfect silence reigned in the King's bedchamber. Catherine, attended by Madame de Fieschi, came to the bedside and gazed at her son with an admirable assumption of grief. She held her handkerchief to her eyes and retreated to the window, where Madame de Fieschi brought her a chair. From thence she could look down into the courtyard.

It had been agreed between Catherine and the Cardinal de Tournon that if Montmorency got safely into the town, he, the cardinal, would come to her, accompanied by the two Gondis; in case of disaster, he was to come alone. At nine in the morning the two Princes of Lorraine, accompanied by their suite, who remained in the hall, came to the King's room. The captain on duty had informed them that Ambroise Paré had but just arrived with Chapelain and three other physicians, prompted by Catherine de' Medici, and all hating Ambroise Paré.

In a few minutes the great hall of the bailliage presented precisely the same appearance as the guardroom at Blois on the day when the Duc de Guise was appointed lieutenant-general of the kingdom, and when Christophe was tortured; with only this difference, that then love and glee reigned in the royal rooms, and that the Guises were triumphant;

whereas now death and grief prevailed, and the Princes of Lorraine felt the power slipping from their grasp.

The maids of honor of the two Queens were grouped on opposite sides of the great fireplace, where an immense fire was blazing.   The room was full of courtiers.

The news, repeated no one knows by whom, of a bold plan of Ambroise Paré's for saving the King's life, brought in every gentleman who had any right to appear at Court.   The outer steps of the house and the courtyard were thronged with anxious groups.   The scaffold erected for the Prince, opposite the convent of the Récollets, astonished all the nobles.   People spoke in whispers, and here, as at Blois, the conversation was a medley of serious and frivolous subjects, of grave and trivial talk.   They were beginning to feel used to turmoils, to sudden rebellion, to a rush to arms, to revolts, to the great and sudden events which marked the long period during which the House of Valois was dying out, in spite of Queen Catherine's efforts.   Deep silence was kept for some distance outside the bedroom door, where two men-at-arms were on guard, with two pages, and the captain of the Scotch company.

Antoine de Bourbon,* a prisoner in his lodgings, finding himself neglected, understood the hopes of the courtiers; he was overwhelmed at hearing of the preparations made during the night for his brother's execution.

In front of the hall fireplace stood one of the finest and grandest figures of his time, the Chancellor de l'Hôpital, in his crimson robes bordered with ermine, and wearing his square cap, in right of his office.   This brave man, regarding his benefactors as the leaders of a rebellion, had espoused the cause of his king, as represented by the Queen-mother; and, at the risk of his head, he had gone to Écouen to consult the Connétable de Montmorency.   No one dared to disturb the meditations in which he was plunged.   Robertet, the secretary of state, two marshals of France, Vieilleville and Saint-

* Antony, King of Navarre, husband of Jeanne d'Albret.

André, and the keeper of the seals, formed a group in front of the chancellor.

The men of the Court were not actually laughing, but their tone was sprightly, especially among those who were disaffected to the Guises.

The cardinal had at last secured Stewart, the Scotchman who had murdered President Minard, and was arranging for his trial at Tours. He had also confined in the Castles of Blois and of Tours a considerable number of gentlemen who had seemed compromised, to inspire a certain degree of terror in the nobles; they, however, were not terrified, but saw in the Reformation a fulcrum for the love of resistance they derived from a feeling of their inborn equality with the King. Now, the prisoners at Blois had contrived to escape, and, by a singular fatality, those who had been shut up at Tours had just followed their example.

"Madame," said the Cardinal de Châtillon to Madame de Fieschi, "if any one takes an interest in the prisoners from Tours, they are in the greatest danger."

On hearing this speech, the chancellor looked round at the group of the elder Queen's maids of honor.

"Yes, for young Desvaux, the Prince de Condé's equerry, who was imprisoned at Tours, added a bitter jest to his escape. He is said to have written a note to Messieurs de Guise to this effect:

"'We have heard of the escape of your prisoners at Blois; it has grieved us so much that we are about to run after them; we will bring them back to you as soon as we have arrested them.'"

Though he relished this pleasantry, the chancellor looked sternly at Monsieur de Châtillon.

At this instant louder voices were heard in the King's bed-chamber. The two marshals, with Robertet and the chancellor, went forward, for it was not merely a question of life and death to the King; everybody was in the secret of the danger to the chancellor, to Catherine, and to her adherents. The silence that ensued was absolute.

Ambroise had examined the King; the moment seemed favorable for the operation; if it were not performed he might die at any moment. As soon as the brothers de Guise came in, he explained to them the causes of the King's sufferings, and demonstrated that in such extremities trepanning was absolutely necessary. He only awaited the decision of the physicians.

"Pierce my son's skull as if it were a board, and with that horrible instrument!" cried Catherine de' Medici. "Master Ambroise, I will not permit it."

The doctors were consulting, but Catherine spoke so loud that, as she intended, her words were heard in the outer room.

"But, madame, if that is the only hope of saving him?" said Mary Stewart, weeping.

"Ambroise," said Catherine, "remember that you answer for the King with your head."

"We are opposed to the means proposed by Master Ambroise," said the three physicians. "The King may be saved by injecting a remedy into the ear which will release the humors through that passage."

The Duc de Guise, who was studying Catherine's face, suddenly went up to her and led her into the window-bay, apart from the throng.

"You, madame," said he, "wish your son to die; you are in collusion with your enemies, and that since we came from. Blois. This morning Councilor Viole told your furrier's son that the Prince de Condé was to be beheaded. That young man, who, under torture, had denied all knowledge of the Prince de Condé, gave him a farewell greeting as he passed the window of the lad's prison. You looked on at

13

your hapless accomplice's sufferings with royal indifference. Now, you are opposed to your eldest son's life being saved. You will force us to believe that the death of the Dauphin, which placed the crown on the head of the late King, was not natural, but that Montecuculi was your——"

"Monsieur le Chancelier!" Catherine called out, and at this signal Madame de Fieschi threw open the double doors of the bedchamber.

The persons assembled in the hall could thus see the whole scene in the King's room : the little King, deadly pale, his features sunk, his eyes dim, but repeating the word "Marie," while he held the hand of the young Queen, who was weeping ; the Duchesse de Guise standing, terrified by Catherine's audacity ; the two Princes of Lorraine, not less anxious, but keeping close to the Queen-mother, and resolved to have her arrested by Maillé-Brézé ; and, finally, the great surgeon Ambroise Paré, with the King's physician.   He stood holding his instruments, but not daring to perform the operation, for which perfect quiet was as necessary as the approbation of the medical authorities.

"Monsieur le Chancelier," said Catherine, "Messieurs de Guise wish to authorize a strange operation on the King's person.   Ambroise proposes to perforate his head.   I, as his mother, and one of the commission of Regency, protest against what seems to me to be high treason.   The three physicians are in favor of an injection which, to me, seems quite as efficacious and less dangerous than the cruel process recommended by Ambroise."

At these words there was a dull murmur in reply.   The cardinal admitted the chancellor, and then shut the bedroom doors.

"But I am lieutenant-general of the realm," said the Duc de Guise, "and you must understand, Monsieur de Chancelier, that Ambroise, surgeon to his majesty, answers for the King's life."

"Well, since this is the state of affairs," said the great Ambroise Paré, "I know what to be doing."

He put out his arm over the bed.

"This bed and the King are mine," said he. "I constitute myself the sole master, and singly responsible; I know the duties of my office, and I will operate on the King without the physicians' sanction."

"Save him!" cried the cardinal, "and you shall be the richest man in France."

"Only go on," said Mary Stewart, pressing Paré's hand.

"I cannot interfere," said the chancellor, "but I shall record the Queen-mother's protest."

"Robertet," the Duc de Guise called out.

Robertet came in, and the Duke pointed to the chancellor.

"You are Chancellor of France," he said, "in the place of this felon. Monsieur de Maillé, take Monsieur de l'Hôpital to prison with the Prince de Condé. As to you, madame," and he turned to Catherine, "your protest will not be recognized, and you would do well to remember that such actions need the support of adequate force. I am acting as a faithful and loyal subject of King Francis II., my sovereign. Proceed, Ambroise," he said to the surgeon.

"Monsieur de Guise," said l'Hôpital, "if you use any violence, either on the person of the King or on that of his chancellor, remember that in the hall without there is enough French nobility to arrest all traitors."

"Gentlemen, gentlemen," said the surgeon, "if you prolong this debate, you may as well shout 'Vive Charles IX.,' for King Francis is dying."

Catherine stood unmoved, looking out of the window.

"Well, then, we will use force to remain masters in the King's bedroom," said the cardinal, trying to keep the door; but he was startled and horrified, for the great hall was quite deserted. The Court, sure that the King was dying, had gone back to Antoine of Navarre.

"Come; do it, do it!" cried Mary Stewart to Ambroise. "I and you, Duchess," she said to Madame de Guise, "will protect you."

"Nay, madame," said Paré, "my zeal carried me too far; the doctors, with the exception of my friend Chapelain, are in favor of the injection; I must yield to them. If I were physician and surgeon-in-chief, he could be saved! Give it to me," he said, taking a small syringe from the hand of the chief physician and filling it.

"Good God!" cried Mary Stewart; "I command you to——"

"Alas! madame," replied Paré, "I am subordinate to these gentlemen."

The young Queen and the Duchesse de Guise stood between the surgeon and the doctors and the other persons present. The chief physician held the King's head, and Ambroise made the injection into the ear. The two Princes of Lorraine were watchful; Robertet and Monsieur de Maillé stood motionless. At a sign from Catherine, Madame de Fieschi left the room unnoticed. At the same instant l'Hôpital boldly threw open the door of the King's bedroom.

"I have arrived in the nick of time," exclaimed a man, whose hasty steps rang through the hall, and who, in another minute, was at the door of the King's room. "What, gentlemen! You thought to cut off my fine nephew, the Prince de Condé's head? You have roused the lion from his lair, and here he is!" added the Connétable de Montmorency. "Ambroise, you are not to stir up my King's brains with your instruments! The Kings of France do not allow themselves to be knocked about in that way unless by their enemies' sword in fair fight! The first Prince of the Blood, Antoine de Bourbon, the Prince de Condé, the Queen-mother, and the chancellor are all opposed to the operation."

"YOU, MADAME, HAVE KILLED YOUR SON!"
SAID MARY STEWART.

To Catherine's great satisfaction, the King of Navarre and the Prince de Condé both made their appearance.

"What is the meaning of this?" said the Duc de Guise, laying his hand on his poniard.

"As lord high constable, I have dismissed all the sentinels from their posts. Blood and thunder! we are not in an enemy's country, I suppose. The King our master is surrounded by his subjects, and the States-General of the realm may deliberate in perfect liberty. I have just come from the Assembly, gentlemen; I laid before it the protest of my nephew de Condé, who has been rescued by three hundred gentlemen. You meant to let the royal blood and to decimate the nobility of France. Henceforth I shall not trust anything you propose, Messieurs de Lorraine. And if you give the order for the King's head to be opened, by this sword, which saved France from Charles V., I say it shall not be done——!"

"All the more so," said Ambroise Paré, "because it is too late, suffusion has begun."

"Your reign is over, gentlemen," said Catherine to the two Guises, seeing from Paré's manner that there was now no hope.

"You, madame, have killed your son!" said Mary Stewart, springing like a lioness from the bed to the window, and seizing the Italian Queen by the arm with a vehement clutch.

"My dear," replied Catherine de' Medici, with a keen, cold look that expressed the hatred she had suppressed for six months past, "you, to whose violent passion this death is due, will now go to reign over your own Scotland—and you will go to-morrow. I am now Regent in fact as well as in name."

The three physicians had made a sign to the Queen-mother.

"Gentlemen," she went on, addressing the Guises, "it is an understood thing between Monsieur de Bourbon—whom I hereby appoint lieutenant-general of the kingdom—and myself that the conduct of affairs is our business. Come, Monsieur le Chancellor."

"The King is dead!" said the Grand Master, obliged to carry out the functions of his office.

"God save King Charles IX.!" cried the gentlemen who had come with the King of Navarre, the Prince de Condé, and the constable.

The ceremonies performed when a King of France dies were carried out in solitude. When the king-at-arms called out three times in the great hall, "The King is dead!" after the official announcement by the Duc de Guise, there were but a few persons present to answer—"God save the King!"

The Queen-mother, to whom the Countess Fieschi brought the Duc d'Orleans, now Charles IX., left the room leading the boy by the hand, and followed by the whole Court. Only the two Guises, the Duchesse de Guise, Mary Stewart, and Dayelle remained in the room where Francis II. had breathed his last, with two guards at the door, the Grand Master's pages and the cardinal's, and their two private secretaries.

"Vive la France!" shouted some of the Reformers, a first cry of opposition.

Robertet, who owed everything to the Duke and the cardinal, terrified by their schemes and their abortive attempts, secretly attached himself to the Queen-mother, whom the ambassadors of Spain, England, the German Empire, and Poland met on the stairs, at their head Cardinal Tournon, who had gone to call them after looking up from the courtyard to Catherine de' Medici just as she was protesting against Ambroise Paré's operation.

"Well, the sons of Louis d'Outre-Mer,* the descendants of Charles de Lorraine, have proved cravens," said the cardinal to the Duke.

"They would have been packed off to Lorraine," replied his brother. "I declare to you, Charles," he went on, "if the crown were there for the taking, I would not put out my hand for it. That will be my son's task."

* From over the sea.

"Will he ever have the army and the church on his side as you have?"

"He will have something better."

"What?"

"The people."

"And there is no one to mourn for him but me—the poor boy who loved me so well!" said Mary Stewart, holding the cold hand of her first husband.

"How can we be reconciled to the Queen?" said the cardinal.

"Wait till she quarrels with the Huguenots," said the Duchess.

The clashing interests of the House of Bourbon, of Catherine, of the Guises, and of the Reformers produced such confusion in Orleans that it was not till three days after that the King's body, quite forgotten where it lay, was placed in a coffin by obscure serving men, and carried to Saint-Denis in a covered vehicle, followed only by the Bishop of Senlis and two gentlemen. When this dismal little procession arrived at the town of Etampes, a follower of the Chancellor de l'Hôpital attached to the hearse this bitter inscription, which history has recorded : "Tanneguy du Chastel, where are you? Yet you, too, were French!" A stinging innuendo, striking at Catherine, Mary Stewart, and the Guises. For what Frenchman does not know that Tanneguy du Chastel spent thirty thousand crowns (a million of francs in these days) on the obsequies of Charles VII., the founder and benefactor of his family?

As soon as the tolling bells announced the death of Francis II., and the Connétable de Montmorency had thrown open the gates of the town, Tourillon went up to his hayloft and made his way to a hiding-place.

"What, can he be dead?" exclaimed the glover.

On hearing the voice, a man rose and replied, "*Prêt à*

*servir*" ("Ready to serve," or "Ready, aye ready"), the watchword of the Reformers of Calvin's sect.

This man was Chaudieu, to whom Tourillon related the events of the past week, during which he had left the preacher alone in his hiding-place with a twelve-ounce loaf for his sole sustenance.

"Be off to the Prince de Condé, brother, ask him for a safe-conduct for me, and find me a horse," cried the preacher. "I must set out this moment."

"Write him a line, then, that I may be admitted."

"Here," said Chaudieu, after writing a few lines, "ask for a pass from the King of Navarre, for under existing circumstances I must hasten to Geneva."

Within two hours all was ready, and the zealous minister was on his way to Geneva, escorted by one of the King of Navarre's gentlemen, whose secretary Chaudieu was supposed to be, and who was the bearer of instructions to the Reformed party in Dauphiné.

Chaudieu's sudden departure was at once permitted, to further the interests of Queen Catherine, who, to gain time, made a bold suggestion which was kept a profound secret. This startling scheme accounts for the agreement so unexpectedly arrived at between the Queen and the leaders of the Protestant party. The crafty woman had, as a guarantee of her good faith, expressed a desire to heal the breach between the two churches in an assembly which could be neither a Synod, nor a Council, nor a Convocation, for which indeed a new name was needed, and, above all else, Calvin's consent. It may be said in passing that, when this mystery came out, it led to the alliance of the Guises with the Connétable de Montmorency against Catherine and the King of Navarre—a strange coalition, known to history as the Triumvirate, because the Maréchal de Saint-André was the third person in this purely Catholic combination, to which Catherine's strange proposal for a meeting gave rise. The Guises were then enabled to judge very shrewdly of Catherine's policy; they saw that the Queen cared little enough for this assembly, and only wanted to temporize with her allies till Charles IX. should be of age; indeed, they deceived Montmorency by making him believe in a collusion between Catherine and the Bourbons, while Catherine was taking them all in. The Queen, it will be seen, had in a short time made great strides.

The spirit of argument and discussion which was then in the air was particularly favorable to this scheme. The Catholics and the Huguenots were all to shine in turn in this tournament of words. Indeed, that is exactly what happened. Is it not extraordinary that historians should have mistaken the Queen's shrewdest craft for hesitancy? Catherine never went more directly to the end she had in view than when she seemed to have turned her back on it. So the King of Navarre, incapable of fathoming Catherine's motives, dispatched Chaudieu to Calvin; Chaudieu having secretly intended to watch the course of events at Orleans, where he ran, every hour, the risk of being seized and hanged without trial, like any man who had been condemned to banishment.

At the rate of traveling then possible Chaudieu could not reach Geneva before the month of February, the negotiations could not be completed until March, and the meeting could not be called until the beginning of May, 1561. Catherine intended to amuse the Court meanwhile, and lull party-feeling by the King's coronation, and by his first bed of justice in the Parlement when L'Hôpital and de Thou passed the royal letter, by which Charles IX. intrusted the government of the kingdom to his mother, seconded by Antoine de Navarre as lieutenant-general of the realm—the weakest prince of his time.

Was it not one of the strangest things of that day to see a whole kingdom in suspense for the Yea or Nay of a French citizen, risen from obscurity, and living at Geneva? The Pope of Rome held in check by the new Pope of Geneva?

The two Princes of Lorraine, once so powerful, paralyzed by a brief concord between the first Prince of the Blood, the Queen-mother, and Calvin?  Is it not one of the most pregnant lessons that history has preserved to kings, a lesson that should teach them to judge of men, to give genius its due without any hesitation, and to seek it out, as Louis XIV. did, wherever God has hidden it?

Calvin, whose real name was not Calvin, but Cauvin, was the son of a cooper at Noyon, in Picardy.  Calvin's birth-place accounts to a certain degree for the obstinacy mingled with eccentric irritability which characterized the arbiter of the destinies of France in the sixteenth century.  No one is less known than this man, who was the maker of Geneva and of the spirit of its people.  Jean-Jacques Rousseau, who knew little of history, was utterly ignorant of this man's influence on his Republic.

At first, indeed, Calvin, dwelling in one of the humblest houses in the upper town, near the Protestant church of Saint-Pierre, over a carpenter's shop—one point of resemblance between him and Robespierre—had no great authority in Geneva.  His influence was for a long time checked by the hatred of the Genevese.

In the sixteenth century Geneva could boast of Farel, one of those famous citizens who have remained unknown to the world, some of them even to Geneva itself.  In the year 1537, or thereabouts, this Farel attached Calvin to Geneva by pointing out to him that it might become the stronghold of a reformation more thorough than that of Luther.  Farel and Cauvin looked on Lutheranism as an incomplete achievement, ineffectual, and with no hold on France.  Geneva, lying between France and Italy, speaking the French tongue, was admirably placed for communicating with Germany, Italy, and France.  Calvin adopted Geneva as the seat of his spiritual fortunes, and made it the citadel of his dogmas.  At Farel's request, the town council of Geneva authorized Calvin to lecture on theology in the month of September, 1538. Calvin left preaching to Farel, his first disciple, and patiently devoted himself to teaching his doctrine. His authority, which in the later years of his life was paramount, took long to establish. The great leader met with serious difficulties; he was even banished from Geneva for some time in consequence of the austerity of his doctrines. There was a party of very good folk who clung to their old luxury and the customs of their fathers. But, as is always the case, these worthy people dreaded ridicule; they would not admit what was the real object of their struggles, and the battle was fought over details apart from the real question.

Calvin insisted on leavened bread being used for the sacrament, and on there being no holy days but Sunday. These innovations were disapproved of at Berne and at Lausanne. The Genevese were required to conform to the ritual of Switzerland. Calvin and Farel resisted; their political enemies made a pretext of this refractoriness to exile them from Geneva, whence they were banished for some years. At a later period Calvin came back in triumph, invited by his flock.

Such persecution is always a consecration of moral power when the prophet can wait. And this return was the era of this Mahomet. Executions began, and Calvin organized his religious terror. As soon as this commanding spirit reappeared, he was admitted to the citizenship of Geneva; but, after fourteen years' residence there, he was not yet on the Council. At the time when Catherine was dispatching a minister to treat with him, this king in the realm of thought had no title but that of pastor of the church of Geneva. Indeed, Calvin never had more than a hundred and fifty francs a year in money, fifteen hundredweight of grain, and two casks of wine for his whole remuneration. His brother, a tailor, kept a shop a few paces away from the Place Saint-Pierre, in a street where one of Calvin's printing-places may still be seen.

Such disinterestedness, which in Voltaire and Bacon was lacking, but which is conspicuous in the life of Rabelais, of Campanella, of Luther, of Vico, of Descartes, of Malebranche, of Spinoza, of Loyola, of Kant, and of Jean-Jacques Rousseau, surely forms a noble setting for these sublime and ardent souls.

Robespierre's life, so like that of Calvin, can alone, perhaps, enable our contemporaries to understand Calvin's.   He, founding his power on a similar basis, was as cruel and as tyrannical as the Arras lawyer.   It is strange, too, that Picardy —Arras and Noyon—should have given to the world these two great instruments of reform.   Those who examine into the motives of the executions ordered by Calvin will find, on a different scale, no doubt, all of 1793 at Geneva.   Calvin had Jacques Gruet beheaded "for having written impious letters and worldly verse, and labored to overthrow church ordinances."   Just consider this sentence, and ask yourself if the worst despotism can show in its annals a more absurdly preposterous indictment.

Valentin Gentilis, condemned to death for involuntary heresy, escaped the scaffold only by making more humiliating amends than ever were inflicted by the Catholic church. Seven years before the conference presently to be held in Calvin's house, on the Queen-mother's proposals, Michel Servet (or Servetus), a Frenchman, passing through Geneva, was put in prison, tried, condemned on Calvin's testimony, and burnt alive for having attacked the mystery of the trinity in a work which had not been either composed or printed at Geneva.   Compare with this the eloquent defense of Jean-Jacques Rousseau, whose book, attacking the Catholic religion, written in France and published in Holland, was indeed burnt by the hand of the executioner ; but the writer, a foreigner, was only banished from the kingdom, where he had been trying to strike at the fundamental truths of religion

NOTE.—Up to 1561 the Lutherans and Calvinists were one.

and government; and compare the conduct of the Parlement with that of the Genevese tyrant.

Bolsée, again, was brought to judgment for having other ideas than Calvin on the subject of predestination. Weigh all this, and say whether Fouquier-Tinville did anything worse. Calvin's fierce religious intolerance was, morally speaking, more intense, more implacable, than the fierce political intolerance of Robespierre. On a wider stage than was offered by Geneva, Calvin would have shed more blood than the terrible apostle of political equality, as compared with Catholic equality.

Three centuries earlier a monk, also a son of Picardy, had led the whole of Western Europe to invade the East. Peter the Hermit, Calvin, and Robespierre, sons of the same soil, at intervals of three centuries, were, in a political sense, the levers of Archimedes. Each in turn was an embodied idea finding its fulcrum in the interests of man.

Calvin is, beyond doubt, the—almost unrecognized—maker of that dismal town of Geneva, where, only ten years since, a man, pointing out a carriage gate—the first in the town, for till then there had only been house-doors in Geneva—said, "Through that gate luxury drove into Geneva." Calvin, by the severity of his sentences and the austerity of his doctrine, introduced the hypocritical feeling that has been well called Puritanism [the nearest English equivalent perhaps to the French word *mômerie*]. Good conduct, according to the *mômiers* or puritans, lay in renouncing the arts and the graces of life, in eating well but without luxury, and in silently amassing money without enjoying it otherwise than as Calvin enjoyed his power—in fancy.

Calvin clothed the citizens in the same gloomy livery as he threw over life in general. He formed in the Consistory a perfect Calvinist inquisition, exactly like the revolutionary tribunal instituted by Robespierre. The Consistory handed over the victims to be condemned by the Council, which

Calvin ruled through the Consistory just as Robespierre ruled the Convention through the Jacobin Club. Thus an eminent magistrate of Geneva was sentenced to two months' imprisonment, to lose his office, and to be prohibited from ever filling any other, because he led a dissolute life and had made friends among Calvin's foes. In this way Calvin was actually a legislator; it was he who created the austere manners, sober, respectable, hideously dull, but quite irreproachable, which have remained unchanged in Geneva to this day; they prevailed there indeed before the English habits were formed that are universally known as Puritanism, under the influence of the Cameronians, the followers of Caméron, a Frenchman who trod in Calvin's steps. These manners have been admirably described by Walter Scott.

The poverty of this man, an absolute sovereign, who treated as a power with other powers, asking for their treasure, demanding armies, and filling his hands with their money for the poor, proves that the Idea, regarded as the sole means of dominion, begets political misers, men whose only enjoyment is intellectual, and who, like the jesuits, love power for its own sake. Pitt, Luther, Calvin, and Robespierre, all these *Harpagons* in greed of dominion, died penniless. History has preserved the inventory made in Calvin's room after his death, and everything, including his books, was valued at fifty crowns. Luther's possessions amounted to as much; indeed, his widow, the famous Catherine de Bora, was obliged to petition for a pension of fifty crowns bestowed on her by a German Elector.

Potemkim, Mazarin, and Richelieu, men of thought and action, who all three founded or prepared the foundations of empires, each left three hundred millions of francs; but these men had a heart, they loved women and the arts, they built and conquered; while, with the exception of Luther, whose wife was the Helen of this Iliad, none of the others could accuse himself of ever having felt his heart throb for a woman.

This brief history was needed to explain Calvin's position at Geneva.

One day early in February, 1561, on one of the mild evenings which occur at that time of year on the shores of Lake Leman, two men on horseback arrived at Pré-l'Evêque, so-called from the ancient residence of the Bishop of Geneva, driven out thirty years before. These two men, acquainted, no doubt, with the laws of Geneva as to the closing of the gates, very necessary then, and absurd enough in these days, rode toward the Porte de Rives ; but they suddenly drew rein at the sight of a man of fifty, walking with the help of a woman-servant's arm, and evidently returning to the town. This personage, rather stout in figure, walked slowly and with difficulty, dragging one foot before the other with evident pain, and wearing broad, laced shoes of black velvet.

"It is he," said Chaudieu's companion, who dismounted, gave his bridle to the preacher, and went forward open-armed to meet the master.

The man on foot, who was in fact Jean Calvin, drew back to avoid the embrace, and cast the severest glance at his disciple. At the age of fifty Calvin looked like a man of seventy. Thick-set and fat, he seemed all the shorter because frightful pain from the stone obliged him to walk much bent. These sufferings were complicated with attacks of the worst form of gout. Anybody might have quaked at the aspect of that face, almost as broad as it was long, and bearing no more signs of good-nature, in spite of its roundness, than that of the dreadful King Henry VIII., whom Calvin, in fact, resembled. His sufferings, which never gave him a reprieve, were visible in two deep furrows on each side of his nose, following the line of his mustache, and ending, like it, in a full gray beard.

This face, though red and inflamed like a drunkard's, showed patches where his complexion was yellow ; still, and in spite of the velvet cap that covered his massive, broad head, it was possible to admire a large and nobly formed fore-head, and beneath it two sparkling brown eyes, which in moments of wrath could flash fire. Whether by reason of his bulk, or because his neck was too thick and short, or, as a consequence of late hours and incessant work, Calvin's head seemed sunk between his broad shoulders, which compelled him to wear a quite shallow, pleated ruff, on which his face rested like John the Baptist's in the charger. Between his mustache and his beard there peeped, like a rose, a sweet and eloquent mouth, small, and fresh, and perfectly formed. This face was divided by a square nose remarkable for its long aquiline outline, resulting in high-lights at the tip, significantly in harmony with the prodigious power expressed in this magnificent head.

Though it was difficult to detect in these features any trace of the constant headaches which tormented Calvin in the intervals of a slow fever that was consuming him, pain, constantly defied by study and a strong will, gave this apparently florid face a terrible tinge, attributable, no doubt, to the hue of the layer of fat due to the sedentary habits of a hard worker. It bore the marks of the perpetual struggle of a sickly temperament against one of the strongest wills known in the history of mankind. Even the lips, though beautiful, expressed cruelty. A chaste life, indispensable to vast projects, and compulsory in such conditions of sickly health, had set its stamp on the face. There was regret in the serenity of that mighty brow, and suffering in the gaze of the eyes, whose calmness was a terror.

Calvin's dress gave effect to his head, for he wore the famous black cloth gown, belted with a cloth band and brass buckle, which was adopted as the costume of Calvinist preachers, and which, having nothing to attract the eye, directed all the spectator's attention to the face.

"I am in too great pain to embrace you, Théodore," said Calvin to the elegant horseman.

Théodore de Bèze, at that time two-and-forty, and, by Calvin's desire, a free citizen of Geneva for two years past, was the most striking contrast to the terrible minister to whom he had given his allegiance. Calvin, like all men of the middle-class who have risen to moral supremacy, like all inventors of a social system, was consumed with jealousy. He abhorred his disciples, would suffer no equal, and could not endure the slightest contradiction. However, between him and Théodore de Bèze the difference was so great; this elegant gentleman, gifted with a charming appearance, polished, courteous, and accustomed to Court life, was, in his eyes, so unlike all his fierce Janissaries, that for him he set aside his usual impulses. He never loved him, for this crabbed lawgiver knew absolutely nothing of friendship; but having no fear of finding his successor in him, he liked to play with Théodore, as Richelieu at a later time played with his cat. He found him pliant and amusing. When he saw that de Bèze succeeded to perfection in every mission, he took delight in the polished tool of which he believed himself to be the soul and guide; so true is it that even those men who seem most surly cannot live without some semblance of affection.

Théodore was Calvin's spoilt child. The great Reformer never scolded him, overlooked his irregularities, his love affairs, his handsome dress, and his choice language. Possibly Calvin was well content to show that the Reformation could hold its own even among Court circles. Théodore de Bèze wanted to introduce a taste for art, letters, and poetry into Geneva, and Calvin would listen to his schemes without knitting his grizzled brows. Thus the contrast of character and person was as complete as the contrast of mind in these two celebrated men.

Calvin accepted Chaudieu's very humble bow, and replied by slightly bending his head. Chaudieu slipped the bridles of both horses over his right arm and followed the two great Reformers, keeping to the right of Théodore de Bèze, who

14

was walking on Calvin's right.  Calvin's housekeeper ran forward to prevent the gate being shut, by telling the captain of the Guard that the pastor had just had a severe attack of pain.

Théodore de Bèze was a native of the Commune of Vézelay, the first to demand for itself corporate government, of which the curious tale has been told by one of the Thierrys.  Thus the spirit of citizenship and resistance which was endemic to Vézelay no doubt contributed an item to the great rising of the Reformers in the person of this man, who is certainly a most singular figure in the history of heresy.

"So you still suffer great pain ?" said Théodore to Calvin.

"The sufferings of the damned, a Catholic would say," replied the Reformer, with the bitterness that colored his least remarks.  "Ah ! I am going fast, my son, and what will become of you when I am gone ?"

"We will fight by the light of your writings," said Chaudieu.

Calvin smiled; his purple face assumed a more gracious expression, and he looked kindly on Chaudieu.

"Well, have you brought me any news !" he asked.  "Have they killed a great many of us?" he added with a smile, and a sort of mocking glee sparkled in his brown eyes.

"No," said Chaudieu; "peace is the order of the day."

"So much the worse, so much the worse !" cried Calvin.  "Every form of peace would be a misfortune if it were not always, in fact, a snare.  Our strength lies in persecution.  Where should we be if the church took up the Reformation ?"

"Indeed," said Théodore, "that is what the Queen-mother seems inclined to do."

"She is quite capable of it," said Calvin.  "I am studying that woman."

"From hence?" cried Chaudieu.

"Does distance exist for the spirit ?" said Calvin severely, regarding the interruption as irreverent.  "Catherine longs for power, and women who aim at that lose all sense of honor and faith.   What is in the wind ? "

" Well, she suggests a sort of Council," said Théodore de Bèze.

" Near Paris? " asked Calvin roughly.

" Yes."

" Ah ! that is well ! " said Calvin.

" And we are to try to come to an understanding, and draw up a public act to consolidate the two churches."

" Ah ! if only she had courage enough to separate the French Church from the Church of Rome, and to create a patriarch in France, as in the Greek Church ! "* cried the Reformer, whose eyes glistened at this idea, which would place him on a throne.  " But, my son, can a Pope's niece be truthful?  She only wants to gain time."

" And do not we need time to recover from our check at Amboise, and to organize some formidable resistance in various parts of the kingdom ? "

" She has sent away the Queen of Scotland," said Chaudieu.

" That is one less, then," said Calvin, as they passed through the Porte de Rives.  " Elizabeth of England will keep her busy.  Two neighboring queens will soon be fighting ; one is handsome, and the other ugly enough—a first cause of irritation ; and then there is the question of legitimacy——"

He rubbed his hands, and his glee had such a ferocious taint that de Bèze shuddered, for he too saw the pool of blood at which his master was gazing.

" The Guises have provoked the House of Bourbon," said de Bèze after a pause ; " they broke the stick between them at Orleans."

" Ay," said Calvin, " and you, my son, did not believe me when, as you last started for Nérac, I told you that we

* He is an absolute ruler ; his title, Ecumenical.

should end by stirring up war to the death between the two
branches of the royal family of France.

"So at last I have a court, a king, a dynasty on my side.
My doctrine has had its effect on the masses. The citizen
class understand me; henceforth they will call those who
go to mass idolaters, those who paint the walls of their place
of worship, and put up pictures and statues there. Oh,
the populace find it far easier to demolish cathedrals and
palaces than to discuss justification by faith or the real presence! Luther was a wrangler, I am an army! He was a
reasoner, I am a system! He, my child, was but a tormentor,
I am a Tarquin!

"Yes, they of the truth will destroy churches, will tear
down pictures, will make millstones of the statues to grind
the bread of the people. There are bodies in great States, I
will have only individuals; bodies are too resistant, and see
clearly when individuals are blind.

"Now, we must combine this agitating doctrine with political interests, to .consolidate it and to keep up the material of
my armies. I have satisfied the logic of thrifty minds and
thinking brains by this bare, undecorated worship which lifts
religion into the sphere of the ideal. I have made the mob
understand the advantages of the suppression of ceremonial.

"Now, it is your part, Théodore, to enlist people's interests. Do not overstep that line. In the way of doctrine
everything has been done, everything has been said; add not
one jot! Why does Caméron, that little pastor in Gascony,
meddle with writing?"

Calvin, Théodore de Bèze, and Chaudieu went along the
streets of the upper town and through the crowd, without
any attention being paid to the men who were unchaining
the mob in cities and ravaging France. After this terrifying
harangue, they walked on in silence, till they reached the
little square of Saint-Pierre, and made their way toward the
minister's dwelling. Calvin's lodging consisted of three

rooms on the third floor of this house, which is hardly known, and of which no one ever tells you in Geneva—where, indeed, there is no statue to Calvin. The rooms were floored and wainscoted with pine, and on one side there were a kitchen and a servant's room. The entrance, as is commonly the case in Genevese houses, was through the kitchen, which opened into a small room with two windows, parlor, dining, and drawing-room in one. Next to this was the study where, for fourteen years, Calvin's mind had carried on the battle with pain, and beyond was his bedroom. Four oak chairs with tapestry seats, placed around a long table, formed all the furniture of the sitting-room. A white earthenware stove in one corner of the room gave out a pleasant warmth; paneling of unvarnished pine covered the walls, and there was no other decoration. The bareness of the place was quite in keeping with the frugal and simple life led by the Reformer.

"Well," said de Bèze, as he went in, taking advantage of a few minutes when Chaudieu had left them to put up the horses at a neighboring inn, "what am I to do? Will you agree to this meeting?"

"Certainly," said Calvin. "You, my son, will bear the brunt of the struggle. Be decisive, absolute. Nobody—neither the Queen, nor the Guises, nor I—wants pacification as a result; it would not suit our purpose. I have much confidence in Duplessis-Mornay. Give him the leading part. We are alone——" said he, with a suspicious glance into the kitchen, of which the door was open, showing two shirts and some collars hung to dry on a line. "Go and shut all the doors. Well," he went on, when Théodore had done his bidding, "we must compel the King of Navarre to join the Guises and the Connétable de Montmorency, by advising him to desert Queen Catherine de' Medici. Let us take full advantage of his weakness; he is but a poor creature. If he prove a turncoat to the Italian woman, she, finding herself bereft of his support, must inevitably join the Prince de Condé and

Coligny.   Such a manœuvre may possibly compromise her so effectually that she must remain on our side——"

Théodore de Bèze raised the hem of Calvin's gown and kissed it.

"Oh, master," said he, " you are indeed great ! "

"Unfortunately, I am dying, my dear Théodore.   If I should die before seeing you again," he went on, whispering in the ear of his Minister for Foreign Affairs, " remember to strike a great blow by the hand of one of our martyrs."

"Another Minard to be killed ?"

"Higher than a lawyer."

"A king ?"

"Higher still.   The man who wants to be king."

"The Duc de Guise ! " cried Théodore, with a gesture of dismay.

"Well," cried Calvin, fancying that he discerned refusal, or at least an instinct of resistance, and failing to notice the entrance of Chaudieu, "have we not a right to strike as we are struck?   Yes, and in darkness and silence !   May we not return wound for wound, and death for death ?   Do the Catholics hesitate to lay snares for us and kill us ?   I trust to you !   Burn their churches.   Go on, my sons !   If you have any devoted youths——"

"I have," Chaudieu put in.

"Use them as weapons of war.   To triumph, we may use every means.   The Balafré, that terrible man of war, is, like me, more than a man ; he is a dynasty, as I am a system ; he is capable of annihilating us !   Death to the Duc de Guise ! "

"I should prefer a peaceful victory, brought about by time and reason," said de Bèze.

"By time ! " cried Calvin, flinging over his chair.   "By reason ?   Are you mad ?   Conquer by reason ?   Do you know nothing of men, you who live among them—idiot?   What is so fatal to my teaching, thrice-dyed simpleton, is that it is based on reason.   By the thunders of Saint Paul, by the sword of the mighty! Pumpkin as you are, Théodore, cannot you see the power that the catastrophe at Amboise has given to my reforms? Ideas can never grow till they are watered with blood. The murder of the Duc de Guise would give rise to a fearful persecution, and I hope for it with all my might! To us reverses are more favorable than success. The Reformation can be beaten and endure, do you hear, oaf? Whereas Catholicism is overthrown if we win a single battle.

"What are these lieutenants of mine? Wet rags and not men! Guts on two legs! Christened baboons! O God, wilt Thou not grant me another ten years to live? If I die too soon, the cause of religion is lost in the hands of such rascals!

"You are as helpless as Antoine de Navarre! Begone! leave me! I must have a better messenger! You are an ass, a popinjay, a poet! Go, write your Catullics, your Tibullics, your acrostics! Hoo!"

The pain he suffered was entirely swamped by the fires of his wrath. Gout vanished before this fearful excitement. Calvin's face was blotched with purple, like the sky before a storm. His broad forehead shone. His eyes flashed fire. He was not like the same man. He let himself give way to this sort of epileptic frenzy, almost madness, which was habitual with him; but, then, struck by the silence of his two listeners, and observing Chaudieu, who said to de Bèze, "The burning bush of Horeb!" the minister sat down, was dumb, and covered his face with his hands, with their thickened joints, and his fingers quivered in spite of their strength.

A few minutes later, while still trembling from the last shocks of this tempest—the result of his austere life—he said in a broken voice—

"My vices, which are many, are less hard to subdue than my impatience! Ah! wild beast, shall I never conquer you?" he exclaimed, striking his breast.

"My beloved master," said de Bèze in a caressing tone,

taking his hands and kissing them, "Jove thunders, but he can smile."

Calvin looked at his disciple with a softened expression.

"Do not misunderstand me, my friends," he said in a milder tone.

"I understand that the shepherds of nations have terrible burdens to bear," replied Théodore. "You have a world on your shoulders."

"I," said Chaudieu, who had become thoughtful under the master's abuse, "have three martyrs on whom we can depend. Stewart, who killed the president, is free——"

"That will not do," said Calvin mildly, and smiling, as a great man can smile when fair weather follows a storm on his face, as if he were ashamed of the tempest. "I know men. He who kills one president will not kill a second."

"Is it absolutely necessary?" said de Bèze.

"What, again?" cried Calvin, his nostrils expanding. "There, go; you will put me in a rage again. You have my decision. You, Chaudieu, walk in your own path, and keep the Paris flock together. God be with you. Dinah! Light my friends out."

"Will you not allow me to embrace you?" said de Bèze with emotion. "Who can tell what the morrow even will bring forth? We may be imprisoned in spite of safe-conducts——"

"And yet you want to spare them?" said Calvin, embracing de Bèze.

He took Chaudieu's hand, saying—

"Mind you, not Huguenots, not Reformers: be Calvinists. Speak only of Calvinism. Alas! this is not ambition, for I am a dying man! Only, everything of Luther's must be destroyed, to the very names of Lutheran and Lutheranism."

"Indeed, divine man, you deserve such honor!" cried Chaudieu.

"Uphold uniformity of creed. Do not allow any further

examination or reconstruction. If new sects arise from among us, we are lost."

To anticipate events and dismiss Théodore de Bèze, who returned to Paris with Chaudieu, it may be said that Poltrot, who, eighteen months later, fired a pistol at the Duc de Guise, confessed, under torture, that he had been urged to the crime by Théodore de Bèze; however, he retracted this statement at a later stage. Indeed, Bossuet, who weighed all the historical evidence, did not think that the idea of this attempt was due to Théodore de Bèze. Since Bossuet, however, a dissertation of an apparently trivial character, *à propos* to a famous ballad, enabled a compiler of the eighteenth century to prove that the song sung throughout France by the Huguenots on the death of the Duc de Guise was written by Théodore de Bèze; and, moreover, that the well-known ballad or lament on Malbrouck—the Duke of Marlborough—is plagiarized from Théodore de Bèze.*

On the day when Théodore de Bèze and Chaudieu reached Paris, the Court had returned thither from Reims, where Charles IX. had been crowned. This ceremony, to which Catherine gave unusual splendor, making it the occasion of great festivities, enabled her to gather round her the leaders of every faction.

After studying the various parties and interests, she saw a choice of two alternatives—either to enlist them on the side of the throne or to set them against each other. The Connétable de Montmorency, above all else a Catholic, whose nephew, the Prince de Condé, was the leader of the Reformation, and whose children also had a leaning to that creed, blamed the Queen-mother for allying herself with that party. The Guises, on their side, worked hard to gain over Antoine de Bourbon, a Prince of no strength of character, and attach him to their faction, and his wife, the Queen of Navarre, informed by de Bèze, allowed this to be done. These diffi-

* See note at the end of this volume.

culties checked Catherine, whose newly acquired authority needed a brief period of tranquillity; she impatiently awaited Calvin's reply by de Bèze and Chaudieu, sent to the great Reformer on behalf of the Prince de Condé, the King of Navarre, Coligny, d'Andelot, and Cardinal de Châtillon.

Meanwhile, the Queen-mother was true to her promises to the Prince de Condé. The chancellor quashed the trial, in which Christophe was involved, by referring the case to the Paris Parlement, and they annulled the sentence pronounced by the Commission, declaring it incompetent to try a Prince of the Blood. The Parlement reopened the trial by the desire of the Guises and the Queen-mother. La Sagne's papers had been placed in Catherine's hands, and she had burnt them. This sacrifice was the first pledge given, quite vainly, by the Guises to the Queen-mother. The Parlement, not having this decisive evidence, reinstated the Prince in all his rights, possessions, and honors.

Christophe, thus released when Orleans was in all its excitement over the King's accession, was excluded from the case, and, as a compensation for his sufferings, was passed as a pleader by Monsieur de Thou.

The Triumvirate—the coalition of interests which were imperiled by Catherine's first steps in authority—was hatching under her very eyes. Just as in chemistry hostile elements fly asunder at the shock that disturbs their compulsory union, so in politics the alliance of antagonistic interests can never last long. Catherine fully understood that, sooner or later, she must fall back on the connétable and the Guises to fight the Huguenots. The convocation, which served to flatter the vanity of the orators on each side, and, as an excuse for another imposing ceremony after that of the coronation, to clear the blood-stained field for the religious war that had, indeed, already begun, was as futile in the eyes of the Guises as it was in Catherine's. The Catholics could not fail to be the losers; for the Huguenots, under the pretense of discussion, would be able to proclaim their doctrine in the face of all France, under the protection of the King and his mother. The Cardinal de Lorraine, flattered by Catherine into the hope of conquering the heretics by the eloquence of the princes of the church, induced his brother to consent. To the Queen-mother six months of peace meant much.

A trivial incident was near wrecking the power which Catherine was so laboriously building up. This is the scene as recorded by history; it occurred on the very day when the envoys from Geneva arrived at the Hôtel de Coligny in the Rue Béthisy, not far from the Louvre. At the coronation, Charles IX., who was much attached to his instructor, Amyot, made him high almoner of France. This affection was fully shared by the Duc d'Anjou (Henry III.), who also was Amyot's pupil.

Catherine heard this from the two Gondis on the way home from Reims to Paris. She had relied on this Crown appointment to gain her a supporter in the church, and a person of importance to set against the Cardinal de Lorraine; she had intended to bestow it on Cardinal de Tournon, so as to find in him, as in l'Hôpital, a second crutch—to use her own words. On arriving at the Louvre, she sent for the preceptor. Her rage at seeing the catastrophe that threatened her policy from the ambition of this self-made man—the son of a shoemaker—was such that she addressed him in this strange speech recorded by certain chroniclers—

"What! I can make the Guises cringe, the Colignys, the Montmorencys, the House of Navarre, the Prince de Condé, and I am to be balked by a priestling like you, who was not content to be Bishop of Auxerre!"

Amyot excused himself. He had, in fact, asked for nothing; the King had appointed him of his own free will to this office, of which he, a humble teacher, regarded himself as unworthy.

"Rest assured, master," for it was by this name that the

Kings Charles IX. and Henri III. addressed this great writer, "that you will not be left standing for twenty-four hours unless you induce your pupil to change his mind."

Between death promised him in such an uncompromising way, and the abdication of the highest ecclesiastical office in the kingdom, the shoemaker's son, who had grown covetous, and hoped perhaps for a cardinal's hat, determined to temporize.   He hid in the abbey of Saint-Germain en Laye.

At his first dinner, Charles IX., not seeing Amyot, asked for him.   Some Guisard, no doubt, told the King what had passed between Amyot and the Queen-mother.

"What!" cried he, "has he been made away with because I created him high almoner?"

He went off to his mother in the violent state of a child when one of his fancies is contravened.

"Madame," said he, as he entered her room, "did I not comply with your wishes and sign the letter you asked of me for the Parlement, by virtue of which you govern my kingdom?   Did you not promise me, when you laid it before me, that my will should be yours? and now the only favor I have cared to bestow excites your jealousy.   The chancellor talks of making me of age at fourteen, three years from hence, and you treat me as a child!   By God, but I mean to be King, and as much a King as my father and grandfather were kings!"

The tone and vehemence with which he spoke these words were a revelation to Catherine of her son's true character; it was like a blow from a bludgeon on her heart.

"And he speaks thus to me," thought she, "to me, who made him King.   Monsieur," she said, "the business of being King in such times as these is a difficult one, and you do not yet know the master minds you have to deal with. You will never have any true and trustworthy friend but your mother, or other adherents than those whom she long since attached to her, and but for whom you would perhaps not be alive at this day.   The Guises are averse both to your position

and your person, I would have you know.  If they could sew
me up in a sack and throw me into the river," said she,
pointing to the Seine, " they would do it to-night.  Those
Lorrains feel that I am a lioness defending her cubs, and that
stays the bold hands they stretch out to clutch  the crown.
To whom, to what is your preceptor attached ? where are his
allies ? what is his authority ? what services can he do you ?
what weight will his words have ?  Instead of gaining a but-
tress to uphold your power, you have undermined it.

" The Cardinal de Lorraine threatens you ; he plays the
King, and keeps his hat on his head in the presence of the
first Prince of the Blood ; was it not necessary to counter-
balance him with another cardinal, invested with authority
equal to his own ?  Is Amyot, a shoemaker who might tie the
bows of his shoes, the man to defy him to his face ?  Well,
well, you are fond of Amyot.  You have appointed him !
Your first decision shall be respected, my lord !  But before
deciding any further, have  the kindness  to  consult me.
Listen to reasons of State, and your boyish good-sense will
perhaps agree with  my old woman's experience before deciding, when you know all the difficulties."

" You must bring back my master ! " said the King, not
listening very carefully to the Queen, on finding her speech
full of reproofs.

" Yes, you shall have him," replied she.  " But not he,
nor even that rough Cypierre, can teach you to reign."

" It is you, my dear mother," he exclaimed, mollified by
his triumph, and throwing off the threatening and sly expression which nature had stamped on his physiognomy.

Catherine sent Gondi to find the high almoner.  When the
Florentine had discovered Amyot's retreat, and the bishop
heard that the courtier came from the Queen, he was seized
with terror, and would not come out of the abbey.  In this
extremity Catherine was obliged to write him himself, and in
such terms that he came back and obtained the promise of her

support, but only on condition of his obeying her blindly in all that concerned the King.

This little domestic tempest being lulled, Catherine came back to the Louvre. It was more than a year since she had left it, and she now held council with her nearest friends as to how she was to deal with the young King, whom Cypierre had complimented on his firmness.

"What is to be done?" said she to the two Gondis, Ruggieri, Birague, and Chiverni, now tutor and chancellor to the Duc d'Anjou.

"First of all," said Birague, "get rid of Cypierre; he is not a courtier, he will never fall in with your views, and will think he is doing his duty by opposing you."

"Whom can I trust?" cried the Queen.

"One of us," said Birague.

"By my faith," said Gondi, "I promise to make the King as pliant as the King of Navarre."

"You let the late King die to save your other children; well, then, do as the grand Signors of Constantinople do: crush this one's passions and fancies," said Albert de Gondi. "He likes the arts, poetry, hunting, and a little girl he saw at Orleans; all this is quite enough to occupy him."

"Then you would be the King's tutor?" said Catherine, to the more capable of the two Gondis.

"If you will give me the necessary authority; it might be well to make me a marshal of France and a Duke. Cypierre is too small a man to continue in that office. Henceforth the tutor of a King of France should be a marshal and Duke, or something of the kind——"

"He is right," said Birague.

"Poetry and hunting," said Catherine, in a dreamy voice.

"We will hunt and make love!" cried Gondi.

"Beside," said Chiverni, "you are sure of Amyot, who will always be afraid of a drugged cup in case of disobedience, and with Gondi you will have the King in leading strings."

"You were resigned to the loss of one son to save the three others and the Crown; now you must have the courage to keep this one *occupied* to save the kingdom—to save yourself perhaps," said Ruggieri.

"He has just offended me deeply," said Catherine.

"He does not know how much he owes you; and if he did, you would not be safe," Birague replied with grave emphasis.

"It is settled," said the Queen, on whom this reply had a startling effect; "you are to be the King's governor, Gondi. The King must make me a return in favor of one of my friends for the concession I have made for that cowardly bishop. But the fool has lost the cardinal's hat; so long as I live I will hinder the Pope from fitting it to his head! We should have been very strong with Cardinal de Tournon to support us. What a trio they would have made: he, as high almoner, with l'Hôpital and de Thou! As to the citizens of Paris, I mean to make my son coax them over, and we will lean on them."

And Gondi was, in fact, made a marshal, created Duc de Retz and tutor to the King, within a few days.

This little council was just over when Cardinal de Tournon came to announce to the Queen the messengers from Calvin. Admiral Coligny escorted them to secure them respectful treatment at the Louvre. The Queen summoned her battalion of maids of honor, and went into the great reception-room built by her husband, which no longer exists in the Louvre of our day.

At that time the staircase of the Louvre was in the clock-tower. Catherine's rooms were in the older part of the building, part of which survives in the Cour du Musée. The present staircase to the galleries was built where the *Salle des ballets* (dancing hall) was before it. A *ballet* at that time meant a sort of dramatic entertainment performed by all the Court.

Revolutionary prejudice led to the most ridiculous mistake as to Charles IX. *à propos* to the Louvre.  During the Revolution a belief defamatory of this King, whose character has been caricatured, made a monster of him.  Chénier's tragedy was written under the provocation of a tablet hung up on the window of the part of the palace that projects toward the quay.  On it were these words, " From this window Charles IX. of execrable memory fired on the citizens of Paris."  It may be well to point out to future historians and studious persons that the whole of that side of the Louvre, now called the Old Louvre—the projecting wing at a right angle to the quay, connecting the galleries with the Louvre by what is called the Galerie d'Apollon, and the Louvre with the Tuileries by the picture gallery—was not in existence in the time of Charles IX.  The principal part of the site of the river-front, where lies the garden known as le Jardin de l'Infante, was occupied by the Hôtel de Bourbon, which belonged, in fact, to the House of Navarre.  It would have been physically impossible for Charles IX. to fire from the Louvre of Henri II. on a boat full of Huguenots crossing the Seine, though he could see the river from some windows, which are now built up, in that part of the palace.

Even if historians and libraries did not possess maps in which the Louvre at the time of Charles IX. is perfectly shown, the building bears in itself the refutation of the error. The several kings who have contributed to this vast structure have never failed to leave their cypher on the work in some form of monogram.  The venerable buildings, now all discolored, of that part of the Louvre that goes down to the quay bear the initials of Henri II. and of Henri IV.; quite different from those of Henri III., who added to his H Catherine's double C in a way that looks like D to superficial observers.  It was Henri IV. who was able to add his own palace, the Hôtel de Bourbon, with its gardens and domain, on to the Louvre.  He first thought of uniting Catherine de'

Medici's palace to the Louvre by finishing the galleries, of which the exquisite sculpture is too little appreciated.

But if no plan of Paris under Charles IX. were in existence, nor the monograms of the two Henrys, the difference in the architecture would be enough to give the lie to this calumny. The rusticated bosses of the Hôtel de la Force, and of this portion of the Louvre, are precisely characteristic of the transition from the architecture of the Renaissance to the architecture of Henri III., Henri IV., and Louis XIII.

This archæological digression, in harmony, to be sure, with the pictures at the beginning of this narrative, enables us to see the aspect of this other part of Paris, of which nothing now remains but that portion of the Louvre, where the beautiful bas-reliefs are perishing day by day.

When the Court was informed that the Queen was about to give audience to Théodore de Bèze and Chaudieu, introduced by Admiral Coligny, every one who had a right to go into the throne-room hastened to be present at this interview. It was about six o'clock; Admiral Coligny had supped, and was picking his teeth as he walked upstairs between the two Calvinists. This playing with a toothpick was a confirmed habit with the admiral; he involuntarily picked his teeth in the middle of a battle when meditating a retreat. " Never trust the admiral's toothpick, the constable's ' No,' nor Catherine's ' Yes,' " was one of the proverbs of the Court at the time. And after the massacre of Saint-Bartholomew, the mob made horrible mockery of the admiral's body, which hung for three days at Montfaucon, by sticking a grotesque toothpick between his teeth. Chroniclers have recorded this hideous jest. And, indeed, this trivial detail in the midst of a tremendous catastrophe is just like the Paris mob, which thoroughly deserves this grotesque parody of a line of Boileau's:

" Le Français, né malin, créa la guillotine."

Or: The Frenchman, a born wag, invented the guillotine.

15

In all ages, the Parisians have made fun before, during, and after the most terrible revolutions.

Théodore de Bèze was in Court dress, black silk long-hose, slashed shoes, full trunks, a doublet of black silk, also slashed, and a little, black velvet cloak, over which fell a fine white ruff, deeply gauffered. He wore the tuft of beard called a *virgule* (a comma) and a mustache, his sword hung by his side, and he carried a cane. All who know the pictures at Versailles, or the portraits by Odieuvre, know his round and almost jovial face, with bright eyes, and the remarkably high and broad forehead, which is characteristic of the poets and writers of that time. De Bèze had a pleasant face, which did him good service. He formed a striking contrast to Coligny, whose austere features are known to all, and to the bitter and bilious-looking Chaudieu, who wore the preacher's gown and Calvinist bands.

The state of affairs in the Chamber of Deputies in our own day, and that, no doubt, in the Convention too, may enable us to understand how at that Court and at that time persons, who six months after would be fighting to the death and waging heinous warfare, would meanwhile meet, address each other with courtesy, and exchange jests.

When Coligny entered the room, Birague, who would coldly advise the massacre of Saint-Bartholomew, and the Cardinal de Lorraine, who would tell his servant Besme not to miss the admiral, came forward to meet him, and the Piedmontese said, with a smile—

"Well, my dear admiral, so you have undertaken to introduce these gentlemen from Geneva?"

"And you will count it to me for a crime perhaps," replied the admiral in jest, "while, if you had undertaken it, you would have scored it as a merit."

"Master Calvin, I hear, is very ill," said the Cardinal de Lorraine to Théodore de Bèze. "I hope we shall not be suspected of having stirred his broth for him!"

"Nay, monseigneur, you would lose too much by that," said Théodore de Bèze shrewdly.

The Duc de Guise, who was examining Chaudieu, stared at his brother and Birague, who were both startled by this speech.

"By God!" exclaimed the cardinal, "heretics are of the right faith in keen politics!"

To avoid difficulties, the Queen, who was announced at this moment, remained standing. She began by conversing with the connétable, who spoke eagerly of the scandal of her admitting Calvin's envoys to her presence.

"But, you see, my dear constable, we receive them without ceremony."

"Madame," said the admiral, approaching Catherine, "these are the two doctors of the new religion who have come to an understanding with Calvin, and have taken his instructions as to a meeting where the various churches of France may compromise their differences."

"This is Monsieur Théodore de Bèze, my wife's very great favorite," said the King of Navarre, coming forward and taking de Bèze by the hand.

"And here is Chaudieu!" cried the Prince de Condé. "My friend the Duc de Guise knows the captain," he added, looking at le Balafré; "perhaps he would like to make acquaintance with the minister."

This sally made everybody laugh, even Catherine.

"By my troth," said the Duc de Guise, "I am delighted to see a man who can so well choose a follower, and make use of him in his degree. One of your men," said he to the preacher, "endured, without dying or confessing anything, the extreme of torture; I fancy myself brave, but I do not know that I could endure so well!"

"Hm!" observed Ambroise Paré, "you said not a word when I pulled the spear out of your face at Calais."

Catherine, in the middle of the semicircle formed right and

left of the maids of honor and Court officials, kept silence. While looking at the two famous Reformers, she was trying to penetrate them with her fine, intelligent, black eyes, and study them thoroughly.

"One might be the sheath and the other the blade," Albert de Gondi said in her ear.

"Well, gentlemen," said Catherine, who could not help smiling, "has your master given you liberty to arrange a public conference where you may convert to the Word of God those modern fathers of the church who are the glory of our realm?"

"We have no master but the Lord," said Chaudieu.

"Well, you acknowledge some authority in the King of France?" said Catherine, smiling, and interrupting the minister.

"And a great deal in the Queen," added de Bèze, bowing low.

"You will see," she went on, "that the heretics will be my most dutiful subjects."

"Oh, madame," cried Coligny, "what a splendid kingdom we will make for you!   Europe reaps great profit from our divisions.   It has seen one-half of France set against the other for fifty years past."

"Have we come here to hear chants in praise of heretics?" said the constable roughly.

"No, but to bring them to amendment," answered the Cardinal de Lorraine in a whisper, "and we hope to achieve it by a little gentleness."

"Do you know what I should have done in the reign of the King's father?" said Anne de Montmorency.   "I should have sent for the provost to hang those two rascals high and dry on the Louvre gallows."

"Well, gentlemen, and who are the learned doctors you will bring into the field?" asked the Queen, silencing the constable with a look.

" Duplessis-Mornay and Théodore de Bèze are our leaders,'' said Chaudieu.

" The Court will probably go to the Castle of Saint-Germain ; and as it would not be seemly that this colloquy should take place in the same town, it shall be held in the little town of Poissy,'' replied Catherine.

"Shall we be safe there, madame?'' asked Chaudieu.

"Oh!'' said the Queen, with a sort of simplicity, "you will, no doubt, know what precautions to take. Monsieur the Admiral will make arrangements to that effect with my cousins de Guise and Montmorency.''

"Fie on it all!'' said the constable ; "I will have no part in it.''

The Queen took Chaudieu a little way apart.

"What do you do to your sectarians to give them such a spirit?'' said she. "My furrier's son was really sublime,'' she added.

"We have faith,'' said Chaudieu.

At this moment the room was filled with eager groups, all discussing the question of this assembly, which, from the Queen's suggestion, was already spoken of as the " Convocation of Poissy.''

Catherine looked at Chaudieu, and felt it safe to say—

"Yes, a new faith.''

"Ah, madame, if you were not blinded by your connection with the Court of Rome, you would see that we are returning to the true doctrine of Jesus Christ, who, while sanctifying the equality of souls, has given all men on earth equal rights.''

"And do you think yourself the equal of Calvin?'' said Catherine shrewdly. "Nay, nay, we are equals only in church. What, really? Break all bonds between the people and the throne?'' cried Catherine. "You are not merely heretics ; you rebel against obedience to the King while avoiding all obedience to the Pope.''

She sharply turned away, and returned to Théodore de Bèze.

"I trust to you, monsieur," she said, "to carry through this conference conscientiously.  Take time over it."

"I fancied," said Chaudieu to the Prince de Condé, the King of Navarre, and Admiral Coligny, " that affairs of State were taken more seriously."

"Oh, we all know exactly what we mean," said the Prince de Condé, with a significant glance at Théodore de Bèze.

The hunchback took leave of his followers to keep an assignation.  This great Prince and party leader was one of the most successful gallants of the Court ; the two handsomest women of the day fought for him with such infatuation that the Maréchale de Saint-André, the wife of one of the coming Triumvirate, gave him her fine estate of Saint-Valery to win him from the Duchesse de Guise, the wife of the man who had wanted to bring his head under the axe ; being unable to wean the Duc de Nemours from his flirtations with Mademoiselle de Rohan, she fell in love, meanwhile, with the leader of the Reformed party.

"How different from Geneva!" said Chaudieu to Théodore de Bèze on the little bridge by the Louvre.

"They are livelier here, and I cannot imagine why they are such traitors," replied de Bèze.

"Meet a traitor with a traitor-and-a-half," said Chaudieu in a whisper.  "I have saints in Paris that I can rely on, and I mean to make a prophet of Calvin.  Christophe will rid us of the most dangerous of our enemies."

"The Queen-mother, for whom the poor wretch endured torture, has already had him passed, by high-handed orders, as pleader before the Parlement, and lawyers are more apt to be tell-tales than assassins.  Remember Avenelles, who sold the secret of our first attempt to take up arms."

"But I know Christophe," said Chaudieu, with an air of conviction, as he and the Calvinist ambassador parted.

Some days after the reception of Calvin's secret envoys by
Catherine, and toward the end of that year—for the year then
began at Easter, and the modern calendar was not adopted
until this very reign—Christophe, still stretched on an armchair, was sitting on that side of the large sombre room where
our story began, in such a position as to look out on the river.
His feet rested on a stool.　Mademoiselle Lecamus and Babette Lallier had just renewed the application of compresses,
soaked in a lotion brought by Ambroise, to whose care Catherine had commended Christophe.　When once he was restored to his family, the lad had become the object of the
most devoted care.　Babette, with her father's permission,
came to the house every morning and did not leave until the
evening.　Christophe, a subject of wonder to the apprentices,
gave rise in the neighborhood to endless tales, which involved
him in poetic mystery.　He had been put to torture, and the
famous Ambroise Paré was exerting all his skill to save him.
What, then, had he done to be treated so?　On this point
neither Christophe nor his father breathed a word.　Catherine,
now all-powerful, had an interest in keeping silence, and so
had the Prince de Condé.　The visits of Ambroise Paré, the
surgeon to the King and to the House of Guise, permitted
by the Queen-mother and the Princes of Lorraine to attend a
youth accused of heresy, added to the singularity of this business, which no one could see through.　And then the priest
of Saint-Pierre aux Bœufs came several times to see his church-
warden's son, and these visits made the causes of Christophe's
condition even more inexplicable.

The old furrier, who had a plan of his own, replied evasively
when his fellows of the guild, traders, and friends spoke of his
son—

"I am very happy, neighbor, to have been able to save
him!　You know! it is well not to put your finger between
the wood and the bark.　My son put his hand to the stake
and took out fire enough to burn my house down!　They im-

posed on his youth, and we citizens never get anything but scorn and harm by hanging on to the great. This quite determines me to make a lawyer of my boy; the law courts will teach him to weigh his words and deeds. The young Queen, who is now in Scotland, had a great deal to do with it; but perhaps Christophe was very imprudent too. I went through terrible grief. All this will probably lead to my retiring from business; I will never go to Court any more. My son has had enough of the Reformation now; it has left him with broken arms and legs. But for Ambroise, where should I be?"

Thanks to these speeches, and to his prudence, a report was spread in the neighborhood that Christophe no longer followed the creed of Colas. Every one thought it quite natural that the old Syndic should wish to see his son a lawyer in the Parlement, and thus the priest's calls seemed quite a matter of course. In thinking of the old man's woes, no one thought of his ambition, which would have been deemed monstrous.

The young lawyer, who had spent ninety days on the bed put up for him in the old sitting-room, had only been out of it for a week past, and still needed the help of crutches to enable him to walk. Babette's affection and his mother's tenderness had touched Christophe deeply; still, having him in bed, the two women lectured him soundly on the subject of religion. Président de Thou came to see his godson, and was most paternal. Christophe, as a pleader in the Parlement, ought to be a Catholic, he would be pledged to it by his oath; and the president, who never seemed to doubt the young man's orthodoxy, added these important words—

"You have been cruelly tested, my boy. I myself know nothing of the reasons Messieurs de Guise had for treating you thus; but now I exhort you to live quietly henceforth and not to interfere in broils, for the favor of the King and Queen will not be shown to such as brew storms. You are not a great enough man to drive a bargain with the King, like the Duke and the cardinal. If you want to be councilor

in the Parlement some day, you can only attain that high
office by serious devotion to the cause of royalty.''

However, neither Monsieur de Thou's visit, nor Babette's
charms, nor the entreaties of Madame Lecamus, his mother,
had shaken the faith of the Protestant martyr. Christophe
clung all the more stoutly to his religion in proportion to
what he had suffered for it.

"My father will never allow me to marry a heretic," said
Babette in his ear.

Christophe replied only with tears, which left the pretty
girl speechless and thoughtful.

Old Lecamus maintained his dignity as a father and a
Syndic; watched his son, and said little. The old man,
having got back his dear Christophe, was almost vexed with
himself, and repentant of having displayed all his affection
for his only son; but secretly he admired him. At no time
in his life had the furrier pulled so many wires to gain his
ends; for he could see the ripe harvest of the crop sown with
so much toil, and wished to gather it all.

A few days since he had had a long conversation with
Christophe alone, hoping to discover the secret of his son's
tenacity. Christophe, who was not devoid of ambition, believed in the Prince de Condé. The Prince's generous speech
—which was no more than the stock-in-trade of princes—was
stamped on his heart. He did not know that Condé had
wished him at the devil at the moment when he bid him such
a touching farewell through the bars of his prison at Orleans.

"A Gascon would have understood," the Prince had said
to himself.

And in spite of his admiration for the Prince, Christophe
cherished the deepest respect for Catherine, the great Queen
who had explained to him in a look that she was compelled
by necessity to sacrifice him, and then, during his torture,
had conveyed to him in another glance an unlimited promise
by an almost imperceptible tear.

During the deep calm of the ninety days and nights he had spent in recovering, the newly made lawyer thought over the events at Blois and at Orleans. He weighed, in spite of himself, it may be said, the influence of these two patrons; he hesitated between the Queen and the Prince. He had certainly done more for Catherine than for the Reformation; and the young man's heart and mind, of course, went forth to the Queen, less by reason of this difference than because she was a woman. In such a case a man will always found his hopes on a woman rather than on a man.

"I immolated myself for her—what will she not do for me?"

This was the question he almost involuntarily asked himself as he recalled the tone in which she had said, "My poor boy!"

It is difficult to conceive of the pitch of self-consciousness reached by a man alone and sick in bed. Everything, even the care of which he is the object, tends to make him think of himself alone. By exaggerating the Prince de Condé's obligations to him, Christophe looked forward to obtaining some post at the Court of Navarre. The lad, a novice still in politics, was all the more forgetful of the anxieties which absorb party leaders, and of the swift rush of men and events which overrule them, because he lived almost in solitary imprisonment in that dark parlor. Every party is bound to be ungrateful when it is fighting for dear life; and when it has won the day, there are so many persons to be rewarded, that it is ungrateful still. The rank and file submit to this oblivion, but the captains turn against the new master who for so long has marched as their equal.

Christophe, the only person to remember what he had suffered, already reckoned himself as one of the chiefs of the Reformation by considering himself as one of its martyrs. Lecamus, the old wolf of trade, acute and clear-sighted, had guessed his son's secret thoughts; indeed, all his manœuvring was based on the very natural hesitancy that possessed the lad.

"Would it not be fine," he had said the day before to Babette, "to be the wife of a councilor to the Parlement? you would be addressed as madame."

"You are crazy, neighbor," said Lallier. "In the first place, where would you find ten thousand crowns a year in landed estate, which a councilor must show, and from whom could you purchase a connection? The Queen-mother and Regent would have to give all her mind to it to get your son into the Parlement; and he smells of the stake too strongly to be admitted."

"What would you give, now, to see your daughter a councilor's wife?"

"You want to sound the depth of my purse, you old fox!" exclaimed Lallier.

Councilor to the Parlement! The words distracted Christophe's brain.

Long after the conference was over, one morning when Christophe sat gazing at the river, which reminded him of the scene that was the beginning of all this story, of the Prince de Condé, la Renaudie, and Chaudieu, of his journey to Blois, and of all he hoped for, the Syndic came to sit down by his son with ill-disguised glee under an affectation of solemnity.

"My boy," said he, "after what took place between you and the heads of the riot at Amboise, they owed you so much that your future might very well be cared for by the House of Navarre."

"Yes," replied Christophe.

"Well," his father went on, "I have definitely applied for permission for you to purchase a legal business in Béarn.* Our good friend Paré undertook to transmit the letters I wrote in your name to the Prince de Condé and Queen Jeanne.

* Then a province of Navarre-Gascony.

Here, read this reply from Monsieur de Pibrac, Vice-Chancellor of Navarre:

"*To Master Lecamus, Syndic of the Guild of Furriers.*

"His Highness the Prince de Condé bids me express to you his regret at being unable to do anything for his fellow-prisoner in the Tour de Saint-Aignan, whom he remembers well, and to whom, for the present, he offers the place of man-at-arms in his own company, where he will have the opportunity of making his way as a man of good heart—which he is.

"The Queen of Navarre hopes for an occasion of rewarding Master Christophe, and will not fail.

"And with this, Monsieur le Syndic, I pray God have you in His keeping.                         PIBRAC,
                                        "*Chancellor of Navarre.*

"Nérac."

"Nérac! Pibrac! Crac!" cried Babette. "There is nothing to be gotten out of these Gascons; they think only of themselves."

Old Lecamus was looking at his son with ironical amusement.

"And he wants to set a poor boy on horseback whose knees and ankles were pounded up for him!" cried the mother. "What a shameful mockery!"

"I do not seem to see you as a councilor in Navarre," said the old furrier.

"I should like to know what Queen Catherine would do for me if I petitioned her," said Christophe, much crestfallen.

"She made no promises," said the old merchant, "but I am sure she would not make a fool of you and would remember your sufferings. Still, how could she make a councilor-at-law of a Protestant citizen?"

"But Christophe has never abjured ! " exclaimed Babettte. " He may surely keep his own secret as to his religious opinions."

" The Prince de Condé would be less scornful of a coun-cilor to the Parlement of Paris," said Lecamus.

" A councilor, father !   Is it possible ? "

" Yes, if you do nothing to upset what I am managing for you.   My neighbor Lallier here is ready to pay two hundred thousand livres, if I add as much again, for the purchase of a fine estate entailed on the heirs male, which we will hand over to you."

"And I will add something more for a house in Paris," said Lallier.

" Well, Christophe ? " said Babette.

" You are talking without the Queen," replied the young lawyer.

Some days after this bitter mortification, an apprentice brought this brief note to Christophe—

"Chaudieu wishes to see his son."

"Bring him in," said Christophe.

" O my saint and martyr ! " cried the preacher, embracing the young man, " have you gotten over your sufferings ? "

" Yes, thanks to Paré ! "

" Thanks to God, who gave you strength to endure them ! But what is this I hear?   You have passed as a pleader, you have taken the oath of fidelity, you have confessed the Whore, the Catholic  Apostolic, Romish Church ? "

" My father insisted."

" But are we not to leave father and mother and children and wife for the sacred cause of Calvinism, and to suffer all things?   Oh, Christophe, Calvin, the great Calvin, the whole party, the whole world, the future counts on your courage and your greatness of soul !   We want your life."

There is this strange feature in the mind of man : the most devoted, even in the act of devoting himself, always builds up a romance of hope even in the most perilous crisis.  Thus, when on the river under the Pont au Change, the prince, the soldier, and the preacher had required Christophe to carry to Queen Catherine the document which, if discovered, would have cost him his life, the boy had trusted to his wit, to chance, to his perspicacity, and had boldly marched on between the two formidable parties—the Guises and the Queen —who had so nearly crushed him.  While in the torture chamber he still had said to himself, "I shall live through it —it is only pain ! "

But at this brutal command, " Die ! " to a man who was still helpless, hardly recovered from the injuries he had suffered, and who clung all the more to life for having seen death so near, it was impossible to indulge in any such illusions.

Christophe calmly asked, " What do you want of me ? "

" To fire a pistol bravely, as Stewart fired at Minard."

" At whom ? "

" The Duc de Guise."

" Assassination ? "

" Revenge !  Have you forgotten the hundred gentlemen massacred on one scaffold !  A child, little d'Aubigné, said as he saw the butchery, ' They have beheaded all France.' "

" We are to take blows and not return them is the teaching of the Gospel," replied Christophe.  " If we are to imitate the Catholics, of what use is it to reform the church ? "

" Oh, Christophe, they have made a lawyer of you, and you argue ! " said Chaudieu.

" No, my friend," the youth replied.  " But principles are ungrateful, and you and yours will only be the playthings of the House of Bourbon."

" Oh, Christophe, if you had only heard Calvin, you would know that we can turn them like a glove !  The Bourbons are the glove, and we the hand."

" Read this," said Christophe, handing Pibrac's letter to the minister.

"Alas, boy! you are ambitious; you can no longer sacrifice yourself;" and Chaudieu went away.

Not long after this visit, Christophe, with the families of Lallier and Lecamus, had met to celebrate the plighting of Babette and Christophe in the old parlor, whence Christophe's couch was removed, for he could now climb the stairs, and was beginning to drag himself about without crutches. It was nine in the evening, and they waited for Ambroise Paré. The family notary was sitting at a table covered with papers. The furrier was selling his house and business to his head-clerk, who was to pay forty thousand livres down for the house, and to mortgage it as security for the stock-in-trade, beside paying twenty thousand livres on account.

Lecamus had purchased for his son a magnificent house in the Rue de Saint-Pierre aux Bœufs, built of stone by Philibert de l'Orme, as a wedding gift. The Syndic had also spent two hundred and fifty thousand livres out of his fortune, Lallier paying an equal sum, for the acquisition of a fine manor and estate in Picardy, for which five hundred thousand livres were asked. This estate being a dependence of the Crown, letters patent from the King—called letters of rescript—were necessary, beside the payment of considerable fines and fees. Thus the actual marriage was to be postponed till the royal signature could be obtained.

Though the citizens of Paris had obtained the right of purchasing manors and lands, the prudence of the Privy Council had placed certain restrictions on the transfer of lands belonging to the Crown; and the estate on which Lecamus had had his eye for the last ten years was one of these. Ambroise had undertaken to produce the necessary permission this very evening. Old Lecamus went to and fro between the sitting-room and the front door with an impatience that showed the eagerness of his ambition.

At last Ambroise appeared.

"My good friend!" exclaimed the surgeon in a great fuss, and looking at the supper-table, "what is your napery like? Very good. Now bring waxlights, and make haste, make haste. Bring out the best of everything you have."

"What is the matter?" asked the priest of Saint-Pierre aux Bœufs.

"The Queen-mother and the King are coming to sup with you," replied the surgeon. "The Queen and King expect to meet here an old councilor, whose business is to be sold to Christophe, and Monsieur de Thou, who has managed the bargain. Do not look as if you expected them; I stole out of the Louvre."

In an instant all were astir. Christophe's mother and Babette's aunt trotted about in all the flurry of housewives taken by surprise. In spite of the confusion into which the announcement had thrown the party, preparations were made with miraculous energy. Christophe, amazed, astounded, overpowered by such condescension, stood speechless, looking on at all the bustle.

"The Queen and the King here!" said the old mother.

"The Queen?" echoed Babette; "but what for, what to do?"

Within an hour everything was altered; the old room was smartened up, the table shone. A sound of horses was heard in the street. The gleam of torches carried by the mounted escort brought all the neighbors' noses to the windows. The rush was soon over; no one was left under the arcade but the Queen-mother and her son, King Charles IX., Charles de Gondi, master of the wardrobe and tutor to the King; Monsieur de Thou, the retiring councilor; Pinard, secretary of state; and two pages.

"Good people," said the Queen as she went in, "the King, my son, and I have come to sign the marriage-contract of our furrier's son, but on condition that he remains a Catholic. Only a Catholic can serve in the Parlement, only a

Catholic can own lands dependent on the Crown, only a Catholic can sit at table with the King—what do you say, Pinard?"

The secretary of state stepped forward, holding the letters patent.

"If we are not all Catholics here," said the little King, "Pinard will throw all the papers into the fire; but we are all Catholics?" he added, looking round proudly enough at the company.

"Yes, Sire," said Christophe Lecamus, bending the knee, not without difficulty, and kissing the hand the young King held out to him.

Queen Catherine, who also held out her hand to Christophe, pulled. him up rather roughly, and leading him into a corner, said—

"Understand, boy, no subterfuges! We are playing an honest game?"

"Yes, madame," he said, dazzled by the splendid reward and by the honor the grateful Queen had done him.

"Well, then, Master Lecamus, the King, my son, and I permit you to purchase the offices and appointments of this good man Groslay, councilor to the Parlement, who is here?" said the Queen. "I hope, young man, that you will follow in the footsteps of your lord president."

De Thou came forward and said—

"I will answer for him, madame."

"Very well, then proceed, notary," said Pinard.

"Since the King, our master, does us the honor of signing my daughter's marriage-contract," cried Lallier, "I will pay the whole price of the estate."

"The ladies may be seated," said the young King graciously. "As a wedding gift to the bride, with my mother's permission, I remit my fines and fees."

Old Lecamus and Lallier fell on their knees and kissed the boy-King's hand.

16

"' By heaven, Sire, what loads of money these citizens have!" said Gondi in his ear.

And the young King laughed.

"Their majesties being so graciously inclined," said old Lecamus, "will they allow me to present to them my successor in the business, and grant him the royal patent as furrier to their majesties?"

"Let us see him," said the King, and Lecamus brought forward his successor, who was white with alarm.

Old Lecamus was shrewd enough to offer the young King a silver cup which he had bought from Benvenuto Cellini* when he was staying in Paris at the Tour de Nesle, at a cost of not less than two thousand crowns.

"Oh, mother! what a fine piece of work!" cried the youth, lifting the cup by its foot.

"It is Florentine," said Catherine.

"Pardon me, madame," said Lecamus; "it was made in France, though by a Florentine. If it had come from Florence, it should have been the Queen's; but being made in France, it is the King's."

"I accept it, my friend," cried Charles IX., "and henceforth I drink out of it."

"It is good enough," the Queen remarked, "to be included among the Crown treasure."

"And you, Master Ambroise," she went on in an undertone, turning to the surgeon, and pointing to Christophe, "have you cured him! Will he walk?"

"He will fly," said the surgeon, with a smile. "You have stolen him from us very cleverly!"

"The abbey will not starve for lack of one monk!" replied the Queen, in the frivolous tone for which she has been blamed, but which lay only on the surface.

The supper was cheerful; the Queen thought Babette pretty, and, like the great lady she was, she slipped a diamond ring

---

* A noted sculptor, engraver, and goldsmith.

"YOU ARE A LOYAL SUBJECT," SAID CATHERINE.

on the girl's finger in compensation for the value of the silver cup.

King Charles IX., who afterward was perhaps rather too fond of thus invading his subjects' homes, supped with a good appetite; then, on a word from his new tutor, who had been instructed, it is said, to efface the virtuous teaching of Cypierre, he incited the president of Parlement, the old retired councilor, the secretary of state, the priest, the notary, and the citizens to drink so deep that Queen Catherine rose to go at the moment when she saw that their high spirits were becoming uproarious.

As the Queen rose, Christophe, his father, and the two women took up tapers to light her as far as the door of the store. Then Christophe made so bold as to pull the Queen's wide sleeve and give her a meaning look. Catherine stopped, dismissed the old man and the women with a wave of her hand, and said to the young man—"What?"

"If you can make any use of the information, madame," said he, speaking close to the Queen's ear, "I can tell you that assassins are plotting against the Duc de Guise's life."

"You are a loyal subject," said Catherine with a smile, "and I will never forget you."

She held out her hand, famous for its beauty, drawing off her glove as a mark of special favor. And Christophe, as he kissed that exquisite hand, was more Royalist than ever.

"Then I shall be rid of that wretch without my having anything to do with it," was her reflection as she put on her glove.

She mounted her mule and returned to the Louvre with her two pages.

Christophe drank, but he was gloomy; Paré's austere face reproached him for his apostasy; however, later events justified the old Syndic. Christophe would certainly never have escaped in the massacre of Saint-Bartholomew; his wealth and lands would have attracted the butchers. History has recorded the cruel fate of the wife of Lallier's successor, a beautiful woman, whose naked body remained hanging by the hair for three days to one of the starlings of the Pont au Change. Babette could shudder then as she reflected that such a fate might have been hers if Christophe had remained a Calvinist, as the Reformers were soon generally called. Calvin's ambition was fulfilled, but not until after his death.

This was the origin of the famous Lecamus family of law-yers. Tallemant des Réaux was mistaken in saying they had come from Picardy. It was afterward to the interest of the Lecamus family to refer their beginning to the time when they had acquired their principal estate, situated in that province.

Christophe's son, and his successor under Louis XIII., was father of that rich Président Lecamus, who in Louis XIV.'s time built the magnificent mansion which divided with the Hôtel Lambert the admiration of Parisians and foreigners, and which is certainly one of the finest buildings in Paris. This house still exists in the Rue de Thorigny, though it was pillaged at the beginning of the Revolution, as belonging to Monsieur de Juigné, archbishop of Paris. All the paintings were then defaced, and the lodgers who have since dwelt there have still further damaged it. This fine residence, earned in the old house in the Rue de la Pelleterie, still shows what splendid results were then the outcome of family spirit. We may be allowed to doubt whether modern individualism, resulting from the repeated equal division of property, will ever raise such edifices.

# PART II.


### THE RUGGIERI'S SECRET.

Between eleven o'clock and midnight, toward the end of October, 1573, two Florentines, brothers, Albert de Gondi, marshal of France, and Charles de Gondi la Tour, master of the wardrobe to King Charles IX., were sitting at the top of a house in the Rue Saint-Honoré on the edge of the gutter. Such gutters were made of stone; they ran along below the roof to catch the rain-water, and were pierced here and there with long gargoyles carved in the form of grotesque creatures with gaping jaws. In spite of the zeal of the present generation in the destruction of ancient houses, there were still in Paris many such gutter-spouts when, not long since, the police regulations as to waste-pipes led to their disappearance. A few sculptured gutters are still to be seen in the Saint-Antoine quarter, where the low rents have kept owners from adding rooms in the roof.

It may seem strange that two persons invested with such important functions should have chosen a perch more befitting cats. But to any one who has hunted through the historical curiosities of that time, and seen how many interests were complicated about the throne, so that the domestic politics of France can only be compared to a tangled skein of thread, these two Florentines are really cats, and quite in their place in a gutter. The devotion to the person of Catherine de' Medici, who had transplanted them to the French Court, required them to shirk none of the consequences of their intrusion there.

But to explain how and why these two courtiers were perched up there, it will be necessary to relate a scene which had just taken place within a stone's throw of this gutter, at the Louvre, in the fine brown room—which is, perhaps, all that remains of Henri II.'s apartments—where the Court was in attendance after supper on the two Queens and the King. At that time middle-class folk supped at six o'clock, and men of rank at seven ; but people of exquisite fashion supped between eight and nine ; it was the meal we nowadays call dinner.

Some people have supposed that etiquette was the invention of Louis XIV.; but this is a mistake ; it was introduced into France by Catherine de' Medici, who was so exacting that the Connétable Anne de Montmorency had more difficulty in obtaining leave to ride into the courtyard of the Louvre than in winning his sword, and even then the permission was granted only on the score of his great age. Etiquette was slightly relaxed under the first three Bourbon Kings, but assumed an Oriental character under Louis the Great, for it was derived from the Lower Empire, which borrowed it from Persia. In 1573 not only had very few persons a right to enter the courtyard of the Louvre with their attendants and torches, just as in Louis XIV.'s time only dukes and peers might drive under the porch, but the functions which gave the privilege of attending their majesties after supper could easily be counted. The Maréchal de Retz, whom we have just seen keeping watch on the gutter, once offered a thousand crowns of that day to the clerk of the closet to get speech of Henry III. at an hour when he had no right of *entrée*. And how a certain venerable historian mocks at a view of the courtyard of the Castle of Blois, into which the draughtsman introduced the figure of a man on horseback !

At this hour, then, there were at the Louvre none but the most eminent persons in the kingdom. Queen Elizabeth of Austria and her mother-in-law, Catherine de' Medici, were seated to the left of the fireplace. In the opposite corner the King, sunk in his armchair, affected an apathy excusable on the score of digestion, for he had eaten like a prince returned from hunting.   Possibly, too, he wished to avoid speech in the presence of so many persons whose interest it was to detect his thoughts.

The courtiers stood, hat in hand, at the farther end of the room.   Some conversed in undertones; others kept an eye on the King, hoping for a glance or a word.   One, being addressed by the Queen-mother, conversed with her for a few minutes.   Another would be so bold as to speak a word to Charles IX., who replied with a nod or a short answer.   A German noble, the Count of Solern, was standing in the chimney-corner by the side of Charles V.'s grand-daughter, with whom he had come to France.   Near the young Queen, seated on a stool, was her lady-in-waiting, the Countess Fieschi, a Strozzi, and related to Catherine.   The beautiful Madame de Sauves, a descendant of Jacques Cœur, and mistress in succession of the King of Navarre, of the King of Poland, and of the Duc d'Alençon, had been invited to supper, but she remained standing, her husband being merely a secretary of state.   Behind these two ladies were the Gondis, talking to them.   They alone were laughing of all the dull assembly.   Gondi, made Duc de Retz and Gentleman of the Bedchamber, since obtaining the marshal's bâton though he had never commanded an army, had been sent as the King's proxy to be married to the Queen at Spires.   This honor plainly indicated that he, like his brother, was one of the few persons whom the King and Queen admitted to a certain familiarity.

On the King's side the most conspicuous figure was the Meréchal de Tavannes, who was at Court on business; Neufville de Villeroy, one of the shrewdest negotiators of the time, who laid the foundation of the fortunes of his family; Messieurs de Birague and de Chiverni, one in attendance on the Queen-mother, the other Chancellor of Anjou and of Poland, who, knowing Catherine's favoritism, had attached himself to Henry III., the brother whom Charles IX. regarded as an enemy; Strozzi, a cousin of Queen Catherine, and a few more gentlemen, among whom were to be noted the old Cardinal de Lorraine and his nephew, the young Duc de Guise, both very much kept at a distance by Catherine and by the King. These two chiefs of the Holy Alliance, afterward known as the League, established some years since with Spain, made a display of the submission of servants who await their opportunity to become the masters; Catherine and Charles IX. were watching each other with mutual attention.

At this Court—as gloomy as the room in which it had assembled—each one had reasons for sadness or absence of mind. The young Queen was enduring all the torments of jealousy, and disguised them ineffectually by attempting to smile at her husband, whom she adored as a pious woman of infinite kindness. Marie Touchet, Charles IX.'s only mistress, to whom he was chivalrously faithful, had come home a month since from the Castle of Fayet, in Dauphiné, whither she had retired for the birth of her child; and she had brought back with her the only son Charles IX. ever had—Charles, at first Comte d'Auvergne and afterward Duc d'Angoulême.

Beside the grief of seeing her rival the mother of the King's son, while she had only a daughter, the poor Queen was enduring the mortification of complete desertion. During his mistress' absence, the King had made it up with his wife with a vehemence which history mentions as one of the causes of his death. Thus Marie Touchet's return made the pious Austrian Princess understand how little her husband's heart had been concerned in his love-making. Nor was this the only disappointment the young Queen had to endure in this matter; till now Catherine de' Medici had seemed to be her friend; but, in fact, her mother-in-law, for political ends, had encouraged her son's infidelity, and preferred to support the mistress rather than the wife. And this is the reason why:

When Charles IX. first confessed his passion for Marie

Touchet, Catherine looked with favor on the girl for reasons affecting her own prospects of dominion. Marie Touchet was brought to Court at a very early age, at the time of life when a girl's best feelings are in their bloom ; she loved the King passionately for his own sake. Terrified at the gulf into which ambition had overthrown the Duchesse de Valentinois, better known as Diane de Poitiers, she was afraid too, no doubt, of Queen Catherine, and preferred happiness to splendor. She thought, perhaps, that a pair of lovers so young as she and the King were could not hold their own against the Queen-mother.

And, indeed, Marie, the only child of Jean Touchet, the lord of Beauvais and le Quillard, King's councilor and lieutenant of the bailiwick of Orleans, half-way between the citizen class and the lowest nobility, was neither altogether a noble nor altogether *bourgeoise*, and was probably ignorant of the objects of innate ambition aimed at by the Pisseleus and the Saint-Valliers, women of family who were struggling for their families with the secret weapons of love. Marie Touchet, alone and of no rank, spared Catherine de' Medici the annoyance of finding in her son's mistress the daughter of some great house who might have set up for her rival.

Jean Touchet, a wit in his day, to whom some poets dedicated their works, wanted nothing of the Court. Marie, a young creature, with no following, as clever and well informed as she was simple and artless, suited the Queen-mother to admiration and won her warm affection.

In point of fact, Catherine persuaded the Parlement to acknowledge the son which Marie Touchet bore to the King in the month of April, and she granted him the title of Comte d'Auvergne, promising the King that she would leave the boy her personal estate, the Counties of Auvergne and Lauraguais. Afterward, Marguerite, Queen of Navarre, disputed the gift when she became Queen of France, and annulled it ; but later still, Louis XIII., out of respect to the royal blood of the

Valois, indemnified the Comte d'Auvergne by making him Duc d'Angoulême.

Catherine had already given Marie Touchet, who asked for nothing, the manor of Belleville, an estate without a title, near Vincennes, whither she came when, after hunting, the King slept at that royal residence. Charles IX. spent the greater part of his later days in that gloomy fortress, and, according to some authors, ended his days there as Louis XII. had ended his. Though it was very natural that a lover so entirely captivated should lavish on the woman he adored fresh proofs of affection when he had to expiate his legitimate infidelities, Catherine, after driving her son back to his wife's arms, certainly pleaded for Marie Touchet as women can, and had won the King back to his mistress again. Whatever could keep Charles IX. employed in anything but politics was pleasing to Catherine ; and the kind intentions she expressed toward this child for the moment deceived Charles IX., who was beginning to regard her as his enemy.

The motives on which Catherine acted in this business escaped the discernment of the Queen, who, according to Brantôme, was one of the gentlest Queens that ever reigned, and who did no harm nor displeasure to any one, even reading her Hours in secret. But this innocent Princess began to perceive what gulfs yawn round a throne, a terrible discovery which might well make her feel giddy ; and some still worse feeling must have inspired her reply to one of her ladies, who, at the King's death, observed to her that if she had had a son she would be Queen-mother and Regent—

" Ah, God be praised that He never gave me a son ! What would have come of it ? The poor child would have been robbed, as they tried to rob the King my husband, and I should have been the cause of it. God has had mercy on the kingdom and has ordered everything for the best."

This Princess, of whom Brantôme thinks he has given an ample description when he had said that she had a complexion of face as fine and delicate as that of the ladies of her Court, and very pleasing, and that she had a beautiful shape though but of middle height, was held of small account at the Court; and the King's state affording her an excuse for her double grief, her demeanor added to the gloomy hues of a picture to which a young Queen less cruelly stricken than she was might have given some brightness. The pious Elizabeth was at this crisis a proof of the fact that qualities which add lustre to a woman in ordinary life may be fatal in a Queen. A Princess who did not devote her whole night to prayer would have been a valuable ally for Charles IX., who found no help either in his wife or in his mistress.

As to the Queen-mother, she was absorbed in watching the King; he during supper had made a display of high spirits, which she interpreted as assumed to cloak some plan against herself. Such sudden cheerfulness was in too strong a contrast to the fractious humor he had betrayed by his persistency in hunting, and by a frenzy of toil at his forge, where he wrought iron, for Catherine to be duped by it. Though she could not guess what statesman was lending himself to these schemes and plots—for Charles IX. could put his mother's spies off the scent—Catherine had no doubt that some plan against her was in the wind.

The unexpected appearance of Tavannes, arriving at the same time as Strozzi, whom she had summoned, had greatly aroused her suspicions. By her power of organization Catherine was superior to the evolution of circumstances; but against sudden violence she was powerless.

As many persons know nothing of the state of affairs, complicated by the multiplicity of parties which then racked France, each leader having his own interests in view, it is needful to devote a few words to describing the dangerous crisis in which the Queen-mother had become entangled. And, as this will show Catherine de' Medici in a new light, it will carry us to the very core of this narrative.

Two words will fully summarize this strange woman, so interesting to study, whose influence left such deep traces on France. These two words are dominion and astrology. Catherine de' Medici was excessively ambitious; she had no passion but for power. Superstitious and fatalist, as many a man of superior mind has been, her only sincere belief was in the occult sciences. Without this twofold light, she must always remain misunderstood; and by giving the first place to her faith in astrology, a light will be thrown on the two philosophical figures of this study.

There was a man whom Catherine clung to more than to her children; this man was Cosmo Ruggieri. She gave him rooms in her Hôtel de Soissons; she had made him her chief counselor, instructing him to tell her if the stars ratified the advice and commonsense of her ordinary advisers.

Certain curious antecedent facts justified the power which Ruggieri exerted over his mistress till her latest breath. One of the most learned men of the sixteenth century was, beyond all doubt, the physician to Catherine's father, Lorenzo de' Medici, Duke of Urbino. This leech was known as Ruggiero the elder (*vecchio Ruggier*, and in French *Roger l'Ancien*, with authors who have written concerning alchemy), to distinguish him from his two sons, Lorenzo Ruggiero, called the Great by writers on the Cabala, and Cosmo Ruggiero, Catherine's astrologer, also known as *Roger* by various French historians. French custom altered their name to Ruggieri, as it did Catherine's from Medici to Medicis.

The elder Ruggieri, then, was so highly esteemed by the family of the Medici that the two Dukes, Cosmo and Lorenzo, were godfathers to his sons. In his capacity of mathematician, astrologer, and physician to the Ducal House—three offices that were often scarcely distinguished—he cast the horoscope of Catherine's nativity, in concert with Bazile, the famous mathematician. At that period the occult sciences were cultivated with an eagerness which may seem surprising to the skeptical spirits of this supremely analytical age, who perhaps may find in this historical sketch the germ of the positive sciences which flourish in the nineteenth century—bereft, however, of the poetic grandeur brought to them by the daring speculators of the sixteenth ; for they, instead of applying themselves to industry, exalted art and vivified thought. The protection universally granted to these sciences by the sovereigns of the period was indeed justified by the admirable works of inventors who, starting from the search for the *great work*,* arrived at astonishing results.

Never, in fact, were rulers more curious for these mysteries. The Fugger family, in whom every modern Lucullus must recognize his chiefs and every banker his masters, were beyond a doubt men of business, not to be caught nodding ; well, these practical men, while lending the capitalized wealth of Europe to the sovereigns of the sixteenth century—who ran into debt quite as handsomely as those of to-day—these illustrious entertainers of Charles V. furnished funds for the retorts of Paracelsus. At the beginning of the sixteenth century, Ruggieri the elder was the head of that secret college whence came Cardan, Nostradamus, and Agrippa, each in turn physician to the Valois ; and all the astronomers, astrologers, and alchemists who at that period crowded to the Courts of the princes of Christendom, and who found especial welcome and protection in France from Catherine de' Medici.

In the horoscope cast for Catherine by Bazile and Ruggieri the elder, the principal events of her life were predicted with an accuracy that is enough to drive disbelievers to despair. This forecast announced the disasters which, during the siege of Florence, affected her early life, her marriage with a Prince of France, his unexpected accession to the throne, the birth and the number of her children. Three of her sons were to reign in succession, her two daughters were to become queens ; all were to die childless. And this was all so exactly

* Magnum opus.

verified that many historians have regarded it as a prophecy after the event.

It is well known that Nostradamus brought to the Castle of Chaumont, whither Catherine went at the time of la Renaudie's conspiracy, a woman who had the gift of reading the future.   Now in the time of Francis II., when the Queen's sons were still children and in good health, before Elizabeth de Valois had married Philip II. of Spain, or Marguerite de Valois had married Henri de Bourbon, King of Navarre, Nostradamus and this soothsayer confirmed all the details of the famous horoscope.

This woman, gifted no doubt with second-sight, and one of the extensive association of indefatigable inquirers for the *magnum opus*, though her life has evaded the ken of history, foretold that the last of these children to wear the crown would perish assassinated.   Having placed the Queen in front of a magical mirror in which a spinning-wheel was reflected, each child's face appearing at the end of a spoke, the soothsayer made the wheel turn, and the Queen counted the number of turns.   Each turn was a year of a reign.   When Henri IV. was placed on the wheel, it went round twenty-two times. The woman—some say it was a man—told the terrified Queen that Henri de Bourbon would certainly be King of France, and reign so many years.   Queen Catherine vowed a mortal hatred of the Béarnais on hearing that he would succeed the last, murdered Valois.

Curious to know what sort of death she herself would die, she was warned to beware of Saint-Germain.   Thenceforth, thinking that she would be imprisoned or violently killed at the Castle of Saint-Germain, she never set foot in it, though, by its nearness to Paris, it was infinitely better situated for her plans than those where she took refuge with the King in troubled times.   When she fell ill, a few days after the Duc de Guise was assassinated, during the assembly of the States-General at Blois, she asked the name of the prelate who came to minister to her. She was told that his name was Saint-Germain.

"I am a dead woman ! " she cried.

She died the next day, having lived just the number of years allotted to her by every reading of her horoscope.

This scene, known to the Cardinal de Lorraine, who ascribed it to the Black Art, was being realized ; Francis II. had reigned for two turns only of the wheel, and Charles IX. was achieving his last. When Catherine spoke these strange words to her son Henri as he set out for Poland, "You will soon return ! " they must be ascribed to her faith in the occult sciences, and not to any intention of poisoning Charles IX. Marguerite de France was now Queen of Navarre ; Elizabeth was Queen of Spain ; the Duc d'Anjou was King of Poland.

Many other circumstances contributed to confirm Catherine's belief in the occult sciences. On the eve of the tournament where Henri II. was mortally wounded, Catherine saw the fatal thrust in a dream. Her astrological council, consisting of Nostradamus and the two Ruggieri, had foretold the King's death. History has recorded Catherine's earnest entreaties that he should not enter the lists. The prognostic and the dream begotten of the prognostic were verified.

The chronicles of the time relate another and not less strange fact. The courier who brought news of the victory of Moncontour arrived at night, having ridden so hard that he had killed three horses. The Queen-mother was roused, and said, "I knew it."

"In fact," says Brantôme, "she had the day before announced her son's success and some details of the fight."

The astrologer attached to the House of Bourbon foretold that the youngest of the Princes in direct descent from Saint-Louis, the son of Antoine de Bourbon, would be King of France. This prophecy, noted by Sully, was fulfilled precisely as described by the horoscope, which made Henry IV.

remark that by dint of lies these astrologers hit on the very truth.

Be this as it may, most of the clever men of the time believed in the far-reaching "science of the Magi," as it was called by the masters of astrology—or sorcery, as it was termed by the people—and they were justified by the verification of horoscopes.

It was for Cosmo Ruggieri, her mathematician and astrologer—her wizard, if you will—that Catherine erected the pillar against the corn-market in Paris, the only remaining relic of the Hôtel de Soissons. Cosmo Ruggieri, like confessors, had a mysterious influence which satisfied him, as it does them. His secret ambition, too, was superior to that of vulgar minds. This man, depicted by romance-writers and playwrights as a mere juggler, held the rich abbey of Saint-Mahé in Lower Brittany, and had refused high ecclesiastical preferment; the money he derived in abundance from the superstitious mania of the time was sufficient for his private undertakings; and the Queen's hand, extended to protect his head, preserved every hair of it from harm.

As to Catherine's devouring thirst for dominion, her desire to acquire power was so great that, in order to grasp it, she could ally herself with the Guises, the enemies of the throne; and to keep the reins of State in her own hands, she adopted every means, sacrificing her friends, and even her children. This woman could not live without the intrigues of rule, as a gambler cannot live without the excitement of play. Though she was an Italian and a daughter of the luxurious Medici, the Calvinists, though they calumniated her plentifully, never accused her of having a lover.

Appreciating the maxim, "Divide to reign," for twelve years she had been constantly playing off one force against another. As soon as she took the reins of government into her hands, she was compelled to encourage discord to neutralize the strength of two rival Houses and save the throne.

This necessary system justified Henri II.'s foresight. Catherine was the inventor of the political see-saw, imitated since by every prince who has found himself in a similar position; she upheld, by turns, the Calvinists against the Guises, and the Guises against the Calvinists. Then, after using the two creeds to check each other in the heart of the people, she set the Duc d'Anjou against Charles IX. After using things to counteract each other, she did the same with men, always keeping the clue to their interests in her own hands.

But in this tremendous game, which requires the head of a Louis XI. or a Louis XVIII., the player inevitably is the object of hatred to all parties, and is condemned to win unfailingly, for one lost battle makes every interest his enemy, until indeed by dint of winning he ends by finding no one to play against him. The greater part of Charles IX.'s reign was the triumph of the domestic policy carried out by this wonderful woman. What extraordinary skill Catherine must have brought into play to get the chief command of the army given to the Duc d'Anjou, under a brave young King thirsting for glory, capable and generous—and in the face of the Connétable Anne de Montmorency! The Duc d'Anjou, in the eyes of all Europe, reaped the honors of Saint-Bartholomew's Day, while Charles IX. had all the odium. After instilling into the King's mind a spurious and covert jealousy of his brother, she worked upon this feeling so as to exhaust Charles IX.'s really fine qualities in the intrigues of rivalry with his brother. Cypierre, their first tutor, and Amyot, Charles IX.'s preceptor, had made their royal charge so noble a man, and had laid the foundations of so great a reign, that the mother hated the son from the very first day when she feared to lose her power after having conquered it with so much difficulty.

These facts have led certain historians to believe that the Queen-mother had a preference for Henri III.; but her behavior at this juncture proves that her heart was absolutely indifferent toward her children. The Duc d'Anjou, when he

17

went to govern Poland, robbed her of the tool she needed to keep Charles IX.'s mind fully occupied by these domestic intrigues, which had hitherto neutralized his energy by giving food to his vehement feelings.  Catherine then hatched the conspiracy of la Mole and Coconnas, in which the Duc d'Alençon had a hand ; and he, when he became Duc d'Anjou on his brother's being made King, lent himself very readily to his mother's views and displayed an ambition which was encouraged by his sister Marguerite, Queen of Navarre.

This plot, now ripened to the point which Catherine desired, aimed at putting the young Duke and his brother-in-law, the King of Navarre, at the head of the Calvinists, at seizing Charles IX., thus making the King, who had no heir, a prisoner, and leaving the throne free for the Duke, who proposed to establish Calvinism in France.  Only a few days before his death, Calvin had won the reward he hoped for—the Reformed creed was called Calvinism in his honor.

La Mole and Coconnas had been arrested fifty days before the night on which this scene opens, to be beheaded in the following April ; and if le Laboureur and other judicious writers had not amply proved that they were the victims of the Queen-mother, Cosmo Ruggieri's participation in the affair would be enough to show that she secretly directed it. This man, suspected and hated by the King for reasons which will be presently sufficiently explained, was implicated by the inquiries.  He admitted that he had furnished la Mole with an image representing the King and stabbed to the heart with two needles.  This form of witchcraft was at that time a capital crime.  This kind of bedevilment (called in French *envoûter*, from the Latin *vultus*, it is said) represented one of the most infernal conceptions that hatred could imagine, and the word admirably expresses the magnetic and terrible process carried on, in occult science, by constantly active malevolence on the person devoted to death ; its effects being incessantly suggested by the sight of the wax figure.  The law at that time considered, and with good reason, that the idea thus embodied constituted high treason. Charles IX. desired the death of the Florentine; Catherine, more powerful, obtained from the Supreme Court, through the intervention of her Councilor Lecamus, that her astrologer should be condemned only to the galleys. As soon as the King was dead, Ruggieri was pardoned by an edict of Henri III.'s,* who reinstated him in his revenues and received him at Court.

Catherine had, by this time, struck so many blows on her son's heart, that at this moment he was only anxious to shake off the yoke she had laid on him. Since Marie Touchet's absence, Charles IX., having nothing to occupy him, had taken to observing very keenly all that went on around him. He had set very skillful snares for certain persons whom he had trusted, to test their fidelity. He had watched his mother's proceedings, and had kept her in ignorance of his own, making use of all the faults she had inculcated in order to deceive her. Eager to efface the feeling of horror produced in France by the massacre of Saint-Bartholomew, he took an active interest in public affairs, presided at the council, and tried by well-planned measures to seize the reins of government. Though the Queen might have attempted to counteract her son's endeavors by using all the influence that maternal authority and her habit of dominion could have over his mind, the downward course of distrust is so rapid that, at the first leap, the son had gone too far to be recalled.

On the day when his mother's words to the King of Poland were repeated to Charles IX., he already felt so ill that the most hideous notions dawned on his mind; and when such suspicions take possession of a son and a king nothing can remove them. In fact, on his death-bed his mother was obliged to interrupt him, exclaiming, "Do not say that, monsieur!" when Charles IX., intrusting his wife and

* In 1573 chosen and crowned King of Poland.

daughter to the care of Henri IV., was about to put him on his guard against Catherine.

Though Charles IX. never failed in the superficial respect of which she was so jealous, and she never called the kings, her sons, anything but monsieur, the Queen-mother had, for some months past, detected in Charles' manner the ill-disguised irony of revenge held in suspense. But he must be a clever man who could deceive Catherine. She held in her hand this conspiracy of the Duc d'Alençon and la Mole, so as to be able to divert Charles' effort at emancipation by this new rivalry of a brother; but before making use of it, she was anxious to dissipate the want of confidence which might make her reconciliation with the King impossible—for how could he leave the power in the hands of a mother who was capable of poisoning him?

Indeed, at this juncture she thought herself so far in danger that she had sent for Strozzi, her cousin, a soldier famous for his death. She held secret councils with Birague and the Gondis, and never had she so frequently consulted the oracle of the Hôtel de Soissons.

Though long habits of dissimulation and advancing years had given Catherine that abbess-like countenance, haughty and ascetic, expressionless and yet deep, reserved but scrutinizing, and so remarkable for any student of her portraits, those about her perceived a cloud over this cold, Florentine mirror. No sovereign was ever a more imposing figure than this woman had made herself since the day when she had succeeded in coercing the Guises after the death of Francis II. Her black velvet hood, with a peak over the forehead, for she never went out of mourning for Henri II., was, as it were, a womanly cowl round her cold, imperious features, to which she could, however, on occasion, give insinuating Italian charms. She was so well-made that she introduced the fashion for women to ride on horseback in such a way as to display their legs; this is enough to prove that hers were of perfect form.   Every lady in Europe thenceforth rode on a side-saddle, *à la planchette,** for France had long set the fashions.

To any one who can picture this impressive figure, the scene in the great room that evening has an imposing aspect. The two Queens, so unlike in spirit, in beauty, and in dress, and almost at daggers drawn, were both much too absent-minded to give the impetus for which the courtiers waited to raise their spirits.

The dead secret of the drama which, for the past six months, the son and mother had been cautiously playing, was guessed by some of their followers ; the Italians, more especially, had kept an attentive lookout, for if Catherine should lose the game, they would all be the victims.   Under these circumstances, at a moment when Catherine and her son were vying with each other in subterfuges, the King was the centre of observation.

Charles IX., tired by a long day's hunting and by the serious reflections he brooded over in secret, looked forty this evening.   He had reached the last stage of the malady which killed him, and which gave rise to grave suspicions of poison. According to de Thou, the Tacitus of the Valois, the surgeon found unaccountable spots in the King's body (*ex causâ incognitâ reperti livores*).   His funeral was even more carelessly conducted than that of Francis II.   Charles the Ninth was escorted from Saint-Lazare to Saint-Denis by Brantôme and a few archers of the Guard commanded by the Comte de Solern. This circumstance, added to the mother's supposed hatred of her son, may confirm the accusations brought against her by de Thou ; at least it gives weight to the opinion here expressed, that she cared little for any of her children, an indifference which is accounted for by her faith in the pronouncement of astrology.   Such a woman could not care for the tools that were to break in her hands.   Henri III. was the

* Lit.: On a shelf.

last King under whom she could hope to reign; and that was all.

In our day it seems allowable to suppose that Charles IX. died a natural death. His excesses, his manner of life, the sudden development of his powers, his last struggles to seize the reins of government, his desire to live, his waste of strength, his last sufferings and his last pleasures, all indicate, to impartial judges, that he died of disease of the lungs, a malady at that time little understood and of which nothing was known; and its symptoms might lead Charles himself to believe that he was poisoned.

The real poison given him by his mother lay in the evil counsels of the courtiers with whom she surrounded him, who induced him to waste his intellectual and physical powers, and who thus were the cause of a disease which was purely incidental and not congenital.

Charles the Ninth, at this period of his life more than at any other, bore the stamp of a sombre dignity not unbecoming in a King. The majesty of his secret thoughts was reflected in his face, which was remarkable for the Italian complexion he inherited from his mother. This ivory pallor, so beautiful by artificial light, and so well suited with an expression of melancholy, gave added effect to his deep blue eyes showing narrowly under thick eyelids, and thus acquiring that keen acumen which imagination pictures in the glance of a King, while their color was an aid to dissimulation. Charles' eyes derived an awe-inspiring look from his high, marked eyebrows —accentuating a lofty forehead—which he could lift or lower with singular facility. His nose was long and broad and thick at the tip—a true lion's nose; he had large ears; light reddish hair; lips of the color of blood, the lips of a consumptive man; the upper lip thin and satirical, the lower full enough to indicate fine qualities of feeling.

The wrinkles stamped on his brow in early life, when terrible anxieties had blighted its freshness, made his face intensely interesting; more than one had been caused by remorse for the massacre of Saint-Bartholomew, a deed which had been craftily foisted on him; but there were two other lines on his face which would have been eloquent to any student who at that time could have had a special revelation of the principles of modern physiology. These lines made a deep furrow from the cheek-bones to each corner of the mouth, and betrayed the efforts made by an exhausted organization to respond to mental strain and to violent physical enjoyment. Charles IX. was worn out. The Queen-mother, seeing her work, must have felt some remorse, unless, indeed, politics stifle such a feeling in all who sit under the purple. If Catherine could have foreseen the effects of her intrigues on her son, she might perhaps have shrunk from them(?).

It was a terrible spectacle. The King, by nature so strong, had become weak; the spirit, so nobly tempered, was racked by doubts; this man, the centre of authority, felt himself helpless; the naturally firm temper had lost confidence in its power. The warrior's valor had degenerated into ferocity, reserve had become dissimulation, the refined and tender passion of the Valois was an insatiable thirst for pleasure. This great man, misprized, perverted, with every side of his noble spirit chafed to a sore, a King without power, a loving heart without a friend, torn a thousand ways by conflicting schemes, was, at four-and-twenty, the melancholy image of a man who has found everything wanting, who distrusts every one, who is ready to stake his all, even his life. Only lately had he understood his mission, his power, his resources, and the obstacles placed by his mother in the way of the pacification of the kingdom; but the light glowed in a broken lamp.

Two men, for whom the King had so great a regard that he had saved one from the massacre of Saint-Bartholomew, and had dined with the other at a time when his enemies accused him of poisoning the King—his chief physician Jean Chapelain, and the great surgeon Ambroise Paré—had been sent for from the country by Catherine, and, obeying the summons in hot haste, arrived at the King's bedtime. They looked anxiously at their sovereign, and some of the courtiers made whispered inquiries, but they answered with due reserve, saying nothing of the sentence each had secretly pronounced. Now and again the King would raise his heavy eyelids and try to conceal from the bystanders the glance he shot at his mother. Suddenly he rose, and went to stand in front of the fireplace.

"Monsieur de Chiverni," said he, "why do you keep the title of Chancellor of Anjou and Poland? Are you our servant or our brother's?"

"I am wholly yours, Sire," replied Chiverni, with a bow.

"Well, then, come to-morrow; I mean to send you to Spain, for strange things are doing at the Court of Madrid, gentlemen."

The King looked at his wife and returned to his chair.

"Strange things are doing everywhere," he added in a whisper to Marshal Tavannes, one of the favorites of his younger days. And he rose to lead the partner of his youthful pleasures into the recess of an oriel window, saying to him—

"I want you; stay till the last. I must know whether you will be with me or against me. Do not look astonished. I am breaking the leading strings. My mother is at the bottom of all the mischief here. In three months I shall either be dead or be really King. As you love your life, silence! You are in my secret with Solern and Villeroy. If the least hint is given, it will come from one of you three. Do not keep too close to me; go and pay your court to my mother; tell her that I am dying, and that you cannot regret it, for that I am but a poor creature."

Charles IX. walked round the room leaning on his old favorite's shoulder, and discussing his sufferings with him, to mislead inquisitive persons; then, fearing that his coldness might be too marked, he went to talk with the two Queens, calling Birague to his side.

Just then Pinard glided in at the door and came up to Queen Catherine, slipping in like an eel, close to the wall. He murmured two words in the Queen-mother's ear, and she replied with an affirmative nod. The King did not ask what this meant, but he went back to his chair with a scowl round the room of horrible rage and jealousy. This little incident was of immense importance in the eyes of all the Court. This exertion of authority without any appeal to the King was like the drop of water that makes the glass overflow. The young Queen and Countess Fieschi withdrew without the King's paying her the least attention, but the Queen-mother attended her daughter-in-law to the door. Though the mis-understanding between the mother and son lent enormous interest to the movements, looks, and attitude of Catherine and Charles IX., their cold composure plainly showed the courtiers that they were in the way; as soon as the Queen had gone they took their leave. At ten o'clock no one re-mained but certain intimate persons—the two Gondis, Ta-vannes, the Comte de Solern, Birague, and the Queen-mother.

The King sat plunged in the deepest melancholy. This silence was fatiguing. Catherine seemed at a loss; she wished to retire, and she wanted the King to attend her to the door, but Charles remained obstinately lost in thought; she rose to bid him good-night, Charles was obliged to follow her example; she took his arm, and went a few steps with him to speak in his ear these few words—

"Monsieur, I have matters of importance to discuss with you."

As she left, the Queen-mother met the eyes of the Gondis reflected in a glass, and gave them a significant glance, which her son could not see—all the more so because he himself was exchanging meaning looks with the Comte de Solern and Vil-leroy; Tavannes was absorbed in thought.

"Sire," said the Maréchal de Retz, coming out of his meditations, "you seem right royally bored. Do you never amuse yourself nowadays? Heaven above us! where are the times when we went gadding about the streets of nights?"

"Yes, those were good times," said the King, not without a sigh.

"Why not be off now?" said Monsieur de Birague, bowing himself out, with a wink at the Gondis.

"I always think of that time with pleasure," cried the Maréchal de Retz.

"I should like to see you on the roofs, Monsieur le Maréchal," said Tavannes. "*Sacré chat d'Italie* (Sacred Italian cat), if you might but break your neck," he added in an undertone to the King.

"I know not whether you or I should be nimblest at jumping across a yard or a street; but what I do know is, that neither of us is more afraid of death than the other," replied the Duc de Retz.

"Well, Sire, will you come to scour the town as you did when you were young?" said the master of the wardrobe to the King.

Thus at four-and-twenty the unhappy King was no longer thought young, even by his flatterers. Tavannes and the King recalled, like two schoolfellows, some of the good tricks they had perpetrated in Paris, and the party was soon made up. The two Italians, being dared to jump from roof to roof across the street, pledged themselves to follow where the King should lead. They all went to put on common clothes.

The Comte de Solern, left alone with the King, looked at him with amazement. The worthy German, though filled with compassion as he understood the position of the King of France, was fidelity and honor itself, but he had not a lively imagination. King Charles, surrounded by enemies, and trusting no one, not even his wife—who, not knowing that his mother and all her servants were inimical to him, had

committed some little indiscretions—was happy to have found
in Monsieur de Solern a devotion which justified complete
confidence. Tavannes and Villeroy were only partly in the
secret. The Comte de Solern alone knew the whole of the
King's schemes; and he was in every way very useful to his
master, inasmuch that he had a handful of confidential and
attached men at his orders who obeyed him blindly. Monsieur de Solern, who held a command in the Archers of the
Guard, had for some days been picking from among his men
some who were faithful in their adherence to the King, to
form a chosen company. The King could think of everything.

"Well, Solern," said Charles IX., "we are needing a pretext for spending a night out of doors. I had the excuse, of
course, of Madame de Belleville; but this is better, for my
mother can find out what goes on at Marie's house."

Monsieur de Solern, as he was to attend the King, asked if
he might not go the rounds with some of his Germans, and
to this Charles consented. By eleven o'clock the King, in
better spirits now, set out with his three companions to ex-
plore the neighborhood of the Rue Saint-Honoré.

"I will take my lady by surprise," said Charles to Tavannes as they went along the Rue de l'Autruche.

To make this nocturnal play more intelligible to those who
may be ignorant of the topography of old Paris, it will be
necessary to explain the position of the Rue de l'Autruche.
The part of the Louvre, begun by Henri II., was still being
built amid the wreck of houses. Where the wing now stands
looking over the Pont des Arts, there was at that time a
garden. In the place of the Colonnade there were a moat
and a drawbridge on which, somewhat later, a Florentine, the
Maréchal d'Ancre, met his death. Beyond this garden rose
the turrets of the Hôtel de Bourbon, the residence of the
princes of that branch till the day when the constable's
treason (after he was ruined by the confiscation of his posses-

sions, decreed by Francis I., to avoid having to decide between him and his mother) put an end to the trial that had cost France so dear, by the confiscation of the constable's estates.

This castle, which looked well from the river, was not destroyed till the time of Louis XIV.

The Rue de l'Autruche ran from the Rue Saint-Honoré, ending at the Hôtel de Bourbon on the quay. This street, named de l'Autriche on some old plans, and de l'Austruc on others, has, like many more, disappeared from the map. The Rue des Poulies would seem to have been cut across the ground occupied by the houses nearest to the Rue Saint-Honoré. Authors have differed, too, as to the etymology of the name. Some suppose it to be derived from a certain Hôtel d'Osteriche (*Osterrichen*), inhabited in the fourteenth century by a daughter of that house who married a French nobleman. Some assert that this was the site of the royal aviaries, whither, once on a time, all Paris crowded to see a living ostrich.

Be it as it may, this tortuous street was made notable by the residences of certain Princes of the Blood, who dwelt in the vicinity of the Louvre. Since the sovereign had deserted the Faubourg Saint-Antoine, where for several centuries he had lived in the Bastille, and removed to the Louvre, many of the nobility had settled near the palace. The Hôtel de Bourbon had its fellow in the old Hôtel d'Alençon in the Rue Saint-Honoré. This, the palace of the Counts of that name, always an appanage of the Crown, was at this time owned by Henry II.'s fourth son, who subsequently took the title of Duc d'Anjou, and who died in the reign of Henri III., to whom he gave no little trouble. The estate then reverted to the Crown, including the old palace, which was pulled down. In those days a prince's residence was a vast assemblage of buildings; to form some idea of its extent, we have only to go and see the space covered by the Hôtel de Soubise, which is still standing in the Marais. Such a palace included all the buildings necessary to these magnificent lives, which may seem almost problematical to many persons who see how poor is the state of a prince in these days. There were immense stables, lodgings for physicians, librarians, chancellor, chaplains, treasurers, officials, pages, paid servants, and lackeys, attached to the prince's person.

Not far from the Rue Saint-Honoré, in a garden belonging to the Hôtel, stood a pretty little house built in 1520 by command of the celebrated Duchesse d'Alençon, which had since been surrounded with other houses erected by merchants. Here the King had installed Marie Touchet. Although the Duc d'Alençon was engaged in a conspiracy against the King at that time, he was incapable of annoying him in such a matter.

As the King was obliged to pass by his lady's door on his way down the Rue Saint-Honoré, where at that time highway robbers had no opportunities within the Barrière des Sergents, he could hardly avoid stopping there. While keeping a lookout for some stroke of luck—a belated citizen to be robbed or the watch to be thrashed—the King scanned every window, peeping in wherever he saw lights, to see what was going on, or to overhear a conversation. But he found his good city in a provokingly peaceful state. On a sudden, as he came in front of the house kept by a famous perfumer named René, who supplied the Court, the King was seized with one of those swift inspirations which are suggested by antecedent observations, as he saw a bright light shining from the topmost window of the roof.

This perfumer was strongly suspected of doctoring rich uncles when they complained of illness; he was credited at Court with the invention of the famous *Élixir à successions*— the Elixir of Inheritance—and had been accused of poisoning Jeanne d'Albret, Henri IV.'s mother, who was buried without her head having been opened, in spite of the express orders of Charles IX., as a contemporary* tells us.   For two months past the King had been seeking some stratagem to enable him to spy out the secrets of René's laboratory, whither Como Ruggieri frequently resorted.   Charles intended, if anything should arouse his suspicions, to take steps himself without the intervention of the police or the law, over whom his mother would exert the influence of fear or of bribery.

It is beyond all doubt that during the sixteenth century, and the years immediately preceding and following it, poisoning had been brought to a pitch of perfection which remains unknown to modern chemistry, but which is indisputably proved by history.   Italy, the cradle of modern science, was at that time the inventor and mistress of these secrets, many of which are lost.   Romancers have made such extravagant use of this fact, that whenever they introduce Italians they make them play the part of assassins and poisoners.

But though Italy had then the monopoly of those subtle poisons of which historians tell us, we must regard her supremacy in toxicology merely as part of her preëminence in all branches of knowledge and in the arts, in which she led the way for all Europe.   The crimes of the period were not hers alone ; she served the passions of the age, as she built magnificently, commanded armies, painted glorious frescoes, sang songs, loved Queens, and directed politics.   At Florence this hideous art had reached such perfection that a woman dividing a peach with a duke could make use of a knife of which one side only was poisoned, and, eating the untainted half, dealt death with the other.   A pair of perfumed gloves introduced a mortal malady by the pores of the hand ; poison could be concealed in a bunch of fresh roses of which the fragrance, inhaled but once, meant certain death. Don Juan of Austria, it is said, was poisoned by a pair of boots.

So King Charles had a right to be inquisitive, and it is easy

* De Thou : " Historia sui Temporis."

to imagine how greatly the dark suspicions which tormented him added to his eagerness to detect René in the act.

The old fountain, since rebuilt, at the corner of the Rue de l'Arbre-Sec, afforded this illustrious crew the necessary access to the roof of a house, which the King pretended that he wished to invade, not far from René's. Charles, followed by his companions, began walking along the roofs, to the great terror of the good folk awakened by these marauders, who would call to them, giving them some coarsely grotesque name, listen to family squabbles or love-makings, or do some vexatious damage.

When the two Gondis saw Tavannes and the King clambering along the roof adjoining René's, the Maréchal de Retz sat down, saying he was tired, and his brother remained with him.

"So much the better," thought the King, glad to be quit of his spies.

Tavannes made fun of the two Italians, who were then left alone in the midst of perfect silence in a place where they had only the sky above them and the cats for listeners. And the brothers took advantage of this position to speak out thoughts which they never would have uttered elsewhere— thoughts suggested by the incidents of the evening.

"Albert," said the Grand Master to the marshal, "the King will get the upper hand of the Queen; we are doing bad business so far as our fortunes are concerned by attaching ourselves to Catherine's. If we transfer our services to the King now, when he is seeking some support against his mother, and needs capable men to rely upon, we shall not be turned out like wild beasts when the Queen-mother is banished, imprisoned, or killed."

"You will not get far, Charles, by that road," the marshal replied. "You will follow your master into the grave, and he has not long to live; he is wrecked by dissipation; Cosmo Ruggieri has foretold his death next year."

"A dying boar has often gored the hunter," said Charles de Gondi. "This plot of the Duc d'Alençon with the King of Navarre and the Prince de Condé, of which la Mole and Coconnas are taking the *onus,* is dangerous rather than useful. In the first place, the King of Navarre, whom the Queen-mother hopes to take in the fact, is too suspicious of her, and will have nothing to do with it. He means to get the benefit of the conspiracy and run none of the risks. And now, the last idea is to place the crown on the head of the Duc d'Alençon, who is to turn Calvinist."

"Foolery! Dolt that you are, do you not see that this plot enables our Queen to learn what the Huguenots can do with the Duc d'Alençon, and what the King means to do with the Huguenots? For the King is temporizing with them. And Catherine, to set the King riding on a wooden horse, will betray the plot which must nullify his schemes."

"Ay!" said Charles de Gondi, "by dint of taking our advice she can beat us at our own game. That is very good."

"Good for the Duc d'Anjou, who would rather be King of France than King of Poland; I am going to explain matters to him."

"You are going, Albert?"

"To-morrow. Is it not my duty to attend the King of Poland? I shall join him at Venice, where the ladies have undertaken to amuse him."

"You are prudence itself."

"*Che bestia!* I assure you solemnly that there is not the slightest danger for either of us at Court. If there were, should I leave? I would stick to our kind mistress."

"Kind!" said the Grand Master. "She is the woman to drop her tools if she finds them too heavy."

"*O coglione!* You call yourself a soldier, and are afraid of death? Every trade has its duties, and our duty is to

Fortune.   When we attach ourselves to monarchs who are
the fount of all temporal power, and who protect and ennoble
and enrich our families, we have to give them such love as
inflames the soul of the martyr for heaven ; when they sacrifice us for the throne we may perish, for we die as much for
ourselves as for them, but our family does not perish.   *Ecco ;*
I have said ! ''

"You are quite right, Albert ; you have got the old duchy
of Retz.''

"Listen to me,'' said the Duc de Retz.   "The Queen has
great hopes of the Ruggieri and their arts to reconcile her to
her son.   When that artful youth refused to have anything to
do with René, our Queen easily guessed what her son's suspicions were.   But who can tell what the King has in his pocket ?
Perhaps he is only doubting as to what fate he intends for his
mother ; he hates her, you understand ?   He said something
of his purpose to the Queen, and the Queen talked of it to
Madame de Fieschi ; Madame de Fieschi carried it on to the
Queen-mother, and since then the King has kept out of his
wife's way.''

"It was high time——'' said Charles de Gondi.

"What to do ?'' asked the marshal.

"To give the King something to do,'' replied the Grand
Master, who, though he was on less intimate terms with
Catherine than his brother, was not less clear-sighted.

"Charles,'' said de Retz gravely, "I have started on a
splendid road ; but if you want to be a Duke, you must, like
me, be our mistress' ready tool.   She will remain Queen ; she
is the strongest.   Madame de Sauves is still devoted to her ;
and the King of Navarre and the Duc d'Alençon are devoted
to Madame de Sauves ; Catherine will always have them in
leading strings under this King, as she will have them under
King Henri III.   Heaven send he may not be ungrateful ! ''

"Why ?''

"His mother does too much for him.''

18

"Hark! There is a noise in the Rue Saint-Honoré," cried Charles de Gondi. "René's door is being locked. Can you not hear a number of men? They must have taken the Ruggieri."

"The devil! What a piece of prudence! The King has not shown his usual impetuosity. But where will he imprison them? Let us see what is going on."

The brothers reached the corner of the Rue de l'Autruche at the moment when the King was entering his mistress' house. By the light of the torches held by the gatekeeper they recognized Tavannes and the Ruggieri.

"Well, Tavannes," the Grand Master called out as he ran after the King's companion, who was making his way back to the Louvre, "what adventures have you had?"

"We dropped on a full council of wizards, and arrested two who are friends of yours, and who will explain for the benefit of French noblemen by what means you, who are not Frenchmen, have contrived to clutch two Crown offices," said Tavannes, half in jest.

"And the King?" asked the Grand Master, who was not much disturbed by Tavannes' hostility.

"He is staying with his mistress."

"We have risen to where we stand by the most absolute devotion to our masters, a brilliant and noble career which you too have adopted, my dear Duke," replied the Maréchal de Retz.

The three courtiers walked on in silence. As they bade each other good-night, rejoining their retainers, who escorted them home, two men lightly glided along the Rue de l'Autruche in the shadow of the wall. These were the King and the Comte de Solern, who soon reached the river-bank at a spot where a boat and rowers, engaged by the German Count, were awaiting them. In a few minutes they had reached the opposite shore.

"My mother is not in bed," cried the King, "she will see us; we have not made a good choice of our meeting-place."

"She will think some duel is in the wind," said Solern. "And how is she to distinguish who we are at this distance?"

"Well! Even if she sees me!" cried Charles IX. "I have made up my mind now."

The King and his friend jumped on shore, and hurried off toward the Pré aux Clercs. On arriving there, the Comte de Solern, who went first, parleyed with a man on sentry, with whom he exchanged a few words, and who then withdrew to a group of others.

Presently two men, who seemed to be princes by the way the outposts saluted them, left the spot where they were in hiding behind some broken fencing, and came to the King, to whom they bent the knee; but Charles IX. raised them before they could touch the ground, saying—

"No ceremony; here we are all gentlemen together."

These three were now joined by a venerable old man, who might have been taken for the Chancellor de l'Hôpital, but that he had died the year before. Then all four walked on as quickly as possible to reach a spot where their conversation could not be overheard by their retainers, and Solern followed them at a little distance to keep guard over the King. This faithful servant felt some doubts which Charles did not share, for to him, indeed, life was too great a burden. The Count de Solern was the only witness present at the meeting on the King's side.

It soon became interesting.

"Sire," said one of the speakers, "the Connétable de Montmorency, the best friend the King, your father, had, and possessed of all his secrets, agreed with the Maréchal de Saint-André that Madame Catherine should be sewn up in a sack and thrown into the river. If that had been done, many good men would be alive now."

"I have executions enough on my conscience, monsieur," replied the King.

"Well, Sire," said the youngest of the four gentlemen, "from the depths of exile Queen Catherine would still manage to interfere and find men to help her. Have we not everything to fear from the Guises, who, nine years since, schemed for a monstrous Catholic alliance, in which your majesty is not included, and which is a danger to the throne? This alliance is a Spanish invention—for Spain still cherishes the hope of leveling the Pyrenees. Sire, Calvinism can save France by erecting a moral barrier between this nation and one that aims at the Empire of the world. If the Queen-mother finds herself in banishment, she will throw herself on Spain and the Guises."

"Gentlemen," said the King, "I will have you to know that, with your help, and with peace established on a basis of confidence, I will undertake to make every soul in the kingdom quake. By God and every sacred relic! it is time that the royal authority should assert itself. Understand this clearly; so far, my mother is right, power is slipping from your grasp, as it is from mine. Your estates, your privileges are bound to the throne; when you have allowed religion to be overthrown, the hands you are using as tools will turn against the Monarchy and against you.

"I have had enough of fighting ideas with weapons that cannot touch them. Let us see whether Protestantism can make its way if left to itself; above all, let us see what the spirit of that faction means to attack. The admiral, God be merciful to him, was no enemy of mine. He swore to me that he would restrain the revolt within the limits of spiritual feeling, and in the temporal kingdom secure mastery to the King and submissive subjects. Now, gentlemen, if the thing is still in your power, set an example, and help your sovereign to control the malcontents who are disturbing the peace of both parties alike. War robs us of all our revenue, and ruins the country; I am weary of this troubled State—so much so that, if it should be absolutely necessary, I would sacrifice my mother. I would do more: I would have about me a like number of Catholics and of Protestants, and I would hang Louis XI.'s axe over their heads to keep them equal. If Messieurs de Guise plot a Holy Alliance which endangers the Crown, the executioner shall begin on them.

"I understand the griefs of my people, and am quite ready to cut freely at the nobles who bring trouble on our country. I care little for questions of conscience; I mean henceforth to have submissive subjects who will work, under my rule, at the prosperity of the State.

"Gentlemen, I give you ten days to treat with your adherents, to break up your plots, and return to me, who will be a father to you. If you are refractory, you will see great changes. I shall make use of smaller men who, at my bidding, will rush upon the great lords. I will follow the example of a king who pacified his realm by striking down greater men than you are who dared to defy him. If Catholic troops are wanting, I can appeal to my brother of Spain to defend a threatened throne; nay, and if I need a Minister to carry out my will, he will lend me the Duke of Alva."

"In that event, Sire, we can find Germans to fight your Spaniards," said one of the party.

"I may remind you, cousin," said Charles IX. coldly, "that my wife's name is Elizabeth of Austria; your allies on that side might fail you. But take my advice; let us fight this alone without calling in the foreigner. You are the object of my mother's hatred, and you care enough for me to play the part of second in my duel with her—well, then, listen. You stand so high in my esteem that I offer you the office of high constable; you will not betray us as the other has done."

The Prince thus addressed took the King's hand in a friendly grasp, exclaiming—

"God's 'ounds, brother, that is indeed forgiving evil!

But, Sire, the head cannot move without the tail, and our tail is hard to drag along. Give us more than ten days. We still need at least a month to make the rest hear reason; by the end of that time we shall be the masters."

"A month, so be it; Villeroy is my only plenipotentiary. Take no word but his, whatever any one may say."

"One month," said the three other gentlemen;"that will be enough time."

"Gentlemen," said the King, "we are but five, all men of mettle. If there is any treachery, we shall know with whom to deal."

The three gentlemen left the King with every mark of deep respect and kissed his hand.

As the King recrossed the Seine, four o'clock was striking by the Louvre clock.

Queen Catherine was still up.

"My mother is not gone to bed," said Charles to the Comte de Solern.

"She too has her forge," said the German.

"My dear Count, what must you think of a king who is reduced to conspiracy?" said Charles IX. bitterly, after a pause.

"I think, Sire, that if you would only allow me to throw that woman into the river, as our young friend said, France would soon be at peace."

"Parricide!—and after Saint-Bartholomew's!" said the King. "No, no—Exile. Once fallen, my mother would not have an adherent or a partisan."

"Well, then, Sire," the Count went on, "allow me to take . her into custody now, at once, and escort her beyond the frontier; for by to-morrow she will have won you round again to her views."

"Well," said the King, "come to my forge; no one can hear us there. Beside, I am anxious that my mother should know nothing of the arrest of the Ruggieri. If she knows I am within, the good lady will suspect nothing, and we will concert the measures for arresting her."

When the King, attended by Solern, went into the low room which served as his workshop, he smiled as he pointed to his forge and various tools.

"I do not suppose," said he, "that of all the kings France may ever have, there will be another with a taste for such a craft. But when I am really King, I shall not forge swords; they shall all be sheathed."

"Sire," said the Comte de Solern, "the fatigues of tennis, your work at the forge, hunting, and—may I say it?—love-making, are chariots lent you by the devil to hasten your journey to Saint-Denis."

"Ah, Solern!" said the King sadly, "if only you could feel the fire they have set burning in my heart and body. Nothing can slake it. Are you sure of the men who are guarding the Ruggieri?"

"As sure as of myself."

"Well, in the course of this day I shall have made up my mind. Think out the means of acting, and I will give you my final instructions at five this evening, at Madame de Belleville's."

The first gleams of daybreak were struggling with the lights in the King's workshop, where the Comte de Solern had left him alone, when he heard the door open and saw his mother, looking like a ghost in the gloom. Though Charles IX. was highly strung and nervous, he did not start, although under the circumstances this apparition had an ominous and grotesque aspect.

"Monsieur," said she, "you are killing yourself——"

"I am fulfilling my horoscopes," he retorted, with a bitter smile. "But you, madame, are you as ill as I am?"

"We have both watched through the night, monsieur, but with very different purpose. When you were setting out to confer with your bitterest enemies in the open night, and hiding it from your mother, with the connivance of Tavannes and the Gondis, with whom you pretended to be scouring the town, I was reading dispatches which prove that a terrible conspiracy is hatching, in which your brother the Duc d'Alençon is implicated with your brother-in-law, the King of Navarre, the Prince de Condé, and half the nobility of your kingdom. Their plan is no less than to snatch the Crown from you by taking possession of your person. These gentlemen have already a following of fifty thousand men, all good soldiers.''

'' Indeed ! '' said the King incredulously.

'' Your brother is becoming a Huguenot,'' the Queen went on.

'' My brother joining the Huguenots ? '' cried Charles, brandishing the iron bar he held.

'' Yes. The Duc d'Alençon, a Huguenot at heart, is about to declare himself. Your sister, the Queen of Navarre, has scarcely a tinge of affection left for you. She loves Monsieur le Duc d'Alençon, she loves Bussy, and she also loves little la Mole.''

'' What a large heart ! '' said the King.

'' Little la Mole, to grow great,'' the Queen went on, '' can think of no better means than making a King of France to his mind. Then, it is said, he is to be high constable.''

'' That damned Margot ! '' cried the King. '' This is what comes of her marrying a heretic——''

'' That would be nothing ; but then there is the head of the younger branch, whom you have placed near the throne against my warnings, and who only wants to see you all kill each other ! The House of Bourbon is the enemy of the House of Valois. Mark this, monsieur, a younger branch must always be kept in abject poverty, for it is born with the spirit of conspiracy, and it is folly to give it weapons when it has none, or to leave them in its possession when it takes them.  The younger branches must be impotent for mischief —that is the law of sovereignty.  The sultans of Asia observe it.

"The proofs are upstairs in my closet, whither I begged you to follow me when we parted last night, but you had other projects.  Within a month, if we do not take a high hand, your fate will be that of Charles the Simple."

"Within a month!" exclaimed Charles, amazed at the coincidence of this period with the term fixed by the princes that very night.  "In a month we shall be the masters," thought he to himself, repeating their words.  "You have proofs, madame?" he asked aloud.

"They are unimpeachable, monsieur; they are supplied by my daughter Marguerite.  Terrified by the probable outcome of such a coalition, in spite of her weakness for your brother d'Alençon, the throne of the Valois lay, for once, nearer to her heart than all her amours.  She asks indeed, as the reward of her revelation, that la Mole shall go scot-free; but that popinjay seems to me to be a rogue we ought to get rid of, as well as the Comte de Coconnas, your brother d'Alençon's right-hand man.  As to the Prince de Condé, that boy would agree to anything so long as I may be' flung into the river; I do not know if that is his idea of a handsome return on his wedding-day for the pretty wife I got him.

"This is a serious matter, monsieur.  You spoke of predictions!  I know of one which says that the Bourbons will possess the throne of the Valois; and if we do not take care, it will be fulfilled.  Do not be vexed with your sister, she has acted well in this matter.

"My son," she went on, after a pause, with an assumption of tenderness in her tone, "many evil-minded persons, in the interest of the Guises, want to sow dissension between you and me, though we are the only two persons in the realm whose interests are identical.  Reflect.  You blame yourself now, I know, for Saint-Bartholomew's night; you blame me for persuading you to it.　But Catholicism, monsieur, ought to be the bond of Spain, France, and Italy, three nations which by a secretly and skillfully worked scheme may, in the course of time, be united under the House of Valois.　Do not forfeit your chances by letting the cord slip which includes these three kingdoms in the pale of the same faith.

"Why should not the Valois and the Medici carry out, to their great glory, the project of Charles V., who lost his head?　Let those descendants, of Jane the Crazy, people the new world at which they are grasping.　The Medici, masters of Florence and Rome, will subdue Italy to your rule; they will secure all its advantages by a treaty of commerce and alliance, and recognize you as their liege lord for the fiefs of Piedmont, the Milanese, and Naples, over which you have rights.　These, monsieur, are the reasons for the war to the death we are waging with the Huguenots.　Why do you compel us to repeat these things?

"Charlemagne made a mistake when he pushed northward. France is a body of which the heart is on the Gulf of Lyons, and whose two arms are Spain and Italy.　Thus we should command the Mediterranean, which is like a basket into which all the wealth of the East is poured to the benefit of the Venetians now, in the teeth of Philip II.

"And if the friendship of the Medici and your inherited rights can thus entitle you to hope for Italy, force, or alliance, or perhaps inheritance, may give you Spain.　There you must step in before the ambitious House of Austria, to whom the Guelphs would have sold Italy, and who still dream of possessing Spain.　Though your wife is a daughter of that line, humble Austria, hug her closely to stifle her!　There lie the enemies of your dominion, since from thence comes aid for the Reformers.　Do not listen to men who would profit by our disagreement, and who fill your head with trouble by representing me as your chief enemy at home.　Have I hindered you from having an heir?　Is it my fault that your mistress has a son and your wife only a daughter? Why have you not by this time three sons, who would cut off all this sedition at the root? Is it my part, monsieur, to reply to these questions? If you had a son, would Monsieur d'Alençon conspire against you?"

As she spoke these words, Catherine fixed her eyes on Charles IX. with the fascinating gaze of a bird of prey on its victim. The daughter of the Medici was beautiful in her way; her real feelings illumined her face, which, like that of a gambler at the green-table, was radiant with ambitious greed. Charles IX. saw her no longer as the mother of one man, but, as she had been called, the mother of armies and empires (*mater castrorum*). Catherine had spread the pinions of her genius, and was boldly soaring in the realm of high politics of the Medici and the Valois, sketching the vast plans which had frightened Henri II., and which, transmitted by the Medici to Richelieu,* were stored in the cabinet of the House of Bourbon. But Charles IX., seeing his mother take so many precautions, supposed them to be necessary, and wondered to what end she was taking them. He looked down; he hesitated; his distrust was not to be dispelled by words.

Catherine was astonished to see what deeply founded suspicion lurked in her son's heart.

"Well, monsieur," she went on, "do you not choose to understand me? What are we, you and I, compared with the eternity of a royal Crown? Do you suspect me of any purposes but those which must agitate us who dwell in the sphere whence empires are governed?"

"Madame," said he, "I will follow you to your closet—we must act——"

"Act?" cried Catherine. "Let them go their way and take them in the act; the law will rid you of them. For God's sake, monsieur, let them see us smiling."

* Reign Louis XIII., son of Henry IV. and Marie de' Medici.

The Queen withdrew. The King alone remained standing for a minute, for he had sunk into extreme dejection.

"On which side are the snares?" he said aloud. "Is it she who is deceiving me, or they? What is the better policy? *Deus! discerne causam meam,*" he cried, with tears in his eyes. "Life is a burden to me. Whether natural or compulsory, I would rather meet death than these contradictory torments," he added, and he struck the hammer on his anvil with such violence that the vaults of the Louvre quaked. "Great God!" he exclaimed, going out and looking up at the sky, "Thou for whose holy religion I am warring, give me the clearness of Thine eyes to see into my mother's heart by questioning the Ruggieri."

The little house inhabited by the Lady of Belleville, where Charles had left his prisoners, was the last but one in the Rue de l'Autruche, near the Rue Saint-Honoré. The street-gate, guarded by two little lodges built of brick, looked very plain at a time when gates and all their accessories were so elaborately treated. The entrance consisted of two stone pillars, diamond-cut, and the architrave was graced with the reclining figure of a woman holding a cornucopia. The gate, of timber covered with heavy iron scroll-work, had a wicket peephole at the level of the eye for spying any one who desired admittance. In each lodge a porter lived, and Charles' caprice insisted that a gatekeeper should be on the watch day and night.

There was a little courtyard in front of the house paved with Venetian mosaic. At that time, when carriages had not been invented, and ladies rode on horseback or in litters, the courtyard could be splendid with no fear of injury from horses or vehicles. We must constantly bear these facts in mind to understand the narrowness of the streets, the small extent of the forecourts, and various other details of the dwellings of the fifteenth century.

The house, of one story above the ground floor, had at the top a sculptured frieze, on which rested a roof sloping up from all the four sides to a flat space at the top. The sides were pierced by dormer windows adorned with architraves and side-posts, which some great artist had chiseled into delicate arabesques. All the three windows of the second-floor rooms were equally conspicuous for this embroidery in stone, thrown into relief by the red-brick walls. On the ground floor a double flight of outside steps, elegantly sculptured—the balcony being remarkable for a true lover's knot—led to the house-door, decorated in the Venetian style with stone cut into pointed lozenges, a form of ornament that was repeated on the window-jambs on each side of the door, a fashion then much in vogue.

A garden laid out in the fashion of the time, and full of rare flowers, occupied a space behind the house of equal extent with the forecourt. A vine hung over the walls. A silver pine stood in the centre of a grass-plot; the flower borders were divided from the turf by winding paths leading to a little bower of clipped yews at the further end. The garden walls, covered with a coarse mosaic of colored pebbles, pleased the eye by a richness of color that harmonized with the hues of the flowers. The garden-front of the house, like the front to the court, had a pretty balcony from the middle window over the door; and on both facades alike the architectural treatment of this middle window was carried up to the frieze of the cornice, with a bow that gave it the appearance of a lantern. The sills of the other windows were inlaid with fine marbles let into the stone.

Notwithstanding the perfect taste evident in this building, it had a look of gloom. It was shut out from the open day by neighboring houses and the roofs of the Hôtel d'Alençon, which cast their shadow over the courtyard and garden; then absolute silence prevailed. Still, this silence, this subdued light, this solitude, were restful to a soul that could give itself up to a single thought, as in a cloister where we may meditate, or in a snug home where we may love.

Who can fail now to conceive of the interior elegance of this dwelling, the only spot in all his kingdom where the last Valois but one could pour out his heart, confess his sufferings, give play to his taste for the arts, and enjoy the poetry he loved—pleasures denied him by the cares of his most ponderous royalty. There alone were his lofty soul and superior qualities appreciated; there alone, for a few brief months, the last of his life, could he know the joys of fatherhood, to which he abandoned himself with the frenzy which his presentiment of an imminent and terrible death lent to all his actions.

In the afternoon of this day, Marie was finishing her toilet in her oratory—the ladies' boudoir of that time. She was arranging the curls of her fine black hair, so as to leave a few locks to turn over a new velvet coif, and was looking attentively at herself in the mirror.

"It is nearly four o'clock! That interminable Council must be at an end by now," said she to herself. "Jacob is back from the Louvre, where they are greatly disturbed by reason of the number of councilors convened and by the duration of the sitting. What can have happened, some disaster? Dear heaven! does *he* know how the spirit is worn by waiting in vain? He is gone hunting, perhaps. If he is amused, all is well. If I see him happy, I shall forget my sorrows——"

She pulled down her bodice around her waist, that there might not be a wrinkle in it, and turned to see how her dress fitted in profile; but then she saw the King reclining on a couch. The carpeted floors deadened the sound of footsteps so effectually that he had come in without being heard.

"You startled me," she said, with a cry of surprise, which she instantly checked.

"You were thinking of me, then?" said the King.

"When am I not thinking of you?" she asked him, sitting down by his side.

She took off his cap and cloak, and passed her hands through his hair as if to comb it with her fingers. Charles submitted without speaking. Marie knelt down to study her royal master's pale face, and discerned in it the lines of terrible fatigue and of a more devouring melancholy than any she had ever been able to scare away. She checked a tear, and kept silence, not to irritate a grief she as yet knew nothing of by some ill-chosen word. She did what tender wives do in such cases; she kissed the brow seamed with precocious wrinkles and the hollow cheeks, trying to breathe the freshness of her own spirit into that careworn soul through its infusion into gentle caresses, which, however, had no effect. She raised her head to the level of the King's, embracing him fondly with her slender arms, and then laid her face on his laboring breast, waiting for the opportune moment to question the stricken man.

"My Charlot, will you not tell your poor anxious friend what are the thoughts that darken your brow and take the color from your dear, red lips?"

"With the exception of Charlemagne," said he, in a dull, hollow voice, "every King of France of the name of Charles has come to a miserable end."

"Pooh!" said she. "What of Charles VIII.?"

"In the prime of life," replied the King, "the poor man knocked his head against a low doorway in the Castle of Amboise, which he was decorating splendidly, and he died in dreadful pain.* His death gave the Crown to our branch."

"Charles VII. reconquered his kingdom."

"Child, he died"—and the King lowered his voice—"of starvation, in the dread of being poisoned by the Dauphin, who had already caused the death of his fair Agnes. .

* April 7, 1498.

The father dreaded his son.   Now, the son dreads his mother!"

"Why look back on the past?" said she, remembering the terrible existence of Charles VI.

"Why not, dear heart?  Kings need not have recourse to diviners to read the fate that awaits them; they have only to study history.   I am at this time engaged in trying to escape the fate of Charles the Simple, who was bereft of his crown, and died in prison after seven years' captivity."

"Charles V. drove out the English!" she cried triumphantly.

"Not he, but du Guesclin; for he, poisoned by Charles of Navarre, languished in sickness."

"But Charles IV.?" said she.

"He married three times and had no heir, in spite of the masculine beauty that distinguished the sons of Philip the Handsome.  The first Valois dynasty ended in him.  The second Valois will end in the same way.  The Queen has only brought me a daughter, and I shall die without leaving any child to come, for a minority would be the greatest misfortune that could befall the kingdom.  Beside, if I had a son, would he live?  Charles is a name of ill-omen, Charlemagne exhausted all the luck attending it.  If I could be King of France again, I would not be called Charles X."

"Who then aims at your crown?"

"My brother d'Alençon is plotting against me.  I see enemies on every side——"

"Monsieur," said Marie, with an irresistible pout.  "Tell me some merrier tales."

"My dearest treasure," said the King vehemently, "never call me *monsieur*, even in jest.  You remind me of my mother, who incessantly offends me with that word.  I feel as if she deprived me of my crown.  She says 'My son' to the Duc d'Anjou; that is to say, the King of Poland."

"Sire," said Marie, folding her hands as if in prayer,

"there is a realm where you are adored, which your majesty fills entirely with glory and strength; and there the word monsieur means my gentle lord."

She unclasped her hands, and with a pretty action pointed to her heart. The words were so sweetly musical—*musiquées,* to use an expression of the period, applied to love-songs—that Charles took Marie by the waist, raised her with the strength for which he was noted, seated her on his knee, and gently rubbed his forehead against the curls his mistress had arranged with such care.

Marie thought this a favorable moment; she ventured on a kiss or two, which Charles allowed rather than accepted; then, between two kisses, she said—

"If my people told the truth, you were scouring Paris all night, as in the days when you played the scapegrace younger son?"

"Yes," said the King, who sat lost in thought.

"Did you not thrash the watch and rob certain good citizens? And who are the men placed under my guard, and who are such criminals that you have forbidden all communication with them? No girl was ever barred in with greater severity than these men, who have had neither food nor drink. Solern's Germans have not allowed any one to go near the room where you left them. Is it a joke? Or is it a serious matter?"

"Yes," said the King, rousing himself from his reverie, "last night I went scampering over the roofs with Tavannes and the Gondis. I wanted to have the company of my old comrades in folly. But our legs are not what they were; we did not dare jump across the streets. However, we crossed two courtyards by leaping from roof to roof. The last time, however, when we alighted on a gable close by this, as we clung to the bar of a chimney, we decided, Tavannes and I, that we could not do it again. If either of us had been alone, he would not have tried it."

"You were the first to jump, I will wager."

19

The King smiled.

"I know why you risk your life so."

"Hah, fair sorceress!"

"You are weary of life."

"Begone with witchcraft! I am haunted by it!" said the King, grave once more.

"My witchcraft is love," said she, with a smile. "Since the happy day when you first loved me, have I not always guessed your thoughts? And if you will suffer me to say so, the thoughts that torment you to-day are not worthy of a King."

"Am I a King?" said he bitterly.

"Can you not be a King? What did Charles VII. do, whose name you bear? He listened to his mistress, my lord, and he won back his kingdom, which was invaded by the English then as it is now by the adherents of the New Religion. Your last act of State opened the road you must follow: Exterminate heresy."

"You used to blame the stratagem," said Charles, "and now——"

"It is accomplished," she put in. "Beside, I am of Madame Catherine's opinion. It was better to do it yourself than to leave it to the Guises."

"Charles VII. had only men to fight against, but I have to battle with ideas," the King went on. "You may kill men; you cannot kill words? The Emperor Charles V. gave up the task; his son, Don Philip, is spending himself in the attempt. We shall die of it, we kings. On whom can I depend? On my right, with the Catholics, I find the Guises threatening me; on my left, the Calvinists will never forgive the death of my poor Father Coligny, nor the blood-letting of August; beside, they want to be rid of us altogether. And in front of me, my mother——"

"Arrest her; reign alone," said Marie, whispering in his ear.

"AM I A KING?" SAID HE, BITTERLY.

"I wanted to do so yesterday—but I do not to-day. You speak of it lightly enough."

"There is no such great distance between the daughter of an apothecary and the daughter of a leech," said Marie Touchet, who would often laugh at the parentage falsely given her.

The King knit his brows.

"Marie, take no liberties. Catherine de' Medici is my mother, and you ought to tremble at——"

"But what are you afraid of?"

"Poison!" cried the King, beside himself.

"Poor boy!" said Marie, swallowing her tears, for so much strength united to so much weakness moved her deeply. "Oh!" she went on, "how you make me hate Madame Catherine, who used to seem so kind; but her kindness seems to be nothing but perfidy. Why does she do me so much good and you so much evil? While I was away in Dauphiné I heard a great many things about the beginning of your reign which you had concealed from me; and the Queen your mother seems to have been the cause of all your misfortunes."

"How?" said the King, with eager interest.

"Women whose soul and intentions are pure rule the men they love through their virtues; but women who do not truly wish them well find a motive power in their evil inclinations. Now the Queen has turned many fine qualities in you into vices, and made you believe that your bad ones were virtues. Was that acting a mother's part? Be a tyrant like Louis XI., make everybody dreadfully afraid of you, imitate Don Philip, banish the Italians, hunt out the Guises, and confiscate the estates of the Calvinists; you will rise to stand in solitude, and you will save the Crown. The moment is favorable; your brother is in Poland."

"We are two infants in politics," said Charles bitterly. "We only know how to love. Alas! dear heart, yesterday I could think of all this; I longed to achieve great things. Puff! my mother has blown down my house of cards. From afar difficulties stand out as clearly as mountain peaks. I say to myself, 'I will put an end to Calvinism; I will bring Messieurs de Guise to their senses; I will cut adrift from the Court of Rome; I will rely wholly on the people of the middle-class;' in short, at a distance everything looks easy, but, when we try to climb the mountains, the nearer we get the more obstacles we discern.

"Calvinism in itself is the last thing the party-leaders care about; and the Guises, those frenzied Catholics, would be in despair if the Calvinists were really exterminated. Every man thinks of his own interests before all else, and religious opinions are but a screen for insatiable ambition. Charles IX.'s party is the weakest of all; those of the King of Navarre, of the King of Poland, of the Duc d'Alençon, of the Condés, of the Guises, of my mother, form coalitions against each other, leaving me alone even in the Council Chamber. In the midst of so many elements of disturbance my mother is the stronger, and she has just shown me that my plans are inane. We are surrounded by men who defy the law. The axe of Louis XI. of which you speak is not in our grasp. The Parlement would never sentence the Guises, nor the King of Navarre, nor the Condés, nor my brothers. It would think it was setting the kingdom in a blaze. What is wanted is the courage to command murder; the throne must come to that, with these insolent wretches who have nullified justice; but where can I find faithful hands? The Council I held this morning disgusted me with everything—treachery on all sides, antagonistic interests everywhere!

"I am tired of wearing the crown; all I ask is to die in peace."

And he sank into gloomy somnolence.

"Disgusted with everything!" echoed Marie Touchet sadly, but respecting her lover's heavy torpor.

Charles was, in fact, a prey to utter prostration of mind and body, resulting from over-fatigue of every faculty, and enhanced by the dejection caused by the vast scale of his misfortunes and the evident impossibility of overcoming them in the face of such a multiplicity of difficulties as genius itself takes alarm at. The King's depression was proportionate to the height to which his courage and his ideas had soared during the last few months; and now a fit of nervous melancholy, part, in fact, of his malady, had come over him as he left the long sitting of the Council he had held in his closet. Marie saw that he was suffering from a crisis when everything is irritating and importunate—even love; so she remained on her knees, her head in the King's lap, as he sat with his fingers buried in her hair without moving, without speaking, without sighing, and she was equally still. Charles IX. was sunk in the lethargy of helplessness; and Marie in the dark despair of a loving woman, who can see the border-line ahead where love must end.

Thus the lovers sat for some little time in perfect silence, in the mood when every thought is a wound, when the clouds of a mental storm hide even the remembrance of past happiness.

Marie believed herself to be in some sort to blame for this terrible dejection. She wondered, not without alarm, whether the King's extravagant joy at welcoming her back, and the vehement passion she could not contend with, were not helping to wreck his mind and frame. As she looked up at her lover, her eyes streaming with tears that bathed her face, she saw tears in his eyes too and on his colorless cheeks. This sympathy, uniting them even in sorrow, touched Charles IX. so deeply that he started up like a horse that feels the spur. He put his arm around Marie's waist, and before she knew what he was doing had drawn her down on to the sumptuous couch.

"I will be King no more!" he said. "I will be nothing

but your lover, and forget everything in that joy.  I will die happy and not eaten up with the cares of a throne."

The tone in which he spoke, the fire that blazed in eyes just now so dull, instead of pleasing Marie, gave her a terrible pang ; at that moment she blamed her love for contributing to the illness of which the King was dying.

"You forget your prisoners," said she, starting up suddenly.

"What do I care about the men?  They have my permission to kill me."

"What?  Assassins ! " said she.

" Do not be uneasy, we have them safe, dear child.  Now, think not of them, but of me.  Say, do you not love me ?" he inquired.

"Sire ! " she cried.

"Sire ! " he repeated, flashing sparks from his eyes, so violent was his first surge of fury at his mistress' ill-timed deference.  "You are in collusion with my mother."

"Great God ! " cried Marie, turning to the picture over her praying-chair, and trying to get to it to put up a prayer. "Oh ! make him understand me ! "

"What ! " said the King sternly.  "Have you any sin on your soul ? "

And still holding her in his arms, he looked deep into her eyes.  "I have heard of the mad passion of one d'Entragues for you," he went on, looking wildly at her, "and since their grandfather, Capitaine Balzac, married a Visconti of Milan, those rascals hesitate at nothing."

Marie gave the King such a look of pride that he was ashamed.  Just then the cry was heard of the infant Charles de Valois from the adjoining room ; he was just awake, and his nurse was no doubt bringing him to his mother.

"Come in, la Bourguignonne," said Marie, taking the child from his nurse and bringing him to the King.  "You are more of a child than he," said she, half angry, but half appeased.

"He is a fine boy," said Charles IX., taking his son in his arms.

"No one but me can know how like you he is," said Marie. "He has your smile and ways already."

"What, so young?" said the King, smiling.

"Men will never believe such things," said she; "but look, my Charlot, play with him, look at him—now, am I not right?"

"It is true," said the King, startled by a movement on the infant's part, which struck him as the miniature reproduction of a trick of his own.

"Pretty flower!" said his mother. "He will never go away from me; he will never make me unhappy."

The King played with the child, tossing it, kissing it with entire devotion, speaking to it in those vague and foolish words, the onomatopœia of mothers and nurses; his voice was childlike, his brow cleared, joy came back to his saddened countenance; and when Marie saw that her lover had forgotten everything, she laid her head on his shoulder and whispered in his ear—

"Will you not tell me, my Charlot, why you put assassins in my keeping, and who these men are, and what you intend to do with them? And whither were you going across the roofs? I hope there was no woman in the case."

"Then you still love me so well?" said the King, caught by the bright flash of one of those questioning looks which women can give at a critical moment.

"You could doubt me?" asked she, as the tears gathered under her beautiful girlish eyelids.

"There are women in my adventure, but they are witches. Where was I?"

"We were quite near here, on the gable of a house," said Marie. "In what street?"

"In the Rue Saint-Honoré, my jewel," said the King, who seemed to have recovered himself, and who, as he recalled his ideas, wanted to give his mistress some notion of the scene that was about to take place here. "As I crossed it in pursuit of some sport, my eyes were attracted by a bright light in a top window of the house inhabited by René, my mother's perfumer and glover—yours too, the whole Court's. I have strong suspicions as to what goes on in that man's house, and if I am poisoned that is where the poison is prepared."

"I give him up to-morrow," said Marie.

"What, you have still dealt with him since I left him?" said the King. "My life was here," he added gloomily, "and here no doubt they have arranged for my death."

"But, my dear boy, I have just come home from Dauphiné with our Dauphin," said she, with a smile, "and I have bought nothing of René since the Queen of Navarre died. Well, go on; you climbed up to René's roof——?"

"Yes," the King went on. "In a moment I, followed by Tavannes, had reached a spot whence, without being seen, I could see into the devil's kitchen, and note certain things which led me to take strong measures. Do you ever happen to have noticed the attics that crown that damned Florentine's house? All the windows to the street are constantly kept shut excepting the last, from which the Hôtel de Soissons can be seen, and the column my mother had erected for her astrologer, Cosmo Ruggieri. There is a room in this top story with a corridor lighted from the inner yard, so that, in order to see what is being done within, a man must get to a perch which no one would ever think of climbing, the coping of a high wall which ends against the roof of René's house. The creatures who placed the alembics there to distill death trusted to the faint hearts of the Parisians to escape inspection; but they counted without their Charles de Valois. I crept along the gutter, and supported myself against the window-jamb with my arm round the neck of a monkey that is sculptured on it."

"And what did you see, dear heart?" said Marie, in alarm.

"A low room where deeds of darkness are plotted," replied

the King. "The first thing on which my eyes fell was a tall, old man seated in a chair, with a magnificent beard like old l'Hôpital's, and dressed, like him, in black velvet. The concentrated rays of a brightly burning lamp fell on his high · forehead, deeply furrowed by hollow lines, on a crown of white hair and a calm, thoughtful face, pale with vigils and study. His attention was divided between a manuscript on parchment several centuries old and two lighted stoves on which some heretical mixtures were cooking. Neither the floor nor the ceiling was visible; they were so covered with animals hung up there, skeletons, dried herbs, minerals, and drugs, with which the place was stuffed; here some books and retorts, with chests full of instruments for magic and astrology; there diagrams for horoscopes, phials, wax-figures, and, perhaps, the poisons he concocts for René in payment for the shelter and hospitality bestowed on him by my mother's glover.

"Tavannes and I were startled, I can tell you, at the sight of this diabolical arsenal; for merely at the sight of it one feels spellbound, and but that my business is to be King of France, I should have been frightened. 'Tremble for us both,' said I to Tavannes.

"But Tavannes' eyes were riveted on the most mysterious object. On a couch by the old man's side lay a girl at full length, of the strangest beauty, as long and slender as a snake, as white as an ermine, as pale as death, as motionless as a statue. Perhaps it was a woman just dug out of her grave, for she seemed to be still wrapped in her shroud; her eyes were fixed, and I could not see her breathe. The old wretch paid no sort of heed to her. I watched him so curiously that his spirit I believe passed into me. By dint of studying him, at last I admired that searching eye, keen and bold, in spite of the chills of age; that mouth, mobile with thoughts that came from what seemed a single fixed desire, graven in a myriad wrinkles. Everything in the man spoke of a hope which nothing can discourage and nothing dismay. His attitude, motionless but full of thrilling life, his features so chiseled, so deeply cut by a passion that has done the work of the sculptor's tool, that mind dead-set on some criminal or scientific purpose, that searching intelligence on the track of nature though conquered by her, and bent, without having broken, under the burden of an enterprise it will never give up, threatening creation with fire borrowed from itself—— I was fascinated for a moment.

"That old man was more a king than I, for his eye saw the whole world and was its master. I am determined to temper no more swords; I want to float over abysses, as that old man does; his science seems to me a sovereignty. In short, I believe in these occult sciences."

"You, the eldest son, and the defender of the Holy Catholic, Apostolic, and Roman Church!" cried Marie.

"I."

"Why, what has come over you? Go on; I will be frightened for you, and you shall be brave for me."

"The old man looked at the clock and rose," the King went on. "He left the room, how I could not see, but I heard him open the window toward the Rue Saint-Honoré. Presently a light shone out, and then I saw another light, answering to the old man's, by which we could perceive Cosmo Ruggieri on the top of the column.

"'Oh, ho! They understand each other,' said I to Tavannes, who at once thought the whole affair highly suspicious, and was quite of my opinion that we should seize these two men, and at once make a search in their abominable workshop. But, before proceeding to a raid, we wanted to see what would happen. By the end of a quarter of an hour the door of the laboratory opened, and Cosmo Ruggieri, my mother's adviser—the bottomless pit in which all the Court secrets are buried, of whom wives crave help against their husbands and their lovers, and husbands and lovers take counsel against faithless women, who gains money out of the past and the future, taking it from every one, who sells horoscopes, and is supposed to know everything—that half-demon came in, saying to the majestic-looking old man, 'Good-evening, brother.'

"He had with him a horrible little old woman, toothless, hunchbacked, crooked, and bent like a lady's marmoset, but far more hideous; she was wrinkled like a withered apple, her skin was of the color of saffron, her chin met her nose, her mouth was a hardly visible slit, her eyes were like the black spots of the deuce on dice, her brow expressed a bitter temper, her hair fell in gray locks from under a dirty coif; she walked with a crutch; she stank of devilry and the stake; and she frightened us, for neither Tavannes nor I believed that she was a real woman; God never made one so horrible as her.

"She sat down on a stool by the side of the fair white serpent with whom Tavannes was falling in love.

"The two brothers paid no heed to either the old woman or the young one, who, side by side, formed a horrible contrast. On one hand life in death, on the other death in life."

"My sweet poet!" cried Marie, kissing the King.

"'Good-evening, Cosmo,' the old alchemist replied. And then both looked at the stove. 'What is the power of the moon to-night?' the old man asked Cosmo. 'Why, dear Lorenzo,' my mother's astrologer replied, 'the high tides of September are not yet over; it is impossible to read anything in the midst of such confusion.' 'And what did the Orient say this evening?' 'He has just discovered,' said Cosmo, 'that there is a creative force in the air which gives back to the earth all it takes from it; he concludes, with us, that everything in this world is the outcome of a slow transformation, but all the various forms are of one and the same matter.' 'That is what my predecessor thought,' said Lorenzo. 'This morning Bernard Palissy was telling me that the metals are a result of compression, and that fire, which parts all things, joins all things also; fire has the power of compressing as well as that of diffusing. That worthy has a spark of genius in him.'

"Though I was placed where I could not be seen, Cosmo went up to the dead girl, and, taking her hand, said, 'There is some one near! Who is it?' 'The King,' said she, very promptly.

"I at once showed myself, knocking on the window-pane; Ruggieri opened the window and I jumped into this wizard's kitchen, followed by Tavannes.

"'Yes, the King,' said I to the two Florentines, who seemed terror-stricken. 'In spite of your furnaces and books, your witches and your learning, you could not divine my visit. I am delighted to see the famous Lorenzo Ruggieri, of whom the Queen my mother speaks with such mystery,' said I to the old man, who rose and bowed. 'You are in this kingdom without my consent, my good man. Whom are you working for here, you, who from father to son have dwelt in the heart of the House of the Medici? Listen to me. You have your hand in so many purses that the most covetous would by this have had their fill of gold; you are far too cunning to plunge unadvisedly into criminal courses, but you ought not either to rush like feather-brains into this kitchen; you must have some secret schemes, you who are not content with gold or with power? Whom do you serve, God or the devil? What are you concocting here? I insist on the whole truth. I am honest man enough to hear and keep the secret of your undertakings, however blamable they may be. So tell me everything without concealment. If you deceive me, you will be sternly dealt with. But Pagan or Christian, Calvinist or Mohammedan, you have my royal word for it that you may leave the country unpunished, even if you have some peccadilloes to confess. At any rate, I give you the remainder of this night and to-morrow morning to examine your consciences, for you are my prisoners, and you must now follow me to a place where you will be guarded like a treasure.'

"Before yielding to my authority, the two Florentines glanced at each other with a wily eye, and Lorenzo Ruggieri replied that I might be certain that no torture would wring their secrets from them; that in spite of their frail appearance, neither pain nor human feeling had any hold on them. Confidence alone could win from their lips what their mind had in its keeping. I was not to be surprised if at that moment they treated on an equal footing with a King who acknowledged no one above him but God, for that their ideas also came from God alone. Hence they demanded of me such confidence as they would grant. So, before pledging themselves to answer my questions without reserve, they desired me to place my left hand in the young girl's and my right hand in the old woman's. Not choosing to let them suppose that I feared any devilry, I put out my hands. Lorenzo took the right and Cosmo the left, and each placed one in the hand of a woman, so there I was like Jesus Christ between the two thieves. All the time the two witches were studying my hands, Cosmo held a mirror before me, desiring me to look at myself, while his brother talked to the two women in an unknown tongue. Neither Tavannes nor I could catch the meaning of a single sentence.

"We set seals on every entrance to this laboratory before bringing away the men, and Tavannes undertook to keep guard till Bernard Palissy and Chapelain, my physician-in-chief, shall go there to make a close examination of all the drugs stored or made there. It was to hinder their knowing anything of the search going on in their kitchen, and to prevent their communicating with any one whatever outside—for they might have sent some message to my mother—that I brought these two demons to be shut up here with Solern's Germans to watch them, who are as good as the stoutest prison-walls. René himself is confined to his room under the eye of Solern's groom, and the two witches also.   And now, sweetheart, as I hold the key of the Cabala, the kings of Thunes, the chiefs of witchcraft, the princes of Bohemia, the masters of the future, the inheritors of all the famous soothsayers, I will read and know your heart, and at last we will know what is to become of us."

"I shall be very glad if they can lay my heart bare," said Marie, without showing the least alarm.

"I know why necromancers do not frighten you; you cast spells yourself."

"Will you not have some of these peaches?" said she, offering him some fine fruit on a silver-gilt plate.   "Look at these grapes and pears; I went myself to gather them all at Vincennes."

"Then I will eat some, for there can be no poison in them but the philters distilled from your fingers."

"You ought to eat much fruit, Charles; it would cool your blood, which you scorch by such violent living."

"And ought I not to love you less, too?"

"Perhaps——" said she.   "If what you love is bad for you—and I have often thought so—I should find power in my love to refuse to let you have it.   I adore Charles far more than I love the King, and I want the man to live without the troubles that make him sad and anxious."

"Royalty is destroying me."

"It is so," replied she.   "If you were only a poor prince like your brother-in-law the King of Navarre, that wretched debauchee who has not a sou or a stitch of his own, who has merely a poor little kingdom in Spain where he will never set foot, and Béarn in France, which yields him scarcely enough to live on, I should be happy, much happier than if I were really Queen of France."

"But are you not much more than the Queen?   King Charles is hers only for the benefit of the kingdom, for the Queen, after all, is part of our politics."

Marie smiled with a pretty little pout, saying—

"We all know that, my liege. And my sonnet—is it finished?"

"Dear child, it is as hard to write verses as to draw up an edict of pacification. I will finish them for you soon. Ah God! life sits lightly on me here; would I could never leave you! But I must, nevertheless, examine the two Florentines. By all the sacred relics, I thought one Ruggieri quite enough in France, and behold there are two! Listen, my dearest heart, you have good mother-wit, you would make a capital lieutenant of police, for you detect everything——"

"Well, Sire, we women take all we dread for granted, and to us what is probable is certain; there is all our subtlety in two words."

"Well, then, help me to fathom these two men. At this moment every determination I may come to depends on this examination. Are they innocent? Are they guilty? Behind them stands my mother."

"I hear Jacob on the winding stair," said Marie.

Jacob was the King's favorite body-servant, who accompanied him in all his amusements; he now came to ask whether his master would wish to speak with the two prisoners.

At a nod of consent, the mistress of the house gave some orders.

"Jacob," said she, "make every one in the place leave the house, except the nurse and Monsieur le Dauphin d'Auvergne —they may stay. Do you remain in the room downstairs; but first of all shut the windows, draw the curtains, and light the candles."

The King's impatience was so great that, while these preparations were being made, he came to take his place on a large settle, and his pretty mistress seated herself by his side in the nook of a wide, white marble chimney-place, where a bright fire blazed on the hearth. In the place of a mirror hung a portrait of the King, in a red velvet frame. Charles rested his elbow on the arm of the seat, to contemplate the two Italians at his ease.

The shutters closed, and the curtains drawn, Jacob lighted the candles in a sort of candelabrum of chased silver, placing it on a table at which the two Florentines took their stand— seeming to recognize the candlestick as the work of their fellow-townsman, Benvenuto Cellini. Then the effect of this rich room, decorated in the King's taste, was really brilliant. The russet tone of the tapestries looked better than by daylight. The furniture, elegantly carved, reflected the light of the candles and of the fire in its shining bosses. The gilding, judiciously introduced, sparkled here and there like eyes, and gave relief to the brown coloring that predominated in this nest for lovers.

Jacob knocked twice, and at a word brought in the two Florentines. Marie Touchet was immediately struck by the grand presence which distinguished Lorenzo in the sight of great and small alike. This austere and venerable man, whose silver beard was relieved against an overcoat of black velvet, had a forehead like a marble dome. His severe countenance, with two black eyes that darted points of fire, inspired a thrill as of a genius emerged from the deepest solitude, and all the more impressive because its power was not dulled by contact with other men. It was as the steel of a blade that has not yet been used.

Cosmo Ruggieri wore the Court dress of the period. Marie nodded to the King, to show him that he had not exaggerated the picture, and to thank him for introducing her to this extraordinary man. "I should have liked to see the witches, too," she whispered.

Charles IX., sunk again in brooding, made no reply; he was anxiously flipping off some crumbs of bread that happened to lie on his doublet and hose.

"Your science cannot work on the sky, nor compel the sun to shine, Messieurs de Florence," said the King, pointing to the curtains which had been drawn to shut out the gray mist of Paris. "There is no daylight."

"Our science, Sire, enables us to make a sky as we will," said Lorenzo Ruggieri. "The weather is always fair for those who work in a laboratory by the light of a furnace."

"That is true," said the King. "Well, father," said he, using a word he was accustomed to employ to old men, "explain to us very clearly the object of your studies."

"Who will guarantee us impunity?"

"The word of a King!" replied Charles, whose curiosity was greatly excited by this question.

Lorenzo Ruggieri seemed to hesitate, and Charles exclaimed—

"What checks you? we are alone."

"Is the King of France here?" asked the old man.

Charles IX. reflected for a moment, then he replied, "No."

"But will he not come?" Lorenzo urged.

"No," replied Charles, restraining an impluse of rage.

The imposing old man took a chair and sat down. Cosmo, amazed at his boldness, dared not imitate his brother.

Charles IX. said, with severe irony—

"The King is not here, monsieur, but you are in the presence of a lady for whose permission you ought to wait."

"The man you see before you, madame," said the grand old man, "is as far above kings as kings are above their subjects, and you shall find me courteous, even when you know my power."

Hearing these bold words, spoken with Italian emphasis, Charles and Marie looked at each other and then at Cosmo, who, with his eyes fixed on his brother, seemed to be asking himself, "How will he get himself out of the awkward position we are in?"

In fact, one person only could appreciate the dignity and skill of Lorenzo Ruggieri's first move; not the King, nor his

20

young mistress, over whom the elder man had cast the spell of his audacity, but his not less wily brother Cosmo. Though he was superior to the cleverest men at Court, and perhaps to his patroness Catherine de' Medici, the astrologer knew Lorenzo to be his master.

The learned old man, buried in solitude, had gauged the sovereigns of the earth, almost all of them wearied out by the perpetual shifting of politics; for at that time great crises were so sudden, so far reaching, so fierce, and so unexpected! He knew their satiety, their lassitude; he knew with what eagerness they pursued all that was new, strange, or uncommon; and, above all, how glad they were to rise now and then to intellectual regions so as to escape from the perpetual struggle with men and things. To those who have exhausted politics, nothing remains but abstract thought; this Charles V. had proved by his abdication.

Charles IX., who made sonnets and swords to recreate himself after the absorbing business of an age when the Throne was in not less ill-odor than the King, and when royalty had only its cares and none of its pleasures, could not but be strangely startled by Lorenzo's audacious negation of his power. Religious impiety had ceased to be surprising at a time when Catholicism was closely inquired into; but the subversion of all religion, assumed as a groundwork for the wild speculations of mystical arts, naturally amazed the King and roused him from his gloomy absence of mind. Beside, a victory to be won over mankind was an undertaking which would make every other interest seem trivial in the eyes of the Ruggieri. An important debt to be paid depended on this idea to be suggested to the King; the brothers could not ask for this, and yet they must obtain it. The first thing was to make Charles IX. forget his suspicions by making him jump at some new idea.

The two Italians knew full well that in this strange game their lives were at stake; and the glances—deferent but proud

—that they exchanged with Marie and the King, whose looks were keen and suspicious, were a drama in themselves.

"Sire," said Lorenzo Ruggieri, "you have asked for the truth. But to show her to you naked, I must bid you sound the well, the pit, from which she will rise. I pray you let the gentleman, the poet, forgive us for saying what the Eldest Son of the Church* may regard as blasphemy—I do not believe that God troubles Himself about human affairs."

Though fully resolved to preserve his sovereign indifference, Charles IX. could not control a gesture of surprise.

"But for that conviction, I should have no faith in the miraculous work to which I have devoted myself. But, to carry it out, I must believe it ; and if the hand of God rules all things, I am a madman. So, be it known to the King, we aim at winning a victory over the immediate course of human nature.

"I am an alchemist, Sire ; but do not suppose, with the vulgar, that I am striving to make gold. The composition of gold is not the end, but only an incident of our researches ; else we should not call our undertaking *magnum opus*, the great work. The great work is something far more ambitious than that. If I, at this day, could recognize the presence of God in matter, the fire of the furnaces that have been burning for centuries would be extinguished to-morrow at my bidding.

"But make no mistake—to deny the direct interference of God is not to deny God. We place the Creator of all things far above the level to which religions reduce Him. Those who hope for immortality are not to be accused of atheism. Following the example of Lucifer, we are jealous of God, and jealousy is a proof of violent love. Though this doctrine lies at the root of our labors, all adepts do not accept it. Cosmo," said the old man, indicating his brother, "Cosmo is devout ; he pays for masses for the repose of our father's soul, and he

* A title of the Kings of France.

goes to hear them.  Your mother's astrologer believes in the
divinity of Christ, in the immaculate conception, and in tran-
substantiation ; he believes in the Pope's indulgences, and in
hell—he believes in an infinite number of things.  His hour
is not yet come, for I have read his horoscope ; he will live to
be nearly a hundred.  He will live through two reigns, and
see two kings of France assassinated——''

"Who will be——?'' asked the King.

"The last of the Valois and the first of the Bourbons,''
replied Lorenzo.  "But Cosmo will come to my way of
thinking.  In fact, it is impossible to be an alchemist and
a Catholic ; to believe in the dominion of man over matter,
and in the supreme power of mind.''

"Cosmo will live to be a hundred?'' said the King, knitting his brows in the terrible way that was his wont.

"Yes, Sire,'' said Lorenzo decisively.  "He will die peacefully in his bed.''

"If it is in your power to predict the moment of your
death, how can you be ignorant of the result of your inquiries?'' asked the King.  And he smiled triumphantly as
he looked at Marie Touchet.

The brothers exchanged a swift look of satisfaction.

"He is interested in alchemy,'' thought they, "so we are
safe.''

"Our prognostics are based on the existing relations of
man to nature ; but the very point we aim at is the complete
alteration of those relations,'' replied Lorenzo.

The King sat thinking.

"But if you are sure that you must die, you are assured of
defeat,'' said Charles IX.

"As our predecessors were,'' replied Lorenzo, lifting his
hand and letting it drop with a solemn and emphatic gesture,
as dignified as his thoughts.  "But your mind has rushed on
to the goal of our attempt, Sire ; we must come back again,
Sire !  Unless you know the ground on which our edifice is

erected, you may persist in saying that it will fall, and judge this science, which has been pursued for centuries by the greatest minds, as the vulgar judge it.''

The King bowed assent.

''I believe, then, that this earth belongs to man, that he is master of it, and may appropriate all the forces, all the elements thereof. Man is not a creature proceeding directly from the hand of God, but the result of the principle diffused throughout the infinite ether, wherein myriads of beings are produced; and these have no resemblance to each other between star and star, because the conditions of life are everywhere different. Ay, my liege, the motion we call life has its source beyond all visible worlds; creation draws from it as the surrounding conditions may require, and the minutest beings share in it by taking all they are able, at their own risk and peril; it is their part to defend themselves from death. This is the sum-total of alchemy.

''If man, the most perfect animal on this globe, had within him a fraction of the Godhead, he could not perish—but he does perish. To escape from this dilemma, Socrates and his school invented the soul. I—the successor of the great unknown kings who have ruled this science—I am for the old theories against the new; I believe in the transmutation of matter which I can see, as against the eternity of a soul which I cannot see. I do not acknowledge the world of souls. If such a world existed, the substances of which the beautiful combination, produces your body—and which in madame are so dazzling—would not separate and resolve themselves after your death to return each to its own place; the water to water, the fire to fire, the metal to metal, just as when my charcoal is burnt its elements are restored to their original molecules.

''Though you say that something lives on, it is not we ourselves; all that constitutes our living self perishes.

''Now, it is my living self that I desire to perpetuate beyond the common term of life; it is the present manifestation for which I want to secure longer duration.   What ! trees live for centuries, and men shall live but for years, while those are passive and we are active; while they are motionless and speechless, and we walk and talk!   No creature on earth ought to be superior to us either in power or permanency. We have already expanded our senses; we can see into the stars.   We ought to be able to extend our life.   I place life above power.   Of what use is power if life slips from us ?

"A rational man ought to have no occupation but that of seeking—not whether there is another life—but the secret on which our present life is based, so as to be able to prolong it at will !   This is the desire that has silvered my hair.   But I walk on boldly in the darkness, leading to battle those intellects which share my faith.   Life will some day be ours."

"But how?" cried the King, starting to his feet.

"The first condition of our faith is the belief that this world is for man ; you must grant me that," said Lorenzo.

"Well and good, so be it !" said Charles de Valois, impatient, but already fascinated.

"Well, then, Sire, if we remove God from this world, what is left but man?   Now let us survey our domain.   The material world is composed of elements; those elements have a first principle within them.   All these principles resolve themselves into one which is gifted with motion.   The number three is the formula of creation : Matter, Motion, Production !"

"Proof, proof?   Pause there !" cried the King.

"Do you not see the effects?" replied Lorenzo.   "We have analyzed in our crucibles the acorn from which an oak would have risen as well as the embryo which would have become a man ; from these small masses of matter a pure element was derived to which some force, some motion would have been added.   In the absence of a Creator, must not that first principle be able to assume the external forms which constitute our world?   For the phenomena of life are everywhere the same. Yes, in metals, as in living beings, in plants as in man, life begins by an imperceptible embryo which develops spontaneously. There is a first principle! We must detect it at the point where it acts on itself, where it is one, where it is a principle before it is a creature, a cause before it is an effect; then we shall see it absolute—formless, but capable of assuming all the forms we see it take.

"When we are face to face with this particle or atom, and have detected its motion from the starting-point, we shall know its laws; we are thenceforth its masters and able to impose on it the form we may choose, among all we see; we shall possess gold, having the world, and can give ourselves centuries of life to enjoy our wealth. That is what we seek, my disciples and I. All our powers, all our thoughts are directed to that search; nothing diverts us from it. One hour wasted on any other passion would be stolen from our greatness! You have never found one of your hunting-dogs neglectful of the game or the death, and I have never known one of my persevering subjects diverted by a woman or a thought of greed.

"If the adept craves for gold and power, that hunger comes of our necessities; he clutches at fortune as a thirsty hound snatches a moment from the chase to drink, because his retorts demand a diamond to consume or ingots to be reduced to powder. Each one has his line of work. This one seeks the secret of vegetable nature, he studies the torpid life of plants, he notes the parity of motion in every species and the parity of nutrition; in every case he discerns that sun, air, and water are needed for fertility and nourishment. Another investigates the blood of animals. A third studies the laws of motion generally and its relation to the orbits of the stars. Almost all love to struggle with the intractable nature of metals; for though we find various elements in everything, we always find metals the same throughout, down to their minutest particles.

"Hence the common error as to our labors.  Do you see all these patient toilers, these indefatigable athletes, always vanquished, and always returning to the assault?  Humanity, Sire, is at our heels, as your huntsman is at the heels of the pack.  It cries to us, 'Hurry on!  Overlook nothing!  Sacrifice everything, even a man—you who sacrifice yourselves!  Hurry onward!  Cut off the head and hands of Death, my foe.'

"Yes, Sire, we are animated by a sentiment on which depends the happiness of generations to come.  We have buried many men—and what men!—who have died in the pursuit.  When we set foot on that road it is not to work for ourselves: we may perish without discovering the secret.  And what a death is that of a man who does not believe in a future life!  We are glorious martyrs; we bear the selfishness of the whole race in our hearts; we live in our successors.  On our way we discover secrets which enrich the mechanical and liberal arts.  Our furnaces shed gleams of light which help society to possess more perfect forms of industry.  Gunpowder was discovered in our retorts; we shall conquer the thunder yet.  Our patient vigils may overthrow politics."

"Can that be possible?" cried the King, sitting up again on the settle.

"Why not?" replied the Grand Master of the New Templars.  "*Tradidit mundum disputationibus!* (God has given us the world.)  Listen to this once again!  Man is lord on earth, and matter is his.  Every means, every power is at his service.  What created us?  A motion.  What power keeps life in us?  A motion.  And should not science grasp this motion?  Nothing on earth is lost, nothing flies off from our planet to go elsewhere; if it were so, the stars would fall on one another.  The waters of the Deluge are all here, and not a drop lost.  Around us, above, below, are the elements whence have proceeded the innumerable millions of men who have trodden the earth, before and since the Deluge.  What is it that remains to be done? To detect the disintegrating force; on the other hand, to discover the combining force. We are the outcome of a visible toil. When the waters covered our globe, men came forth from them who found the elements of life in the earth's covering, in the atmosphere, and in food. Earth and air, then, contain the first principle of human transformations; these go on under our eyes, by the agency of what is under our eyes; hence we can discover the secret by not confining our efforts to the span of one man's life, but making the task endure as long as mankind itself. We have, in fact, attacked matter as a whole; Matter, in which I believe, and which I, Grand Master of our Order, am bent on penetrating.

" Christopher Columbus gave a world to the King of Spain; I am seeking to give the King of France a people that shall never die. I, an outpost on the remotest frontier which cuts us off from the knowledge of things, a patient student of atoms, I destroy forms, I dissolve the bonds of every combination, I imitate Death to enable me to imitate Life. In short, I knock incessantly at the door of Creation, and shall still knock till my latest day. When I die, my knocker will pass into other hands not less indefatigable, as unknown giants bequeathed it to me.

" Fabulous images, never understood, such as those of Prometheus, of Ixion, of Adonis, of Pan, etc., which are part of the religious beliefs of every people and in every age, show us that this hope had its birth with the human race. Chaldæa, India, Persia, Egypt, Greece, and the Moors have transmitted Magian lore, the highest of all the occult sciences, the storehouse of the results of generations of watchers. Therein lay the bond of the noble and majestic Order of the Temple. When he burned the Templars, a predecessor of yours, Sire, only burned men; their secrets remain with us. The reconstruction of the Temple is the watchword of an unrecognized people, a race of intrepid seekers, all looking to the Orient of life, all brethren, all inseparable, united by an idea, stamped with the seal of toil. I am the sovereign of this people, their chief by election and not by birth. I guide them all toward the essence of life ! Grand Master, Rosicrucians, companions, adepts, we all pursue the invisible molecule which escapes our crucibles, and still evades our sight ; but we shall make ourselves eyes manifold more powerful than those bestowed on us by nature ; we shall get to the primitive atom, the corpuscular element so perseveringly sought by all the sages who have preceded us in the sublime pursuit.

"Sire, when a man stands astride on that abyss, and has at his command divers so intrepid as my brethren, other human interests look very small ; hence, we are not dangerous. Religious disputes and political struggles are far from us ; we are immeasurably beyond them. Those who contend with nature do not condescend to take men by the throat.

"Moreover, every result in our science is appreciable ; we can measure every effect, we can predict it, whereas in the combinations which include men and their interests everything is unstable. We shall submit the diamond to our crucible ; we shall make diamonds ; we shall make gold ! Like one of our craft at Barcelona, we shall make ships move by the help of a little water and fire. We shall dispense with the wind, nay, we shall make the wind, we shall make light and renew the face of empires by new industries. But we will never stoop to mount a throne to be *gehennaed* by nations."

Notwithstanding his desire to avoid being entrapped by Florentine cunning, the King, as well as his simple-minded mistress, was by this time caught and carried away in the rhetoric and rhodomontade of this pompous and specious flow of words. The lovers' eyes betrayed how much they were dazzled by the vision of mysterious riches spread out before them ; they saw, as it were, subterranean caverns in long perspective full of toiling gnomes. The impatience of curiosity dissipated the alarms of suspicion.

"But, then," exclaimed the King, "you are great politicians, and can enlighten us."

"No, Sire," said Lorenzo simply.

"Why not?" asked the King.

"Sire, it is given to no one to be able to predict what will come of a concourse of some thousands of men; we may be able to tell what one man will do, how long he will live, and whether he will be lucky or unlucky; but we cannot tell how several wills thrown together will act, and any calculation of the swing of their interests is even more difficult, for interests are men *plus* things; only in solitude can we discern the general aspect of the future. The Protestantism that is devouring you will be devoured in its turn by its practical outcome, which, in its day, will become a theory, too. Europe, so far, has not gone further than religion; to-morrow it will attack royalty."

"Then the night of Saint-Bartholomew was a great conception?"

"Yes, Sire; for when the people triumph, they will have their Saint-Bartholomew. When religion and royalty are swept away, the people will attack the great, and after the great they will fall upon the rich. Finally, when Europe is no more than a dismembered herd of men for lack of leaders, it will be swallowed up by vulgar conquerors. The world has presented a similar spectacle twenty times before, and Europe is beginning again. Ideas devour the ages as men are devoured by their passions. When man is cured, human nature will cure itself perhaps. Science is the soul of mankind, and we are its pontiffs; and those who study the soul care but little for the body."

"How far have you gone?" asked the King of this strange and learned man.

"We move but slowly; but we never lose what we have once conquered."

"So you, in fact, are the King of the Wizards," said

Charles IX., piqued at finding himself so small a personage in the presence of this man.

The imposing Grand Master of Adepts flashed a look at him that left him thunder-stricken.

"You are the King of men," replied he; "I am the King of ideas. Beside, if there were real wizards, you could not have burned them!" he added, with a touch of irony. "We too have our martyrs."

"But by what means," the King went on, "do you cast nativities? How did you know that the man near your window last night was the King of France? What power enabled one of your race to foretell to my mother the fate of her three sons? Can you, the Grand Master of the Order that would fain knead the world—can you, I say, tell me what the Queen my mother is thinking at this moment?"

"Yes, Sire."

The answer was spoken before Cosmo could pull his brother's coat to warn him.

"You know why my brother, the King of Poland, is returning home?"

"Yes, Sire."

"And why?"

"To take your place."

"Our bitterest enemies are our own kith and kin," cried the King, starting up in a fury and striding up and down the room. "Kings have no brothers, no sons, no mother! Coligny was right; my executioners are in the conventicles, they are at the Louvre. You are either impostors or regicides! Jacob, call in Solern."

"My lord!" said Marie Touchet, "the Ruggieri have your word of honor. You have chosen to eat of the fruit of the tree of knowledge; do not complain of its bitterness."

The King smiled with an expression of deep contempt; his material sovereignty seemed small in his eyes in comparison with the supreme intellectual sovereignty of old Lorenzo Ruggieri. Charles IX. could scarcely govern France; the Grand Master of the Rosicrucians commanded an intelligent and submissive people.

"Be frank; I give you my word as a gentleman that your reply, even if it should contain the avowal of the worst crimes, shall be as though it had never been spoken," the King said. "Do you study poisons?"

"To know what will secure life, it is needful to know what will cause death."

"You have the secret of many poisons?"

"Yes, but in theory only, and not in practice; we know them, but do not use them."

"Has my mother asked for any?"

"The Queen-mother, Sire, is far too clever to have recourse to such means. She knows that the sovereign who uses poison shall perish by poison; the Borgias, and Bianca, Grand Duchess of Tuscany, are celebrated examples of the dangers incurred by those who use such odious means. At Court everything is known. You can kill a poor wretch outright; of what use, then, is it to poison him? But if you attempt the life of conspicuous persons, what chance is there of secrecy? Nobody could have fired at Coligny but you, or the Queen-mother, or one of the Guises. No one made any mistake about that. Take my word for it, in politics poison cannot be used twice with impunity; beside, princes always have successors.

"As to smaller men, if, like Luther, they become sovereigns by the power of ideas, by killing them you do not kill their doctrine. The Queen is a Florentine; she knows that poison can only be the instrument of private vengeance. My brother, who has never left her since she came to France, knows how deeply Madame Diane aggrieved her; she never thought of poisoning her, and she could have done so. What would the King your father have said? No woman would

have been more thoroughly justified or more certain of impunity.   But Madame de Valentinois is alive to this day."

"And the magic of wax images?" asked the King.

"Sire," said Cosmo, "those figures are so entirely innocu-
ous that we lend ourselves to such magic to satisfy blind
passions, like physicians who give bread-pills to persons who
fancy themselves sick.   A desperate woman imagines that by
stabbing the heart of an image she brings disaster on the
faithless lover it represents.   What can we say!   These are
our taxes."

"The Pope sells indulgences," said Lorenzo Ruggieri,
smiling.

"Does my mother make use of such images?"

"Of what use would such futile means be to her who can
do what she will?"

"Could Queen Catherine save you at this moment?"
asked Charles ominously.

"We are in no danger, Sire," said Lorenzo calmly.   "I
knew before I entered this house that I should leave it safe
and sound, as surely as I know the ill-feeling that the King
will bear my brother a few days hence; but, even if he should
run some risk, he will triumph.   Though the King reigns by
the sword, he also reigns by justice," he added, in allusion to
the famous motto on a medal struck for Charles IX.

"You know everything; I shall die before long, and that
is well," returned the King, hiding his wrath under feverish
impatience.   "But how will my brother die, who, according
to you, is to be Henri III.?"

"A violent death."

"And Monsieur d'Alençon?"

"He will never reign."

"Then Henri de Bourbon will be King?"

"Yes, Sire."

"And what death will he die?"

"A violent death."

"And when I am dead, what will become of madame?" asked the King, turning to Marie Touchet.

"Madame de Belleville will marry, Sire."

"You are impostors! Send them away, my lord," said Marie Touchet.

"Dear heart, the Ruggieri have my word as a gentleman," said Charles, smiling. "Will Marie have children?"

"Yes—and madame will live to be more than eighty."

"Must I have them hanged?" said the King to his mistress. "And my son, the Comte d'Auvergne?" said Charles, rising to fetch the child.

"Why did you tell him that I should marry?" said Marie Touchet to the two brothers during the few moments when they were alone.

"Madame," replied Lorenzo with dignity, "the King required us to tell the truth, and we told it."

"Then it is true?" said she.

"As true as that the Governor of Orleans loves you to distraction."

"But I do not love him," cried she.

"That is true, madame," said Lorenzo. "But your horoscope shows that you are to marry the man who at this present loves you."

"Could you not tell a little lie for my sake?" said she with a smile. "For if the King should believe your forecast he might——"

"Is it not necessary that he should believe in our innocence?" said Cosmo, with a glance full of meaning. "The precautions taken by the King against us have given us reason, during the time we spent in your pretty gaol, to suppose that the occult sciences must have been maligned in his ears."

"Be quite easy," replied Marie; "I know him, and his doubts are dispelled."

"We are innocent," said the old man haughtily.

"So much the better; for at this moment the King is

having your laboratory searched and your crucibles and phials examined by experts."

The brothers looked at each other and smiled.

Marie took this smile for the irony of innocence; but it meant: "Poor simpletons! Do you suppose that if we know how to prepare poisons, we do not also know how to conceal them?"

"Where are the King's people, then?" asked Cosmo.

"In René's house," replied Marie; and the Ruggieri exchanged a glance which conveyed from each to each the same thought, "The Hotel de Soissons is inviolable!"

The King had so completely thrown off his suspicions, that when he went to fetch his son, and Jacob intercepted him to give him a note written by Chapelain, he opened it in the certainty of finding in it what his physician told him concerning his visit to the laboratory, where all that had been discovered bore solely on alchemy.

"Will he live happy?" asked the King, showing his infant son to the two alchemists.

"This is Cosmo's concern," said Lorenzo, turning to his brother.

Cosmo took the child's little hand and studied over it very carefully.

"Monsieur," said Charles IX. to the elder man, "if you are compelled to deny the existence of the spirit to believe that your enterprise is possible, tell me how it is that you can doubt that which constitutes your power. The mind you desire to annihilate is the torch that illumines your search. Ah, ha! Is not that moving while denying the fact of motion?" cried he, and, pleased at having hit on this argument, he looked triumphantly at his mistress.

"Mind," said Lorenzo Ruggieri, "is the exercise of an internal sense, just as the faculty of seeing various objects and appreciating their form and color is the exercise of our sight. That has nothing to do with what is assumed as to another life.  Mind—thought—is a faculty which may cease even during life with the forces that produce it."

"You are logical," said the King with surprise.  "But alchemy is an atheistical science."

"Materialist, Sire, which is quite a different thing.  Materialism is the outcome of the Indian doctrines transmitted through the mysteries of Isis to Chaldæa and Egypt, and brought back to Greece by Pythagoras, one of the demi-gods among men;  his doctrine of transmigration is the mathematics of materialism, the living law of its phases.  Each of the different creations which make up the earthly creation possesses the power of retarding the impulse that drags it into another form."

"Then alchemy is the science of sciences!" cried Charles IX., fired with enthusiasm.  "I must see you at work."

"As often as you will, Sire.  You cannot be more eager than the Queen your mother."

"Ah!  That is why she is so much attached to you!" cried the King.

"The House of Medici has secretly encouraged our research for almost a century past."

"Sire," said Cosmo, "this child will live nearly a hundred years; he will meet with some checks, but will be happy and honored, having in his veins the blood of the Valois."

"I will go to see you," said the King, who had recovered his good humor.  "You can go."

The brothers bowed to Marie and Charles IX. and withdrew.  They solemnly descended the stairs, neither looking at each other nor speaking; they did not even turn to look up at the windows from the courtyard, so sure were they that the King's eye was on them; and, in fact, as they turned to pass through the gate, they saw Charles IX. at a window.

As soon as the alchemist and the astrologer were in the Rue de l'Autruche, they cast a look in front and behind to see that no one was either following them or waiting for them.

21

and went on as far as the Louvre moat without speaking a word ; but there, finding that they were alone, Lorenzo said to Cosmo in the Florentine Italian of the time—

"*Affè d'Iddio ! como le abbiamo infinocchiato !*"   (By God, we have caught them finely !)

"*Gran mercès ! a lui sta di spartojarsi*"—(Much good may it do him ; he must make what he can of it)—said Cosmo. "May the Queen do as much for me !  We have done a good stroke for her."

Some days after this scene, which had struck Marie Touchet no less than the King, in one of those moments when in the fullness of joy the mind is in some sort released from the body, Marie exclaimed—

"Charles, I understand Lorenzo Ruggieri ; but Cosmo said nothing."

" That is true," said the King, startled by this sudden flash of light, " and there was as much falsehood as truth in what they said.  Those Italians are as slippery as the silk they spin."

This suspicion explains the hatred of Cosmo that the King betrayed on the occasion of the trial on the conspiracy of la Mole and Coconnas.  When he found that Cosmo was one of the contrivers of that plot, the King believed himself duped by the two Italians ; for it proved to him that his mother's astrologer did not devote himself exclusively to studying the stars, fulminating powder and final atoms.  Lorenzo had then left the country.

In spite of many persons' incredulity of such things, the events which followed this scene confirmed the prophecies uttered by the Ruggieri.

The King died three months later.  The Comte de Gondi followed Charles IX. to the tomb, as he had been told that he would by his brother, the Maréchal de Retz, a friend of the Ruggieri, and a believer in their foresight.

Marie Touchet married Charles de Balzac, Marquis d'Entragues, Governor of Orleans, by whom she had two daughters. The more famous of these two, the Comte d'Auvergne's half-sister, was Henri IV.'s mistress, and at the time of Biron's conspiracy tried to place her brother on the throne of France and oust the Bourbons.

The Comte d'Auvergne, made Duc d'Angoulême, lived till the reign of Louis XIV. He coined money in his province, altering the superscription; but Louis XIV. did not interfere, illegal as it was, so great was his respect for the blood of the Valois.

Cosmo lived till after the accession of Louis XIII.; he saw the fall of the House of Medici in France and the overthrow of the Concini. History has taken care to record that he died an atheist—that is to say, a materialist.

The Marquise d'Entragues was more than eighty when she died.

Lorenzo and Cosmo had for their disciple the famous Comte de Saint-Germain, who became notorious under Louis XV. The great alchemist was not less than a hundred and thirty years old, the age to which some biographers say Marion Delorme attained. The Count may have heard from the Ruggieri anecdotes of the Massacre of Saint-Bartholomew and of the reigns of the Valois, in which they could at pleasure assume a part by speaking in the first person. The Comte de Saint-Germain is the last professor of alchemy who explained the science well, but he left no writings. The doctrine of the Cabala set forth in this volume was derived from that mysterious personage.

It is a strange thing! Three men's lives, that of the old man from whom this information was obtained, that of the Comte de Saint-Germain, and that of Cosmo Ruggieri, embrace European history from the reign of Francis I. to that of Napoleon. Only fifty lives of equal length would cover the time to as far back as the first known epoch of the world.

"What are fifty generations for studying the mysteries of life?" the Comte de Saint-Germain used to say.

PARIS, *November-December,* 1836.

[NOTE.—Charles de Balzac, mentioned on page 323, was not in any way connected with the family of the author.  The Comte d'Auvergne, Duc d'Angoulême, was, of course, the child of Charles IX. and Marie Touchet.]

# PART III

### THE TWO DREAMS.

In 1786 Bodard de Saint-James, treasurer to the Navy, was of all the financiers of Paris the one whose luxury gave rise to most remark and gossip. At that time he was building his famous Folly at Neuilly, and his wife bought, to crown the tester of her bed, a plume of feathers of which the price had dismayed the Queen. It was far easier then than now to make one's self the fashion and be talked of by all Paris; a witticism was often quite enough, or the caprice of a woman.

Bodard lived in the fine house in the Place Vendôme which the farmer-general Dangé had not long since been compelled to quit. This notorious epicurean was lately dead; and on the day when he was buried, Monsieur de Bièvre, his intimate friend, had found matter for a jest, saying that now one could cross the Place Vendôme without danger (or Dangé). This allusion to the terrific gambling that went on in the deceased man's house was his funeral oration. The house is that opposite to the Chancellerie.

To complete Bodard's history as briefly as possible, he was a poor creature, he failed for fourteen millions of francs after the Prince de Guéménée. His clumsiness in not anticipating that serene bankruptcy—to use an expression of Lebrun-Pindare's—led to his never even being mentioned. He died in a garret, like Bourvalais, Bouret, and many others.

Madame de Saint-James indulged an ambition of never receiving any but people of quality—a stale absurdity that is ever new. To her the cap of a lawyer in the Parlement was but a small affair; she wanted to see her rooms filled with persons of title who had at least the minor privileges of *entrée* at Versailles. To say that many blue ribbons were to be seen in the lady's house would be untrue ; but it is quite certain that she had succeeded in winning the civility and attention of some members of the Rohan family, as was proved subsequently in the too famous case of the Queen's necklace.

One evening—it was, I believe, in August, 1786—I was greatly surprised to see in this millionaire's room, precise as she was in the matter of proofs of rank, two new faces, which struck me as being of decidedly inferior birth.

She came up to me as I stood in a window recess, where I had intentionally ensconced myself.

"Do tell me," said I, with a questioning glance at one of these strangers, "who is that specimen?  How did he get into your house?"

"He is a charming man."

"Do you see him through the prism of love, or am I mistaken in him?"

"You are not mistaken," she replied, laughing ; "he is as ugly as a toad ; but he has done me the greatest service a woman can accept from a man."

As I looked at her with mischievous meaning, she hastened to add—"He has entirely cured me of the ugly red patches which spoilt my complexion and made me look like a peasant woman."

I shrugged my shoulders with disgust.

"A quack !" I exclaimed.

"No," said she, "he is a physician to the Court pages. He is clever and amusing, I assure you ; and he has written books too.  He is a very learned physicist."

"If his literary style is like his face !" said I, smiling. "And the other?"

"What other?"

"That little prim man, as neat as a doll, and who looks as if he drank verjuice."

"He is a man of good family," said she.  "He has come from some province—I forget which.  Ah ! yes, from Artois.

He is in Paris to wind up some affair that concerns the cardinal, and his eminence has just introduced him to Monsieur de Saint-James. They have agreed in choosing Monsieur de Saint-James to be arbitrator. In that the gentleman from the provinces has not shown much wisdom. What are people thinking of when they place a case in that man's hands? He is as gentle as a lamb and as shy as a girl. His eminence is most kind to him."

"What is it about?" said I.

"Three hundred thousand livres," said she.

"What! a lawyer?" I asked, with a little start of astonishment.

"Yes," replied she.

And, somewhat disturbed by having to make this humiliating confession, Madame Bodard returned to her game of faro.

Every table was made up. I had nothing to do or to say. I had just lost two thousand crowns to Monsieur de Laval, whom I had met in a courtesan's drawing-room. I went to take a seat in a deep chair near the fire. If ever on this earth there was an astonished man, it certainly was I on discovering that my opposite neighbor was the controller-general. Monsieur de Calonne seemed to be drowsy, or else he was absorbed in one of those brown studies which come over a statesman. When I pointed out the Minister to Beaumarchais, who came to speak to me, the creator of "Figaro" explained the mystery without speaking a word. He pointed first to my head and then to Bodard's in an ingeniously significant way, by directing his thumb to one and his little finger to the other, with the rest of the fingers closed. My first impulse was to go and say something sharp to Calonne, but I sat still; in the first place, because I intended to play the favorite trick, and also because Beaumarchais had somewhat familiarly seized my hand.

"What is it, monsieur?" said I.

With a wink he indicated the Minister.

"Do not wake him," he said in a low tone; "we may be only too thankful when he sleeps."

"But even sleeping is a scheme of finance," said I.

"Certainly it is," replied the statesmen, who had read our words by the mere motion of our lips. "And would to God we could sleep a long time; there would not be such an awakening as you will see!"

"Monseigneur," said the play-writer, "I owe you some thanks."

"What for?"

"Monsieur de Mirabeau is gone to Berlin. I do not know whether in this matter of the waters we may not both be drowned."

"You have too much memory and too little gratitude," replied the Minister drily, vexed at this betrayal of one of his secrets before me.

"Very possibly," said Beaumarchais, greatly nettled. "But I have certain millions which may square many accounts."

Calonne affected not to have heard.

It was half-past twelve before the card-tables broke up. Then we sat down to supper—ten of us: Bodard and his wife, the controller-general, Beaumarchais, the two strangers, two pretty women whose names may not be mentioned, and a farmer-general named, I think, Lavoisier. Of thirty persons whom I had found on entering the drawing-room but these ten remained. And the two "specimens" would only stay to supper on the pressing invitation of the lady of the house, who thought she could discharge her debt to one by giving him a meal, and asked the other perhaps to please her husband, to whom she was doing the civil—wherefore I know not. Monsieur de Calonne was a power, and if any one had cause to be annoyed it would have been I.

The supper was at first deadly dull. The two men and the farmer-general weighed on us. I signed to Beaumarchais to make the son of Esculapius, by whom he was sitting, drink till he was tipsy, giving him to understand that I would deal with the lawyer. As this was the only kind of amusement open to us, and as it gave promise of some blundering impertinence on the part of the two strangers, which amused us by anticipation, Monsieur de Calonne smiled on the scheme. In two seconds the ladies had entered into our Bacchic plot. By significant glances they expressed their readiness to play their part, and the wine of Sillery crowned our glasses again and again with silvery foam. The surgeon was easy enough to deal with; but as I was about to pour out my neighbor's second glass, he told me with the cold politeness of a money-lender that he would drink no more.

At this time, by what chance I know not, Madame de Saint-James had turned the conversation on the wonderful suppers to the Comte de Cagliostro, given by the Cardinal de Rohan. My attention was not too keenly alive to what the mistress of the house was saying; for since her reply I had watched, with invincible curiosity, my neighbor's pinched, thin face, of which the principal feature was a nose at once wide and sharp, which made him at times look very much like a ferret. Suddenly his cheeks flushed as he heard Madame de Saint-James disputing with Monsieur de Calonne.

"But I assure you, monsieur," said she in a positive tone, "that I have seen Queen Cleopatra."

"I believe it, madame," said my neighbor. "I have spoken to Catherine de' Medici."

"Oh! oh!" said Monsieur de Calonne.

The words spoken by the little provincial had an indescribably sonorous tone—to use a word borrowed from physical science. This sudden clearness of enunciation, from a man who till now had spoken very little and very low, in the best possible taste, surprised us in the highest degree.

"Why, he is talking!" exclaimed the surgeon, whom Beaumarchais had worked up to a satisfactory condition.

"His neighbor must have touched a spring," replied the satirist.

Our man colored a little as he heard these words, though they were spoken in a murmur.

"And what was the late lamented Queen like?" asked Calonne.

"I will not assert that the person with whom I supped last night was Catherine de' Medici herself; such a miracle must seem as impossible to a Christian as to a philosopher," replied the lawyer, resting his finger-tips lightly on the table, and leaning back in his chair as if preparing to speak at some length. "But, at any rate, I can swear that that woman was as like to Catherine de' Medici as though they had been sisters. The lady I saw wore a black velvet dress, absolutely like that which the Queen is wearing in the portrait belonging to the King; on her head was the characteristic black velvet cap; her complexion was colorless, and her face the face you know. I could not help expressing my surprise to his eminence. The suddenness of the apparition was all the more wonderful because Monsieur le Comte de Cagliostro* could not guess the name of the personage in whose company I wished to be. I was utterly amazed. The magical spectacle of a supper where such illustrious women of the past were the guests robbed me of my presence of mind. When, at about midnight, I got away from this scene of witchcraft, I almost doubted my own identity.

"But all these marvels seemed quite natural by comparison with the strange hallucination under which I was presently to fall. I know not what words I can use to describe the condition of my senses. But I can declare, in all sincerity of heart, that I no longer wonder that there should have been, of old, spirits weak enough—or strong enough—to believe in the mysteries of magic and the power of the devil. For my part, till I have ampler information, I regard the apparitions of

* Joseph Balsamo, a sorcerer.

which Cardan and certain other thaumaturgists have spoken as quite possible.''

These words, pronounced with incredible eloquence of tone, were of a nature to rouse extreme curiosity in those present. Our looks all centred on the orator, and we sat motionless. Our eyes alone showed life as they reflected the bright wax-lights in the candlesticks. By dint of watching the stranger we fancied we could see an emanation from the pores of his face, and especially from those of his brow, of the inner feelings that wholly possessed him. This man, apparently so cold and strictly reserved, seemed to have within him a hidden fire, of which the flame came forth to us.

''I know not,'' he went on, ''whether the figure I had seen called up made itself invisible to follow me; but as soon as I had laid my head on my pillow, I saw the grand shade of Catherine rise before me. I instinctively felt myself in a luminous sphere; for my eyes, attracted to the Queen with painful fixity, saw her alone. Suddenly she bent over me——''

At these words the ladies with one consent betrayed keener curiosity.

''But,'' said the lawyer, ''I do not know whether I ought to go on; although I am inclined to think that it was but a dream, what remains to be told is serious.''

''Does it bear on religion?'' asked Beaumarchais.

''Or is it in any way indecent?'' asked Calonne. ''These ladies will forgive it.''

''It bears on government,'' replied the lawyer.

''Go on,'' said the Minister. ''Voltaire, Diderot, and their like have done much to educate our ears.''

The controller-general was all attention, and his neighbor, Madame de Genlis, became absorbed. The stranger still hesitated. Then Beaumarchais exclaimed impetuously—

''Come, proceed, master! Do you not know that when the laws leave folk so little liberty, people revenge themselves by laxity of manners?''

So the lawyer went on—

"Whether it was that certain ideas were fermenting in my soul or that I was prompted by some unknown power, I said to her—

"'Ah, madame, you committed a very great crime.'

"'Which?' she asked in a deep voice.

"'That for which the signal was given by the Palace clock on the 24th of August.'

"She smiled scornfully, and some deep furrows showed on her pallid cheeks.

"'Do you call that a crime?' replied she; 'it was only an accident. The undertaking was badly managed, and the good result we looked for failed—for France, for all Europe, and for the Catholic Church. How could we help it? Our orders were badly carried out. We could not find so many Montlucs as we needed. Posterity will not give us credit for the defective communications which hindered us from giving our work the unity of impulse which is necessary to any great *Coup d'État;* that was our misfortune. If by the 25th of August not the shadow of a Huguenot had been left in France, I should have been regarded to the remotest posterity as a noble incarnation of Providence. How often have the clear-seeing spirits of Sixtus V., of Richelieu, of Bossuet, secretly accused me of having failed in my undertaking, after daring to conceive of it! And how many regrets attended my death!

"'The disease was still rife thirty years after that Saint-Bartholomew's night; and it had caused the shedding of ten times more noble blood in France than was left to be shed on August 26, 1572. The revocation of the Edict of Nantes, for which you had medals struck, cost more tears, more blood and money, and killed more prosperity in France than three Saint-Bartholomews. Letellier, with a dip of ink, carried into effect the decree which the Crown had secretly desired since my day; but though on August 25, 1572, this tremendous execution was necessary, on August 25, 1685, it was useless.   Under Henri de Valois' second son heresy was scarcely pregnant ; under Henri de Bourbon's second son the teeming mother had cast her spawn over the whole world.

" ' You accuse me of crime and you raise statues to the son of Anne of Austria !   But he and I aimed at the same end. He succeeded ; I failed ; but Louis XIV. found the Protestants disarmed, while in my day they had powerful armies, statesmen, captains, and Germany to back them.'

" On hearing these words slowly spoken, I felt within me a tremulous thrill.   I seemed to scent the blood of I know not what victims.   Catherine had grown before me.   She stood there like an evil genius, and I felt as if she wanted to get into my conscience to find rest there——"

" He must have dreamed that," said Beaumarchais, in a low voice.   " He certainly never invented it."

" ' My reason is confounded,' said I to the Queen.   'You pride yourself on an action which three generations have condemned and held accursed, and——'

" ' Add,' said she, ' that writers have been more unjust to me than my contemporaries were.   No one undertakes my defense.   I am accused of ambition—I who was so rich and a Queen.   I am taxed with cruelty—I who have but two decapitations on my conscience.   And to the most impartial minds I am still, no doubt, a great riddle.   Do you really believe that I was governed by feelings of hatred, that I breathed only vengeance and fury?'   She smiled scornfully. ' I was as calm and cold as Reason itself.   I condemned the Huguenots without pity, but without anger ; they were the rotten orange in my basket.   If I had been Queen of England, I should have judged the Catholics in the same way, if they had been seditious.   To give our power any vitality at that period, only one God could be allowed in the State, only one faith and one master.   Happily for me, I left my excuse recorded in one sentence.   When Birague brought me a false report of the loss of the battle of Dreux.   " Well and good," said I, "then we will go to sermon." Hate the leaders of the New Religion? I esteemed them highly, and I did not know them. If I ever felt an aversion for any political personage, it was for that cowardly Cardinal de Lorraine, and for his brother, a wily and brutal soldier, who had me watched by their spies. They were my children's enemies; they wanted to snatch the crown from them; I saw them every day, and they were more than I could bear. If we had not carried out the plan for Saint-Bartholomew's Day, the Guises would have done it with the help of Rome and its monks. The League, which had no power till I had grown old, would have begun in 1573.'

" 'But, madame,' said I, 'instead of commanding that horrible butchery—excuse my frankness—why did you not employ the vast resources of your political genius in giving the Reformers the wise institutions which made Henry IV.'s reign so glorious and peaceful?'

"She smiled again, shrugging her shoulders, and her hollow wrinkles gave her pale features an ironical expression full of bitterness.

" 'After a furious struggle a nation needs repose,' said she. 'That is the secret of that reign. But Henri IV. committed two irremediable blunders: He ought neither to have abjured Protestantism nor to have left France Catholic after his own conversion. He alone has ever been in a position to change the face of France without a shock. Either not a single stole or not a single conventicle! That is what he ought to have seen. To leave two hostile principles at work in a government with nothing to balance them is a crime in a King; it is sowing the seed of revolutions. It belongs to God alone to leave good and evil for ever at odds in the work of His hand. But this sentence was, perhaps, inscribed at the foundations of Henri IV.'s policy, and, maybe, it was what led to his death. It is impossible that Sully should not have cast a covetous eye on the immense possessions of the clergy—though the clergy were not their sole masters, for the nobles dissipated at least two-thirds of the church revenues. Sully the Reformer owned abbeys nevertheless.' She paused, to think, as it seemed.

"'But does it occur to you,' said she, 'that you are asking a Pope's niece her reason for remaining Catholic?' Again she paused. 'And, after all, I would just as soon have been a Calvinist,' she went on, with a gesture of indifference. 'Can the superior men of your age still think that religion had really anything to do with that great trial, the most tremendous of those that Europe has been required to decide— a vast revolution retarded by trivial causes, which will not hinder it from overflowing the whole world since I failed to stop it. A revolution,' said she, with a look of deep meaning, 'which is still progressing, and which you may achieve. Yes, *You*, who hear me!'

"I shuddered.

"'What! Has no one yet understood that old interests on one hand, and on the other new interests, had taken Rome and Luther to be their standards of battle! What! When Louis IX., to avoid a somewhat kindred struggle, dragged after him a population a hundred times greater than that I condemned to death, and left them in the sands of Egypt, he earned the title of saint, while I,' she added, 'failed.'

"She looked down and stood silent for a minute. It was no longer a Queen that I beheld, but rather one of those Druidesses of old who sacrificed men, and could unroll the pages of the future while exhuming the lore of the past. But she presently raised her royal and majestic face.

"'By directing the attention of the middle-classes to the abuses of the Roman Church,' said she, 'Luther and Calvin gave birth in Europe to a spirit of investigation which inevitably led the nations to examine everything. Examination leads to doubt. Instead of the faith indispensable to social existence, they brought in their train, and long after them, an inquisitive philosophy, armed with hammers, and greedy of destruction. Science, with its false lights, sprang glittering from the womb of heresy. Reform in the church was not so much what was aimed at as the indefinite liberty of man, which is fatal to power. I have seen that. The result of the successes of the Reformers in their contest against the priest-hood—even at that time better armed and more formidable than the Crown—was the destruction of the monarchical power raised with so much difficulty by Louis XI. on the ruins of feudality. Their aim was nothing less than the anni-hilation of religion and royalty, and over their wreck the middle-classes of all lands were to join in a common compact. Thus this contest was war to the death between these new allies and ancient laws and beliefs. The Catholics were the representative expression of the material interests of the Crown, the nobility, and the priesthood.

" 'It was a duel to the death between two giants; the night of Saint-Bartholomew was, unfortunately, only a wound. Remember that, to save a few drops of blood at the right moment, a torrent had to be shed at a later day. There is a misfortune which the intelligence that looks down on a king-dom cannot avert: that, namely, of having no peers by whom to be judged when he succumbs under the burden of events. My peers are few; fools are in the majority; these two prop-ositions account for everything. If my name is held in exe-cration in France, the inferior minds which constitute the mass of every generation are to blame.

" 'In such great crises as I have been through, reigning does not mean holding audience, reviewing troops, and sign-ing decrees. I may have made mistakes; I was but a woman. But why was there no man then living who was superior to the age? The Duke of Alva had a soul of iron, Philip II. was stultified by Catholic dogmas, Henri IV. was a gambler and a libertine, the admiral was systematically pig-headed. Louis XI. had lived too soon; Richelieu came too late.

Whether it were virtuous or criminal, whether the Massacre of Saint-Bartholomew is attributed to me or not, I accept the burden.   I shall always stand between those two great men as a visible link in an unrecognized chain.   Some day paradoxical writers will wonder whether nations have not sometimes given the name of executioner to those who, in fact, were victims.   Not once only will mankind be ready to immolate a God rather than accuse itself!   You are all ready to shed tears for two hundred louts, when you refuse them for the woes of a generation, of a century, of the whole world!   And you also forget that political liberty, the peace of a nation, and science itself are gifts for which Fate demands a heavy tax in blood!'

"'May the nations never be happy at less cost?' cried I, with tears in my eyes.

"'Great Truths leave their wells only to find fresh vigor in baths of blood.   Christianity itself, the essence of all truth, since it proceeds from God, was not established without martyrs.   Has not blood flowed in torrents?   Must it not for ever flow?   You will know—you who are to be one of the builders of the social edifice founded by the apostles.   As long as you use your instruments to level heads, you will be applauded; then, when you want to take up the trowel, you will be killed.'

"'Blood! blood!'—the words rang in my brain like the echo of a bell.

"'According to you,' said I, ' Protestantism has the same right as you have to argue thus?'

"But Catherine had vanished as though some draught of air had extinguished the supernatural light which enabled my mind to see the figure which had grown to gigantic proportions.   I had suddenly discerned in myself an element which assimilated the horrible doctrines set forth by the Italian Queen.

"I awoke in a sweat and in tears; and at the moment

22

when reason, triumphing within me, assured me in her mild tones that it was not the function of a King, nor even of a nation, to practice these principles, worthy only of a people of atheists——"

"And how are perishing monarchies to be saved?" asked Beaumarchais.

"God is above all, monsieur," replied my neighbor.

"Well, then," said Monsieur de Calonne, with the flippancy which characterized him, "we have always the resource of believing ourselves to be instruments in the hand of God, as the gospel according to Bossuet has it."

As soon as the ladies understood that the whole scene was a conversation between the Queen and the lawyer, they had begun whispering. Indeed, I have spared the reader the exclamations and interruptions with which they broke into the lawyer's narrative. However, such phrases as, "What a deadly bore!" and "My dear, when will he have done?" reached my ear.

When the stranger ceased speaking, the ladies were silent. Monsieur Bodard was asleep. The surgeon being half-drunk, Lavoisier, Beaumarchais, and I alone had been listening; Monsieur de Calonne was playing with the lady at his side.

At this moment the silence was almost solemn. The light of the tapers seemed to me to have a magical hue. A common sentiment linked us by mysterious bonds to this man who, to me, suggested the inexplicable effects of fanaticism. It needed nothing less than the deep hollow voice of Beaumarchais' neighbor to rouse us.

"I too dreamed!" he exclaimed.

I then looked more particularly at the surgeon and felt an indescribable sentiment of horror. His earthy complexion, his features, large but vulgar, were the exact expression of what I must be allowed to call *la canaille*, the rough mob. A few specks of dull blue and black dotted his skin like spots of mud, and his eyes flashed with sinister fires. The face looked more ominous perhaps than it really was, because a powdered wig *à la frimas* (rimy or like hoar-frost) crowned his head with snow.

"That man must have buried more than one patient," said I to my neighbor.

"I would not trust my dog to his care," he replied.

"I hate him involuntarily," said I.

"I despise him," replied he.

"And yet how unjust!" cried I.

"Oh! bless me, by the day after to-morrow he may be as famous as Volange the actor," replied the stranger.

Monsieur de Calonne pointed to the surgeon with a gesture that seemed to convey, "This fellow might amuse us."

"And did you too dream of a queen?" asked Beaumarchais.

"No, I dreamed of a people," said he with emphasis, making us laugh. "I was attending a patient whose leg I was to amputate the next day——"

"And you found a people in your patient's thigh?" asked Monsieur de Calonne.

"Exactly so!" replied the surgeon.

"Is he not amusing?" cried Madame de Genlis.

"I was greatly surprised," the speaker went on, never heeding these interruptions, and stuffing his hands into his breeches pockets, "to find some one to talk to in that leg. I had the strange power of entering into my patient. When I first found myself in his skin, I discerned there an amazing number of tiny beings, moving, thinking, and arguing. Some lived in the man's body and some in his mind. His ideas were creatures that were born, grew, and died; they were sick, gay, healthy, sad—and all had personal individuality. They fought or fondled. A few ideas flew forth and went to dwell in the world of intellect. Suddenly I understood that there are two worlds—the visible and the invisible universe; that the earth, like man, has a body and a soul. A new light was cast on nature, and I perceived its immensity when I saw the ocean of beings everywhere distributed in masses and in species, all of one and the same living matter, from marble rocks up to God.   A magnificent sight !   In short, there was a universe in my patient.   When I inserted my lancet in his gangrened leg, I destroyed a thousand such beings.   You laugh, ladies, at the idea that you are a prey to a thousand creatures——"

"No personalities," said Monsieur de Calonne, "speak for yourself and your patient."

"My man, horrified at the outcry of his animalcules, wanted to stop the operation ; but I persisted, telling him that malignant creatures were already gnawing at his bones.   He made a motion to resist me, not understanding that what I was doing was for his good, and my lancet pierced me in the side——"

"He is too stupid," said Lavoisier.

"No, he is drunk," replied Beaumarchais.

"But, gentlemen, my dream has a meaning," cried the surgeon.

"Oh, oh !" cried Bodard, waking, "my leg is asleep !"

"Your animalcules are dead," said his wife.

"That man has a vocation," put in my neighbor, who had imperturbably stared at the surgeon all the time he was talking.

"It is to monsieur's vocation what action is to speech or the body to the soul," said the ugly guest.

But his tongue was heavy, and he got confused ; he could only utter unintelligible words.   Happily, the conversation took another turn.   By the end of half an hour we had forgotten the surgeon to the Court pages and he was asleep.

When we arose from table, the rain was to be seen pouring in torrents.

"The lawyer is no fool," said I to Beaumarchais.

"Oh, he is dull and cold.   But you see the provinces can still produce good folk who take political theories and the history of France quite seriously. It is a leaven that will spread."

"Have you a carriage?" Madame de Saint-James asked me.

"No," said I shortly. "I did not know that I should want it this evening. You thought, perhaps, that I should take home the controller-general? Did he come to your house *en polisson?*" (the fashionable name at the time for a person who drove his own carriage at Marly dressed as a coachman). Madame de Saint-James left me hastily, rang the bell, ordered her husband's carriage, and took the lawyer aside.

"Monsieur de Robespierre, will you do me the favor of seeing Monsieur Marat home, for he is incapable of standing upright?" said she.

"With pleasure, madame," replied Monsieur de Robespierre with an air of gallantry; "I wish you had ordered me to do something more difficult."

PARIS, *January*, 1828.

# NOTE.

This is the song published by the Abbé de la Place in his collection of interesting fragments, in which may be found the dissertation alluded to. [It will be seen that it goes to the old tune of *Malbrouk s'en va-t-en guerre.*]

## THE DUC DE GUISE'S BURIAL.

Qui veut ouïr chanson?　(*Bis.*)
C'est du Grand Duc de Guise;
　Et bon bon bon bon,
　Di dan di dan don,
C'est du Grand Duc de Guise!
(This last line was spoken, no doubt, in a comic tone.)
*Qui est mort et enterré.*

Qui est mort et enterré.　(*Bis.*)
Aux quatre coins du poêle,
　Et bon bon bon bon,
　Di dan di dan don,
*Quatre gentilshomm's y avoit.*

Quatre gentilshomm's y avoit.　(*Bis.*)
L'un portoit son grand casque,
　Et bon, etc.
*Et l'autre ses pistolets.*

Et l'autre ses pistolets,　(*Bis.*)
Et l'autre son épée,
　Et bon, etc.
*Qui tant d'Hugu'nots a tués.*

Qui tant d'Hugu'nots a tués.　(*Bis.*)
·Venoit le quatrième,
　Et bon, etc.
*Qui étoit le plus dolent.*

Qui étoit le plus dolent;　(*Bis.*)
Après venoient les pages,
　·Et bon, etc.
*Et les valets de pied.*

(342)

> Et les valets de pied, (*Bis.*)
> Avecque de grands crêpes,
>     Et bon, etc.
> *Et des souliers cirés.*
>
> Et des souliers cirés, (*Bis.*)
> Et des beaux bas d'estame,
>     Et bon, etc.
> *Et des culottes de piau.*
>
> Et des culottes de piau.   (*Bis.*)
> La cérémonie faite,
>     Et bon, etc.
> *Chacun s'alla coucher.*
>
> Chacun s'alla coucher : (*Bis.*)
> Les uns avec leurs femmes,
>     Et bon, etc.
> *Et les autres tout seuls.*

The discovery of these curious verses seems to prove, to a certain extent, the guilt of Théodore de Bèze, who tried to mitigate the horror caused by this murder by turning it to ridicule. The principal merit of this song lay, it would appear, in the tune.

# THE EXILES.



In the year 1308 few houses were yet standing on the island formed by the alluvium and sand deposited by the Seine above the city, behind the church of Notre-Dame. The first man who was so bold as to build on this strand, then liable to frequent floods, was a constable of the watch of the City of Paris, who had been able to do some service to their reverences the chapter of the cathedral; and in return the bishop leased to him twenty-five perches of land, with exemption from all feudal dues or taxes on the buildings he might erect.

Seven years before the beginning of this narrative, Joseph Tirechair, one of the sternest of Paris constables, as his name [Tear Flesh] would indicate, had, thanks to his share of the fines collected by him for delinquencies committed within the precincts of the city, been able to build a house on the bank of the Seine just at the end of the Rue du Port-Saint-Landry. To protect the merchandise landed on the strand, the municipality had constructed a sort of breakwater of masonry, which may still be seen on some old plans of Paris, and which preserved the piles of the landing-place by meeting the rush of water and ice at the upper end of the island. The constable had taken advantage of this for the foundation of his house, so that there were several steps up to his door.

Like all the houses of that date, this cottage was crowned by a peaked roof, forming a gable-end to the front, of half a diamond. To the great regret of historians, but two or three examples of such roofs survive in Paris. A round opening gave light to a loft, where the constable's wife dried the linen of the chapter, for she had the honor of washing for the cathedral—which was certainly not a bad customer. On the second floor were two rooms, let to lodgers at a rent, one year with another, of forty sous *Parisis** each, an exorbitant sum, that was however justified by the luxury Tirechair had lavished on their adornment. Flanders tapestry hung on the walls, and a large bed with a top valance of green serge, like a peasant's bed, was amply furnished with mattresses, and covered with good sheets of fine linen. Each room had a stove called a *chauffe-doux* (heat for one); the floor, carefully polished by Dame Tirechair's apprentices, shone like the woodwork of a shrine. Instead of stools, the lodgers had deep chairs of carved walnut, the spoils probably of some raided castle. Two chests with pewter mouldings, and tables on twisted legs, completed the fittings, worthy of the most fastidious knights-banneret whom business might bring to Paris.

The windows of those two rooms looked out on the river. From one you could only see the shores of the Seine and the three barren islands, of which two were subsequently joined together to form the Ile Saint-Louis; the third was the Ile de Louviers. From the other could be seen, down a vista of the Port-Saint-Landry, the buildings on the Grève, the bridge of Notre-Dame, with its houses, and the tall towers of the Louvre, but lately built by Philippe-Auguste to overlook the then poor and squalid town of Paris, which suggests so many imaginary marvels to the fancy of modern romancers.

The first floor of Tirechair's house consisted of a large hall, where his wife's business was carried on, through which the lodgers were obliged to pass on their way to their own rooms up a stairway like a mill-ladder. Behind this were a kitchen and a bedroom, with a view over the Seine. A tiny garden, reclaimed from the waters, displayed at the foot of this modest dwelling its beds of cabbages and onions, and a few rose-bushes, sheltered by palings, forming a sort of hedge. A little structure of lath and mud served as a kennel for a big dog, the indispensable guardian of so lonely a dwelling. Beyond this

* A small Paris coin, or token.

kennel was a little plot, where the hens cackled whose eggs were sold to the canons. Here and there on this patch of earth, muddy or dry according to the whimsical Parisian weather, a few trees grew, constantly lashed by the wind, and teased and broken by the passer-by—willows, reeds, and tall grasses.

The Eyot, the Seine, the landing-place, the house, were all overshadowed on the west by the huge basilica of Notre-Dame casting its cold gloom over the whole plot as the sun moved. Then, as now, there was not in all Paris a more deserted spot, a more solemn or more melancholy prospect. The noise of waters, the chanting of priests, or the piping of the wind were the only sounds that disturbed this wilderness, where lovers would sometimes meet to discuss their secrets when the church-folk and clergy were safe in church at the services.

One evening in April in the year 1308, Tirechair came home in a remarkably bad temper. For three days past everything had been in good order on the King's highway. Now, as an officer of the peace, nothing annoyed him so much as to feel himself useless. He flung down his halbert in a rage, muttered inarticulate words as he pulled off his doublet, half-red and half-blue, and slipped on a shabby camlet jerkin. After helping himself from the bread-box to a hunch of bread, and spreading it with butter, he seated himself on a bench, looked round at his four white-washed walls, counted the beams of the ceiling, made a mental inventory of the household goods hanging from the nails, scowled at the neatness which left him nothing to complain of, and looked at his wife, who said not a word as she ironed the albs and surplices from the sacristy.

"By my halidom," he said, to open the conversation, "I cannot think, Jacqueline, where you go to catch your apprenticed maids. Now, here is one," he went on, pointing to a girl who was folding an altar-cloth, clumsily enough, it must be owned, "who looks to me more like a damsel rather free of her person than a sturdy, country wench. Her hands are as white as a fine lady's! By the mass! and her hair smells of essences, I verily believe, and her hose are as fine as a queen's. By the two horns of Old Nick, matters please me but ill as I find them here."

The girl colored, and stole a look at Jacqueline, full of alarm not unmixed with pride. The mistress answered her glance with a smile, laid down her work, and turned to her husband.

"Come now," said she, in a sharp tone, "you need not harry me. Are you going to accuse me next of some underhand tricks? Patrol your roads as much as you please, but do not meddle here with anything but what concerns your sleeping in peace, drinking your wine, and eating what I set before you, or else, I warn you, I will have no more to do with keeping you healthy and happy. Let any one find me a happier man in all the town," she went on, with a scolding grimace. "He has silver in his purse, a gable over the Seine, a stout halbert on one hand, an honest wife on the other, a house as clean and smart as a new pin! And he growls like a pilgrim smarting from Saint Anthony's fire!"

"Hey-day!" exclaimed the sergeant of the watch, "do you fancy, Jacqueline, that I have any wish to see my house razed down, my halbert given to another, and my wife standing in the pillory?"

Jacqueline and the dainty journeywoman turned pale.

"Just tell me what you are driving at," said the washerwoman sharply, "and make a clean breast of it. For some days, my man, I have observed that you have some maggot twisting in your poor brain. Come up, then, and have it all out. You must be a pretty coward indeed if you fear any harm when you have only to guard the common council and live under the protection of the chapter! Their reverences the canons would lay the whole bishopric under an interdict if Jacqueline brought a complaint of the smallest damage.''

As she spoke, she went straight up to her husband and took him by the arm.

''Come with me,'' she added, pulling him up and out on to the steps.

When they were down by the water in their little garden, Jacqueline looked saucily in her husband's face.

'' I would have you to know, you old gaby, that when my lady fair goes out, a piece of gold comes into our savings-box.''

''Oh, ho!'' said the constable, who stood silent and meditative before his wife. But he presently said, '' Any way, we are done for. What brings the dame to our house?''

''She comes to see the well-favored young clerk who lives overhead,'' replied Jacqueline, looking up at the window that opened on to the vast landscape of the Seine valley.

''The devil's in it!'' cried the man. ''For a few base crowns you have ruined me, Jacqueline. Is that an honest trade for a sergeant's decent wife to ply? And, be she Countess or Baroness, the lady will not be able to get us out of the trap in which we shall find ourselves caught sooner or later. Shall we not have to square accounts with some puissant and offended husband? for, by the mass, she is fair to look upon!''

''But she is a widow, I tell you, gray gander! How dare you accuse your wife of foul play and folly? And the lady has never spoken a word to yon gentle clerk; she is content to look on him and think of him. Poor lad! he would be dead of starvation by now but for her, for she is as good as a mother to him. And he, the sweet cherub! it is as easy to cheat him as to rock a new-born babe. He believes his pence will last for ever, and he has eaten them through twice over in the past six months.''

''Woman,'' said the sergeant, solemnly pointing to the Place de Grève, ''do you remember seeing, even from this spot, the fire in which they burnt the Danish woman the other day?"

"When then?" said Jacqueline, in a fright.

"What then?" echoed Tirechair. "Why, the two men who lodge with us smell of scorching, and neither chapter nor Countess nor protector can serve them. Here is Easter come around; the year is ending; we must turn our company out of doors, and that at once. Do you think you can teach an old constable how to know a gallows-bird? Our two lodgers were on terms with la Porette, that heretic jade from Denmark or Norway, whose last cries you heard from here. She was a brave witch; she never blenched at the stake, which was proof enough of her compact with the devil. I saw her as plain as I see you; she preached to the throng, and declared she was in heaven and could see God.

.. "And since that, I tell you, I have never slept quietly in my bed. My lord, who lodges over us, is of a surety more of a wizard than a Christian. On my word as an officer, I shiver when that old man passes near me; he never sleeps of nights; if I wake, his voice is ringing like a bourdon of bells, and I hear him uttering incantations in the language of hell. Have you ever seen him eat an honest crust of bread or a hearth-cake made by a good Catholic baker? His brown skin has been scorched and tanned by hell-fires. Marry, and I tell you his eyes hold a spell like those of serpents. Jacqueline, I will have none of those two men under my roof. I see too much of the law not to know that it is well to have nothing to do with it. You must get rid of our two lodgers; the elder, because I suspect him; the youngster, because he is too pretty. They neither of them seem to me to keep Christian company. The boy is ever staring at the moon, the stars, and the clouds, like a wizard watching for the hour when he shall mount his broomstick; the other old rogue certainly makes some use of the poor boy for his black art. My house stands too close to the river as it is, and that risk of ruin is bad enough without bringing down fire from heaven, or the love affairs of a countess. I have spoken. Do not rebel."

In spite of her sway in the house, Jacqueline stood stupefied as she listened to the edict fulminated against his lodgers by the sergeant of the watch. She mechanically looked up at the window of the room inhabited by the old man, and shivered with horror as she suddenly caught sight of the gloomy, melancholy face, and the piercing eye that so affected her husband, accustomed as he was to dealing with criminals.

At that period, great and small, priests and laymen, all trembled before the idea of any supernatural power. The word "magic" was as powerful as leprosy to root up feelings, break social ties, and freeze pity in the most generous soul. It suddenly struck the constable's wife that she never, in fact, had seen either of her lodgers exercising any human function. Though the younger man's voice was as sweet and melodious as the tones of a flute, she so rarely heard it that she was tempted to think his silence the result of a spell. As she recalled the strange beauty of that pink-and-white face, and saw in memory the fine fair hair and moist brilliancy of those eyes, she believed they were indeed the artifices of the devil. She remembered that for days at a time she had never heard the slightest sound from either room. Where were the strangers during all those hours?

Suddenly the most singular circumstances recurred to her mind. She was completely overmastered by fear, and could even discern witchcraft in the rich lady's interest in this young Godefroid, a poor orphan who had come from Flanders to study at the University of Paris. She hastily put her hand into one of her pockets, pulled out four livres of Tournay in large silver coinage, and looked at the pieces with an expression of avarice mingled with terror.

"That, at any rate, is not false coin," said she, showing the silver to her husband. "Beside," she went on, "how can I turn them out after taking next year's rent paid in advance?"

"You had better inquire of the dean of the chapter," replied Tirechair. "Is it not his business to tell us how we should deal with these extraordinary persons?"

"Ay, truly extraordinary," cried Jacqueline. "To think of their cunning; coming here under the very shadow of Notre-Dame! Still," she went on, "or ever I ask the dean, why not warn that fair and noble lady of the risk she runs?"

As she spoke, Jacqueline went into the house with her husband, who had not missed a mouthful. Tirechair, as a man grown old in the tricks of his trade, affected to believe that the strange lady was in fact a work-girl; still, this assumed indifference could not altogether cloak the timidity of a courtier who respects a royal incognito. At this moment six was striking by the clock of Saint-Denis du Pas, a small church that stood between Notre-Dame and the Port-Saint-Landry—the first church erected in Paris, on the very spot where Saint-Denis was laid on the gridiron, as chronicles tell. The hour flew from steeple to tower all over the city. Then suddenly confused shouts were heard on the left bank of the Seine, behind Notre-Dame, in the quarter where the schools of the University harbored their swarms.

At this signal, Jacqueline's elder lodger began to move about his room. The sergeant, his wife, and the strange lady listened while he opened and shut his door, and the old man's heavy step was heard on the steep stair. The constable's suspicions gave such interest to the advent of this personage that the lady was startled as she observed the strange expression of the two countenances before her. Referring the terrors of this couple to the youth she was protecting—as was natural in a lover—the young lady awaited, with some uneasiness, the event thus heralded by the fears of her so-called master and mistress.

The old man paused for a moment on the threshold to scrutinize the three persons in the room, and seemed to be looking for his young companion. This glance of inquiry, unsuspicious as it was, agitated the three. Indeed, nobody, not even the stoutest man, could deny that nature had bestowed exceptional powers on this being, who seemed almost supernatural. Though his eyes were somewhat deeply shaded by the wide sockets fringed with long eyebrows, they were set, like a kite's eyes, in eyelids so broad, and bordered by so dark a circle sharply defined on his cheek, that they seemed rather to be prominent. These singular eyes had in them something indescribably domineering and piercing, which took possession of the soul by a grave and thoughtful look, a look as bright and lucid as that of a serpent or a bird, but which held one fascinated and crushed by the swift communication of some tremendous sorrow, or of some super-human power.

Every feature was in harmony with this eye of lead and of fire, at once rigid and flashing, stern and calm. While in this eagle eye earthly emotions seemed in some sort extinct, the lean, parched face also bore traces of unhappy passions and great deeds done. The nose, which was narrow and aquiline, was so long that it seemed to hang on by the nostrils. The bones of the face were strongly marked by the long, straight wrinkles that furrowed the hollow cheeks. Every line in the countenance looked dark. It would suggest the bed of a torrent where the violence of former floods was recorded in the depth of the water-courses, which testified to some terrible, unceasing turmoil. Like the ripples left by the oars of a boat on the waters, deep lines, starting from each side of his nose, marked his face strongly, and gave an expression of bitter sadness to his mouth, which was firm and straight-lipped. Above the storm thus stamped on his countenance, his calm brow rose with what may be called boldness, and crowned it as with a marble dome.

The stranger preserved that intrepid and dignified manner that is frequently habitual with men inured to disaster, and fitted by nature to stand unmoved before a furious mob and to face the greatest dangers. He seemed to move in a sphere apart, where he poised above humanity. His gestures, no less than his look, were full of irresistible power; his lean hands were those of a soldier; and if your own eyes were forced to fall before his piercing gaze, you were no less sure to tremble when by word or action he spoke to your soul. He moved in silent majesty that made him seem a king without his guard, a god without his rays.

His dress emphasized the ideas suggested by the peculiarities of his mien and face. Soul, body, and garb were in harmony, and calculated to impress the coldest imagination. He wore a sort of sleeveless gown of black cloth, fastened in front, and falling to the calf, leaving the neck bare with no collar. His doublet and boots were likewise black. On his head was a black velvet cap like a priest's, sitting in a close circle above his forehead, and not showing a single hair. It was the strictest mourning, the gloomiest habit a man could wear. But for a long sword that hung by his side from a leather belt which could be seen where his surcoat hung open, a priest would have hailed him as a brother. Though of no more than middle height, he appeared tall; and, looking him in the face, he seemed a giant.

"The clock has struck, the boat is waiting; will you not come?"

At these words, spoken in bad French, but distinctly audible in the silence, a little noise was heard in the other top room, and the young man came down as lightly as a bird.

When Godefroid appeared the lady's face turned crimson; she trembled, started, and covered her face with her white hands.

Any woman might have shared her agitation at the sight of

23

this youth of about twenty, of a form and stature so slender that at a first glance he might have been taken for a mere boy, or a young girl in disguise. His black cap—like the *beret* worn by the Basque people—showed a brow as white as snow, where grace and innocence shone with an expression of divine sweetness—the light of a soul full of faith. A poet's fancy would have seen there the star which, in some old tale, a mother entreats the fairy godmother to set on the forehead of an infant abandoned, like Moses, to the waves. Love lurked in the thousand fair curls that fell over his shoulders. His throat, truly a swan's throat, was white and exquisitely round. His blue eyes, bright and liquid, mirrored the sky. His features and the mould of his brow were refined and delicate enough to enchant a painter. The bloom of beauty, which in a woman's face causes men such indescribable delight, the exquisite purity of outline, the halo of light that bathes the features we love, were here combined with a masculine complexion, and with strength as yet but half developed, in the most enchanting contrast. His was one of those melodious countenances which, even when silent, speak and attract us. And yet, on marking it attentively, the incipient blight might have been detected which comes of a great thought or a passion, the faint yellow tinge that made him seem like a young leaf opening to the sun.

No contrast could be greater or more startling than that seen in the companionship of these two men. It was like seeing a frail and graceful shrub that has grown from the hollow trunk of some gnarled willow, withered by age, blasted by lightning, standing decrepit; one of those majestic trees that painters love; the trembling sapling takes shelter there from storms. One was a god, the other was an angel; one the poet that feels, the other the poet that expresses—a prophet in sorrow, a Levite in prayer.

They went out together without speaking.

"Did you mark how he called him to him?" cried the

sergeant of the watch when the footsteps of the couple were no longer audible on the strand. "Are they not a demon and his familiar?"

"Phooh!" puffed Jacqueline. "I felt smothered! I never marked our two lodgers so carefully. 'Tis a bad thing for us women that the devil can wear so fair a mien!"

"Ay, cast some holy water on him," said Tirechair, "and you will see him turn into a toad. I am off to tell the office all about them."

On hearing this speech the lady roused herself from the reverie into which she had sunk and looked at the constable, who was donning his red-and-blue jacket.

"Whither are you off?" she asked.

"To tell the justices that wizards are lodging in our house very much against our will."

The lady smiled.

"I," said she, "am the Comtesse de Mahaut," and she rose with a dignity that took the man's breath away. "Beware of bringing the smallest trouble on your guests. Above all, respect the old man; I have seen him in the company of your lord the King, who entreated him courteously; you will be ill-advised to trouble him in any way. As to my having been here—never breathe a word of it, as you value your life."

She said no more, but relapsed into thought.

Presently she looked up, signed to Jacqueline, and together they went up into Godefroid's room. The fair Countess looked at the bed, the carved chairs, the chest, the tapestry, the table, with a joy like that of the exile who sees on his return the crowded roofs of his native town nestling at the foot of a hill.

"If you have not deceived me," said she to Jacqueline, "I promise you a hundred crowns in gold."

"Behold, madame," said the woman, "the poor angel is confiding—here is all his treasure."

As she spoke, Jacqueline opened a drawer in the table and showed some parchments.

"God of mercy!" cried the Countess, snatching up a document that caught her eye, on which she read, *Gothofredus Comes Gantiacus* (Godefroid, Count of Ghent).

She dropped the parchment, and passed her hand over her brow; then, feeling, no doubt, that she had compromised herself by showing so much emotion, she recovered her cold demeanor.

"I am satisfied," said she.

She went downstairs and out of the house. The constable and his wife stood in their doorway, and saw her take the path to the landing-place.

A boat was moored hard by. When the rustle of the Countess' approach was audible, a boatman suddenly stood up, helped the fair laundress to take her seat in it, and rowed with such strength as to make the boat fly like a swallow down the stream.

"You are a sorry fellow," said Jacqueline, giving the officer's shoulder a familiar slap. "We have earned a hundred gold crowns this morning."

"I like harboring lords no better than harboring wizards. And I know not, of the two, which is the more like to bring us to the gallows," replied Tirechair, taking up his halbert. "I will go my rounds over by Champfleuri; God protect us, and send me to meet some pert jade out in her bravery of gold rings to glitter in the shade like a glow-worm!"

Jacqueline, alone in the house, hastily went up to the unknown lord's room to discover, if she could, some clue to this mysterious business. Like some learned men who give themselves infinite pains to complicate the clear and simple laws of nature, she had already invented a chaotic romance to account for the meeting of these three persons under her humble roof. She hunted through the chest, examined everything, but could find nothing extraordinary. She saw nothing on the table but a writing-case and some sheets of parchment ; and as she could not read, this discovery told her nothing. A woman's instinct then took her into the young man's room, and from thence she descried her two lodgers crossing the river in the ferry-boat.

" They stand like two statues," said she to herself.  " Ah, ha !  They are landing at the Rue du Fouarre.  How nimble he is, the sweet youth !  He jumped out like a bird.  By him the old man looks like some stone saint in the cathedral. They are going to the old school of the Four Nations. Presto ! they are out of sight.  And this is where he lives, poor cherub ! " she went on, looking about the room.  " How smart and winning he is !  Ah ! your fine gentry are made of other stuff than we are."

And Jacqueline went down again after smoothing the bed-coverlet, dusting the chest, and wondering for the hundredth time in six months—

" What in the world does he do all the blessed day ?  He cannot always be staring at the blue sky and the stars that God has hung up there like lanterns.  That dear boy has known trouble.  But why do he and the old man hardly ever speak to each other ? "

Then she lost herself in wonderment and in thoughts which, in her addled woman's brain, were tangled like a skein of silken thread.

The old man and his young companion had gone into one of the schools for which the Rue du Fouarre was at that time famous throughout Europe.  At the moment when Jacqueline's two lodgers arrived at the old school des Quatre Nations, the celebrated Sigier, the most noted Doctor of Mystical Theology of the University of Paris, was mounting his pulpit in a spacious, low room on a level with the street.  The cold stones were strewn with clean straw, on which several of his disciples knelt on one knee, writing on the other, to enable them to take notes from the Master's improvised discourse, in the shorthand abbreviations which are the despair of modern decipherers.

The hall was full, not of students only, but of the most distinguished men belonging to the clergy, the Court, and the legal faculty. There were some learned foreigners, too—soldiers and rich citizens. The broad faces were there, with prominent brows and venerable beards, which fill us with a sort of pious respect for our ancestors when we see their portraits from the Middle Ages. Lean faces, too, with burning, sunken eyes, under bald heads yellow from the labors of futile scholasticism, contrasted with young and eager countenances, grave faces, warlike faces, and the ruddy cheeks of the financial class.

These lectures, dissertations, theses, sustained by the brightest geniuses of the thirteenth and fourteenth centuries, roused our forefathers to enthusiasm. They were to them their bull-fights, their Italian opera, their tragedy, their dancers; in short, all their drama. The performance of Mysteries* was a later thing than these spiritual disputations, to which, perhaps, we owe the French stage. Inspired eloquence, combining the attractions of the human voice skillfully used, with daring inquisition into the secrets of God, sufficed to satisfy every form of curiosity, appealed to the soul, and constituted the fashionable entertainment of the time. Not only did theology include the other sciences, it was science itself, as grammar was science to the ancient Greeks; and those who distinguished themselves in these duels, in which the orators, like Jacob, wrestled with the Spirit of God, had a promising future before them. Embassies, arbitrations between sovereigns, chancellorships, and ecclesiastical dignities were the meed of men whose rhetoric had been schooled in theological controversy. The professor's chair was the tribune of the period.

This system lasted till the day when Rabelais gibbeted

* A rude drama : The passion play, at Ober-Ammergau, is a survival.

dialectics by his merciless satire, as Cervantes demolished chivalry by a narrative-comedy.

To understand this amazing period and the spirit which dictated its voluminous, though now forgotten, masterpieces, to analyze it, even to its barbarisms, we need only examine the constitutions of the University of Paris and the extraordinary scheme of instruction that then obtained. Theology was taught under two faculties—that of Theology properly so called, and that of Canon Law. The faculty of Theology, again, had three sections—Scholastic, Canonical, and Mystic. It would be wearisome to give an account of the attributes of each section of the science, since one only, namely, Mystic, is the subject of this *Étude* (study).

Mystical Theology included the whole of Divine Revelation and the elucidation of the Mysteries. And this branch of ancient theology has been secretly preserved with reverence even to our own day; Jacob Bœhm, Swedenborg, Martinez Pasqualis, Saint-Martin, Molinos, Madame Guyon, Madame Bourignon, and Madame Krudener, the extensive sect of the Ecstatics, and that of the Illuminati, have at different periods duly treasured the doctrines of this science, of which the aim is indeed truly startling and portentous. In Doctor Sigier's day, as in our own, man has striven to gain wings to fly into the sanctuary where God hides from our gaze.

This digression was necessary to give a clue to the scene at which the old man and the youth from the island under Notre-Dame had come to be audience; it will also protect this narrative from all blame on the score of falsehood and hyperbole, of which certain persons of hasty judgment might perhaps suspect me.

Doctor Sigier was a tall man in the prime of life. His face, rescued from oblivion by the archives of the University, had singular analogies with that of Mirabeau. It was stamped with the seal of fierce, swift, and terrible eloquence. But the doctor bore on his brow the expression of religious faith that his modern double had not.   His voice, too, was of persuasive sweetness, with a clear and pleasing ring in it.

At this moment the daylight, that was stintingly diffused through the small, heavily-leaded window-panes, tinted the assembly with capricious tones and powerful contrasts from the checkered light and shade.   Here, in a dark corner, eyes shone brightly, their dark heads under the sunbeams gleamed light above faces in shadow, and various bald heads, with only a circlet of white hair, were distinguished among the crowd like battlements silvered by moonlight.   Every face was turned toward the doctor, mute but impatient.   The drowsy voices of other lecturers in the adjoining schools were audible in the silent street like the murmuring of the sea; and the steps of the two strangers, as they now came in, attracted general attention.   Doctor Sigier, ready to begin, saw the stately senior standing, looked round for a seat for him, and then finding none, as the place was full, came down from his place, went to the new-comer, and, with great respect, led him to the platform of his professor's chair, and there gave him his stool to sit upon.   The assembly hailed this mark of deference with a murmur of approval, recognizing the old man as the orator of a fine thesis admirably argued not long since at the Sorbonne.

The stranger looked down from his raised position on the crowd below with that deep glance that held a whole poem of sorrow, and those who met his eyes felt an indescribable thrill.   The lad, following the old man, sat down on one of the steps, leaning against the pulpit in a graceful and melancholy attitude.   The silence was now profound, and the doorway and even the street were blocked by scholars who had deserted the other classes.

Doctor Sigier was to-day to recapitulate, in the last of a series of discourses, the views he had set forth in the former lectures on the Resurrection, Heaven, and Hell.   His strange doctrine responded to the sympathies of the time, and gratified the immoderate love of the marvelous, which haunts the mind of man in every age.  This effort of man to clutch the infinite, which for ever slips through his ineffectual grasp, this last tourney of thought against thought was a task worthy of an assembly where the brightest luminaries of the age had met, and where the most stupendous human imagination ever known, perhaps, at that moment shone.

The doctor began by summing up in a mild and even tone the principal points he had so far established :

"No intellect was the exact counterpart of another.  Had man any right to require an account of his Creator for the inequality of powers bestowed on each ?  Without attempting to penetrate rashly into the designs of God, ought we not to recognize the fact that by reason of their general diversity intelligences could be classed in spheres ?  From the sphere where the least degree of intelligence gleamed, to the most translucent souls who could see the road by which to ascend to God, was there not an ascending scale of spiritual gift ?  And did not spirits of the same sphere understand each other like brothers in soul, in flesh, in mind, and in feeling ?"

From this the doctor went on to unfold the most wonderful theories of sympathy.  He set forth in Biblical language the phenomena of love, of instinctive repulsion, of strong affinities which transcend the laws of space, of the sudden mingling of souls which seem to recognize each other.  With regard to the different degrees of strength of which our affections are capable, he accounted for them by the place, more or less near the centre, occupied by beings in their respective circles.

He gave mathematical expression to God's grand idea in the coördination of the various human spheres.  "Through man," he said, "these spheres constituted a world intermediate between the intelligence of the brute and the intelligence of the angels." As he stated it, the divine Word nourishes the spiritual Word, the spiritual Word nourishes the living Word, the living Word nourishes the animal Word, the animal Word nourishes the vegetable Word, and the vegetable Word is the expression of the life of the barren Word. These successive evolutions, as of a chrysalis, which God thus wrought in our souls, this infusorial life, so to speak, communicated from each zone to the next, more vivid, more spiritual, more perceptive in its ascent, represented, rather dimly no doubt, but marvelously enough to his inexperienced hearers, the impulse given to nature by the Almighty. Supported by many texts from the Sacred Scriptures, which he used as a commentary on his own statements to express by concrete images the abstract arguments he felt to be wanting, he flourished the Spirit of God like a torch over the deep secrets of creation, with an eloquence peculiar to himself, and accents that urged conviction on his audience. As he unfolded his mysterious system and all its consequences, he gave a key to every symbol and justified the vocation, the special gifts, the genius, the talent of each human being.

Then, instinctively becoming physiological, he remarked on the resemblance to certain animals stamped on some human faces, accounting for them by primordial analogies and the upward tendency of all creation. He showed his audience the workings of nature, and assigned a mission and a future to minerals, plants, and animals. Bible in hand, after thus spiritualizing Matter and materializing Spirit, after pointing to the Will of God in all things, and enjoining respect for His smallest works, he suggested the possibility of rising by faith from sphere to sphere.

This was the first portion of his discourse, and, by adroit digressions, he applied the doctrine of his system to feudalism. The poetry—religious and profane—and the abrupt eloquence of that period had a grand opening in this vast theory, wherein the doctor had amalgamated all the philosophical systems of

the ancients, and from which he brought them out again classi-
fied, transfigured, purified.  The false dogmas of two adverse
principles and of Pantheism were demolished at his word,
which proclaimed the Divine Unity, while ascribing to God
and His angels the knowledge, the ends to which the means
shone resplendent to the eyes of man.  Fortified by the dem-
onstrations that proved the existence of the world of Matter,
Doctor Sigier constructed the scheme of a spiritual world
dividing us from God by an ascending scale of spheres, just
as the plant is divided from man by an infinite number of
grades.  He peopled the heavens, the stars, the planets, the
sun.

Quoting Saint Paul, he invested man with a new power;
he might rise, from globe to globe, to the very Font of eternal
life.  Jacob's mystical ladder was both the religious formula
and the traditional proof of the fact.  He soared through
space, carrying with him the passionate souls of his hearers
on the wings of his word, making them feel the infinite, and
bathing them in the heavenly sea.  Then the doctor accounted logically for hell by circles placed in inverse order to
the shining spheres that lead to God, in which torments and
darkness take the place of the Spirit and of light.  Pain was
as intelligible as rapture.  The terms of the comparison were
present in the conditions of human life and its various atmos-
pheres of suffering and of intellect.  Thus the most extraordinary traditions of hell and purgatory were quite naturally
conceivable.

He gave the fundamental *rationale* of virtue with admirable
clearness.  A pious man, toiling onward in poverty, proud of
his good conscience, at peace with himself, and steadfastly
true to himself in his heart in spite of the spectacle of exultant
vice, was a fallen angel doing penance, who remembered his
origin, foresaw his guerdon, accomplished his task, and obeyed
his glorious mission.  The sublime resignation of Christians
was then seen in all its glory.  He depicted martyrs at the

burning stake, and almost stripped them of their merit by
stripping them of their sufferings. He showed their inner
angel as dwelling in the heavens, while the outer man was
tortured by the executioner's sword. He described angels
dwelling among men, and gave tokens by which to recognize
them.

He next strove to drag from the very depths of man's understanding the real sense of the word fall, which occurs in every
language. He appealed to the most widely spread traditions
in evidence of this one true origin, explaining, with much
lucidity, the passion all men have for rising, mounting—an
instinctive ambition, the perennial revelation of our destiny.

He displayed the whole universe at a glance, and described
the nature of God Himself circulating in a full tide from the
centre to the extremities, and from the extremities to the
centre again. Nature was one and homogeneous. In the
most seemingly trivial, as in the most stupendous work,
everything obeyed that law; each created object reproduced
in little an exact image of that nature—the sap in the plant,
the blood in man, the orbits of the planets. He piled proof
on proof, always completing his idea by a picture musical with
poetry.

And he boldly anticipated every objection. He thundered
forth an eloquent challenge to the monumental works of science and human excrescences of knowledge, such as those
which societies use the elements of the earthly globe to produce. He asked whether our wars, our disasters, our de-
pravity could hinder the great movement given by God to all
the globes; and he laughed human impotence to scorn by
pointing to their efforts everywhere in ruins. He cried upon
the names of Tyre, Carthage, and Babylon; he called upon
Babel and Jerusalem to appear; and sought, without finding
them, the transient furrows made by the ploughshare of civilization. Humanity floated on the surface of the earth as a ship
whose wake is lost on the calm level of ocean.

These were the fundamental notions set forth in Doctor Sigier's address, all wrapped in the mystical language and strange school-Latin of the time. He had made a special study of the Scriptures, and they supplied him with the weapons with which he came before his contemporaries to hasten their progress. He hid his boldness under his immense learning, as with a cloak, and his philosophical bent under a saintly life. At this moment, after bringing his hearers face to face with God, after packing the universe into an idea, and almost unveiling the idea of the world, he gazed down on the silent, throbbing mass, and scrutinized the stranger with a look. Then, spurred on, no doubt, by the presence of this remarkable personage, he added these words, from which I have eliminated the corrupt Latinity of the Middle Ages:

"Where, think you, may a man find these fruitful truths if not in the heart of God Himself? What am I? The humble interpreter of a single line left to us by the greatest of the Apostles—a single line out of thousands all equally full of light. Before us, Saint Paul said, '*In Deo vivimus movemur et sumus.*' In our day less believing and more learned, or better instructed and more skeptical, we should ask the Apostle, 'To what end this perpetual motion? Whither leads this life divided into zones? Wherefore an intelligence that begins with the obscure perfection of marble and proceeds from sphere to sphere up to man, up to the angel, up to God? Where is the Font, where is the ocean, if life, attaining to God across worlds and stars, through Matter and Spirit, has to come down again to some other goal?'

"You desire to see both aspects of the universe at once. You would adore the Sovereign on condition of being suffered to sit for an instant on His throne. Mad fools that we are! We will not admit that the most intelligent animals are able to understand our ideas and the object of our actions; we are merciless to the creatures of the inferior spheres, and exile them from our own; we deny them the faculty of divining human thoughts, and yet we ourselves would fain master the highest of all ideas—the Idea of the Idea!

"Well, go then, start! Fly by faith up from globe to globe, soar through space! Thought, love, and faith are its mystical keys. Traverse the circles, reach the throne! God is more merciful than you are; He opens His Temple to all His creatures. Only, do not forget the pattern of Moses: put your shoes from off your feet, cast off all filth, leave your body far behind; otherwise you shall be consumed; for God —God is Light!"

Just as Doctor Sigier spoke these grand words, his face radiant, his hand uplifted, a sunbeam pierced through an open window, like a magic jet from a font of splendor, a long triangular shaft of gold that lay like a scarf over the whole assembly. They all clapped their hands, for the audience accepted this effect of the sinking sun as a miracle. There was a universal cry of—

"*Vivat! Vivat!*" (Bravo! Bravo!)

The very sky seemed to shed approval. Godefroid, struck with reverence, looked from the old man to Doctor Sigier; they were talking together in an undertone.

"All honor to the master!" said the stranger.

"What is such transient honor?" replied Sigier.

"I would I could perpetuate my gratitude," said the older man.

"A line written by you is enough!" said the doctor "It would give me immortality, humanly speaking."

"Can I give what I have not?" cried the elder.

Escorted by the crowd, which followed in their footsteps, like courtiers around a king, at a respectful distance, Godefroid, with the old man and the doctor, made their way to the oozy shore, where as yet there were no houses, and where the ferryman was waiting for them. The doctor and the stranger were talking together, not in Latin nor in any Gallic tongue, but in an unknown language, and very gravely. They

pointed with their hands now to heaven and now to the earth.
Sigier, to whom the paths by the river were familiar, guided
the venerable stranger with particular care to the narrow
planks which here and there bridged the mud ; the following
watched them inquisitively; and some of the students envied
the privileged boy who might walk with these two great masters of speech.  Finally, the doctor took leave of the stranger,
and the ferry-boat pushed off.

At the moment when the boat was afloat on the wide river,
communicating its motion to the soul, the sun pierced the
clouds like a conflagration blazing up on the horizon, and
poured forth a flood of light, coloring slate roof-tops and
humbler thatch with a ruddy glow and tawny reflections,
fringed Philippe Auguste's towers with fire, flooded the sky,
dyed the waters, gilded the plants, and aroused the half-
sleeping insects.  The immense shaft of light set the clouds
on fire.  It was like the last verse of the daily hymn.  Every
heart was thrilled ; nature in such a moment is sublime.

As he gazed at the spectacle, the stranger's eyes moistened
with the tenderest of human tears : Godefroid, too, was weeping ; his trembling hand touched that of the elder man, who,
looking round, confessed his emotion.  But thinking his dignity as a man compromised, no doubt, to redeem it, he said in
a deep voice—

" I weep for my native land.  I am an exile !  Young man,
in such an hour as this I left my home.  There, at this hour,
the fireflies are coming out of their fragile dwellings and
clinging like diamond sparks to the leaves of the iris.  At
this hour the breeze, as sweet as the sweetest poetry, rises up
from a valley bathed in light, bearing on its wings the richest
fragrance.  On the horizon I could see a golden city like the
heavenly Jerusalem—a city whose name I may not speak.
There, too, a river winds.  But that city and its buildings,
that river of which the lovely vistas, and the pools of blue
water, mingled, crossed, and embraced each other, which

gladdened my sight and filled me with love—where are they?

"At that hour the waters assumed fantastic hues under the sunset sky, and seemed to be painted pictures; the stars dropped tender streaks of light, the moon spread its pleasing snares; it gave another life to the trees, to the color and form of things, and a new aspect to the sparkling water, the silent hills, the eloquent buildings. The city spoke, it glittered, it called to me to return!

"Columns of smoke rose up by the side of the ancient pillars, whose marble sheen gleamed white through the night; the lines of the horizon were still visible through the mists of evening; all was harmony and mystery. Nature would not say farewell; she desired to keep me there. Ah! It was all in all to me; my mother and my child, my wife and my glory! The very bells bewailed my condemnation. Oh, land of marvels! It is as beautiful as heaven. From that hour the wide world has been my dungeon. Beloved land, why hast thou rejected me?

"But I shall triumph there yet!" he cried, speaking with an accent of such intense conviction and such a ringing tone, that the boatman started as at a trumpet call.

The stranger was standing in a prophetic attitude and gazing southward into the blue, pointing to his native home across the skyey regions. The ascetic pallor of his face had given place to a glow of triumph, his eyes flashed, he was as grand as a lion shaking his mane.

"But you, poor child," he went on, looking at Godefroid, whose cheeks were beaded with glittering tears, "have you, like me, studied life from blood-stained pages? What can you have to weep for, at your age?"

"Alas!" said Godefroid, "I regret a land more beautiful than any land on earth—a land I never saw and yet remember. Oh, if I could but cleave the air on beating wings, I would fly——"

"Whither?" asked the exile.

"Up there," replied the boy.

On hearing this answer, the stranger seemed surprised; he looked darkly at the youth, who remained silent. They seemed to communicate by an unspeakable effusion of the spirit, hearing each other's yearnings in the teeming silence, and going forth side by side, like two doves sweeping the air on equal wing, till the boat touching the strand of the island, roused them from their deep reverie.

Then, each lost in thought, they went together to the sergeant's house.

"And so the boy believes that he is an angel exiled from heaven!" thought the tall stranger. "Which of us all has a right to undeceive him? Not I—I, who am so often lifted by some magic spell so far above the earth; I who am dedicate to God; I who am a mystery to myself. Have I not already seen the fairest of the angels dwelling in this mire? Is this child more or less crazed than I am? Has he taken a bolder step in the way of faith? He believes, and his belief no doubt will lead him into some path of light like that in which I walk. But though he is as beautiful as an angel, is he not too feeble to stand fast in such a struggle?"

Abashed by the presence of his companion, whose voice of thunder expressed to him his own thoughts, as lightning expresses the will of heaven, the boy was satisfied to gaze at the stars with a lover's eyes. Overwhelmed by a luxury of sentiment, which weighed on his heart, he stood there timid and weak—a midge in the sunbeams. Sigier's discourse had proved to them the mysteries of the spiritual world; the tall, old man was to invest them with glory; the lad felt them in himself, though he could in no way express them. The three represented in living embodiment Science, Poetry, and Feeling.

On going into the house, the Exile shut himself into his

room, lighted the inspiring lamp, and gave himself over to the ruthless demon of Work, seeking words of the silence and ideas of the night. Godefroid sat down on his window-sill, by turns gazing at the moon reflected in the water, and studying the mysteries of the sky. Lost in one of the trances that were frequent with him, he traveled from sphere to sphere, from vision to vision, listening for obscure rustlings and the voices of angels, and believing that he heard them; seeing, or fancying that he saw, a divine radiance in which he lost himself; striving to attain the far-away goal, the source of all light, the font of all harmony.

Presently the vast clamor of Paris, brought down on the current, was hushed; lights were extinguished one by one in the houses; silence spread over all; and the huge city slept like a tired giant.

Midnight struck. The least noise, the fall of a leaf, or the flight of a jackdaw changing its perching-place among the pinnacles of Notre-Dame, would have been enough to bring the stranger's mind to earth again, to have made the youth drop from the celestial heights to which his soul had soared on the wings of rapture.

And then the old man heard with dismay a groan mingling with the sound of a heavy fall—the fall, as his experienced ear assured him, of a dead body. He hastened into Godefroid's room, and saw him lying in a heap with a long rope tight round his neck, the end meandering over the floor.

When he had untied it, the poor lad opened his eyes.

"Where am I?" he asked with a hopeful gleam.

"In your own room," said the older man, looking with surprise at Godefroid's neck, and at the nail to which the cord had been tied, and which was still in the knot.

"In heaven?" said the boy, in a voice of music.

"No; on earth!"

Godefroid rose and walked along the path of light traced on the floor by the moon through the window, which stood open ; he saw the rippling Seine, the willows and plants on the island. A misty atmosphere hung over the waters like a smoky floor.

On seeing the view, to him so heartbreaking, he folded his hands over his bosom, and stood in an attitude of despair; the Exile came up to him with astonishment on his face.

"You meant to kill yourself?" he asked.

"Yes," replied Godefroid, while the stranger passed his hand about his neck again and again to feel the place where the rope had tightened on it.

But for some slight bruises, the young man had been but little hurt. His friend supposed that the nail had given way at once under the weight of the body, and the terrible attempt had ended in a fall without injury.

"And why, dear lad, did you try to kill yourself?"

"Alas!" said Godefroid, no longer restraining the tears that rolled down his cheeks, "I heard the Voice from on high ; it called me by name. It had never named me before, but this time it bade me to heaven! Oh, how sweet is that voice! As I could not fly to heaven," he added artlessly, "I took the only way we know of going to God."

"My child! oh, sublime boy!" cried the old man, throwing his arms round Godefroid, and clasping him to his heart. "You are a poet; you can boldly ride the whirlwind! Your poetry does not proceed from your heart; your living, burning thoughts, your creations, move and grow in your soul. Go, never reveal your ideas to the vulgar! Be at once the altar, the priest, and the victim!"

"You know heaven, do you not? You have seen those myriads of angels, white-winged, and holding golden sistrums, all soaring with equal flight toward the Throne, and you have often seen their pinions moving at the breath of God as the trees of the forest bow with one consent before the storm. Ah, how glorious is unlimited space! Tell me."

The stranger clasped Godefroid's hand convulsively, and

they both gazed at the firmament, whence the stars seemed to shed gentle poetry which they could hear.

"Oh, to see God!" murmured Godefroid.

"Child!" said the old man suddenly, in a sterner voice, "have you so soon forgotten the holy teaching of our good master, Doctor Sigier? In order to return—you to your heavenly home and I to my native land on earth—must we not obey the voice of God? We must walk on resignedly in the stony paths where His almighty finger points the way. Do not you quail at the thought of the danger to which you exposed yourself? Arriving there without being bidden, and saying, 'Here I am!' before your time, would you not have been cast back into a world beneath that where your soul now hovers? Poor outcast cherub! Should you not rather bless God for having suffered you to live in a sphere where you may hear none but heavenly harmonies? Are you not as pure as a diamond, as lovely as a flower?

"Think what it is to know, like me, only the City of Sorrows! Dwelling there, I have worn out my heart. To search the tombs for their horrible secrets; to wipe hands steeped in blood, counting them over night after night, seeing them rise up before me imploring forgiveness which I may not grant; to mark the writhing of the assassin and the last shriek of his victim; to listen to appalling noises and fearful silence, the silence of a father devouring his dead sons; to wonder at the laughter of the damned; to look for some human form among the livid heaps wrung and trampled by crime; to learn words such as living men may not hear without dying; to call perpetually on the dead, and always to accuse and condemn! Is that living?"

"Cease!" cried Godefroid; "I cannot see you or hear you any further! My reason wanders, my eyes are dim. You light a fire within me which consumes me."

"And yet I must go on!" said the senior, waving his hand with a strange gesture that worked on the youth like a spell.

For a moment the old man fixed Godefroid with his large, weary, lightless eyes; then he pointed with one finger to the ground. A gulf seemed to open at his bidding. He remained standing in the doubtful light of the moon; it lent a glory to his brow which reflected an almost solar gleam. Though at first a somewhat disdainful expression lurked in the wrinkles of his face, his look presently assumed the fixity which seems to gaze on an object invisible to the ordinary organs of sight. His eyes, no doubt, were seeing then the remoter images which the grave has in store for us.

Never, perhaps, had this man presented so grand an aspect. A terrible struggle was going on in his soul, and reacted on his outer frame; strong man as he seemed to be, he bent as a reed bows under the breeze that comes before a storm. Godefroid stood motionless, speechless, spellbound; some inexplicable force nailed him to the floor; and, as happens when our attention takes us out of ourselves while watching a fire or a battle, he was wholly unconscious of his body.

"Shall I tell you the fate to which you were hastening, poor angel of love? Listen! It has been given to me to see immeasurable space, bottomless gulfs in which all human creations are swallowed up, the shoreless sea whither flows the vast stream of men and of angels. As I made my way through the realms of eternal torment, I was sheltered under the cloak of an immortal—the robe of glory due to genius, and which the ages hand on—I, a frail mortal! When I wandered through the fields of light where the happy souls play, I was borne up by the love of a woman, the wings of an angel; resting on her heart, I could taste the ineffable pleasures whose touch is more perilous to us mortals than are the torments of the worser world.

"As I achieved my pilgrimage through the dark regions below I had mounted from torture to torture, from crime to crime, from punishment to punishment, from awful silence to heartrending cries, until I reached the uppermost circle of

Hell. Already, from afar, I could see the glory of Paradise shining at a vast distance; I was still in darkness, but on the borders of day. I flew, upheld by my Guide, borne along by a power akin to that which, during our dreams, wafts us to spheres invisible to the eye of the body. The halo that crowned our heads scared away the shades as we passed, like impalpable dust. Far above us the suns of all the worlds shone with scarce so much light as the twinkling fireflies of my native land. I was soaring toward the fields of air where, around about Paradise, the bodies of light are in closer array, where the azure is easy to pass through, where worlds innumerable spring like flowers in a meadow.

"There, on the last level of the circles where those phantoms dwell that I had left behind me, like sorrows one would fain forget, I saw a vast shade. Standing in an attitude of aspiration, that soul looked eagerly into space; his feet were riveted by the will of God to the topmost point of the margin, and he remained for ever in the painful strain by which we project our purpose when we long to soar, as birds about to take wing. I saw the man; he neither looked at us nor heard us; every muscle quivered and throbbed; at each separate instant he seemed to feel, though he did not move, all the fatigue of traversing the infinite that divided him from Paradise where, as he gazed steadfastly, he believed he had glimpses of a beloved image. At this last gate of Hell, as at the first, I saw the stamp of despair even in hope. The hapless creature was so fearfully held by some unseen force that his anguish entered into my bones and froze my blood. I shrank closer to my Guide, whose protection restored me to peace and silence.

"Suddenly the Shade gave a cry of joy—a cry as shrill as that of the mother bird that sees a hawk in the air or suspects its presence. We looked where he was looking, and saw, as it were, a sapphire, floating high up in the abyss of light. The glowing star fell with the swiftness of a sunbeam when it flashes over the horizon in the morning and its first rays shoot across the world. The Splendor became clearer and grew larger; presently I beheld the cloud of glory in which the angels move—a shining vapor that emanates from their divine substance, and that glitters here and there like tongues of flame. A noble face, whose glory none may endure that have not won the mantle, the laurel, and the palm—the attribute of the Powers—rose above this cloud as white and pure as snow. It was Light within light. His wings as they waved shed dazzling ripples in the spheres through which he descended, as the glance of God pierces through the universe. At last I saw the archangel in all his glory. The flower of eternal beauty that belongs to the angels of the Spirit shone in him. In one hand he held a green palm branch, in the other a sword of flame: the palm to bestow on the pardoned soul, the sword to drive back all the hosts of Hell with one sweep. As he approached, the perfumes of Heaven fell upon us as dew. In the region where the archangel paused, the air took the hues of opal, and moved in eddies of which he was the centre. He paused, looked at the Shade, and said—

"'To-morrow.'

"Then he turned heavenward once more, spread his wings, and clove through space as a vessel cuts through the waves, hardly showing her white sails to the exiles left on some deserted shore.

"The Shade uttered appalling cries, to which the damned responded from the lowest circle, the deepest in the immensity of suffering, to the more peaceful zone near the surface on which we were standing. This worst torment of all had appealed to all the rest. The turmoil was swelled by the roar of a sea of fire which formed a bass to the terrific harmony of endless millions of suffering souls.

"Then suddenly the Shade took flight through the doleful city, and down to its place at the very bottom of Hell; but as suddenly it came up again, turned, soared through the endless circles in every direction, as a vulture, confined for the first time in a cage, exhausts itself in vain efforts. The Shade was free to do this; he could wander through the zones of Hell—icy, fetid, or scorching—without enduring their pangs; he glided into that vastness as a sunbeam makes its way into the deepest dark.

"'God has not condemned him to any torment,' said the Master, 'but not one of the souls you have seen suffering their various punishments would exchange his anguish for the hope that is consuming this soul.'

"And just then the Shade came back to us, brought thither by an irresistible force which condemned him to parch on the verge of Hell. My divine Guide, guessing my curiosity, touched the unhappy Shade with his palm-branch. He, who was perhaps trying to measure the age of sorrow that divided him from that ever-vanishing 'To-morrow,' started and gave a look full of all the tears he had already shed.

"'You would know my woe?' said he sadly. 'Oh, I love to tell it. I am here, Teresa is above; that is all. On earth we were happy, we were always together. When I saw my loved Teresa Donati for the first time, she was ten years old. We loved each other even then, not knowing what love meant. Our lives were one; I turned pale if she were pale, I was happy in her joy; we gave ourselves up to the pleasure of thinking and feeling together; and we learned what love was, each through the other. We were wedded at Cremona; we never saw each other's lips but decked with the pearls of a smile; our eyes always shone; our hair, like our desires, flowed together; our heads were always bent over one book when we read, our feet walked in equal step. Life was one long kiss, our home was a nest.

"'One day, for the first time, Teresa turned pale and said, "I am in pain!" And I was not in pain!

"'She never rose again. I saw her sweet face change, her golden hair fade—and I did not die! She smiled to hide her sufferings, but I could read them in her blue eyes, of which I could interpret the slightest trembling. "Honorino, I love you!" said she, at the very moment when her lips turned white, and she was clasping my hand still in hers when death chilled them. So I killed myself that she might not lie alone in her sepulchral bed, under her marble sheet. Teresa is above, and I am here. I could not bear to leave her, but God has divided us. Why, then did He unite us on earth? He is jealous! Paradise was no doubt so much the fairer on the day when Teresa entered in.

"'Do you see her? She is sad in her bliss; she is parted from me! Paradise must be a desert to her.'

"'Master,' said I with tears, for I thought of my love, 'when this one shall desire Paradise for God's sake alone, shall he not be delivered?' And the Father of Poets mildly bowed his head in sign of assent.

"We departed, cleaving the air, and making no more noise than the birds that pass overhead sometimes when we lie in the shade of a tree. It would have been vain to try to check the hapless Shade in his blasphemy. It is one of the griefs of the angels of darkness that they can never see the light even when they are surrounded by it. He would not have understood us."

At this moment the swift approach of many horses rang through the stillness, the dog barked, the constable's deep growl replied; the horsemen dismounted, knocked at the door; the noise was so unexpected that it seemed like some sudden explosion.

The two exiles, the two poets, fell to earth through all the space that divides us from the skies. The painful shock of this fall rushed through their veins like strange blood, hissing as it seemed, and full of scorching sparks. Their pain was like an electric discharge. The loud, heavy step of a man-at-arms sounded on the stairs with the iron clank of his sword, his cuirass, and spurs; a soldier presently stood before the astonished stranger.

"We can return to Florence," said the man, whose bass voice sounded soft as he spoke in Italian.

"What is that you say?" asked the old man.

"The *Bianchi* are triumphant."

"Are you not mistaken?" asked the poet.

"No, dear Dante!" replied the soldier, whose warlike tones rang with the thrill of battle and the exultation of victory.

"To Florence! To Florence! Ah, my Florence!" cried Dante Alighieri, drawing himself up, and gazing into the distance. In fancy he saw Italy; he was gigantic.

"But I—when shall I be in heaven?" said Godefroid, kneeling on one knee before the immortal poet, like an angel before the sanctuary.

"Come to Florence," said Dante in compassionate tones. "Come! when you see its lovely landscape from the heights of Fiesole you will fancy yourself in Paradise."

The soldier smiled. For the first time, perhaps for the only time in his life, Dante's gloomy and solemn features wore a look of joy; his eyes and brow expressed the happiness he has depicted so lavishly in his vision of Paradise. He thought, perhaps, that he heard the voice of Beatrice.

A light step and the rustle of a woman's gown were audible in the silence. Dawn was now showing its first streaks of light. The fair Comtesse de Mahaut came in and flew to Godefroid.

"Come, my child, my son! I may at last acknowledge you. Your birth is recognized, your rights are under the protection of the King of France, and you will find Paradise in your mother's heart."

"I hear, I know, the voice of heaven!" cried the youth in rapture.

The exclamation roused Dante, who saw the young man

folded in the Countess' arms.  He took leave of them with a look, and left his young companion on his mother's bosom.

"Come away!" he cried in a voice of thunder.  "Death to the Guelphs!"

Paris, *October*, 1831.

# THE MESSAGE.

Translated by ELLEN MARRIAGE.

*To M. le Marquis Damaso Pareto.*

I HAVE always longed to tell a simple and true story, which should strike terror into two young lovers and drive them to take refuge each in the other's heart, as two children cling together at the sight of a snake by a woodside. At the risk of spoiling my story and of being taken for a coxcomb, I state my intention at the outset.

I myself played a part in this almost commonplace tragedy; so, if it fails to interest you, the failure will be in part my own fault, in part owing to historical veracity. Plenty of things in real life are superlatively uninteresting; so that it is one-half of art to select from realities those which contain possibilities of poetry.

In 1819 I was traveling from Paris to Moulins. The state of my finances obliged me to take an outside place. Englishmen, as you know, regard those airy perches on the top of the coach as the best seats; and for the first few miles I discovered abundance of excellent reasons for justifying the opinion of our neighbors. A young fellow, apparently in somewhat better circumstances, who came to take the seat beside me from preference, listened to my reasoning with inoffensive smiles. An approximate nearness of age, a similarity in ways of thinking, a common love of fresh air and of the rich landscape scenery through which the coach was lumbering along—these things, together with an indescribable magnetic something, drew us before long into one of those short-lived traveler's intimacies, in which we unbend with the more complacency because the intercourse is by its very nature transient and makes no implicit demands upon the future.

(380)

We had not come thirty leagues before we were talking of women and of love. Then, with all the circumspection demanded in such matters, we proceeded naturally to the topic of our lady-loves. Young as we both were, we still admired "the woman of a certain age," that is to say, the woman between thirty-five and forty. Oh! any poet who should have listened to our talk, for heaven knows how many stages beyond Montargis, would have reaped a harvest of flaming epithet, rapturous description, and very tender confidences. Our bashful fears, our silent interjections, our blushes as we met each other's eyes, were expressive with an eloquence, a boyish charm, which I have ceased to feel. One must remain young, no doubt, to understand youth.

Well, we understood one another to admiration on all the essential points of passion. We had laid it down as an axiom at the very outset, that in theory and practice there was no such piece of driveling nonsense in this world as a certificate of birth; that plenty of women were younger at forty than many a girl of twenty; and, to come to the point, that a woman is no older than she looks.

This theory set no limits to the age of love, so we struck out, in all good faith, into a boundless sea. At length, when we had portrayed our mistresses as young, charming, and devoted to us, women of rank, women of taste, intellectual and clever; when we had endowed them with little feet, a satin, nay, a delicately fragrant skin, then came the admission—on his part that Madame Such-an-one was thirty-eight years old, and on mine, that I worshiped a woman of forty. Whereupon, as if released on either side by some kind of vague fear, our confidences came thick and fast, when we found that we were of the same confraternity of love. It was which of us should overtop the other in sentiment.

One of us had traveled six hundred miles to see his mistress for an hour. The other, at the risk of being shot for a wolf, had prowled about her park to meet her one night. Out came all our follies in fact.　If it is pleasant to remember past dangers, is it not at least as pleasant to recall past delights? We live through the joy a second time.　We told each other everything, our perils, our great joys, our little pleasures, and even the humors of the situation.　My friend's countess had lighted a cigar for him; mine made chocolate for me, and wrote to me every day when we did not meet; his lady had come to spend three days with him at the risk of ruin to her reputation; mine had done even better, or worse, if you will have it so.　Our countesses, moreover, were adored by their husbands; these gentlemen were enslaved by the charm possessed by every woman who loves; and, with even supererogatory simplicity, afforded us that just sufficient spice of danger which increases pleasure.　Ah! how quickly the wind swept away our talk and our happy laughter!

When we reached Pouilly, I scanned my new friend with much interest, and, truly, it was not difficult to imagine him the hero of a very serious love affair.　Picture to yourselves a young man of middle height, but very well proportioned, a bright, expressive face, dark hair, blue eyes, moist lips, and white and even teeth.　A certain not unbecoming pallor still overspread his delicately cut features, and there were faint, dark circles about his eyes, as if he were recovering from an illness.　Add, furthermore, that he had white and shapely hands, of which he was as careful as a pretty woman should be; add that he seemed to be very well informed and was decidedly clever, and it should not be difficult for you to imagine that my traveling companion was more than worthy of a countess.　Indeed, many a girl might have wished for such a husband, for he was a vicomte with an income of twelve or fifteen thousand livres, " to say nothing of expectations."

About a league out of Pouilly the coach was overturned. My luckless comrade, thinking to save himself, jumped to the edge of a newly ploughed field, instead of following the fortunes of the vehicle and clinging tightly to the roof, as I did. He either miscalculated in some way, or he slipped; how it happened I do not know, but the coach fell over upon him, and he was crushed under it.

We carried him into a peasant's cottage, and there, amid the moans wrung from him by horrible sufferings, he contrived to give me a commission—a sacred task, in that it was laid upon me by a dying man's last wish. Poor boy, all through his agony he was torturing himself in his young simplicity of heart with the thought of the painful shock to his mistress when she should suddenly read of his death in a newspaper. He begged me to go myself to break the news to her. He bade me look for a key which he wore on a ribbon about his neck. I found it half-buried in the flesh, but the dying boy did not utter a sound as I extricated it as gently as possible from the wound which it had made. He had scarcely given me the necessary directions—I was to go to his home at La Charité-sur-Loire for his mistress' love-letters, which he conjured me to return to her—when he grew speechless in the middle of a sentence; but, from his last gesture, I understood that the fatal key would be my passport in his mother's house. It troubled him that he was powerless to utter a single word to thank me, for of my wish to serve him he had no doubt. He looked wistfully at me for a moment, then his eyelids drooped in token of farewell, and his head sank, and he died. His death was the only fatal accident caused by the overturn.

"But it was partly his own fault," the coachman said to me.

At La Charité, I executed the poor fellow's dying wishes. His mother was away from home, which in a manner was fortunate for me. Nevertheless, I had to assuage the grief of an old woman-servant, who staggered back at the tidings of her young master's death, and sank half-dead into a chair when she saw the blood-stained key. But I had another and more dreadful sorrow to think of, the sorrow of a woman who had lost her last love; so I left the old woman to her prosopopeia, and carried off the precious correspondence, carefully sealed by my friend of a day.

The Countess' castle was some eight leagues beyond Moulins, and then there was some distance to walk across country. So it was not exactly an easy matter to deliver my message. For divers reasons into which I need not enter, I had barely sufficient money to take me to Moulins. However, my youthful enthusiasm determined to hasten thither on foot as fast as possible. Bad news travels swiftly, and I wished to be first at the castle. I asked for the shortest way, and hurried through the field-paths of the Bourbonnais, bearing, as it were, a dead man on my back. The nearer I came to the Castle of Montpersan, the more aghast I felt at the idea of my strange self-imposed pilgrimage. Vast numbers of romantic fancies ran in my head. I imagined all kinds of situations in which I might find this Comtesse de Montpersan, or, to observe the laws of romance, this "Juliette," so passionately beloved of my traveling companion. I sketched out ingenious answers to the questions which she might be supposed to put to me. At every turn of a wood, in every beaten pathway, I rehearsed a modern version of the scene in which Sosie describes the battle to his lantern. To my shame be it said, I had thought at first of nothing but the part that *I* was to play, of my own cleverness, of how I should demean myself; but now that I was in the country, an ominous thought flashed through my soul like a thunderbolt tearing its way through a veil of gray cloud.

What an awful piece of news it was for a woman whose whole thoughts were full of her young lover, who was looking forward hour by hour to a joy which no words can express, a woman who had been at a world of pains to invent plausible pretexts to draw him to her side. Yet, after all, it was a cruel deed of charity to be the messenger of death! So I hurried on, splashing and bemiring myself in the by-ways of the Bourbonnais.

Before very long I reached a great chestnut avenue with a pile of buildings at the farther end—the Castle of Montpersan stood out against the sky like a mass of brown cloud, with sharp, fantastic outlines. All the doors of the castle stood open. This in itself disconcerted me, and routed all my plans; but I went in boldly, and in a moment found myself between a couple of dogs, barking as your true country-bred animal can bark. The sound brought out a hurrying servant-maid; who, when informed that I wished to speak to Mme. la Comtesse, waved a hand toward the masses of trees in the English park which wound about the castle, with " Madame is out there——"

"Many thanks," said I ironically. I might have wandered for a couple of hours in the park with her "out there" to guide me.

In the meantime, a pretty little girl, with curling hair, dressed in a white frock, a rose-colored sash, and a broad frill at the throat, had overheard or guessed the question and its answer. She gave me a glance and vanished, calling in shrill, childish tones—

"Mother! here is a gentleman who wishes to speak to you!"

And, along the winding alleys, I followed the skipping and dancing white frill, a sort of will-o'-the-wisp, that showed me the way among the trees.

I must make a full confession. I stopped behind the last shrub in the avenue, pulled up my collar, rubbed my shabby hat and my trousers with the cuffs of my sleeves, dusted my coat with the sleeves themselves, and then gave them a final cleansing rub one against the other. I buttoned my coat carefully so as to exhibit the inner, always the least worn, side of the cloth, and finally had turned down the bottom of my trousers over my boots, artistically cleaned in the grass. Thanks to

25

this Gascon toilet, I could hope that the lady would not take me for the local tax-collector; but now, when my thoughts travel back to that episode of my youth, I sometimes laugh at my own expense.

Suddenly, just as I was composing myself, at a turning in the green walk, among a wilderness of flowers lighted up by a hot ray of sunlight, I saw Juliette—Juliette and her husband. The pretty little girl held her mother by the hand, and it was easy to see that the lady had quickened her pace somewhat at the child's ambiguous phrase. Taken aback by the sight of a total stranger, who bowed with a tolerably awkward air, she looked at me with a coolly courteous expression and an adorable pout, in which I, who knew her secret, could read the full extent of her disappointment. I sought, but sought in vain, to remember any of the elegant phrases so laboriously prepared.

This momentary hesitation gave the lady's husband time to come forward. Thoughts by the myriad flitted through my brain. To give myself a countenance, I got out a few sufficiently feeble inquiries, asking whether the persons present were really M. le Comte and Mme. la Comtesse de Montpersan. These imbecilities gave me time to form my own conclusions at a glance, and, with a perspicacity rare at that age, to analyze the husband and wife whose solitude was about to be so rudely disturbed.

The husband seemed to be a specimen of a certain type of nobleman, the fairest ornaments of the provinces of our day. He wore big shoes with stout soles to them. I put the shoes first advisedly, for they made an even deeper impression upon me than a seedy black coat, a pair of threadbare trousers, a flabby cravat, or a crumpled shirt collar. There was a touch of the magistrate in the man, a good deal more of the councilor of the prefecture, all the self-importance of the mayor of the arrondissement, the local autocrat, and the soured temper of the unsuccessful candidate who has never been returned since the year 1816. As to countenance—a weazened, wrinkled, sunburned face, and long, sleek locks of scanty gray hair; as to character—an incredible mixture of homely sense and sheer silliness; of a rich man's overbearing ways, and a total lack of manners; just the kind of husband who is almost entirely led by his wife, yet imagines himself to be the master; apt to domineer in trifles, and to let more important things slip past unheeded—there you have the man! A typical French "farmer-gentleman."

But the Countess! Ah, how sharp and startling the contrast between husband and wife! The Countess was a little woman, with a flat, graceful figure and enchanting shape; so fragile, so dainty was she that you would have feared to break some bone if you so much as touched her. She wore a white muslin dress, a rose-colored sash, and rose-colored ribbons in the pretty cap on her head; her chemisette was moulded so deliciously by her shoulders and the loveliest rounded contours, that the sight of her awakened an irresistible desire of possession in the depths of the heart. Her eyes were bright and dark and expressive, her movements graceful, her foot charming. An experienced man of pleasure would not have given her more than thirty years, her forehead was so girlish. She had all the most transient delicate detail of youth in her face. In character she seemed to me to resemble the Comtesse de Lignolles and the Marquise de B——, two feminine types always fresh in the memory of any young man who has read Louvet's romance.

In a moment I saw how things stood, and took a diplomatic course that would have done credit to an old ambassador. For once, and perhaps for the only time in my life, I used tact, and knew in what the special skill of courtiers and men of the world consists.

I have had so many battles to fight since those heedless days, that they have left me no time to distill all the least actions of daily life, and to do everything so that it falls in with those rules of etiquette and good taste which wither the most generous emotions.

"Monsieur le Comte," I said with an air of mystery, "I should like a few words with you," and I fell back a pace or two.

He followed my example. Juliette left us together, going away unconcernedly, like a wife who knew that she can learn her husband's secrets as soon as she chooses to know them.

I told the Comte briefly of the death of my traveling companion. The effect produced by my news convinced me that his affection for his young collaborator was cordial enough, and this emboldened me to make reply as I did.

"My wife will be in despair," cried he; "I shall be obliged to break the news of this unhappy event with great caution."

"Monsieur," said I, "I addressed myself to you in the first instance, as in duty bound. I could not, without first informing you, deliver a message to Madame la Comtesse, a message intrusted to me by an entire stranger; but this commission is a sort of sacred trust, a secret of which I have no power to dispose. From the high idea of your character which he gave me, I felt sure that you would not oppose me in the fulfillment of a dying request. Madame la Comtesse will be at liberty to break the silence which is imposed upon me."

At this eulogy, the Count swung his head very amiably, responded with a tolerably involved compliment, and finally left me a free field. We returned to the house. The bell rang, and I was invited to dinner. As we came up to the house, a grave and silent couple, Juliette stole a glance at us. Not a little surprised to find her husband contriving some frivolous excuse for leaving us together, she stopped short, giving me a glance—such a glance as women only can give you. In that look of hers there was the pardonable curiosity of the mistress of the house confronted with a guest dropped down upon her from the skies, and innumerable doubts, certainly warranted by the state of my clothes, by my youth and my expression, all singularly at variance; there was all the disdain of the adored mistress, in whose eyes all men save one are as nothing; there were involuntary tremors and alarms; and, above all, the thought that it was tiresome to have an unexpected guest just now, when, no doubt, she had been scheming to enjoy full solitude for her love. This mute eloquence I understood in her eyes, and all the pity and compassion in me made answer in a sad smile. I thought of her, as I had seen her for one moment, in the pride of her beauty; standing in the sunny afternoon in the narrow alley with the flowers on either hand; and, as that fair wonderful picture rose before my eyes, I could not repress a sigh.

"Alas! madame, I have just made a very arduous journey——, undertaken solely on your account."

"Sir!"

"Oh! it is on behalf of one who calls you Juliette that I am come," I continued. Her face grew white.

"You will not see him to-day."

"Is he ill?" she asked, and her voice sank lower.

"Yes. But for pity's sake, control yourself—— He intrusted me with secrets that concern you, and you may be sure that never messenger could be more discreet nor more devoted than I."

"What is the matter with him?"

"How if he loved you no longer?"

"Oh! that is impossible!" she cried, and a faint smile, nothing less than frank, broke over her face. Then all at once a kind of shudder ran through her and she reddened, and she gave me a wild, swift glance as she asked—

"Is he alive?"

Great God! What a terrible phrase! I was too young to bear that tone in her voice; I made no reply, only looked at the unhappy woman in helpless bewilderment.

"Monsieur, monsieur, give me an answer!" she cried with vehemence.

"Yes, madame."

"Is it true?  Oh! tell me the truth; I can hear the truth. Tell me the truth!  Any pain would be less keen than this suspense."

I answered by two tears wrung from me by that strange tone of hers.  She leaned against a tree, with a faint, sharp cry.

"Madame, here comes your husband!"

"Have I a husband?" and with those words she fled away out of sight.

"Well," cried the Count, "dinner is growing cold.  Come, monsieur."

Thereupon I followed the master of the house into the dining-room.  Dinner was served with all the luxury which we have learned to expect in Paris.  There were five covers laid, three for the Count and Countess and their little daughter; my own, which should have been *his;* and another for the canon of Saint-Denis, who said grace, and then asked—

"Why, where can our dear Countess be?"

"Oh! she will be here directly," said the Count.  He had hastily helped us to the soup, and was dispatching an ample plateful with portentous speed.

"Oh! nephew," exclaimed the canon, "if your wife was here, you would behave more rationally."

"Papa will make himself ill!" said the child with a mischievous look.

Just after this extraordinary gastronomical episode, as the Count was eagerly helping himself to a slice of venison, a housemaid came in with, "We cannot find madame anywhere, sir!"

I sprang up at the words with a dread in my mind, my fears written so plainly in my face that the old canon came out after me into the garden.  The Count, for the sake of appearances, came as far as the threshold.

" Don't go, don't go ! " called he. " Don't trouble your-selves in the least," but he did not offer to accompany us.

We three—the canon, the housemaid, and I—hurried through the garden-walks and over the bowling-green in the park, shouting, listening for an answer, growing more uneasy every moment. As we hurried along, I told the story of the fatal accident, and discovered how strongly the maid was at-tached to her mistress, for she took my secret dread far more seriously than the canon. We went along by the pools of water; all over the park we went; but we neither found the Countess nor any sign that she had passed that way. At last we turned back, and under the walls of some outbuildings I heard a smothered, wailing cry, so stifled that it was scarcely audible. The sound seemed to come from a place that might have been a granary. I went in at all risks, and there we found Juliette. With the instinct of despair, she had buried herself deep in the hay, hiding her face in it to deaden those dreadful cries—pudency even stronger than grief. She was sobbing and crying like a child, but there was a more poignant, more piteous sound in the sobs. There was nothing left in the world for her. The maid pulled the hay from her, her mistress submitting with the supine listlessness of a dying animal. The maid could find nothing to say but " There ! madame; there, there——"

" What is the matter with her? What is it, niece ? " the old canon kept on exclaiming.

At last, with the girl's help, I carried Juliette to her room, gave orders that she was not to be disturbed, and that every one must be told that the Countess was suffering from a sick headache. Then we came down to the dining-room, the canon and I.

Some little time had passed since we left the dinner-table ; I had scarcely given a thought to the Count since we left him under the peristyle ; his indifference had surprised me, but my amazement increased when we came back and found him seated philosophically at table. He had eaten pretty nearly all the dinner, to the huge delight of his little daughter; the child was smiling at her father's flagrant infraction of the Countess' rules. The man's odd indifference was explained to me by a mild altercation which at once arose with the canon. The Count was suffering from some serious complaint. I cannot remember now what it was, but his medical advisers had put him on a very severe regimen, and the ferocious hunger familiar to convalescents, sheer animal appetite, had overpowered all human sensibilities. In that little space I had seen frank and undisguised human nature under two very different aspects, in such a sort that there was a certain grotesque element in the very midst of a most terrible tragedy.

The evening that followed was dreary. I was tired. The canon racked his brains to discover a reason for his niece's tears. The lady's husband silently digested his dinner; content, apparently, with the Countess' rather vague explanation, sent through the maid, putting forward some feminine ailment as her excuse. We all went early to bed.

As I passed the door of the Countess' room on the way to my night's lodging, I asked the servant timidly for news of her. She heard my voice, and would have me come in, and tried to talk, but in vain—she could not utter a sound. She bent her head, and I withdrew. In spite of the painful agitation, which I had felt to the full as youth can feel, I fell asleep, tired out with my forced march.

It was late in the night when I was awakened by the grating sound of curtain rings drawn sharply over the metal rods. There sat the Countess at the foot of my bed. The light from a lamp set on my table fell full upon her face.

"Is it really true, monsieur, quite true?" she asked. "I do not know how I can live after that awful blow which struck me down a little while since; but just now I feel calm. I want to know everything."

"What calm!" I said to myself as I saw the ghastly pallor

of her face contrasting with her brown hair, and heard the guttural tones of her voice. The havoc wrought in her drawn features filled me with dumb amazement.

Those few hours had bleached her; she had lost a woman's last glow of autumn color. Her eyes were red and swollen, nothing of their beauty remained, nothing looked out of them save her bitter and exceeding grief; it was as if a gray cloud covered the place through which the sun had shone.

I gave her the story of the accident in a few words, without laying too much stress on some too harrowing details. I told her about our first day's journey, and how it had been filled with recollections of her and of love. And she listened eagerly, without shedding a tear, leaning her face toward me, as some zealous doctor might lean to watch any change in a patient's face. When she seemed to me to have opened her whole heart to pain, to be deliberately plunging herself into misery with the first delirious frenzy of despair, I caught at my opportunity, and told her of the fears that troubled the poor dying man, told her how and why it was that he had given me this fatal message. Then her tears were dried by the fires that burned in the dark depths within her. She grew even paler. When I drew the letters from beneath my pillow and held them out to her, she took them mechanically; then, trembling from head to foot, she said in a hollow voice—

"And *I* burned all his letters! I have nothing of him left! Nothing! nothing!"

She struck her hand against her forehead.

"Madame——" I began.

She glanced at me in the convulsion of grief.

"I cut this from his head, this lock of his hair."

And I gave her that last imperishable token that had been a very part of him she loved. Ah! if you had felt as I felt then, her burning tears falling on your hands, you would know what gratitude is, when it follows so closely upon the benefit. Her eyes shone with a feverish glitter, a faint ray of happiness gleamed out of her terrible suffering, as she grasped my hands in hers, and said, in a choking voice and with grievous sobs—

"Ah! you love! May you be happy always. May you never lose her whom you love."

She broke off, and fled away with her treasure.

Next morning, this night-scene among my dreams seemed like a dream; to make sure of the piteous truth, I was obliged to look fruitlessly under my pillow for the packet of letters. There is no need to tell you how the next day went. I spent several hours of it with the Juliette whom my poor comrade had so praised to me. In her lightest words, her gestures, in all that she did and said, I saw proofs of the nobleness of soul, the delicacy of feeling which made her what she was, one of those beloved, loving, and self-sacrificing natures so rarely found upon this earth.

In the evening the Comte de Montpersan came himself as far as Moulins with me. There he spoke with a kind of embarrassment—

"Monsieur, if it is not abusing your good-nature and acting very inconsiderately toward a stranger to whom we are already under obligations, would you have the goodness, as you are going to Paris, to remit a sum of money to M. de—— (I forget the name), in the Rue du Sentier; I owe him an amount, and he asked me to send it as soon as possible?"

"Willingly," said I. And in the innocence of my heart I took charge of a rouleau of twenty-five louis d'or, which paid the expenses of my journey back to Paris; and only when, on my arrival, I went to the address indicated to repay the amount to M. de Montpersan's correspondent, did I understand the ingenious delicacy with which Julie had obliged me. Was not all the genius of a loving woman revealed in such a way of lending, in her reticence with regard to a poverty easily guessed?

And what rapture to have this adventure to tell to a woman who clung to you more closely in dread, saying, "Oh, my dear, not you! *you* must not die!"

Paris, *January*, 1832.